The Yarn of the Mitten

R. Lewis Jessop

Library of Congress Catalog Number 98-66983
ISBN Number 1-57087-420-4

Professional Press
Chapel Hill, NC 27515-4371

Manufactured in the United States of America
02 01 00 99 98   10 9 8 7 6 5 4 3 2 1

Dedication

For my father Earl and my late wife Evelyn
for the gifts of their inspiration,
patience and understanding.

Acknowledgments

The research for this book was done from many sources. Some that I valued highly were the direct account of early pioneers as recorded in the *Michigan History Quarterlies* published by The Michigan Historical Society. For general American History I made good use of *The Oxford History of the American People* by Samuel Eliot Morrison. For details of the Civil War, *The Concise Illustrated History of the Civil War*, a National Historical Society publication, was important. Also important was *The Civil War Handbook* by William H. Price, and information obtained from the *Burton Collection*.

There are many to whom I would like to express a sincere thank you for their help and support. First, to the staff of the *Burton Collection* in The Detroit Public Library for some very fine help. Also to Pam Church for retyping the manuscript in computer format. For the staff of Professional Press, a special thanks for their expert guidance and quality workmanship. To my present wife, Doris Marsh-Jessop, for her loving support, and most especially, to my daughter, Lorraine Jessop Davis for doing a good deal of the work which made the publishing of *The Yarn* possible.

Table of Contents

Part One
Chapter One

The lake steamer Chippewa left the open water of Lake Erie for the Detroit River while the morning sun was still a blinding haze. A heavy fog rose slowly over the marshes along the river bank. Ribbons of trailing herring gulls screamed and circled. The gray overcast lowered to meet the fog, and the sun disappeared, replaced by a cold drizzle.

Traveling north, into the swift current of the river, the side wheeler heeled as the captain fought the treacherous eddies off the Isle Aux Bois Blanc and moved slowly past the remains of once proud Fort Malden at Amherstberg. Captain Barclay's British fleet had sailed out of Fort Malden to meet Oliver Hazard Perry in September 1813, already twenty-four years ago.

On the deck of the Chippewa a hundred or more passengers crowded against the deck houses and peered from underneath sodden bits of canvas as the brief warmth of the morning sun faded and the chill wet of early spring pierced their motley clothing.

Only the steerage passengers and those lucky enough to occupy below-deck cabins were fortunate enough to enjoy the heat from the two wood stoves, one at each end of the steerage. Deck passengers were excess baggage on an immigrant boat and the only heat they could hope to enjoy was that which radiated from the throbbing steam plant in the center of the boat. Those who could, crowded to this area, trying to reach a share of the warmth.

By mid morning the river narrowed and on the east shore appeared long strips of cleared land. Starting at the river bank, they cut broad gashes into the wooded hills, extending back as far as the eye could see. These were the ribbon farms of the early french inhabitants who had occupied them since the early 1700's, land grants of Louis XIV, administered by Antoine De Cadillac. These grants had been laid out in narrow strips so that each occupant could enjoy the water frontage so important in those early days.

Soon another series of these cultivated strips appeared on the west bank, and as if their appearance were some sort of signal, a murmur of excitement rose from deep within the ship. At first it could be felt more than heard: A change in the steady vibration, the neighing of a horse somewhere below, deck passengers, stretching and shivering to the crowded rails.

Then, as the morning garbage went overboard, life on the Chippewa came alert. The streamers of gulls which had trailed the boat since it left Buffalo became a blizzard of black-tipped wings. Where only a moment before, the gulls had flown in thin and lazy lines, now space itself seemed to give up its bounty of screaming birds, swirling, soaring, and diving, to settle like snow on the trail of offal.

Somewhere at the rail the laugh of a well-dressed gentleman cut through the drizzle. "They are just like us," he said, waving his arm towards the screaming gulls. "President Jackson tosses out eight million acres of new land and we come fighting and clawing for a choice morsel. We are vultures, hungry, just as they are, for a crumb or a fortune, whichever it is our lot to find."

"With four million acres sold last year," said his companion, "we will be lucky to find an empty bed in a tavern and a peg to hang our hat on."

"True, but I guess better men than we are have slept in stables. We will survive."

From out of the crowd of immigrants a small boy squeezed his way to the rail, pushed back a shock of blonde hair from his forehead, and looking up, spoke with youthful anticipation. "I hope I see an Indian."

From the lee of the deckhouse an infant squealed as a passing gull swooped close to its face. The cry sounded plaintive and foreign in this cold, rough setting.

The gentleman at the rail turned, and enjoying the audience, spoke loudly. "It seems they are even leaving the cradle to come to Michigan. I suppose some have not heard of the dangers of cholera and the ague."

For a moment silence settled over the deck passengers, then next to the dark–haired girl who held the infant, the big mackinawed form of a man called Ganus the Serb turned and looked hard and long at the stranger. Then he spoke slowly in reply. His voice was low, like the silver call of an oboe, but it carried easily on the wet morning air so that all could hear.

"We have heard, my friend. We have heard of the mud, the mosquitoes and the cholera. We have heard of the heat of the summers and the cold of the winters. We have heard of the endless swamps, the trees to be cut and the red men to be reckoned with. All of these we fear.

"We have heard also of the rich eastern gentleman who come to buy Michigan land for a dollar and twenty–five cents an acre so that they can re-sell it back to their countrymen in another year for ten times that amount."

He paused, as though finished, then turned again to face the rail. "We come this year, now! Because land to us is important, and to our children it will be important. We come now because we cannot afford to wait. We come now and we will stay. We will clear the land and build our homes. We will raise our families and our cattle. We will work until our backs ache and our hands bleed. But we will sell only that which we bring forth with the sweat of our bodies and the will of God. And, God willing, we will grow strong like the land, while your kind will return east to your homes to count the dollars that earned themselves but built nothing."

He turned now to the others around him. "I come here from old Serbia. There, in those hills, I have known the heel of the Ottoman Turk. But I survived, and here, too, I and my family will survive. This I know."

A murmur of approval swelled through the deck passengers. And at the rail an old lady shook a thin fist at the gentleman and laughed a shrill laugh. "Jah! reech man, you buy plenty arrow root and quinine too, 'cause cholera and the ague, they don't know you rich."

The gentleman and his companion turned and left the rail in disgust and threaded their way along the crowded deck and back to their cabin.

Ganus Michaelovic brushed the rain from his big shoulders and, putting an arm around his young wife, he pulled her from the protection of the deck house. Then, leading the way, he took her to the unprotected bow of the boat. There, among the rows of wagon wheels tied securely to the rigging, he found a spot where they could be alone, and turning his back to the cold drizzle he pulled the girl and the baby within the protection of his big mackinaw and spoke to them softly.

"Mina, what the man said is true. Michigan is still a wild new state. Fever and the ague kill many settlers. There will be many months of hard work before you have a roof above you, a table to work on, a comfortable bed to sleep on or a floor in your cabin. There will be wolves howling through the cold winter nights, many clothes to mend...."

"There will be hot, dry summer days and cold winter

nights when the snow will pile itself higher than our cabin roof.... " The girl, Mina, spoke then, her eyes glowing brightly as the fire of her French ancestry burned hot.

"But in the spring, like my brother Milan has told us, the fresh smell of pine trees will fill the air, meadowlarks will sing from the hillsides, the sun will warm our skins and our hearts, the lakes will shine blue and clear like the Mediterranean our mothers knew.... and Toma will love it.

"Oui, my husband, for sure there will be hard times. But we have known hard times before. Serbia was a hard place for Christians and France was a hard place for a Huguenot, but we both survived and grew strong, perhaps because of those hard times.

"Now we are here, my Ganus, in Michigan where we can afford land of our own. Land where you can forget the blackness of the mines and work the soil in clean air and sunshine."

"This does sound good, Mina."

"And best of all it will be our own soil where nobody can say, Go from it, and when you and I are gone our Toma will have the good land for his own, and we will call him Thomas Michaels, American."

"So we go on?" Ganus was bright with his broad grin now. A grin which exposed the real nature of the big, weathered man and set little flames dancing in his piercing blue eyes.

Mina pushed a thatch of unruly hair back beneath his woolen cap and laughed. "We go on."

A long blast from the Chippewa's whistle broke the stillness. Mina shuddered as the sound cut through the fog and echoed from the wooded shores. The Chippewa also shuddered as the big paddle wheels slowed and finally stopped, leaving only the dripping of water to fill the silence.

After hours of constant churning, the quiet seemed to cut almost as deeply as the sound of the whistle. As though something was needed to fill the void, the voice of a deckhand picked up a song, and slowly others throughout the boat joined in . . . .

Come all ye Yankee farmers who wish to change your lot
Who've spunk enough to travel beyond your native spot?
And leave behind the village where Ma and Pa still stay
Come follow me to settle in Michigania . . . .

Chapter Two

Detroit, the City of the Straight, had recovered quickly after the great fire which had leveled it in 1805. Fine wide streets had been laid out and after the War of 1812 and 1813, Fort Shelby had been torn down, the land used for expansion and a new capital had been built on the edge of the forests north of town.

Now nearly eight thousand people lived in the area. While the crash of falling trees could still be heard on the outskirts, the inhabitants, a strange mixture of early French settlers, provincial soldiers, Indians, half–breeds, and the colorful coureurs-de-bois, tugged and pulled in the direction of their own personal interests.

The old residents watched the transformation with interest and grew wealthy as their land holdings tripled in value, cabins were replaced by taverns, trading posts became stores, trees became board walks and trails became long muddy streets.

The character of the people changed also as immigrant Yankees, foreign–born Dutch, and educated Germans appeared, bringing wives and children with them. Four churches were built by those who believed. For those who did not there was a semblance of order, with a judge, a marshall, and a whipping post prominently displayed near the marketplace. This served mostly as a warning but was still used on occasion. The city was still in a frontier stage, but as the forest of maple, oak, and birch was slowly pushed back, a degree of order was appearing where, for thousands of years, only the laws of nature and the primitive codes of the red men had prevailed.

The city in the spring of 1837 was throbbing with activity. The Treaties of Chicago and Washington in 1821 and 1836 had opened up the entire western and northern portions of the peninsula for public sale, and with Black Hawk and his Sauk and Fox warriors now quiet the settlers were pouring in to buy cheap land.

Few of those who arrived in 1836 had been prepared for the rough frontier life they found here and had shaken themselves free of the winter snows piled high on half–finished cabins to find that they were in desperate need of supplies of all kinds. Supplies merchants with bare shelves could not furnish until the first boats began to arrive in the spring.

To add to the problem the ice was slow to leave the river that spring and the boats were two weeks late reaching the docks with their first cargoes. Then came the warm spring rains, filling the swamps with water and turning the streets and trails into rivers of clinging mud.

During this period, only four months after Michigan and her southern sister, Arkansas, were accepted as new members of the Union, the Chippewa appeared churning her way past the Huron and Potawatomi villages and the homes of the French farmers south of town. In another twenty minutes it had wheezed out of the swift current and into a spot between two schooners already disgorging their cargoes onto the docks. There, like a smithy's bellows, the Chippewa gave a throaty gasp and collapsed into majestic silence.

On the waterfront, horses struggling through the mud with loaded wagons or two wheeled French carts glared sidewise at the quivering hulk, panic showing in the whites of their eyes and in the tension of their dancing feet. Drivers drew on the leather reins, driving the bits into their throats and, clinging to their wagon seats, cursed them into submission in French, Italian, and a dozen other languages. Small boys dropped their fishing poles and watched with open mouths as the boat hands leaped from boat to dock and skillfully secured the lines. Merchants, their aprons still tied around their middles, headed for the pier to claim their trade goods and everywhere the silent Indians stood like copper statues, some dressed in their own colorful buckskins and others in varying combinations of white man's garb. One regal old chief even wore a gentleman's frock coat and a tall beaver hat.

Mina Michaelovic's intent blue eyes passed searchingly

over the gathering crowd.

"Do you see him, Mina?"

"Not yet."

Mina's mind was probing the past for the picture that would tell her how he would look, all the time certain that when their eyes met there would be no doubt.

Milan had been only seventeen when he left France as a boy-man with a stubborn will, a fierce pride, and a recklessness that invited trouble.

Father René had watched him with concern and grown quiet. The deep differences in France had built up animosities that he knew would long outlive the Edicts of Louis XVI, and the high villages of the Cevennes were far from the courts of Paris and Marseilles. Nearly every family in France could still name a relative among the twelve thousand killed in the massacre of St. Bartholemew, and in these very hills the blood of the Canisards was still flowing.

"We already have three graves on the LaVoy hillside," said René. "We want no more. You will go to America, my son. There they have made it possible for a man to think and to worship as he sees fit. There you will be an honor to us and to America." Sixteen years had now passed, years of a very few letters, a beaver pelt, soft as the down of a new–born goose, and descriptions of a strange watery country where Milan and his voyageur friends traded guns and trinkets to the red men for furs like the one he had sent to Mina. His stories had been too strange for

Mina's mind to comprehend, but her hope of following him to America had never dimmed. So when the plague had taken her father and mother she had quickly sought passage.

The crowd grew, but now Mina had eyes for only one person, a tall, curly–haired Frenchman with broad, flat shoulders and very narrow thighs. He dressed in soft Indian buckskins and sat back from the crowd, straight and easy on a shining chestnut mare. Mon Dieu! How he had changed.

His eyes swept the boat with a slow sureness and met hers. The years melted away as she remembered the unruly hair and the smile which seemed to turn the corners of his mouth both up and down at the same time. "Oh God! Is he handsome."

Now he was dismounting, and raising his arms he came through the crowd like a boy in a field of grain. Then he lifted her and Toma from the gang plank before they could reach the ground and carried them squealing to the back of the chestnut mare.

"Mina," he said, holding her from him, "You are beautiful. And this is Toma. Welcome to Michigan. Come, I have a place where we can talk." And with one arm around Ganus's big shoulders he led the mare and its riders past the marketplace, busy with its bales of furs coming in from the back country, on past the whipping post, the sweating horses of the dray men, and up a muddy hill.

The fireplace in the Steamboat Hotel on Woodbridge Street was stocked with wood and Milan brought ribs to roast over the open fire. The day and long into the night was spent in the firelight, talking of their lives during the years they had been apart. There were sixteen years of separation to relive, the story of Ganus's strange past to hear, and how he had met Mina on the docks of New York, each alone, frightened, speaking only a little English, but ready to laugh and start a new life together.

"Think I'll go up into town a spell, Mina," said Ganus next morning.

"Curiosity getting the best of you, Gan?"

"That some, and there's a lot we have to learn about this country. It's a heap different than old Serbia, and France too, I'm betting. Looks to me like every street ends up in a swamp or some Frenchman's barnyard."

Ganus pulled on his big coat and with his old cap down over his ears he left the hotel. Women with baskets on their arms were already searching the shelves behind weathered gray storefronts. Easterners like the two he had met on the boat were out in spite of the weather, as bearded trappers in wool mackinaws and moosehide Indian boots were heading for the marketplace, still carrying their long muskets and smelling of the smoke of distant campfires. French farmers on rickety two–wheeled wagons were searching out passable routes through muddy streets, and the Indians, unmindful of the rain, silently watched from street benches.

The land office was crowded beyond belief but Ganus found a spot beneath a slabwood awning and, dry for the moment, he set to listening. Near the doorway a group of men had gathered to talk land. Some appeared to be the usual hangers-on making a show of knowing. Some he recognized as immigrants who had arrived on the Chippewa. Others appeared to be squatters, back to file claim or more likely to threaten any moneyed newcomer bent on beating them to the purchase.

One man was obviously acting for wealthy speculators. He had taken up a prominent spot on the boardwalk and was passing out some printed matter. "There's little doubt about it, men," his voice was loud and convincing, "Port Sheldon will soon be the most prosperous town in Michigan. Where is it, did you ask? Eighty–five miles west of Detroit on Pigeon Bayou, our best port on Lake Michigan and the gateway to the West. More fresh water than old England ever saw, soil so rich you have to jump back after you plant a seed, and more blue sky than the birds can handle.

"But no fooling, men, if a business lot is what you want, or a town home in good country, Port Sheldon is your buy."

"Seems as though we couldn't go wrong, could we?" Ganus turned. It was Bill Sugars, the tall Yankee he had met on the Chippewa, standing beside him.

"Good morning, Bill. How did your wife stand the trip?"

"Tolerable," said Bill, his usual easy grin spread generously across a rather thin face and his old hat pushed way back on his head. "She's mean anyways. That usually means she's in good health. But as for that 'good morning', I have known ducks that wouldn't be seen in weather like this. Mother England, go home."

Ganus laughed. Bill Sugars was not serious. He had never seemed serious about anything, even though his slight build did not seem to be proper backing for the optimism he showed. Ganus guessed that was why he had liked him from the first. A serious man needs someone like Bill around to remind him of what he's missing. Yet he had the feeling that Bill Sugars had what it takes to do well for himself.

"I hear the land offices are accepting only hard money."

"Yes, I just heard that," said Ganus. "Orders from President Jackson."

"Don't guess it matters much," said Bill. "We never went much for spending other people's money. Trouble is we never get past the first sock, and we can't seem to keep that one mended. I keep telling Mary that we should start saving a little for a rainy day. She all'us says, that's a fine idea, Bill, but it just seems to keep drizzlin' all the time."

Bill brushed the water from his old hat. "Don't know that we will buy land anyway. I'm not much for farming. Like fishing better," and he grinned his likeable grin. "Not so much work between the plantin' and the platter. May just buy a few acres fer Mary to plant and find me a little business. Here, son, I'll take one of those maps of that little gold mine."

"Yes sir! Mister, a lot in Port Sheldon is a key to future wealth and happiness, a mill, wide streets and the Ottawa House, the finest hotel in the West, are all under construction."

"He's got a good spiel, but my figuring tells me it's more like one hundred and sixty miles to Lake Michigan than eighty–five. I reckon if a man can lie that much there ain't much truth in him.

Picked your poison yet, Mr. Michaelovic?"

"No, not really. Mina's brother seems to favor going north to the wild country. Says the eastern speculators have bought up so much land in the south that it might take months to find a good location south of the Grand River."

"Could be," said Bill. "I heard that one man latched on to eighteen hundred acres this morning. He sure ain't figuring to clear that much land himself. And the way it looks now he might be getting four times the government's price for it in another year. The President should set a limit on the acres a man can buy. I guess you cain't legislate the poison out of a rattlesnake, though."

"The north country sounds good," said Ganus. "The way Milan tells it, and he knows the country well. But I'm not sure. From all that I can learn that's sand country. Sand and Pine. A man can starve in sand and pine country."

"Less'n he likes to fish," grinned Bill Sugars. "One

thing sure, you will get first choice in that country. Everyone here right now has got one mind, Yankee Springs or Ionia. Ionia is a new country, but they say that already the settlers are spreading out through the woods like pancakes on a cold griddle. If we spend too much time looking this year we might as well go back to rocky old New England."

"We will stay," grinned Ganus, "somewhere."

"Me, too, I guess," said Bill. "Once a man pulls stakes he seldom plants them again in the same holes." Bill hitched his pants up a bit higher on his bony hips and took in another notch.

"Ever hear of Farmington?" asked a wiry New Englander who had stopped to listen. "They tell me it's Quaker, and still has land. A man seldom goes wrong picking Quaker land."

"I'll go along with that," said Bill.

"Sounds a lot safer than that Fort Sheldon place, and a lot handier. Sometimes people all seem to take off for far places and maybe overlook something good close by. I think I'll take a look." The man found the hand of the scrawny boy who had been energetically kicking pebbles off of the board walk and wandered off into the crowd.

"Everybody to his own, I guess," said Bill. "But me, not wanting a lot of land, I think I'll prospect a little like the rest of the snakes. Then if I can get another sock filled I might look you up, up in that fishing country."

"I wish you would, Bill. It sure would pleasure us to

have you and Mary for neighbors."

It's interesting, thought Ganus, as he started back to the hotel. Bill taking it for sure that we're going to the north country, and I knew from the start what he was up to. He's a Yankee dealer, and a sharp one, too. I'll bet he could buy from a Jew and sell to a Scotchman and double his money. It would be nice if he and Mary come north, though. They would be amiable neighbors.

Back around the fire that night Milan stood before the big farmers map on the wall and pointed out places and told stories. It seemed that he had been everywhere and as he talked people gathered quickly to listen.

"How about the Indians?" they asked. "Are they still out there? What are they like?"

Now Milan hesitated. How could he possibly explain ways of living and ways of thinking as different as he had known? These people would call them ignorant, but he had known many who were far from it. They would call them dirty, and in their manner of living, most Indians certainly were. They would call them lazy, but even he could not answer that. Their actions were too dependent on circumstances. Theirs was a way of life that had known no boundaries, no fences, no claims, no guiding bibles, no laws. Only understandings set by traditions and the strength of their neighbor's tomahawks.

"The great ones I have known are no longer there," said Milan, now struggling for words to explain feelings he knew these people could never understand. "Mateo,

Topinabee, and Shingabawassin are gone or fading into age. Probably Pontiac and Okemos are the last, and they are broken men, overwhelmed by the settlers and broken by their liquor."

Milan's mind kept carrying him back to the meetings at Chicago where he had gone with Governor Cass. He was seeing the stately Mateo as he rose to speak, and the other chiefs sitting around in a circle of respectful silence. After a long pause to make sure he had total attention, Mateo had spoken, his voice strong with emotion. . . .

"My friends, you, Black Cloud, Mukutay Oquot; you, Cowpemossay, The Walker. You Windecowiss and Keeshaowash, and all of my other brothers, listen to my words. We have watched and listened as our friend, the prophet, told us that we must join together and fight the Long Knives. The prophet was also my brother and a brave man, but he also was a fool." There was a murmur of question from the chiefs, but Mateo went on. "The Long Knives are as many as the red leaves that fall after the hard frosts of winter and the Shawnee would not see this. Their guns are like the lightning from the skies and their sicknesses are to us only death. Who will care for our women and children if we continue to follow in his path and to fight them and to die? Who will bring food to our families when they are hungry and skins when they are cold if there are only a few of us left?

"Our old ones have told us that once before we were driven from our hunting grounds. Our enemies then were the tribes of the Iroquois. But we were not defeated. Our fathers found a new home and we lived well among our hills and lakes. Our Manitou was good to us and perhaps he will again show us a good way. There are still many forests and rich lands to the west, and to the north are swamps rich with game and hills of rock where the white man's plows can never harm the good earth. It is to these places, my brothers, that we must go.

"The time has come when we must listen to Robinson and to Mr. Cass who are our friends. They are telling us that this is our only choice."

Cowpemossay had grunted quietly at this but the others remained silent.

"They are telling us that we should go to Washington where the Great White Father will bargain with us fairly for our lands. I know that you will say no, our lands are dear to us. We have watched the sun come up over the hills and waters there for many moons. We have fed the land and been fed by it. We have traveled its rivers and climbed its hills. We know when to make the good sugar and where to find the sweetest berries and the fattest game. We have fought for it and paid for it with our blood. . . . It is our home.

"But now, my brothers, we must again be wise. Listen! It is Mateo speaking. Already the white settlers are in our woods. Everyday the chi-cheemauns bring more Long Knives up our river from the east. How many more winters will we be able to hold our lands? One? Two?" He had raised his fingers to make it clearer. "Perhaps three or four. But when the winters of one hand are gone and the summer sun rises again over the big waters, the white man will be all around us in our hunting grounds. His iron axes will be cutting our trees and his oxen will be turning our soil. What then can we do? Will we then be able to go to the Great White Father and say, we will smoke the pipe; we will make peace with you; we will sell you our lands? And if we do will he then hear us, or will he know that the Long Knives have already taken our lands, and he will laugh?"

Milan's eyes came back to the people in the room. Mina was looking at him with eyes that questioned his long silence. He smiled back, understanding. These were good people, gathered here around him in the firelight, strong and ready to make their own way in a raw new state. But among them he saw none, not even big Ganus, who could compare with the noble Mateo, or even the thoughtful Windecowiss who looked straight through everyone with those dark piercing eyes. How could he explain this to these people?

He looked again, and knowing that they would never know the likes of those great leaders he would have to find another way to explain the Algonquians.

Finally he said, "If you want, I will tell you two stories that may help you to understand the Indians." He rose and walked again to the map.

"Here, near the mouth of the Saint Mary's River,

between Lake Superior and Lake Huron, there was once an Indian village of about forty lodges. They were of the Chippewa Clan and they had lived along this river for many years, and with good reason. Here where the Saint Mary's slides out of old Missisagaigon the river tumbles over a series of rocky shelves. In the rapids were fine trout, and in the deep water below were the good whitefish just waiting to be speared or netted by the red men. They liked the food. It was there for the taking, and in the hills nearby were maple trees with sap to make their sugar. These were rich Indians."

Milan's voice was rich and pleasant. Mina settled down with Toma on her lap and watched the firelight dance on the heavy beamed ceiling.

"Late one day, after the first wet snow had fallen in November, a canoe appeared, coming down the river from the north. A young white man was starting to run the rapids in a big canoe. He was alone except for two big bundles of furs lashed to the middle struts. It was an unusual time for trader to be bringing down furs from the north country but this one had missed the trading season and was trying to make a late fall run.

"It was clear to the Chippewas that he did not know the river for he came down much too close to the west bank where the current eddied off of the rocky shoreline and made it hard to hold a bark steady with the flow. Faster he came and plunged into the rapids built up heavy by the fall rains. He cleared the first hundred yards of the white water without problems, but when the rocks began to throw the cold spray up into his face he became blinded and just before he reached the last rocky shelf a strong eddy caught the bark, sucked it into a deep trough and threw it sidewise to the current. Before he could straighten it out, it struck a great boulder and turned over.

The young braves set up a shout of laughter at the young white man but, without a moment of hesitation, Chief Sassaba stopped them and ordered them out into the rapids in their canoes.

"An hour later the braves found the man far downriver huddled beneath his canoe, exhausted by his battle with the river and with fingers too nearly frozen to start a fire. They started his fire, wrapped him in a blanket, and when he was warm and dry they put him into clothing of their own and carried him back to their village. There he was taken to the lodge of a young widow. She covered him with a warmed trader's blanket and a bearskin to stop his chills and fed him maple sugar and balsam tea to check the scurvy that had weakened him.

"It was spring before the young man was strong enough to repair his canoe and travel on to Fort Mackinac. Never during that time, though, was he allowed to go hungry, and before he left their village the good Chief Sassaba took him by the shoulders and said to him, 'You are a brave man, Frenchman, foolish but brave. Come back to us again, the Frenchmen are our brothers.'"

Milan added another stick to the fire as the chill spring

air crept into the lodge, then turned again, his face now serious as his memory carried him back to those trying times.

"That was one kind of Indian, the good Chippewas of Sault Saint Marie. I will always remember them, and well I should, because I was that young Frenchman. Still young and foolish, I had spent my first season working for the Company at La Point. Here." He had gone again to the map and was pointing to an island far up along the southwest shore of Lake Superior.

"I had quickly learned that I had no liking for the work with the Company so when some friendly Chippewa offered to sell me furs of my own I foolishly defied the Company and headed for Mackinaw Island alone. If I could not sell them there, where the Company controlled the trade, I planned to go all the way to Detroit. But November is not the time to travel the lakes. A young man has to learn these things and only the lucky or smart survive."

Milan laughed his carefree laugh. "I know for sure that I was one of the lucky ones, for if it had not been for Chief Sassaba and the good Chippewas of Sault Saint Marie my life as an independent trader would have been a short one."

The little group was silent, not quite understanding, perhaps, but aware that Milan was changing their perception of the Red Men.

Milan stretched his long legs and continued. "The other

kind of Indians I met several years later. I was traveling with Governor Cass and a party of men, including
twenty–three soldiers, with the idea of learning more
about the unexplored areas in the northwest Michigan
Territory.

"We pulled our canoes from a river one night where an
Indian village had been built high up on the river bank.
While we were pitching our tents and preparing a meal
Governor Cass sent word to the chiefs that he would like
to meet with them around a council fire.

"About dusk they came, three of them dressed in their
best buckskins and a few other braves with touches of
paint showing on their faces. All of them were noticeably
armed with knives, tomahawks, and two of them had
good flintlock rifles.

"Mr. Cass had gifts of blankets, axes, and guns brought
out and laid before them, but their chief made the sign
that they should not touch them. They were very quiet,
their eyes showing that they did not like the soldiers and
were suspicious of our party.

"But they allowed the pipe to be passed many times
and finally Mr. Cass began to speak. He told them that he
had big medicine to make with them. The chiefs laid
down the pipe and waited.

"'I have been sent to remind you,' he said, 'that the
land where our fires now burn and where your village
stands was treatied to the American white people twenty-
five years ago at the Treaty of Greenville down in the land

of the Miami! This was after your people were defeated at The Timbers.

"'You have been allowed to live here because you are our friends and because the land has not been important to our people. But time has passed. Your friends, the English, have tried to take our lands from us and the river has become more important. Before many more summer moons come and go there will be big canoes like you have seen at Mackinaw and the Island coming up this river. The English may try to prevent this and our soldiers will have to protect them.'

"The Indians still squatting around the fire looked angry now, but also confused. They looked first at one another then at Governor Cass. Then their second chief drew his knife from his belt and drove it into the ground in front of him. He had made his decision.

"Governor Cass hesitated. I am sure he was not certain that he should go on. His knowing of the Indian ways was telling him that we were in trouble. There were probably forty or fifty young braves in the village who would welcome a fight with the uniformed soldiers. They might already be waiting in the forest behind the camp and the chiefs could easily turn them loose. But Mr. Cass had been given a job to do and he was not one to back away.

"He looked directly at the chief and, acting as though he had not even noticed their threats, he went on.

"'To you it should not be a big change. You may still fish wherever you like in the river and make your sugar from the forests.' Then Mr. Cass' voice became stern. 'But you must move your lodges from the high ground where they are now built and rebuild your homes farther down the river. This is the wish of the Great White Father.'

"For a few minutes the chief said nothing. He was looking straight back at Governor Cass and back around at his braves as if asking if they were ready. Once he looked directly at me and the hate in his eyes was something to see as he again faced our leader.

"'No! he finally said. No! We will not move our lodges. The land is ours and we will keep it, and rising to his feet in one quick move he kicked the gifts from in front of him into the fire, picked up the pipe, broke it into pieces and led his people out into the dark of the night.

"Within minutes the squaws and children could be seen leaving the village. The young braves were yipping like hungry dogs and striping themselves with paint and a British flag was raised over the chief's lodge to show their defiance of the American visitors. We could only watch as our soldiers and voyageurs formed their half circle around us prepared for the fight which appeared sure to come. We were only a small group against all the men of the village so it looked as though we could not hope to escape without some, and perhaps all, of us being killed just as so many others have been in the past."

Milan hesitated, as if not knowing how to end his story. The fire crackled on and the people waited.

"This was the second kind of Indian. The ones who

have seen the white people come not as friends and neighbors but like fathers of small boys. They come not as sharers but as takers, and not as individuals or families but in ever increasing numbers. So they are confused and afraid. Even with their little knowing they can see that they are slowly losing their lands. The lakes and forests were where their fires have burned for generations and where their rights were bought with the blood of their fathers. Land that has furnished them with food, clothing, and simple pleasures. In the eyes of a white man this may not seem like much, but to them it is everything. It is life itself and they would have killed us gladly to defend it."

The silence was finally broken by Mina. "And did they fight you?"

"No." Milan was smiling again now. "They didn't, or I would not be here with you tonight. No, that day we were lucky. Among the Indians the words of their women carry much weight. With them that night was Mrs. John Johnson, an Indian princess in her own right, the daughter of a chief and the wife of a white trader. She knew that if we were killed, more soldiers would come and her people would be destroyed. The Chippewas were coming to see that there was no possible way that the Algonquian tribes could hold onto their lands. They had fought well at Detroit, at Fallen Timbers, and with the British at Thames River, but had always failed. After a long council she convinced the chiefs to return. A few days later a treaty was signed giving the Americans sixteen miles of their most prized river property, and we continued our journey."

The thoughtful Ganus had been carefully weighing Milan's words. "And where were these second Indians, Milan?"

Milan rose and walked again to the map. "Right here," he said and pointed again to the same falls on the Saint Mary's River. "The chief who was willing and ready to murder our entire party was Sassaba. The same one who had taken me from the river, covered me with robes, and cared for me like one of his own a few years before. The one who said, 'Come back, you are now our brother.'

"Time changes many things and in a few short years the Algonquians had come to look at the Americans, the English, and finally the French as their enemies, not as their friends. A good Indian is a good Indian only as long as he trusts you. Lie to him or cheat him in ways that he can understand and he will be your enemy forever and will aim to destroy you in a hundred murderous ways. Governor Cass learned this that day. I have known him for many years since that time and never again have I ever known him to lie to an Indian."

The door of the inn had slammed shut as Milan finished his story and a stranger tossed a wet coat onto a peg. He was not tall, but was very thick, and probably older than his broad shape suggested. Or perhaps he was young, with age prematurely written into the deep lines of his forehead. He was heavily bearded and out of the beard deep–set eyes showed dark, dark with the glint of bad memories and red with the fire of cheap whiskey.

"From what I hear, we won't have to look at Indians much longer," he said, backing up to the fire as if hesitant to face its brightness. "President Jackson is sending troops to drive them west to Kansas Territory. Good place for them. Nothin' there but grass and buffler."

"And Mandans and the Sioux who have already been fighting the Chippewas for years," said Milan, without looking up, but with a ring of steely hardness in his tone. "Leave them alone. Give them enough land to live on and let them work it or no. Most of them will learn to live like white men if the white men will let them. The rest will move north or west by themselves. No need to send more soldiers to stir things up. There's been too much stirring already."

"Give them land, hell! Give them nothing. They took. We take. Even your old friend, Cass, agrees to that, Frenchy. He said, 'The land should belong to those who will work it for the common good,' and you know that. I say, I hope they are stirred some more. All the way to Kansas. Hurrah for President Jackson." And he laughed, the cold, nervous laugh of the unsure speaking surely.

Milan remained silent, but Ganus smiled a little, knowing in his quiet way that differences of opinion are not always the root of a disagreement. Some men cannot stand the quiet strength of another more competent and content within himself. These strengths offer challenges to the strong and the half strong, and especially the strong gone unsure.

The stranger also remained in stony, challenging silence until the firewarmth added fire to his liquor. The flames danced on the wetness of his beard. He showed no awe for the strength of the Frenchman, more concerned, perhaps, with his own thoughts and his show of defiance.

Finally he turned and stomped his way to the stairs, dragging one leg unevenly behind him. Half way up, however, he stopped. His watery eyes turned belligerently to the little group below him, made a full circle then came back to Milan. This time his voice was hushed with emotion. "Maybe you wouldn't have so much love for those red niggers, Frenchy, if you had been with me at Raisin River." His voice slowly rose as memories swelled within him. "Maybe if you had saw the hair of your best friend hanging from a Pawnee belt and heard the screams of dying men all around you in the bloody snow. . . . Maybe. . . ." But the liquor was stirring too much, or the lack of enough of it brought him the knowledge that women's faces, white and strained, were looking up at him from the dancing shadows. He stopped, rubbed a dirty sleeve across his eyes, mumbled a half apology, and stumbled on into the darkness of the loft.

The sound of the dragging leg grated harshly through the quieted room, then stopped. A door creaked open, then closed.

Milan added a stick to the fire. It crackled to life. This

was not the first time he had heard of Raisin River, or Red Run, or Mackinaw, or any of the other Indian massacres. But there were good Indians and bad Indians. And there were reasons and there were results.

After a while Ganus broke the silence. "Now tell us, Milan, where are we going to find the best Michigan land?"

Milan's love of life was clearly reflected in his quick reply, and Mina smiled as she heard it. "The best for fishing, the best for farming, or the best for living?"

"The best for farming, of course, "someone answered. "How else does a man earn a living?"

Milan smiled now. "Well, those ignorant red niggers have been making out for quite a spell, but if it's work you want, I am always told that the best soil is in the lower counties. Most anywhere south of the Maple River, I would guess. They also have the most muskrats and the biggest mosquitoes."

"Prairie Ronde, that's the place to buy."

Ganus's eyes shifted to the man who spoke. He was one of the smooth–talking speculators Ganus had seen at the land office.

"They tell me that Yankee Springs is the best." This speaker was a young man who had come up on the boat, hardly old enough to grow a beard but sturdy and quick of eye. "All oak openings, good water, and plenty of rich soil."

"And plenty of trees to be cut and stumps to pull before

you can plant a crop," said the Easterner. "Prairie Ronde has twenty thousand acres without a tree."

"You mean it had twenty thousand acres before you buyers moved in," replied the boy. "Besides, I ain't feared of cuttin' trees and burnin' if'n I can get good land cheap. Pa and me did plenty of it back in Pennsylvany. Course I ain't got Pa now. But I can still cut and burn."

"I still believe, Ganus, that you and Mina would like the land that I have told you about in the north."

"Nothing but sand hills, pine trees and cedar swamps," scoffed the Easterner. "I can sell you eighty acres at Prairie Ronde for eight hundred and fifty dollars. All clear and ready for the plow."

Ganus, who had been sitting quietly with his back to the fire, spoke in challenge, directing his deep voice upward. "At a profit of seven hundred and fifty dollars," he said. "Besides, if you had, good Prairie Ronde land, stranger, you would be at Prairie Ronde, selling it where the good land sells itself. We want no burned over edges where the stumps and roots still fill the soil."

Milan's laugh showed his respect for Ganus.

The young man added, "That's right, mister. When they burned low they pull hard. My dad always said, 'cut them high and set them true and they make a damn good fence for you.'"

As the night wore on, the newcomers drifted off and Ganus, Milan, and Mina were left alone at the fire. Milan became more serious. "There is still good land in these southern counties," he said, "but the best of it has been taken. To get good land there now means paying the high prices to those like this man who bothers us or taking land heavy with timber and dotted with swamps.

"Farther to the north," he said, "beyond the Muskingum and the White Rivers there is a range of rolling hills. Here, within sight of Lake Michigan, is a strip of land so rich that it grows pine trees two hundred feet tall, there is none of this smell of pigs, and the swamp fever is rare."

Ganus looked up. A new light grew in his eyes as he heard those words. "How about the soil, Milan? Is it not too light?"

"It is lighter than in the south," agreed Milan, "but it is dark and rich. I believe there have been no fires here to burn the trees and the soil. I am not a farmer, but I have seen the Indians raising fine pumpkins and potatoes. But best of all there is fine fruit, Indian pear, crab apples, hackberry, and blueberries big as musket balls."

Ganus was hesitant. All the stories he had heard had told him that this was poor country for farming. But nobody starves where there is fruit. And there was a call to it that was hard to resist. Perhaps it was the call of the Serbian high country of his ancestors. After all, they had done well before the coming of the Turks, and fruit had been their pride. Perhaps it was not right to resist that call. This would be what Milan calls living country. A healthy country where a boy like Toma would grow up strong.

Chapter Three

The next morning broke clear. The early sunlight slanting across from the Canadian shore of the Detroit River tempered the chill of the night, warmed the board walks along Woodbridge Street, and sent little wisps of steam drifting upward. Merchants called to one another as they swept briskly at their store fronts and a drayman labored silently with long poles and piles of straw, trying valiantly to extricate his wagon and steaming horses from the mud of Jefferson Avenue.

Ganus was awake with the sun. Mina still slept, the rhythm of her breathing sounding peaceful and satisfied. Ganus looked at her and, as always, felt the pride of a man well satisfied with his woman. He turned his head to where Toma lay quietly, eyes wide awake to the breaking day but content in his nest on the floor of their room.

Ganus lay back and traced the cracks in the beams of their rough lodging. How many like him had passed through these doors on their way to a new life in the wilderness that stretched out to the west of them? Where were they now, all of those who had passed through this gateway? Were they happy with what they had found? Were their bellies full and their children warm, or was hard work and hunger dogging their new lives?

He smiled, knowing full well that the human lot was as varied as it had been since the beginning of time, and that success or failure was dependent as always on the wit and will of the animal.

He slipped quietly from the bed and went to the window. Like a waking dog the town was stretching to a new day. The merchants had finished their sweeping and left their doors open to the sun. The town dogs were prancing on the boardwalk and a lone boy in blue homespun went barefoot towards the waterfront bouncing a long fishpole on his shoulder and carrying a can of worms in the other hand. He stopped as a muffled clatter approached from the south.

Ganus turned, too, and saw two Indian boys running alongside the road and between them, as if under escort, was Milan, riding the dancing chestnut mare and leading two other bridled horses.

Ganus wondered, does this man ever sleep? For it had been midnight at this same window when he had watched him ride south out of town into the darkness of the night. He had said nothing to Mina. There were already stories enough being told about this big Frenchman.

Mostly they were about how he would appear in Detroit only now and then and that he always came in a canoe well loaded with bales of the finest furs which always brought the best price. Slept on by Indians, was said to be his secret. An old trapper had told this to Ganus. Every one polished by the touch of human flesh.

But not only was he on good terms with the red men, he was known to be friendly, too, with Governor Mason, the boy Governor who was well thought of by all with whom Ganus had talked. And it was well known that he held an even closer relationship with Ex–Governor Cass.

Perhaps it was these friendships which made his services of such value to Ganus and Mina. The horses, for instance; Ganus knew that they were very scarce. He had been told that the only ones in Detroit were either the big animals of the French farmers, the few coming in on each immigrant boat, or those being held closely by the Indians. These last were the offspring of the cavalry horses stolen from the Americans or the English during the battles with the British in 1812 and 1813. Most likely Milan had tapped this source, for these were good–looking animals.

They spent the next two days preparing for their journey. During this time Milan's help was priceless. Seeds and muskets were bought from the French farmers by assuring them that they could easily replace them during the summer trading season. Axes and blankets were brought from the merchant's back rooms when he cocked the long musket and slammed it noisily across the counter to add emphasis to the devil–may–care look in his eyes. If they were not brought out, Milan walked into the back rooms himself and, brushing aside the objections with a careless laugh, made sure that there was nothing held back that might be important to them. More than once he returned with that big boyish grin on his face, carrying an armful of choice merchandise.

"Take your pick, Mina. It is all for sale. They just hold it for their friends in town or for the high prices they hope to get tomorrow."

Then he would look at the merchant. "Right, M'sieur? Look at it well, Mina, and if you need another blanket there is a fine one on a bed back there yet."

Then from the back room came a woman's voice. "You come back here again, Milan, you wild Frenchman, and you will need more than that big musket. I'll scratch your French eyes out."

At that challenge, Milan disappeared again into the back room. There was a scream with a hint of pleasure in it, a long tirade in French, and Milan reappeared with a fine English wool blanket and added it to the pile with a laugh.

By evening most of their needs were accounted for and they were back at the inn enjoying the leaping flames of Uncle Ben's fire. All, that is, except Milan who had remembered an errand and had again ridden off into the night.

In about an hour he was back, obviously pleased with himself, and presented Toma with a very useful gift. "It is not from me," he said. "It is from Mary Singing Wind, one of my favorite girl friends. And she say, 'No money. This is for little Toma, to make his back strong and straight like the Ottawa. Different, yes? from these thieving Yankees.'"

So the gift was examined. A board of cedar, it was, to which had been woven a strange narrow basket of finely woven willow, bound with buckskin and decorated with colored trader's beads.

"Stand up, my Mina," he said. And as she stood by the glowing fire he strapped the strange basket to her back. Then, picking up Toma, he dropped him roughly into the basket and tied him firmly with crossed straps of buckskin. With this Mina could carry Toma on her back, Indian fashion, or tie him in front of her to a pack horse during their journey.

Next morning was departure time and Milan and Ganus were up early, packing and preparing the horses. Milan had not favored a wagon. To use one would have meant taking the long way over the muddy Chicago Trail then north through Yankee Springs. They would take the shorter trail west by north to Grand Rapids. "There," said Milan, "my friends on the river will furnish us with more supplies and we will go on by canoe."

To Mina, that first day of riding was hardest of all. They had scarcely left the wide expanse of Woodward Avenue when they plunged into long stretches of mosquito–infested swamps. Here the road was either clinging mud or the rough corduroy over which their horses slipped and pranced, disliking the unevenness of the wet logs.

They moved in silence, Mina trying hard not to show the weariness the jolting horses soon produced. Ganus rode silently, stubbornly, concerned about both Mina and Toma.

The sun had appeared briefly in the morning, then faded into misty cloud cover. By noon the cover had thickened and rain was falling steadily. They pulled on their rubber capes and these helped to keep them dry, but they were heavy and airless and added to the discomfort of riding.

Milan took Toma, as the rain started to fall, and fashioned a willow circle over his carrying frame. Over the willow he stretched a small piece of canvas tied firmly with a leather thong. With this folded down his back he carried him securely on his broad shoulders, with Toma making faces and sputtering, but dry and happy.

"This one," said Milan, "is going to be a good traveler."

At noon Milan passed out food from the pack, but they stopped for only a short time. Then they were on their way again, still eating as they rode. "We are lucky," he called back to them as they ate. "This rain keeps the mosquitoes down. We travel three more hours, then we will be out of the worst swamps and I find you a warm cabin for the night. This I know is true, and tomorrow will be better."

After a while the swamps gave way to gentle rises, and the trees changed from cedars and birches to maple, beeches and oaks. There were openings now along the trail and in many of these were cabins. Squat and unkempt looking, they were, with the bark hanging loose from yearling logs like feathers from moulting chickens. There was white smoke drifting lazily from the chimneys, though, fields still dotted with stumps and shocks of corn, and here and there a half open shelter with a cow lazing contentedly inside.

"Take your pick," said Milan, "the latch string is out on every one. That is the way it is here. In a few more years this will change, but now news from the outside is scarce and that alone is enough pay for a night's lodging."

A little farther on a husky young man was splitting wood beside a very new cabin. "Haloo," Milan shouted. Obviously these people had not had time to properly prepare for winter and their wood supply was nearly exhausted by the long, cold spring. Milan's quick eye saw that they could help.

A young man came from behind the shed. "Caleb Hawkins," he said, with a hand thrust forward. Milan took it and introduced the rest.

Soon Mina was talking woman talk with the young mother of two, from Vermont. The children, five and seven, were moving from silent shyness to enthusiastic friendliness as they used Toma to bridge the gap. Ganus and Milan were quickly building up the pile of fresh–cut wood while Caleb brought extra water from the creek. Milan, first checking carefully the shed at the back of the cabin to make sure that meat was available, added a fat rabbit that he had shot that afternoon.

Their food was stew cooked in an iron kettle over the open fire and their beds were their own blankets spread before the fire. But they were warm and dry. Conversation continued far into the night as the rain muttered steadily against the thin roof. The fire in the big grate died to a steady glow in the darkness of a friendly new land.

"We will see deer today," Milan predicted the next morning. "The grass is turning green in the clearings and they will be coming out of their winter swamping yards to find it."

And soon they did. Milan, who was always in the lead, stopped slowly on the trail and sat motionless. Mina and Ganus, coming up behind him, stopped also and saw on the side of a juniper–dotted hill three young doe raising their heads from the spring grass. The deer stood and watched them. Only their gently moving ears betrayed the presence of life. Finally they continued their grazing, only to dance out of sight in long, graceful leaps as Milan started forward.

"Buck and two more doe back in the poplars," said Milan, but Mina had seen only the three.

But if I miss much I also see much, thought Mina. And she stopped. From the top branch of a fire–scarred oak, a mourning dove twitched its pointed tail and called to a distant mate. The sound, soft as velvet on the morning air, came clear from a hundred yards away. From a cedar above a quiet run of water a cardinal appeared, rested briefly in the sunlight of a budding maple, then disappeared. This flash of flame was followed at each move by a puff of smoke, its mate.

Turning on her horse, Mina looked back at Ganus and laughed as he ducked the branch she had held on passing.

Ganus was happy to leave Detroit. He had tired quickly of the ceaseless activity, the press of numbers, and the urgency to obtain lodging, supplies, and information. He was amused by the oozing mud, never allowed to rest for the turning of wheels and the plodding of feet. But he was also mindful of the faces lined by need and haunted by losses from the fire that had burned the city in 1805, the cholera plagues that ended the lives of one out of every ten residents in 1832 and 1834, and the hardships that had accompanied the wars with the English and with Chief Pontiac. He knew that some of these people had been held for ransom during those times. Others had seen their families split by a war which pitted brother against brother and husband against in–laws. For here only the thin line of the Detroit River had separated the two sides, a river never before looked upon as a dividing line.

Other faces he remembered were those of the weak or the unfortunate coming back from the frontiers that had brought them only deaths from the fever or failure to cope with the wilderness.

But while he was reading these things in the faces of Detroit, he wondered what they had read in his.

He thought he knew what they saw. A big plodding man. Not quick enough to make a sharp deal and not fiery enough to bend the will of those he met. This Ganus knew was true and could not be hid. The quickness and the fire must be left to men like Milan. My coals burn more slowly. But, although this was true, the heat was steady and with this he could be satisfied. I'll just continue to plod and win my days with hard work and common sense. That is my way. Let Milan and those like him enjoy theirs. Then he smiled a little to himself. And let those who will, laugh that we let Milan take us north to the tall tree country where the soil is light and the hills are dry. There are many ways for a man to make a living if he is willing to work. We will find one.

I don't believe that I was made for riding a horse, though, I feel like a gum that has just had its tooth pulled.

They reached another high clearing. Mina sat on her horse waiting for Ganus to catch up and wondered whether it would help to dismount for a moment or whether she should just stay on the horse and wait for the morning soreness to pass. She decided on the latter and shifted to look eastward from where they had come. The little cluster of cabins called Brighton had been passed through in the early morning and was now only a few wisps of smoke on the horizon. The road had disappeared completely and if there was a trail, only Milan could see it. She merely followed where he led and marveled that he never had to turn back to get around a swamp or to find a suitable crossing through a creek.

Far behind now and already dim in her memory was Detroit. Only two days back, she reminded herself, but already they seemed in a different world, a world of silence yet one that mingled all the wild, chirping calls of the woods and meadows.

Detroit was gone, to be set aside in her memory along with Buffalo, Albany, New York and all of the other little hamlets in between. The river, too, would settle into its channel in her memory along with the Hudson, the Mohawk, and that little stream that splashed so gaily through their hills back in France. Fading, too, were the long miles of the Erie Canal and the songs of the boaters with their strange talk of horned breezes, ash winds, and long waters.

Miles and years stretched out between these memories of places and people. Now all of them seemed far away and long ago; another new world, with another whole book of new pages was unfolding. If it were not for the reunion with Milan, my faith in Ganus, and the beauty of this country, she thought, it might seem like too much. But Milan is right: take away the backaches and the mosquitoes and this country and its people can stir one's blood. If the hills where he is taking us are still higher and greener than these, I am sure I will be glad that we came.

Ganus's pinto plodded out of the woods and stopped at her side. "Tired, Mina?"

Ganus did not take to horses as well as she did and she

knew that his bones must be weary of the trail. But his thoughts were of her. She smiled back.

"Tired, yes. Sometimes I think my bones are all aching at once. Especially after this first hour in the morning, and again late in the afternoon. Other things I hate, the swamps, the mosquitoes, the deer flies that stick in my hair, and the briers that tear at my legs: the trailing vines that trip my horse and the cold rains and the sharp winds.

"But just when everything seems wrong there comes a morning like this when the sun shines warm on my back and the wind is full of flowers. I know then that there will be even better days ahead and I feel good and everything seems right again. I am French, Ganus, and I will have those days.

"How about you, Ganus?"

Ganus just grinned.

Milan was riding ahead, watching for game, he said. Mina suspected that there were other reasons. Milan liked people, but his years on the trails made him alert to every sound and movement. Each one told him a story and everything that interrupted that story could be annoying to him. Mina had become sensitive to this, and many of their hours on the trail were spent in silence.

Then, like her, there were other times when his mood would change and he would burst into song or talk loudly and joke freely on the trials of the journey.

Toma rode in his basket on a back or tied to the shady side of a horse. He was the best traveler of all but was impatient with any delay. He liked the swaying of the horses and the jingle of bridles. He would flay the air with his arms and laugh when a leafy branch brushed across his face and sputter in disgust when it was a mosquito. When they were forced to pass through swamps, Milan would smear bear tallow on his face and cover his hands with little buckskin mittens as protection from these pests.

"Not bad yet," he would say. "But in another month these swamps will be so full of mosquitoes that they will be carrying off the bobcats for winter food."

This was slow travel for Milan and he did not always hide well his impatience to be getting on. The wooded hills which to Mina and Ganus were new and wild were too close to civilization for him. Here he could still smell the woodsmoke from settlers cabins and hear the distant bawl of cows and the crowing of roosters. His mind forged ahead, on to the tall pine trees and the open meadows of the sand and hill country where he could stretch his eyes from one hilltop to another and drink in the freshness of the air. Even more he longed for the far north where the sand hills turned to rocky ridges, the rivers thundered and fell fast and deep into the clear waters of Lake Superior, and the good Chippewa still welcomed a stranger to their fires. But that must wait.

It was near the end of the fifth day from Detroit that they reached the banks of a clear, stony river bordered by cedar trees and clumps of white birch. The trails here were showing signs of use and although they saw no Indians, Milan told them that the village of the little Chief Okemos was not far to the south and this was their hunting grounds. Okemos had led his people to their last battle with Chief Pontiac at Detroit, though, and would be friendly.

They crossed the river on a gravelly shoal and passed on through groves of huge oak trees where rare black squirrels scampered from tree to tree. "Here," said Milan, pointing to the big trees, "the women from the village gather acorns for winter food. They make a bitter stew, but boiled acorns with an occasional raccoon or porcupine added for flavor has kept many an Ottawa from starving during a hard winter."

The day passed. The afternoon tiredness settled into Mina's back and her legs turned numb from the steady contact with the jolting horse. During this part of the day she and Ganus would ride in silence. The mosquitoes became more unbearable and the beauty of the hills was lost behind thoughts of the night camp and warm blankets.

Only Milan stayed fresh and strong. He would cut a strip of dried venison from his pack and give it to Toma to stop his fretting, then break into a song as though he was fresh on the trail.

"Split Rock ahead," he finally called. Time to make camp. No taverns, no cabins, nothing tonight but the trees overhead and the stars at our feet."

It was Ganus's job to gather firewood while Mina and Milan broke open the packs. Soon a fire was warming the evening air and Mina was roasting two spruce hens that Milan had shot earlier in the day.

Later, after they had eaten their fill and were sitting around the fire with a light breeze rustling the trees above them, Mina asked Milan about the huge boulder standing nearly as high as she was tall and appearing to have been split through the middle by a maple tree which grew tall and straight between the two great halves of solid stone.

"Where does such a stone come from in a country where there are no mountains?" she asked. "And did the tree really split the stone apart as it appears?"

Milan leaned back against the warm face of the boulder and puffed thoughtfully on the pipe which he often lit in the evenings. He seemed hesitant to tell the story he himself found hard to believe. Then he started, and in a strange, roundabout way told a fascinating story.

"Many years ago, soon after I came to Michigan Territory, I spent a winter trapping and trading with the Chippewas in the Mauvais country far to the north and west. In the spring, about like now, I load my canoe heavy with furs and come to Detroit to get the big price.

"After I leave Lake Superior and come down through the Sault of the Sainte Marie into the Lake of the Hurons I know that I have been seen by many Indian and white trappers. I was still young then and afraid that some of these might try to rob me of my furs, so from there I traveled only at night and arrived at Detroit early one morning.

"While I was pulling my canoe from the water I noticed a big man watching me. I say, bon jour, stranger. You want something?' I was young then and full of fight. Not as smart as now.

"The man looked for a long time at my canoe and my furs and the Sioux moccasins I wear and I can see that he is smart about these things.

"'You look like a strong young man, Frenchy,' he say. 'How would you like to go on a long trip with me?'

"'My name is Milan LaVoy,' I say, 'and I just been on a long trip. All I want now is a short beer.'

"He laughs and shakes my hand and say, 'I am Lewis Cass, I'm pleas' to meet you. Those are fine furs you bring, but that buffalo robe, that don't come from Michigan Territory. You been all the way to Sioux country, Frenchy?'

"I don't like stranger to ask so many questions, but this stranger I like. So I tell him, 'No, just Chippewa country. The robe was a gift from my friend Charette, who gets some things from the Sioux.'

"Mr. Cass looked at me for a long time, then he say, 'Simon Charette, of the South West Post at Lac Du Flambeau, I bet. Frenchy, you have had a long trip.'

"Now I was surprised, because Lac Du Flambeau is far up in Lac Superior country. Only Indians and trappers ever go there. So I wonder how in hell this fat tenderfoot could know Simon Charette. But he knew him all right, and he asked me how was old Simon's wife and were the Chippewas still friendly up on the Mauvais, and about Brazil Durante and the Court Oreille. This was like old times and we soon become good friends.

"And when I left Detroit I shook hands and said, 'When you get ready for that long trip, let me know.'

"Almost a year later I got word from Mr. Cass, Come to Detroit, we leave by the end of May. He don't say where we are going, or why, just come. I like that, so I load my furs and start my long trip to Detroit. I know now who he is though. Charette has now told me. He is the Governor of the whole damn Michigan Territory and was a general during the war." Milan took Mina by the hand. "I was going to work for a big man, Mina, and learn many things that were good for this wild young Frenchman.

"Back in Detroit Mr. Cass called us together one day and said, 'Men, you probably wonder where we are going, and why. It is right that you know and I will tell you the best I can. I am the Governor of Michigan Territory by appointment of our President Madison in Washington. Our boundaries now run north to Lake Superior, Missisagaigon, to many of you, and west to the Mississippi River. We know much about lower Michigan but there are many things yet to be learned about the North Country, and about the West, we know little. We do not even know exactly where the Territory ends because no one has properly mapped the upper regions of this river. We have reason to believe that there are minerals in these hills, and Chippewa, Ottawa, Sioux, Menominee, Fox, and a dozen other tribes of red men in the woods. If I am to represent our people well it is important that I know more about all of these things. It is to learn these things that we make our journey.

"'Among you are men who have already traveled through most of these places. You have all been carefully chosen and we appreciate your help. And when I say we, I am speaking for all of the people of the Territory as well as myself and our great President in Washington.

"'But let me remind you. There will be many hard times. Those of you who have traveled the swamps between the St. Louis and the Mississippi rivers know well the nature of that country.'

"Some of our voyageurs shouted their agreement here, and old françois Brunot spoke up loud, 'Seven leagues it is of tamarack bog between the St. Louis and the Savanna, and forty more hard leagues before you reach Sandy Lake. Swamps up to your armpits, mosquitoes so big they carry off your paddles, and it takes a strong man carrying a canoe or a pack nineteen pauses to cross.

"'This is no country for boys or fat men, Mr. Cass.'

"Mr. Cass just laugh and say, 'I make it, François. I will make it or you men will carry me.'

"But françois says, 'I carry no man, Mr. Cass. You will wade like the rest of us or drown in the swamps.'

"But Mr. Cass just looks at the men, 'You have heard

what françois has said. There will be bad days and good days. If any of you are afraid of the hard times please leave us now. Don't wait until the hard times are with us and someone else has to carry your load.'

"He told us much more, but not a man dropped out. These were good men and they all knew that Mr. Cass was a good leader.

"There were thirty–eight of us when we started. Mr. Cass had ordered three big canoes to be made by the Chippewas, who make them best. These were over thirty feet long and wide as a man is tall. I was one of ten Voyageurs who would handle canoes and guide where we knew the country. Ten Indians were to paddle another canoe and carry packs, and eight soldiers came along to eat up all the damn food. Then there were some friends of Mr. Cass who had jobs to do, like making maps, checking the soil and the rocks and learning about the Indians. These all seemed useless to me at first, then, like I say, I begin to learn many things and I started to say, maybe these men are all right.

"Anyway, we have a good party and I get acquainted again with many old friends like the white Shawnee, Joe Parks, Wyang Ding the Chippewa, and fine Frenchmen like Jean Baptiste Dufrene and Medarde Gavin. We have already had many good times together."

Milan leaned back and stretched his legs, enjoying the reliving of those days. Ganus selected a few good sticks of wood and Milan waited until the new burst of flame had subsided, then continued.

"We were gone from the last of May until the frost came in the fall. We knew good times and hard times. But when we returned, there were still the thirty–eight of us, and we had traveled more than four thousand miles. Much of it in country that white men had never seen before.

"You tired now, Mina, or you want to hear more?"

"Oh, more, please, Milan! I am just beginning to know you."

"That is the reason I tell you these things, Mina. That trip did much to change your wild brother. I sat many hours around campfires and in our canoes with these good men and learned many things. Mr. Cass and Mr. Schoolcraft spent many hours teaching us to speak the English, the Algonquian, and the Sioux tongues.

"One of the other things I learned may explain this big boulder. I would not tell this to many people because it is hard to understand. But I will tell it to you as Mr. Schoolcraft told it to me, and you can believe it or no.

"Mr. Schoolcraft was called Pawgwabecanega by the Chippewas. To them this means 'worker among the rocks.' They called him this because he spent much time studying the rocks wherever he went and told us many things about them.

"One day he say to me, 'Come here, Milan, you wild Frenchman. Would you believe that this stone I hold came from a mountain many miles north of here?'

"I looked at the stone. It looked like any other stone to

me and I say, 'You crazy, Hank. I saw you pick it up from the ground right here. What you try to tell me?'"

Milan was enjoying his story now.

"He smile and say, 'Milan, my friend, that stone is quartz. There is no quartz in this country.'

"'That one is in this country,' I say.

"'But it was not always here. Sometime, maybe a thousand years ago, this stone was part of a mountain many miles north of here; North beyond the lake of the Hurons.'

'How do you know this?' I ask.

'I have read that this can be so and I have seen those mountains along the canoe trail you voyageurs call the Great Trace, just as you have. Those hills are solid white quartz, the same as this.'

"'No, I don't believe.' But I am beginning to wonder, because I have seen these white mountains many times and the stone was like them, just as he say.

"'It is true, Milan, my friend. It was carried here by a glacier of ice many years ago. This I have come to believe.'

"I say, 'Pawgwabeconega, you better sit down. Here, I get you a drink of water.'"

Ganus was chuckling now as he enjoyed Milan's humor.

"But, my Mina, old Pawgwabecanega has made me to think, and by and by I have come to believe that he could be right. I have seen many signs since, and Mr. Schoolcraft showed me many other reasons to believe that this did happen.

"Now I have knives in my head, like him. Everywhere I go I pick up the stones and say, 'little stone, where in hell you come from?'"

"So you are saying that this big rock may also have been carried here the same way. Is that true, Milan?"

"I have come to believe that this is true, Mina. If you want to ask Pawgwabecanega, he now lives at the Sault St. Marie. We can take the long canoe ride and you can ask him for yourself."

"No thank you, Milan. The rocks might get into my head, too. Then there would be three of us."

Slowly the fire died to a heap of glowing embers in a circle of gray ash. The night sounds of the woods chirped and rustled. The ripple of the little river in the mountains of France lingered in Mina's mind. The nearer memories of the day pushed the past aside. She thought again of what Milan had told them, and knew now that the free–spirited big brother she had known in France, who had shown little interest in schooling, had truly changed.

She lay back in her blanket to think. A star found a hole in the trees above her, flickered, and disappeared. She was asleep.

Milan smiled at Ganus and added a stout chunk of oak to the dying fire. It smoked briefly, glowed and burst into flame. Dead wood, like lost memories, has a right to return to new life.

Chapter Four

It was the evening of the second day from split rock. Mina was busy preparing the evening meal. Toma was swinging his arms and bouncing merrily in his basket which Ganus had hung from the limb of a nearby tree. Ganus and Milan were down by the broad river that Milan called the Grand, drinking of the beauty of the late evening.

Suddenly Mina became aware that Toma had stopped his bouncing. She sensed a movement behind her and turned to look squarely into the dark face of an old Indian.

Mina had seen many Indians since she came to Michigan but never before had one been so close to her that she could catch the smell of it, and never had she seen one with such a menacing appearance as this one.

He was not tall, but was very broad of shoulder and thick of chest. His legs were decidedly bowed and this crookedness was accentuated by his dirty buckskin breeches with their rows of worn fringe from ankle to thigh. His only other clothing was a pair of greasy moccasins, once finely decorated with beads, but now in much need of repair. His hair was coarse and black and hung into a dirty blanket of trader's wool, drawn about his bare shoulders in the manner of an old lady's shawl. The most striking part of his features, though, were the eyes. Deep set and hostile among leathery wrinkles, they seemed to smoulder and glow like those of an owl, and the huge, crooked nose that separated them accentuated his owlish appearance.

The scream that Mina could not hold back left her breathless yet wondering if the sound had really came forth. The hot blood pounded through her temples and she felt weak as she moved instinctively between Toma and the red man. She was half aware of Ganus pounding up the hill, with Milan's voice, sharp and edgy behind him, saying, "Easy, boy! Easy!" Then she felt Ganus' strong arms around her and heard Milan's voice changed to a relieved chuckle as he faced the old man.

"Cugiascum, you old devil, what are you doing here?" he asked, extending his hand to the old Indian.

The old man looked at the two spruce hens browning over the fire, and then up at Milan. There was the hint of friendliness in his dark eyes that Milan always brought from these people. "Meat, good," he said in halting English, still showing no sign of excitement or emotion. Then he trailed off into the Ottawa tongue and, without waiting to be invited, he laid down his battered rifle and sat cross–legged on the ground close to the fire.

"Well, let's give it a try then," said Milan, and, after digging another set of utensils from the pack, shared the food with the older man. He ate silently and hungrily, answering Milan's questions with only the faintest grunt or nod of the head.

When the last of the food had disappeared, he rose, wiped his mouth on a corner of the dirty blanket, and walked into the darkness as silently as he had come.

Around the fire that night, Milan stirred the coals with a long stick and told them another strange story.

"In 1821," he said, "Squatters were moving into Michigan and starting to settle on Indian land south of the Grand River. Governor Cass was afraid of trouble between the Indians and the squatters so he decided that he must try to get control of the Indian lands before the problem became serious. He called for a meeting of all chiefs of western Michigan.

"I went with Mr. Cass to the meeting. We reached the place, called Chicago, at night. Already the river bank and the lake shore were bright with the council fires of the Indians.

"Mr. Cass wasted no time. He went to the black trader who runs the post there and tells him, no more whiskey is to be sold to the Indians while the council fires still burn. The chiefs of the first rank like this because they know that this will help them to control the lesser chiefs and their braves.

"Then Mr. Cass visits the council fires and the pipes are

passed many times.

"During the next week the fires are kept burning and great Indian speakers spent long hours telling how their people feel about the white settlers. The handsome Potawatomi, Matea, spoke long.

"'My people want only peace with their white brothers,' he said. 'Many of my people have already been driven from far east of the Lake of the Eries, and east of the Iroquois hunting grounds. Now, in Michigan, they can go no farther. Across the big lake are the Foxes and the Winnebagoes, the Menominees and the great nation of the Sioux, with whom our brothers the Chippewa are already at war. We want only that which is ours, our land is our home and our hunting ground. Leave us these and go in peace.'

"The Ottawa, Topinabee, also spoke for a long time.

"'The white men are like the snowflakes in winter,' he said. 'They are many and we are few. We cannot fight so many. They come like the locusts come across the plains during the hot summer moons. They settle on everything left uncovered and chew and destroy all that lives. We already have little left. Our hunting grounds provide little meat, our sugar trees are being destroyed and our garden lands taken. Without these the Indians cannot live.'

"Governor Cass listened and was sad. What the Indians said was true. It was also true that the way of the Indians was a wasteful use of land. The white settlers could not allow it to remain idle for use only as hunting grounds.

They needed it and would put it to much more productive use. It was a clash of two cultures, sad but not new. The Indians were asking for something that could not be. They would have to change or die. Governor Cass probably knew what the answer would be. His job was an unpleasant one, but it must be done.

"On the fourth night he got to his feet. The chiefs waited. It is not the way of an Algonquian to interrupt, and after one has spoken it is customary to spend a few minutes in silence, to make sure that the speaker is finished, or to allow him to add anything he may have forgotten. These courtesies were given to Mr. Cass.

"'I come to you as a friend,' he said. 'You, Topinabee, and you' Matea, I have met before. Also you, Black Cloud-Mukutay Oquot, and you, Cobmoosa-the Flat River Ottawa. You know I will speak to you with a single tongue. But I cannot speak to you with the words of truth and tell you what you wish to hear.' He waited, but there was no reply.

"'I am sad, as you are sad, when I see this movement of my people onto your hunting grounds and garden lands. What Topinabee says is the truth, the white settlers are many. They will continue to come like the locusts come, until all of the good black soil of Michigan has been claimed by them. Nothing that you can do, and nothing that I can do, will stop this movement. These people come from far away where their fathers have been killed in bloody wars. They have known the rocky soils of the mountains and the hunger that this brings. The Michigan soil is good. They will come and come and come, until the good land has all been taken.

"'You are all chiefs. You are wise in the ways of your people and wise in the ways of the white people. You know that I speak the truth. Many of you fought with Chief Pontiac and with Okemos and with the Prophet. You know that fighting is no longer a wise path to take. There is left to you then only a few narrow paths. Let me show them to you as a white brother, then let the wisdom of your leaders choose, as they do on a long journey, the one which it is wise to follow.

"'First, if I am to speak the truth, I must speak hard words. Do not try to hold to your lands south of the Grand River. This country is rich with the dark soil that is prized by the white settlers. They will continue to drive you and your squaw from it. Better to be pierced by the arrow only once than to feel it many times.'

"There were grunts of anger and a movement of eyes, but Mr. Cass was allowed to continue.

"'If you are to remain in Michigan, you must move your people north of the Grand River to the sand country, or even farther to the rocky hills beyond the big lakes to where the white man's plow is useless and the growing season is short. In those hills are ridges, and valleys where there is heavy soil for your gardens. Use them wisely and you will have pumpkins and corn for the winters. There are hills covered with maple trees for your sugar, not as many as in the south, but some are there. I have seen them. As for meat, it is as plentiful there as near your villages. Kill it sparingly for skins. Do not waste it and I believe that you can live well.'

"There are more days and nights of council. Mr. Cass reminds them often that the wave of white settlers will continue to come whether or not they sell their lands, and if they wait too long their claim to it may be forgotten.

"I believe the Indians knew this, and it was this knowing that broke them down.

"Finally, one night after a long day of speeches, and after Mr. Cass had promised them five hundred dollars a year, a rifle and other gifts, a dark, eagle–eyed chief came forward. He was ready. His Flat River country was already dotted with the cabins of the squatters. He would sign the paper that would sell his land to the Great White Father in Washington. That chief was Cugiascum, Chief Long Nose of the Flat River tribe. The money and the gifts had led him to be the first to step forward. After that, others quickly followed and all of the remaining land south of the Grand River became government land.

"But Cugiascum was never allowed to receive that bonus. Like many others, the Grand River Ottawas had counciled and sworn that the first chief among them to step forward to sign this treaty would be killed.

"That was Cugiascum whom we just fed. The strange part is that now, after sixteen years, he is still alive. He has paid dearly for his folly, though. His family has been poisoned, he has been close to death many times, and is a wandering exile from his own people.

"It is a sad story, Mina, but it tells you much about the ways of the frontier."

The fire burned low, then as a low night wind rustled the trees it grew bright and burst into flames as though, like the people around it, it was not yet fitted for sleep.

So Milan told more stories, stories of the two beautiful daughters of Jane Johnston and grand–daughters of Chief Waubjeeg. These girls had been well educated in white men's schools and became the wives of two of his best friends, one of them being Mr. Schoolcraft.

When Mina asked him about them, he told them more about the canoe trips he had made among those islands of Lake Huron where mountains of stone as white as Italian marble rise out of the water along the route of the voyageurs. A land of blue bays, fast streams, and quiet lakes of clear water where the Indians catch their fill of whitefish, trout, and the sweet–flavored perch. This is the land of the Ottawas and the Hurons, and the first country to be traveled by the voyageurs.

The fire died again. A light, cool breeze rustled through the trees. Indians, canoes, and memories from three different corners of the earth twinkled like the stars and faded. Dreams of the future dimmed and the little party slept.

There was another day of steady travel over hills rolling a little higher and a little sandier and dotted more often with the junipers that liked the lighter soil. There were little meadows, greening with new spring grass. Once in a while now there were cabins of newly peeled logs squatting against the hills and sending ribbons of wood smoke upward into the light wind.

Towards evening they prodded their horses to the crest of a hill, orange with Indian paintbrush, white with daisies, and dotted with the stumps of freshly cut trees. From here the country sloped gently downward, and shining in the distance were the broad rapids of the Grand River and the village which had risen along its banks.

Back to the east, the river appeared from the trees of the hills over which they had traveled. It took a lazy turn, then at the point where the town had been built it narrowed and dropped noisily over a series of limestone shelves which extended entirely across it. Here a mill had been built and its wheel was squeaking in noisy competition with the roar of the falls.

The village itself centered around the mill and extended each way along the river bank and back from it until the streets, with their log and farm houses dissolved into farms and freshly plowed fields. These continued, spread evenly along a well–defined trail leading into the wooded hills to the south.

On the north bank of the river the ground rose abruptly then leveled to a broad flat meadow. Here, with wisps of smoke rising from many of them, spread the log buildings of Rev. Slater's Christian Mission. Beyond this, scattered as though a giant hand had carelessly tossed them, was a vast array of bark huts and the small cultivated fields of the Ottawas.

As the little party rode down the hill, the Indian dogs announced their coming with much barking and sniffing at the horses' hooves.

Gray, wiry Rev. Slater came forward to greet them. "Bonjour, Milan. Bonjour my friend," he said, taking Milan's big hand in his two thin ones.

Then from everywhere came the Indians, some to greet them with a "Bon Jour, Bonjour Milan," for many of these Indians had been educated at Rev. Slater's school. Others came timidly, to stand in silence and observe with big black eyes while the women stole the look of the curious from behind doorways.

Mrs. Slater was a tiny, energetic wisp of a woman, only chest–high to Milan as she gave him a motherly embrace. She greeted Ganus briefly then turned her attention to Mina and little Toma. "Now my pretty ones, you come with me," she said, and lifting Toma from his carrier, she led the way through the waves of curious Indians to the nearest of the log cabins.

Inside, a dark–eyed Indian girl, dressed neatly in a cotton skirt and shirt blouse, was already preparing a bath in a huge wood tub.

"Mina, this is Louise," said Mrs. Slater.

The reply came back in soft, perfect English. "I am pleased to meet you, Mina.

May your stay with us be pleasant. Come, you may use my room," and she led the way to a neat room with a clean, comfortable bed and a homemade chest with a real glass mirror.

At the door, and with just the hint of a friendly smile, she said, softly, "As long as you wish to stay, this yours." Mina felt sure that in one brief moment of meeting the mysterious bonds of friendship were securely tied. She also noticed that the dropping of the word was the first hint that Louise had not been born to speak the English language. Mina doubted if she could do as well.

"Oh, such luxury!" said Mina. "This is my first real bath since we left Detroit. The settlers are nice, but so poor."

Mrs. Slater looked at her searchingly, and reading the fears and questions in Mina's eyes, she sat down close to her. "Not really poor, my dear, just new," she said gently. "Most of the settlers along the trails you traveled are just recovering from their first winter here. The work of building their cabins and clearing their land left them scant time to prepare for the winter. They have had no time to think of luxuries yet, my child, just the bare, hard necessities of life. Give them two or three years to clear their fields and lay up some harvest and for those who have the courage to remain, and most of these people do, material wealth will follow. In the meantime the country is beautiful and other compensations are many."

"And the people," asked Mina, "are they as fine, as

courageous, and as friendly as my Ganus thinks?."

Mrs. Slater thought for a long moment, then sat slowly down again. "I believe, my child, that they cannot be otherwise. On a frontier, qualities of courage and fineness are as necessary for survival as food and drink. If these are not present, the wolves, the Indians, and the very stillness of the nights will prod and nip and worry until the weaklings quietly leave."

Mina spread her elbows wide on the sides of the wooden tub, and rested her chin on her hands. She looked up at the older woman for a long time, her eyes a little wet from the knowing. Finally she placed a wet hand on one of Mrs. Slater's and said, warmly, "Thank you, mother Slater, thank you so much."

The next day found Louise waiting for her. "Come, we will watch the fun. Suckers and pickerel are running in the river. There will be no school today. We all have a holiday."

So after a quick breakfast, they gathered up Toma and went down to the river. Here, the Indians had already gathered to watch the fun. Indians boys in high spirits and shy little Indian girls by the dozens, all dressed neat and clean in cotton store clothes, round Indian women with their little ones playing on blankets, and everybody warm–faced and glowing with the fun of the day.

At every vantage point below the falls the Indians had erected long fir booms with the thin end extended out over the water. These long poles were lashed loosely to a fulcrum of upright supports and from the extended end of each pole were hung dip nets of wood and rawhide from three to six feet square. These were then weighted at the corners with stones so that they would sink to the bottom of the river when the butt end of each pole was raised. Then, when fish were sighted over the net, or the intuition of the fisherman told him that the time was right, the butt end of the pole was weighted down with the many boys always available and the net was raised quickly from the water to bring the silvery fish swinging to shore.

Smokehouses of logs were already fired with green hickory or apple wood to cure the meat. The heads and guts were sent to speed the growth of corn and pumpkins.

"Here, Mina, try some," laughed Louise, bringing pieces of fish from the smokehouse.

Mina found that the fresh pickerel, properly cured, was delicious.

"Here, Toma, you can have some too," and Louise showed Mina how to peel the meat from near the tail, where therer would be no bones, and gave him a very small piece.

"You have been carrying him on the Indian board," she said, feeling the back of his head. "That is good. It will make the back straight and strong. He will be the handsome one. But now, while you are here we will make his legs strong. This one will be walking soon. No more hanging in the trees then, except the ones he will climb by himself.

Mina wanted to ask, and Louise read the questions in her eyes.

"Yes, I once had a man," she said, brushing a long black braid back over her shoulder. "A good white man who was a trader across the river. We had many good times, like you and I have today. But he was not strong and the fever came often. The swamps to the south do not well suit white people. Finally I lost him, partly to the fever and partly to the white settlers. I am not sure which hurt him the more deeply. Perhaps I should not have gone to him.

"So I returned across the river to teach my people."

"I am sure you are a fine teacher."

"Mr. Slater tells me that I am. And I believe that my people are learning well, but I am not sure that it is best for them."

"You do not think that learning is always good?"

"I am not sure. One thing I cannot teach them. I cannot teach them to have a white skin, and as long as their skin is red I may be helping them to make a pie which they will not be allowed to eat."

"I am sorry there are that kind, Louise. Perhaps this will change."

"I believe that it will, Mina, but not in time. I have watched the houses climb the hill across the river and now the land to the north, too, has been sold to the white people. The Mission will go and the good Slaters with it.

We have been told that we must go to Kansas, but we will not go." She looked quietly up at Mina, then down again, Indian fashion, at the friendly river. "I see nothing but poor tomorrows for my people."

Milan and Ganus had taken the long list of things that Mina would need to start a home and, taking a young Indian, Jimmy Colby, with them, had gone down the river. As they pulled their canoe up the river bank in front of a long log building, a huge white man came out to greet them.

"Milan LaVoy! How long has it been? Three, four years now?"

"That and more, I think."

"Guard up, boy, and let's see if you are yet the man." Raising a huge right arm, he waited for Milan to seize it in his, then elbow to elbow and foot to foot, they accepted a friendly challenge of strength.

For a few minutes neither of them gave an inch. Their faces reddened and the veins stood out in their necks as each tested the will and the strength of the other.

The trader laughed. "You never make it, Milan. You are the good young buck but the old man is still the best. Give?"

"I never give. You know that, Rix. You take, if you can."

But Milan was no match for the old trader. Inch by inch, as their breath whistled from the strain, his head and shoulders were forced back until the trader let out a wild shout, and with a mighty heave drove him crashing to the ground.

Milan was up like a cat to embrace the man in a warm embrace. "It has been a long time, but you are still the good man," he said, brushing the grass from his buckskins. "How is Singing River?"

"She is fine."

"And the little ones?"

"Well and fit, but not so little anymore. The big one is tall as Jim Colby here, and nearly as handsome. Rutted too much in this Yankee valley, I think, but we are well.

"I think of you often, Milan. You and Medarde and the old times. But a leaf blows for only a little while, then it must settle somewhere and prepare to rot."

"Not much rot in that right arm, my friend."

"No, but the rot starts in the heartwood, Milan. The limbs are the last to lose their green. But we are well, and business is good. Not like old times, when the furs were here and no one else to buy or sell. But I have ways. I have the river, all the way from Chicago and Buffalo right to my door. And I still have the Ottawas."

Milan laughed. "And the other traders?"

"They are learning. They are building a riverboat now. But I will make out, look!" He led them into a back room. There he showed them piles of goods, even furniture, the likes of which they had not seen, even in Detroit.

"You have learned fast, Rix. How about oxen and gear?"

"Ho! oxen for you, Milan? That I don't believe. You

want hair ribbons too?"

Milan laughed, too, knowing his own distaste for the dull animals.

"But if your brother wants oxen, I will get them. I will need two months, though."

"And good milk cows, too?" Ganus asked. "Toma will need plenty of milk."

"Cows, too," said Rix, "and a mirror from me to your sister, Milan. If she is as handsome as you, she should have a glass."

Three days they stayed at the rapids, pleasant days for all of them, for Grand Rapids was not yet a big, dirty city like Detroit. Here there was more sand and clean water, good food and good people.

"Good bye, Mrs. Slater. Good bye, Louise." Good–byes were hard, but this time it seemed harder than ever before. The Slaters and Louise were so good. They were laughing now. Toma had learned to wave his hand, and to take a few faltering steps, too. But his nest in the center of the canoe was not the place for that.

There was a chorus of "Au Revoir, Milan" from the likable Ottawas, and they were again on their way.

Ganus learned the art of paddling quickly, but the reaching motions of a paddler set into action muscles seldom required of a digger. He suffered through the morning, but by mid afternoon the muscles deep down among his ribs were aching painfully and he gasped for breath as the wiry Frenchman in the stern called gaily, "More right,

Ganus, now left a bit, now hold it there." As the current sent them swishing past huge glacial boulders he wondered if they would have been wiser to have remained with the bouncing horses. He hid his pain until they had reached calmer water, then he shouted back to Mina. "This French brother of yours is a devil. He leads us sweating over the hills on horseback until we are just beginning to feel like we belong on a horse, then he hands us these devilish paddles and says, 'Now you are a voyageur, ahoy, ahoy, let us be gone? To hell with you, Milan! I rest."

To Milan, the river was like an old, old friend. From his kneeling position in the stern, legs spread wide and back firm against the ash strut, he became a part of the good Chippewa birch. He read the story of the water ahead, he talked to it, he listened to it, he swayed with it, and sang to it. He splashed it on Toma, he dipped his hands in it and wiped it on his face. He knew every bird, animal and reptile along its wooded edges. He saw the fish flashing from the riffles and a hundred things that Mina could not bring into focus.

She watched him with pleasure as the broad, flat muscles of his shoulders flowed like the current then, when needed, drove deep and sent the good birch ahead like a thing alive to reach a safe channel through a dangerous stretch of water. The clear, fast waters were his home. They belonged to him and he to them. Whether the going was silent and smooth through deep, still swamps where brown–eyed deer stood and gazed unafraid, or they were swaying recklessly down a boulder–strewn wash, with the spray stinging their eyes and great spotted trout darting from their path, it made no difference to Milan. All of it he loved, with a deep, wild, reckless, exhilarating love.

On the second day the river slowed its pace. The gravel in the shallows was replaced by clean white sand. The air took on a clean sharp tang. The oaks and maples along the river banks were replaced by cedars, birches, and towering pines through which the wind sighed and sent out pungent, sweet odors.

In the late afternoon they rounded a bend and moved swiftly again as the river narrowed into a cut between the two towering hills of windswept sand. It widened again on the other side and they glided out into a bay protected by a wide, pebbly bar. The bay in turn widened into a horizonless expanse of blue–green water, water so clear that Mina could see fish swimming twenty feet below them. They had reached the great Lake Michigan, the lake of the Illinois, about which Milan had told them.

The canoe slowly began to rise and fall as the rolling surf reached threateningly into the bay. They beached the canoe on the north shore, lazed for a while in the warm sand of the beach which stretched back for a hundred feet from the water, then prepared a camp in the protection of the cedars at the base of the yellow dunes.

Mina was preparing a meal and Ganus was gathering wood for the evening fire when they heard Milan let out a great whoop. They turned to see another birch canoe sweep majestically out between the towering hills of sand. It curved smoothly towards their camp and, with two paddles dipping evenly, it carried its two Indian occupants onto the sandy beach.

Only then did Mina recognize the girl who jumped quickly from the canoe and embraced her in warm, buckskin–covered arms.

"Louise!" she finally cried, "and Jimmy Colby."

"We come, too," he said, simply.

Travel during the next few days was continued only when and if, as Milan said, the Great Spirit allowed. Usually during the daytime hours and sometimes at night great curling breakers came swirling in with the capricious westerlies to pile clear water in sparkling mountains onto the sandy beach. Here it would spend itself in a vicious surge up the sloping sand, then dissolve and slide slowly back to be met by the thunder of the next one.

When night approached, the wind would usually soften like the waves on the beach. Whippoorwills would start a rhythmic chant up among the pine trees on the sandy hills. Night hawks would appear; climbing up, up, up until they were fluttering specks in the green of the sunset sky then, with wings folded, drop like stones towards the surface of the quieting water. There at the last moment they would spread their wings and air–vibrating, stiffened pinions would produce the thrilling whoom whoom, whoom, which Ganus and Mina loved to hear.

Milan would climb to the top of the nearest dune and wait, watching the heron gulls and sometimes a circling eagle and listening intently. If the wind did not return they would push their canoes out to the moonlit waters and paddle smoothly into the north, always staying within sight of the wooded hills, the canoes leaving long, silver streaks in the water.

Four, five nights they traveled, and two nights sought shelter from persistent winds. Late one night, when the moon was dim in the western sky, they rounded a point of land and Milan stopped paddling.

As the canoe occupied by Louise and Jimmy glided close by, he pointed to a range of high smooth hills of sand, glowing like yellow butter in the moonlight. Jim Colby nodded in agreement and Milan spoke.

"There, Ganus and Mina, beyond those mountains of white sand, lies a lake of clear, blue water. It has a stream running from it which empties into yonder bay. On the opposite shore of the lake a hill rises slowly then flattens to a rolling plateau. This plain is rich with the light, rich earth of which I have told you and bordered by hills covered with pine trees the like of which you have never seen. On that hill overlooking the lake, those sandy hills on its western shore, and on across Lake Michigan, I believe you will build your home. Jimmy and Louise will probably build their cabin among the pine trees on the shore of the lake below you."

The word "home" brought a quick intake of breath to

Mina. The journey from Pennsylvania had appeared end-less. But now, with the end near and the picture of a new home rising here in this beautiful wilderness, she was overcome. As she looked up at big, kind, capable Ganus, then down at the sleeping Toma, tears welled up into her dark eyes and she was glad for the darkness of the night.

While he was speaking, Milan had moved the canoes quietly to the shore where a wide stream flowed out of the hills. Quickly he emptied the canoe which Jimmy and Louise occupied. Then he stepped to Mina, gave her a long, warm hug and kissed her gently. Then he turned to shake hands with Ganus.

"I leave you now, Ganus. When I return I will have the animals. By then you will have your home laid." He turned to Mina. "This Ganus, he is the clumsy ox with a paddle, but with the axe, he is plenty good. You will have a good home soon."

As if to avoid further "Au revoirs," Milan said his quick adieus to Louise and Jimmy, pushed the canoe out into the lake and disappeared into the darkness.

Chapter Five

The years passed swiftly for Ganus and Mina Michaelovic. Their dirt–floored cabin above the lake was home for six years.

On the seventh, Allen Harcourt, an old English sailor and ship's carpenter appeared and he and Ganus built two new cottages, one for each family, with milled siding and smooth wood floors.

Those first years were hard ones. Fruit and pasture were not yet established, rain refused to fall on their sandy fields when they needed it most, and their crops of corn and potatoes withered in the August heat. They were forced to exist much the same as the Indians had, on berries, fish, and wild game.

Mina watched Ganus grow thin from the fever and ague he had contracted on the journey from Detroit. They talked many times of leaving the north country. Of finding land farther south where the soil was heavier and moisture would lay longer on the crops. But the speculators had pushed the prices high, and here the lake and the hills had cast their spell over them. Now leaving the fresh lake air for the south seemed unthinkable. So they stayed.

Each year in the hills cost them something. Time, sweat, and worry. A withered crop. A broken axe handle or a worn–out plow. But obstacles were overcome and placed on the scrap heap of memory along with the triumphs that kept hope alive.

Once passed, each milestone, even though it may have been a disaster at the moment, rested on the memory as another victory. And as time wore on, they learned the ways of the harsh country and the trials became more bearable and the joys more numerous.

The coming of good people like their old friends Bill and Mary Sugars and the Hollanders Carl and Nancy VanBolt brought new life and children to laugh with and to share with. The days became lighter and the hills more alive.

The hard times were mostly behind them now, though hunger was still close by. With others to joke with and to help, the troubles seemed lighter and as they learned to make their sandy hills more productive, they even looked now to the future. Those hillsides where the big pine trees soared to the sky were looked upon with reverence and were slowly bought up section by section with dollars brought from the old country or hoarded from the sale of animals, furs, and fruit.

Carl VanBolt dammed the creek and built a small mill where the town would rise. Another newcomer Nicholas Vaino Tanner set up a forge and his hammer added its music to the swish of the mill and the squeak of wagon wheels. The quiet hills came slowly alive and the people self–sustaining.

Coming alive, too, was young Tom Michaels. The board and the basket was another remembered milestone, but the straight back and the broad flat shoulders already showing above sturdy legs and a ready laugh were a tribute to wisdom of the Indian way. The hills were his playground. With his uncle Milan often at his side he learned the ways of the forest, the lakes, and the wildlife as they are seldom learned.

For Mina this learning was not enough and during the winter months she added book learning. The quietly competent Louise now had children of her own to teach. Soon a small schoolhouse was built on a hill west of the budding village and the mission–educated Ottawa became the teacher.

So the little settlement in the forested hills of Michigan grew. And as it developed, so did the new American nation grow. By May of 1790 the thirteen colonies had become thirteen United States of a new Union. One by one, as the many–colored yarns of the lands across the seas shuttled through the ports of New York, Boston, and Baltimore they wove a pattern farther and farther westward. By 1860 a total of thirty–three States were bound together into the loose fabric of a new democratic nation, bearing the woof of many lands but always the warp colored with the language and customs of Mother England.

Among the people who found their way to these shores

were representatives of many nations and cultures: French, fleeing the upheavals of a political revolution and years of religious persecution; refugees from the Low Countries, suffering the domination of Napoleon; Germanic people of both high and peasant classes, disappointed with their country's failure to form a constitutional republic; English lords and thieves, prostitutes and princes, some fleeing the suppression of the Crown, others enjoying grants of land and money to stimulate trade or get indigents off the public dole. There were also Irish peasants by the thousands, looking for any place that could put food on tables emptied by the famine of 1846 and that would allow them to honor their Catholic faith.

Inevitably this mixing of cultures and languages brought problems of many kinds. The mixing of Irish Catholics into formerly Protestant New York brought on political and religious street fighting reminiscent of the French Revolution. The conflicts between revolutionary patriots and English loyalists separated families and friends, and religious and cultural differences drove minorities, such as the Mormons, the Mennonites, and the Jews, into enclaves of their own. But among the problems caused by these belief variables within the new Union, only one persisted and grew worse as the middle of the nineteenth century was passed.

Among the many people who found their way into the fabric of the Union was one group who came unwillingly and without hope. These were the black Africans who had been sold like cattle by their own countrymen and greedy Europeans for profit. Slavery had been outlawed in England in 1833 and in the French Antilles in 1848. Even South America had freed most of its slaves by 1854. But in the Southern states of the country where freedom was guaranteed and liberty was a byword, it persisted.

Three times between 1825 and 1849 gradual, compensated emancipation had been proposed, and each time the South had turned it down, fearing that the freeing of the slaves would be devastating to the South unless they were returned to Africa, and believing them necessary to the good life the upper classes enjoyed.

Now, as a new decade began, the problem which had festered for forty years had become an open sore. The question of expansion of the slave trade into the new Territories, particularly Kansas, had brought bloodshed and popularized a new Republican Party strongly supported by the abolitionists. In 1860 that party's Presidential candidate carried every free state; a country lawyer named Abraham Lincoln became the country's sixteenth President. On Christmas Eve of that same year South Carolina declared that the union now subsisting between Carolina and other states, under the name of the United States of America, was dissolved.

By the eighth of February, 1861, Mississippi, Florida, Alabama, Georgia, Louisiana and Texas had joined with South Carolina to form the Confederate States of America. The new nation, dedicated to liberty and solidarity, was now a divided nation.

Every state knew its grief at this moment. The State of Tennessee, though, had different problems. Not only was it a border state, lying in a narrow corridor between slave and free territories, it was part rolling farm country and part mountain highland. And as its countryside varied, so did its people differ. It was not surprising, then, that Tennesseans were pulled one way and another by the strong tides of Union and anti–Union sentiment.

Franklin County, Tennessee, had long been the home of a strong–minded and proud breed of pioneers. It was only to be expected that these hardy people would be among the first to voice their own opinions on the matter of secession, and it was typical of them that they would do it in a unique and forceful way.

It started when, on February the sixth, the people of Tennessee rejected, by a majority of 68,000 votes, a proposal that the State secede from the Union and join with her sister states to the south in the formation of the Confederate States of America.

The reaction of the people of Franklin County was immediate and defamatory. Within days a meeting was set up to correct this grievous wrong in a most unusual way.

Up at his little farm in the hills east of Winchester, Ben Campbell walked into his kitchen that day. It was warm from the wood range and rich with the smell of baking corn bread. The troubles of the Union seemed far away. Ben stood at the north window for a while contemplating the sweep of mountain–tops that rose up from the fields beyond the little valley. It was pretty country. Just looking at it was restful to the soul and pleasant to Ben's eyes. But today his mind was busy. His wife, Morina, watched as he fingered the heavy watch chain his father had brought with him from Scotland. She guessed, as women often do, the thoughts that troubled her husband.

"I reckon I'll mosey into town, Morina," he said finally. "There's a meeting at the courthouse this evening and I'm thinking I should be there."

"Another secessionist meeting, I suppose." Morina sighed, wiping the last of the baking dishes and tossing the towel on its peg. "It seems as though there must be another way, Ben." Her voice was low and unexpectedly pleasant, but the fear of a mother facing bad times was in her words.

"I expect it is, Morey," said Ben, ignoring her last statement. Things had already gone too far to hope for compromises. "Secession and President Lincoln. They are the topics of the day in Franklin County, Morey, and nothing either you or I can do will change that. Reckon I should be there, though. It's a man's duty to speak his mind. If he don't, he might as well not have one."

The excitement of it was gnawing at him, too. Morina knew that. It had been a long winter.

"Where's Poke?"

"Out in the hills somewhere. He took Heinie and his gun. Ginny went with him, too."

Ben squeaked open the back door. There were patches

of snow melting along the path that led to the privy and on to the chicken house. The snow steamed a little as the early spring sun melted it from the roof of the cow's shed, and the fresh smell of it mingled with the stink of rotting manure and the fresh clean tang of high mountain air. Snow lay deeper among the scattered sheds that housed the mules and the tools that were needed on a small farm. There were fresh tracks leading out past the hay–stack. The deep throated bay of the big, German short–hair hound boomed out of the hills to the east.

Ben turned back. "Just as well he ain't home," he said.

"These meetings don't make much sense sometimes. Probably best fer him not to get mixed up in them."

Morina watched him go, the old wagon jolting through the stony creek and down the steep trail leading west out of the wooded hills. She knew Ben too well to look lightly on these town meetings. He would go to listen, and maybe to calm down some of the hotheads, but before the meeting was over, Ben's opinions would grow into words and his lacking of fear would raise tempers. Maybe it would have been better if Poke had gone along. His being there might hold Ben in.

It was nearly fourteen miles to Winchester from Ben's high valley but it was a pleasant drive and Ben's mind worked easy with the turning of wheels. It was mid afternoon when he arrived.

The village was lively, yet February was too early for folks to be busy. The fields were still wet and frozen where the snow had not laid a protective cover. Building and harness repairs had been made and everything the farmers could do was done and waiting for the planting season. The lazy ones, and this county had its share of them, would never catch up, anyway. They would be the first ones into town, though. They would be at Birney Casey's tavern and probably never would get to the meeting.

Around the sides of the square where the clapboard courthouse stood, more than the usual scattering of horses and a few teams of oxen already worried at their ties. Some stood with lowered heads, lazing in the touch of warmth from the February sun. Others, and Ben smiled at the likeness of the animals and owners, were sharp–eyed and fidgety. Martin Beaker's polished bay stallion was there, alert and sharp–eyed as a true grandson of Diomed should be. Ben Campbell tied his mules to the same rail and walked across the square to Birney Casey's.

An hour later, when he left the tavern, Martin Beaker's horse had been moved to an unused rail on the far side of the courthouse. Ben casually untied the mules, rode once around the square and again tied them beside of the bay stallion. The arrogance of some men rankled him and it gave him pleasure, down inside, to irritate them. He supposed it was a weakness in himself. Certainly not arrogance. Still he grinned a self–pleasured grin as he tied old Pat and Mike to the cross rail.

"Nothing like good company to sort of lift a body up. Right, Pat?" And he gave the mule's soft gray nose a friendly rub.

Marty Cowans and Gordon Ross were on a bench along the far wall. Ben made his way to them.

"If y'err nyme be Campbell we've a spot o' room ferr ye." Gordon rolled the words and the sound of it was music to Ben's ear. "Aye! It's an open meetin', it is, and I'll be a fightin' any Hinglishman that bars me way," Ben replied.

The room was filling now. They watched with interest as all found places among their own kind. Men, the gregarious creatures that they are, all have their levels of scorn and respect, like the pecking order of chickens. Without always knowing why, or realizing that they do it, they flock to the side of natural leaders. Mostly, Ben thought, they just bunch up like grapes, each one becoming more and more like the other ones of their bunch. And now our states are doing the same thing. It will take a miracle to get them back on the same vine again.

There were no big slaveholders in Franklin County. Martin and Cal Beaker had the most. About a dozen each, Ben had heard, but he was sure that Calvin had more than that. In their crowd were the holders of the bigger farms to the southwest. They were the best aristocrats Franklin County could afford. Tagging along with this group were the small–minded nigger–haters. Share croppers or holders of little parcels of leftover bottom land, they had little hope but to enjoy the infrequent touch and sometimes the charity of the big planters. They were an embarrassment at times but nevertheless tolerated because they would add to the voting power.

The middle class were farmers from the rich valleys, Jacksonian Democrats frustrated by the politics of the times. They had been satisfied with the Missouri Compromise but were angered by the bloodshed which followed the Kansas–Nebraska Act which replaced it. Some of them owned a slave or two, often a family which worked alongside them in their fields and helped with the laundry and the cooking. They didn't talk strong for or against slavery, but back in their heads had been planted the seeds of a dream, the dream of a day when they might have more land, more slaves, and a big white house. This dream had grown in the minds of most Southerners and would not go away. They called themselves state' righters, and they probably were. Those eastern mountains were a firm barrier between them and their friends in the seaboard states. Mostly, though, this was a screen to hide behind while their minds became more and more set on the possibility of a prosperous new Confederacy.

The hill people were a different breed. Freedom was their joy, the freedom to hunt and fish and roam their hills. Freedom to remain poor in wealth but rich in their enjoyment of their little mountain valleys was their choice. They loved the Union which had provided them with that freedom and felt a strong kinship with the new President Lincoln who was so much like them. Ben Campbell was one of these, a reader, a free thinker, and a hard worker up to a point which he insisted on setting.

Now, as he looked out over the crowd, he saw a group divided, just as Tennessee was divided. Just as the whole country was divided. Franklin County, though, nestled up close to Alabama on the south, and, mostly, the discontent of the Deep South was in the eyes of these men.

The room filled now and was quieting. Everyone was expectant and anxious for the meeting to get underway.

There was a stirring up front and Martin Beaker stood, his handsome face and white hair outlined against the fading afternoon light.

"This open meeting of the people of Franklin County is called to order." He waited for the murmur of voices to die.

The troubled bawling of a cow bereft of its calf was filling the room. Sheriff Wheeler closed the courthouse door. The bawling faded to a distant, steady rhythm. The squeak of a pump stopped. Martin Beaker's clear voice came out of the semi–dark.

"Since this is a special, open meeting it has been suggested that the usual reports and minutes be set aside so that all of our time can be spent on the business at hand. Do I hear any objections?"

"Keep goin', Mart." It was the deep, impatient voice of Martin's brother, Calvin, urging him on.

Ben stretched upward to see Cal's heavy frame planted firmly in the front row. He lacked the good looks and the polish that made Martin popular, but he was not short of ambition. As the owner of Sycamore Farm, up Tullahoma way, he controlled some of the best soil in the county, and, while his methods excited little respect, he had shrewdly chosen his land, his negroes, and his foreman, and the rich soil produced good crops of cotton and corn.

Martin voice continued. "Since February 6, when the people of Tennessee rejected the proposal to separate from the Union, many citizens of Franklin County have repeatedly asked if there might be some way in which Franklin County could express its opposition to that dishonorable decision. We are here today to tell you that that way has been found. Resolutions have been written and petitions prepared which will allow the people of Franklin County to speak out in a manner befitting good Southern blood."

Much time was spent reading the Resolves, but Ben Campbell found little of interest in these. They were the usual condemnations of Northern hypocrisy and renewals of the people's praise for Calhoun and Davis. But, after a while, the resolutions petered out and the real business of the meeting was at hand.

It was big Milt Carson who was called on to present the important proposals. Milt was a well–respected middle–of–the–road Democrat, and a firm believer in states rights. He spoke with the easy drawl of a South Carolinian.

"We'all were plumb confused, Mr. Chairman," he said, as the room settled to a more attentive silence, "by all the resolves that were put in front of us. But since we knew well enough what these committees were getting at, we prepared two separate petitions for you all to vote on and the committees have approved them."

Martin Beaker hesitated a moment as if wondering whether this quiet room full of rough men was qualified and ready to make the kind of decisions they were attacking. Ben Campbell, in his seat along the far wall, wondered, too. Martin was not really a leader, but the prodding of his older brother pushed him on. His glance went to Calvin now and what he saw must have strengthened him. Martin turned to the assembly and his words came out sharp and tense, like the ring of an axe against good pin oak. "Read the first one," he said.

Milt stood a little straighter, paper in hand, an expression of mixed concern and humility on his broad face. Like others, he had spoken strong words during the heat of the arguments at Birney Casey's. Now, with the real action taken and the papers in his hand which could change the course of history, he wondered at the wisdom of his own words.

Ben Campbell read this in his eyes and thought better of the man for his doubting.

Marty Cowans saw it, too, and quoted: "Ponder the path of thy feet and let thy ways be established on wisdom."

"Amen," added Gordon Ross.

Milt rubbed a big hand across his chin, raised the paper against the fading light, and waited for the bawling of the cow to quiet.

"On this day, February 24, 1861, we the people of Franklin County, Tennessee, gathered together in open meeting and objecting to the failure of the people of Tennessee to separate from the Union of the United States and to join with our sister states of the South in a new Southern Confederacy, do hereby petition to secede at once from the Sovereign State of Tennessee."

There was a strained silence in the room as everybody waited expectantly for more. The words were strong but unexpectedly brief.

Milt Carson looked back, grinning apologetically. "That's it," he said. "The committee saw no need for more words. I reckon we've already had plenty of them."

Birney Casey was laughing. "You'll have to excuse us, Milt. We ain't never done this before."

Cal Beaker's big frame was up now. "I have an objection," he was saying, "to 'Sovereign'. Thet word stinks of old England. Sounds like an authority nobody's got no right to question. I say, leave that word out. We came to this country to get away from a Sovereign State. Just plain 'State of Tennessee,' thet's good enough."

As Cal spoke there was a rustling at the door. It opened slowly inch by inch and old Mike Shay backed through it and turned unsteadily inside. His battered wool cap was turned well around over his left ear, a sure sign that he had had a good day at Birney's. As Cal's words seeped slowly into his narrowed range of perception he steadied himself against the heavy door and raised his arms in agreement. "Rrright," he spoke, louder than he had intended. "Good ol' Ten'see, that's good enough." Then, as though the words had been the only thing holding him up he slid slowly down against the closed door.

"There ye be, Cal!" piped up little Marty Cowans. "Ye got a weak second to match a weak motion."

Martin Beaker was holding up his arms for quiet now. Ignoring Mike Shay he pursued the business of the meeting. "Do I hear a second to the dropping of the word Sovereign?"

"I say leave it in," said a young stranger. "It was the people of Tennessee, not our state government, who voted to stay with the Union. The word is proper and the statement is strong enough."

A second came from the crowd. With Mike Shay ignored, the motion failed. These men were ready to move strong, but with most, Cal Beaker didn't much count, and they wanted him to know it.

Milt Carson was waiting to speak again now. Slowly the crowd quieted. Milt was liked by most all who knew him. He had come to the bottom lands west of town years ago and had built up a good reputation as a corn and hog farmer. He kept one family of negroes to help out but was never known to have trouble with them and probably worked harder in his fields than they did. Milt's voice was a deep and pleasant one. Tonight it was thoughtful.

"I reckon I have spoke out before, maybe too often and too loud. That's probably how I got the job of writing these petitions. If'n you will listen jest one more time, though, I have a few things I would like to say.

"Like most of you I came to Tennessee Territory when I

was jest a young'n. 1838 I'm thinkin' it was. I wasn't much over fourteen years old at the time and something I saw as we came up through north Georgia impressed me deep hard.

"Back in South Carolina I can remember hearing people saying, Why don't the Indians learn to live like white people? If'n they wern't so ignorant and lazy they would work the land and go to church. Then they would be welcome amongst us.

"Mostly, I guess, this was true. But back where I came from I know an Indian boy as a friend. I called him Butternut, and he was not ignorant and not really lazy. Mostly he was just different. He wan't much fer schoolin' and he never went to church, but he taught me a lot of things most white boys never learn. Mostly about fishing and hunting it was, and how to follow a trail and how to lay easy in the sun when the time was right and get my thinking lined up straight with my feet.

"But while I was still a lad, Butternut and his people were driven out of their homes on the Saluda River and I watched them disappear into the west followed by a troop of soldiers. I could never understand then why my friend was made to leave his home when so much land was free for the taking and only white trash moved in to take their place. To me, Butternut was no different than me. I had never thought of him as being different. He was just my friend.

"A few years later my family tired of South Carolina and started west towards Tennessee. One day we met a man who told us about land being distributed by lottery in Georgia, so we bent our journey north to check it out. What we found when we came down out of those hills I have never forgot.

"There was some right pretty country south of the Tennessee River with wooded hills and good rich valleys. In those valleys the Cherokees had settled and were living like high style white people. They were working the land and building homes, schools, and churches. A smart young halfbreed named Sequoia had made up a Cherokee alphabet and they had printed the bible and school books and were putting out a weekly newspaper. I was told later that they had even set up a constitution and a legislature. Hell! They were more civilized than most of us white settlers.

"But they had made one mistake. They had found gold in those hills, and where gold is, the worst of white people follow. So even though fifteen thousand of them had signed petitions asking President Van Buren to support their treaty of 1791 which had given them this land, they were again being driven out. To our government in Washington an Indian is an Indian, and the complaints of voting settlers are to be honored. So Winfield Scott's soldiers were forcing those good Cherokees west again to Indian Territory. And standing there among them was my friend, Butternut. These were his people, the same as my family are my people. The good Indian, Sequoia, was his uncle, George Grist, of whom he had been quite some proud.

"I was saddened by what I saw that day. I think for once in my life I was ashamed to be a white boy, and too ashamed to go to my friend, Butternut Grist."

Ben rested a moment, looking steady out of the east window to where the setting sun was painting the mountaintops to blue and gold.

"I was young then and these doings set heavy on my mind. I have never forgiven our people in Washington for letting it happen, and since that day I have always believed that the best government is the government closest to the people being governed. If Georgia had sent those troops to drive out the Cherokees it would have been just as bad. But it is easier to send someone else to do a dirty job than it is to do it yourself. I have always felt that if Georgia people had done it at least they would have known what they were doing and, in knowing, they might have drawn back. I am sure that those people in Washington did not rightfully know what those good Indians had accomplished, and Winfield Scott could only obey his orders.

"Likewise I don't believe those people in Washington know a whole lot about conditions in the South. They know little about the amount of hand labor that goes into the raising of cotton, indigo, and tobacco. They don't know that many of our negroes are happy and content with their lot. Neither do they, or I, know much about Kansas and the territories to the west. If the people in those territories say that they need blacks to run their kind of farms who are we, back here in Tennessee or Mr. Lincoln in Washington, to tell them if'n they are right or wrong?

"Like I said, I ain't strong fer slavery. I own my family of four and sometimes I wonder if they are wuth what I paid fer 'em. But one thing I am sure of. That black family I have is a whole lot better off with me than those Cherokees were with our Union soldiers.

"But putting all of that aside, if giving up my blacks would hold our country together, I would free them gladly. If giving up my hopes for states' rights would hold it together, I would give that up, too. But you men know, and I know, that giving those things up wouldn't make a whit of difference. The division between the North and the South is now too wide and too deep. Our Southern leaders no longer want to continue as members of the Union on any terms, and that is the real truth. The line has been drawn. The fence is being built. Tennessee is plumb astraddle of it. Somebody has to move or lose their britches. The only question we can settle here tonight is, Do we, as citizens of Franklin County, want to end up on the North or the South side of the fence? Our sister States have made their positions clear. Representatives from South Carolina, Georgia, Alabama, Mississippi, Florida, Louisiana and Texas are right now meeting only two hundred miles south of here in Montgomery. Tennessee still dallies. I say, whatever our reasons, let's get Franklin County in and hope that the rest of Tennessee will follow. If they do, and Virginia, Kentucky, and Missouri follow, I do not believe the North will fight."

He looked down at the papers in his hand. "I wrote these petitions. I did it with my share of deep thinking and sorrow. I did it knowing that some of our fathers and grandfathers gave their lives to put together what we are tearing apart.

"But the Union is already broken." His voice was quiet now. "We, here in Franklin County, cannot put it back together. We cain't mend it or shape it. We can only choose our position, the same as those good men did who joined it together, and hope that we are doing right."

With that, Milt Carson sat quietly down.

Ben Campbell looked at Gordon Ross. Both he and Marty Cowans sat silent. They had come here expecting a hell–raising shouting match between Cal Beaker and the hill people. Milt's quiet, middle–of–the–road speech was not in the order of things.

Only Cal Beaker and the bereaved cow were unaffected, and Ben Campbell was thinking that the similarity between the two was striking.

He was on his feet now, Cal Beaker, that is, his big shoulders looming black against the wall lamps that Sheriff Wheeler had lighted as the cold sun slid over the hills to the west.

Someone had found a chair for Mike Shay and he was sleeping comfortably with his chin resting on his chest.

Marty Cowans nudged Ben. "Back in Ashley we were too poor to have a town drunk. So we took turns," he chuckled.

The lamps flickered as someone opened the door to spit out into the darkening night. The oily smell of lamp oil blended with the heady odors of stale tobacco and fresh cow manure. Cal waited, nervous and impatient to be heard. Martin stood up also and slowly the hall became quiet again.

"I jest wan't to remind y'all," Cal began, "that there are some of us here in Franklin County that have problems with our Northern brothers that go far beyond the removal of a few Cherokee Indians or states' rights. They go back to the Republican Party and its Chicago Platform that wants to take away our rights and has elected a president to do it, a backwoods railsplitter who aims to blockade our ports, suspend our postal deliveries, and do away with our trade with England.

"Besides, the battle for states' rights has been fought many times before, on the floors of our legislatures, on the steps of the Capital and with canes in a bloody aisle of the Senate Chamber, by Calhoun with Nullification and by South Carolina against the Tariff, and it has always failed and it always will fail except in the Southern Confederacy like Jeff Davis is a fixin' to set up. A real honest–to–God government of our own."

Ben saw Martin Beaker's white hair as he moved along the wall to Cal's left. He grinned and nudged Marty Cowans. Cal could be hot–headed. Martin wanted to be able to hold him in check.

Cal turned now and put a hand on Milt Carson's shoulder. "Milt and I and most of you here tonight are looking for the same things. We want the freedom to run our farms, our families, and our businesses in our own way. We want what we would have if the Northern majority would allow us states' rights. For forty years our patience has been tested and we have been driven close to civil war. Now we have only that one honorable road left. That is the road our sisters to the south are already preparing. Are we a-going to march with them or are we going to lie belly down in the gutter like yellow dogs and whine for another forty years about the things that you and I and Milt Carson believed in but were not willing to fight for?"

Cal's voice slowed as the fire of his strong feelings overcame him.

Ben Campbell squirmed uneasily on his bench, irritated by the chicanery of the big planter. Cal knew that the likeable Milt had a following and he was trying to make Milt Carson's people his people.

"But while we have little to lose, we have much to gain. Those of you who have traveled through Georgia, Alabama, or North Carolina have seen what can be produced by good Southern soil. Once freed from the politics that are holding us down, the South, with its cotton and tobacco, can build a country richer than hell.

"Already Mobile, Macon, and Montgomery are full of the big homes of the wealthy. Their plantations are producing fortunes for them and there is room for more in Louisiana, Arkansas, and right here in Tennessee. Only those Northerners up there in Washington are keeping us right here in Franklin County from sharing in that good English money.

"Of course, the Northerners are telling us that we can farm without our blacks, the same as they do. But do they raise cotton, rice, or indigo? They tell us that England kept on prospering after they freed their slaves back in '33. But England's money comes from her mines and her mills, the same as our North, and it is our cotton raised by the blacks that England refused to feed that kept their mills a-turning.

"And how about England's islands in the West Indies; did they prosper? No! Like us they had no mines or mills. When their labor was taken from them their good land stopped producing sugar cane and rum. Most of the landowners were killed by the black Africans they had been feeding and the good land went back to jungle.

"This, my friends, is what could happen to us. The South is farm country. We are America's Caribbean. Take away our black help and our land, too, will return to weeds and jungle, the same as it did on the Islands.

"For many years we have tried to make this clear to our Northern brothers. They have refused to listen. Now we have given ourselves another choice. We can now join with the new Confederacy. Our money will make Charleston, Savannah, and New Orleans the Bostons and New Yorks of the South. Southern cotton will be shipped in Southern ships. Southern money will go into Southern banks, and our blacks that have been raised out of the jungles of Africa to the blessings of civilization can be pulled out of the gutters of poverty.

"If the rest of Tennessee wants to dally, let them do it. We in Franklin County are ready. If it means war against the North our fightin' should be with our sisters of the South. What they need, we need and by God we're a-goin' to get it."

There was a rumble of approval from the dark room. In spite of their dislike of Cal Beaker as a man, in spite of knowing his ways of dealing with his blacks, these were the words most of them had come to hear and they showed it in their eyes and in the excited sound of their voices.

Outside, the bellowing of the cow stopped for a moment, then came back in a long, sad bawl.

"E'en the cow couldn't stomach that," whispered Marty Cowans.

Cal wanted to say more but words had left him. He had released his pent–up feelings and nothing more would come out. He turned for another look at the crowd then lowered his big frame onto his bench.

Ben Campbell sat quietly dismayed. Cal Beaker had spoke out strong. Ben had not thought that he had it in him. He could now see little hope of turning the tide.

Martin was back in front again and confronting him was a rush of standing men. Farmers like Ben Campbell who worked the little mountain valleys. Men who didn't give a damn about the price of cotton. Men from the worn out land of South Carolina and Georgia who had watched the big plantations grow and prosper while they struggled to feed their families from the marginal land the big planters didn't want or had worn out. Then one by one they sat down as they saw Ben Campbell on his feet. Ben would say what they wanted said and he could do it best. The room grew still. The wall lamps flickered along the sides of the room and drew sharp lines from craggy faces. The cow worried on in the distance and a hound complained to a hazy, rising moon.

Mike Shay stirred, disturbed by the quiet. Still Ben waited, tempting Cal Beaker to object. Finally he began, his voice cutting the darkness, clear, high–pitched and Lincoln–like, as if he were talking to a small child.

"I am aware that in this room tonight I am speaking for a minority. Most of you came here with your minds made up, the same as I did. The same as the minds of most of the people of our country are long set by years of bitter disagreement. I know I have little hope of turning minds so long hardened by hate and prejudice or heads looking towards those big white houses. I can only speak for those of us who, because our way of life leads us up a different, more solitary road, can help us see beyond the politics of the present and into the realities of the future."

Marty Cowans looked at Gordon Ross.

"Mostly we are from those mountain valleys."

He waved a thin arm into the northeast. "One of the things you red dirt farmers should do more often is to saddle up a mule and climb to the top of one of those rocky peaks. There is nothing like the top of a mountain to put a man in proper perspective with the world around him. and nothing like a quiet mountain valley to allow you to think out the problems you think you have without a lot of outside interference.

"After climbing my mountain, looking down at our country spread out below me and doing some hard thinking, it occurred to me that the first thing this country, and men like Cal Beaker, needs to settle is whether or not owning black slaves is legal under our Constitution and then is it right or wrong under the laws of God? Because if it fails to survive either of these tests, we who practice it have no right to be called honest citizens of this great country of ours or civilized human beings under Christian moral law.

"Neither should we be holding meetings to change something already settled by the highest law of the land and the first laws of the Christian Scriptures. The only thing we can be doing, then, is looking for ways to break those legal laws of our country and the moral laws of God." Ben's voice grew firm. "And that is exactly what you promoters of secession aim to do."

Cal Beaker's voice came booming out of the darkness. "There ain't no law that says I cain't own my niggers, Ben Campbell, and you know it."

Ben took no notice.

"Now it doesn't take much thinking to tell us that we

can easily find some way to justify the breaking of the first one. The human mind is real good at finding justifications. But that second one? That one has been in the books for nigh on to two thousand years and anyone who starts to belittling that Do Unto Others law is going to be chipping at the very foundation stone of civilization. Does anyone here want to argue that point? Do you, Cal Beaker?

"And getting back to point one, can you, Cal," and Ben directed his attention straight at Cal Beaker, "or anyone else in this room truthfully say that our country's Constitution was made hastily and without due consideration? Isn't it more true that from the very moment our good founding fathers gathered together to bind that document for our country their first thoughts were that certain things were self–evident, namely that all men were born equal and that with that borning comes certain rights such as life, liberty, and the pursuit of happiness? If the men sitting now in Montgomery can start any better than that I will be a wantin' to hear their words.

"It may be true that our fathers thought of these things first because they had just recently been reminded that they were the political slaves of his Royal Highness King George, and were not happy under this condition. A few years later, though, when these same men had thrown off the harness that George had thrown over their backs and were riding high and free in their own saddles, they had a lapse of memory. Just as you men are today they began to think how nice it was having those uncivilized black Africans pursue that happiness for them.

"Then came along a few more good men: English, Dutch, and Scotsmen who had had a more recent experience. Men who still remembered when they had stood on the deck of the ship that had brought them to this country and heard men with money in their pockets put a price on their heads, and listened to the bargain being made that would send them into eight, maybe ten years of forced labor as indentured servants to pay the cost of their passage to these shores. They remembered, too, how they had no choice but to do the bidding of their owners until the long years of their servitude were up and they were again free men.

"One by one these men rose to be heard in the states of the North. One by one they reread those words which had been written into their Constitution and one by one they decided that since they had fought seven and a half years of bloody war to win those liberties, it was damned inconsistent of them to deprive their servants of those rights because their skins were of a different color. So one by one they set out once more to wipe all forms of slavery from their States and one by one they did it.

"So for a second time the rightness of this principle was upheld." Ben looked over the darkened faces. "Do we need to challenge its rightness again? Has anything happened to make slavery more right now than it was eighty years ago? Would you still consider it necessary if your own skin was black? Isn't it true that when any practice is declared a necessary evil, that that practice immediately becomes more and more necessary and less and less evil?"

Ben turned now, his clear voice directed at Cal Beaker, his dark eyes glowing. "As for me, it is my opinion that slavery as practiced with the kindness of Milt Carson is a tolerable wrong. But when it is exercised by the likes of you, Cal Beaker, it is a moral embarrassment to us all and should be driven from the face of the earth. This is the same difference which allowed a few good planters in the West Indies to continue to live and to employ their black labor while the rest were being hanged from trees in their own front yards.

"As to need, you can say, of course, as Calhoun does, that the North is different. That they did not start with big grants of rich land. That they had cheap labor from Ireland, Finland, and the Balkans. But is this true? Were the five–thousand acre estates cut from Henry McCullouch's forty–thousand in North Carolina different from Van Rensalaer's twenty–four by forty–eight miles on the Hudson? No! But labor came to them because there was a living wage or a share of a crop being allowed to men who could remain free."

Mike Shay was awake now and looking steadily at Ben, impressed by his challenge of big Cal Beaker. A drizzle of tobacco juice ran from the corner of his mouth and added a brown stain to his already dirty wool sweater.

"To me, Ben Campbell, the hill farmer, my points have been made. My arguments are properly supported and the meeting should be over. But I am aware that most of your minds have not been changed. I have not missed the determination on your faces. But I also see beyond you to the faces of wives, mothers and children who are hit the hardest when a war strikes. It is for them that I ask you to be patient a little longer and allow me to say what I believe should be said.

"You men have come here tonight dead set on voting to leave the Union. But have you considered well the other choices or have you allowed your heads to be turned like weathervanes by the winds directed at you by Calhoun and Davis? Most of you claim respect for President Jackson. Have you forgotten that Andrew Jackson, before he died, said that he had only two regrets, 'That my horse never beat a Diomed filly named Haynies Maria, and that I did not not hang John C. Calhoun'?

"Don't you believe that Jackson had his reasons for saying that?

Have you considered that Franklin County could be the pivot on which Tennessee and other divided states like Kentucky, Virginia, and Missouri might turn, and on which the fate of the entire country might be balanced? It is a grave decision that you face, my friends. Consider it well. One much deeper and broader than just our own Franklin County."

Out in the room a sea of dark faces looked back at him.

Good men most of them, humble, hard–working farm people. The light from the oil lamps carved deep lines in their set features. Many of them had sons, as he did, and their lives and the lives of these men themselves could be at stake. Could he make them see this?

"I believe that many of you are convinced that President Lincoln, like Buchanan, when faced with the hard decision, will not fight. Friends and neighbors, I can only say bluntly, you are wrong. Even without Virginia and Tennessee you are wrong."

Ben removed a crumpled copy of the Washington Tribune from his pocket. "This is what President Lincoln said last month at his inauguration-

> 'Into your hands, my dissatisfied country-
> men, and not in mine is the momentous
> issue of civil war. The Government will not
> assail you. You can have no conflict with-
> out yourselves being the aggressor. You
> have no oath registered in heaven to
> destroy this Government, while I have the
> most solemn one to preserve it, protect it
> and defend it.'

"Do those, my friends, sound like the words of a timid President? No! Like you, his mind is made up. He will not hesitate to lead the remaining Union States into war if he believes it necessary to preserve the Union. This I believe and this you must consider carefully."

He waited again and saw Milt Carson look up, questions and respect showing in his eyes.

"We're wasting a hell of a lot of time," Cal Beaker's voice said out of the darkness.

"We have time," said Milt. "Let him finish."

"I have only one more point to make. We already know that our Southern leaders are set on forming a confederacy of their own. They are at work on it right now down in Montgomery. I have tried to convince you that the Union will fight. That brings up the big question. If civil war comes to our country, who will win?

"First of all, nobody will win. Wars seldom produce winners, only losers. But as fathers of sons and daughters, and husbands of wives who may be deeply affected by our decisions here tonight, we have a responsibility to look soberly for an answer.

"I had a good and wise father who put it this way. 'If ye'r lookin' to fight, laddie, look well at the other bye. If he looks stronger than ye, spare yourself. If he looks to be weaker, perhaps in fairness ye should spare him.'

"If a fight appears close there are other places to look for common sense, too. Take bears. If any of you men have ever seen two bears having one of their disagreements you know that first off they mutter and growl and sort of pass a lot of legislation to build up their courage. About the same as our politicians have been doing for the last ten years.

"Then after a while they get to the bluffing stage. They stand up on their hind legs, raise their neck ha'rs and look as big and dangerous as they know how.

"The South is now at that stage.

"But with bears, about here one or the other of them begins to see a glimmer of the truth, and maybe a fifty–pound weight advantage. It might even take a serious charge or two and a few wallops of a forty pound paw to finish the convincing. But hardly ever more than that. A bear's mind is not cluttered with what our politicians call contingent alternatives. His mind tells him loud and clear exactly at what point he is in a fair way of losing the fight and exactly what he must do about it if he hopes to survive. Right there he uses the best kind of judgment. He takes a long last estimate of that other bear, then he turns his big ass around and runs.

"A goose is another tough fighter. I saw one once protecting its nest from a big wolf. It would charge that big dog like a gray thunderbolt, screaming and beating him with those big wings until he completely lost his appetite for goose meat. When that wolf came back with help, though, and that goose saw two more wolves closing in, and knew that it didn't have a chance, it didn't let a set mind stand in the way of a fast retreat and survival.

"What I am trying to say is that men have a weakness that animals do not. a weakness we like to call pride, but which can sometimes be a blind, childish passion to have our own way when logic is calling us to have the sense of a goose."

The stallion in the dark of the courtyard let out a loud

whinny as if speaking for Martin Beaker himself. The men sat quiet, knowing full well that what Ben was saying was the truth, and they respected him for it. But pride was a strong feeling. It was not that easy to push it aside. And those states to the south had already seceded. It was too late to talk of disciplining minds and changing directions. They could be just as dead fighting for the North as for the South. Milt Carson was right. All they could do was to pick their side of the fence, and it looked like there might be plenty of fighting on both sides.

Ben Campbell's voice continued out of the dark. "I tell you this because it has been shown by history that the hunger of the human mind can lead men and nations to destroy themselves. I tell you also because my logic tells me that, if war comes,. .the South will lose."

There were many eyes raised at these words. Eyes smouldering and unbelieving, but forced to hear because, whether they agreed with him or not, they had respect for Ben Campbell.

"I will give you my reasons for believing this," said Ben. "First, in plain arithmetic, and excluding Tennessee and Virginia who I agree may join with the Confederacy, nineteen free states can count a population of close to ten million people. The South, not over six million.

"Second, with little industry compared to the North, the South will need help. Where will they look for it? To England, because Liverpool needs her cotton. Will she get it?" Ben hesitated and spoke slowly. "Only as much as a blockade of our ports will allow and as much as our cotton will pay for. The people of England will allow no more as long as slavery exists in the Southern states. The Confederacy will be fighting to maintain a social system that England, and most of the civilized world, has thrown out."

Ben turned to Cal. "Your very cause, Cal Beaker, will be a millstone around your neck."

Mike Shay was sitting up straight now and looking steadily at Ben. Of all the people in the room only Mike appeared to have been truly turned by his words. The hill people had already been with him. The rest had come with the fiery words of Calhoun still ringing in their ears and the picture of that big white house glowing in their minds. The fires of defiance in their hearts could not be so easily put out.

Ben reached down and gave Mike's cap a quarter turn back to the one o'clock position merited by his improved condition, then sadly made his way to his seat between Marty Cowans and Gordon Ross. He had done his duty. He could do no more.

Martin Beaker was again at the front of the room, his handsome face and Jacksonian white hair commanding the lamp light. He waited, copying Ben Campbell's style, then spoke...

"It now appears that we have given the supporters of all sides of the question their fair chance to be heard. Are we ready to go on?"

"We're ready," muttered Cal, and a rolling sound of agreement supported him.

"We now have the second petition to present to you, then the vote will be taken. I will read this one myself." He waited.

Even the cow was quiet now, as worn as they were by sad necessity.

Martin backed up to the wall lamp, better to see Milt Carson's script, and spoke evenly, his deep voice happy with its own sound.

"We the people of Franklin County, Tennessee, on this twenty–fourth day of February, eighteen hundred and sixty–one, having voted to secede from the state of Tennessee, do hereby petition the state of Alabama to so alter the line between the states of Alabama and Tennessee so as to transfer Franklin County into the state of Alabama.

"It is understood by all the undersigned that in so doing, the people of Franklin County are proudly seceding from the National Union of States and joining with the Confederacy of Southern States of which Alabama is a part."

There was a moment of silence in the darkened room. Then, as the strength of these words penetrated and stirred these hard Tennessee farmers, a cautious murmur of approval rose from them and grew until it became a rousing cheer. As the sound carried into the night, the village hounds joined in and lighted lamps appearing at windows showed that the women of the town had heard and had recognized the portent of the sound. This was action. Men had been talking discontent and gathering hatred in their hearts for forty years. Twice before they had been on the brink of secession and had drawn back. Now they were really doing it. It was a heady feeling.

Ben Campbell's words were quickly forgotten as this call touched their high spirits. Many of them knew that they were wrong. Knew that they were the pawns of the Southern rich, a class of which they would never be a part. But they were South. Those great plantations were theirs, too. The currents of public opinion had swept them up and carried them on until they could no longer turn against it. For better or for worse they had picked their side of the fence.

Both referendums quickly passed.

Ben Campbell rode slowly over the long trail home. Where the road passed over the bridge at Boiling Fork Creek he stopped the mules and rested in the music of the swift water. A thin moon floated over the near peaks of the Cumberland mountains, painting the late frost on the sycamore trees to blue and silver. It was a pretty sight.

But tonight Ben's thoughts were on other things. Poke was a good enough boy, but he had spirit. Like those farmers back there at the meeting, he had spirit enough to get him into a peck of trouble if a war came. And it looked as though this country was sure enough heading straight for it.

Part Two
Chapter Six

The stage from the east made its last river crossing only a few miles east of Lansing. Here the driver ignored the new wooden bridge and, swinging off of the road to the south, he halted in mid stream long enough to allow the horses to quench their thirst and the wheels of the stage to tighten. With the horses refreshed, it left the gravel of the river bottom with a jerk, jolted over a stretch of old plank road bordered by cedar, birch and mottled sycamore trees and, reaching higher ground, whirred smoothly over a sandy road towards the new capital city.

Inside the stage Michigan's new governor, Austin Blair, adjusted his cravat and watched the coming and going of the farms along the road, estimating, as he did so, the number of cattle in each herd, the quality of the land, the sheep and the farmers who tended them.

Across from the Governor, Tom Michaels fingered the diploma still tied in a tight curl in his inside pocket, made similar observations concerning the corn, the land, and the farmers who tended them and mused, "Lord! Will it ever seem good to be home."

The man sitting beside the Governor finally laid down the copy of the *Tribune* which he had been reading with much difficulty. "Our friend, Greeley, still persists in his thinking that peaceful separation from the Confederacy is the best answer to our country's problems." His voice carried a note of cynicism.

"I believe," replied Governor Blair, "that our friends in the East are becoming more concerned with the security of their accumulating fortunes and too little concerned with the security of the Union. Certainly Governor Wisner left no doubt about his opinion on this matter. I can still remember his very words.... 'This is no time for timid and vacillating councils, when the cry of treason and rebellion is ringing in our ears.' It is frightening to think that I have been chosen to carry on the work of a man like him. Especially after the strength the South has shown at Bull Run and Shiloh."

"But your task is already well begun," replied the stranger. "Already we have contributed thirteen regiments to the Union cause."

Governor Blair came quickly alert and his hand struck his knee with a resounding smack. "Please, let's not speak of this as a contribution. It is a loan. A loan of the bravest and best and our state can offer, and I pray that the loan may be quickly and safely returned."

The rest of the ride was made in silence, a silence encouraged by the wisps of dust which rose from beneath the wheels and hooves and eventually filtered into the stage. Pride was plainly visible, however, in the eyes of the Governor and his companion as the stage veered past a huge split boulder with a tree growing through the middle and there, looking west down a well–surveyed stretch of road, the spire of the state capital building shone out white and new in the distance.

There were two more days of travel before the stage passed through Grand Rapids. Days without the illustrious company of the state's new Governor.

There were two more days of travel before the lightness of the air and the pungent sweetness of pine and brake brought Tom alert. The stage passed through Coopersville and Grand Haven. The pines and birches were taller and greener now, and now and then there were glimpses of the blue-green water of Lake Michigan high against the western horizon between the hills.

The nameless little clusters of cabins Tom remembered were larger and cleaner now, filled with the smell of fresh–cut wood and wide with meadows dotted with livestock as the forests were pushed farther and farther back. Tom leaned back and stretched his frame as best he could in the cramped quarters of the rolling stage. He felt good. These hardy pioneers were doing well.

Another hour passed before the steady beat of the horses slowed and the hills leveled out onto the swampy flowway of the Muskegon River. Muskegon town had been a tired little fishing village when he had seen it last, built flat and friendly against the river where it joined the blue expanse of Lake Michigan.

Now, almost overnight, it seemed, it had burst forth into a city, bustling, prosperous, and dirty. Most of the cabins were gone and clapboard houses were falling into formation along well–defined streets reaching from the blue-green water of the big lake to the quiet blue of the smaller one formed by the river's push against the lake dunes. Here, though, nestled along the front streets, was something new to the north country, a row of pretentious houses of white paint and wide, friendly verandas, surrounded by beautiful black iron fences. These were obviously the homes of the newly rich. Sawdust castles to honor the vanity of an ambitious bourgeoisie. Behind them and fronting on the lake rose the source of their wealth, mills, a dozen or more of them. Big, two–storied, barnlike buildings belching smoke and sawdust into the clear lake air.

Back from the river and the town the hills rose slowly from swamp and marsh and as they rose their slopes lay barren, completely stripped of their covering of pines. Trees which had stood tall for one hundred and fifty, perhaps two hundred, years had been felled as if by a single blow, and with them all else that stood in their way. Left in their place was a tangled mass of limbs, stumps and dying tops, slowly wilting and drying in the spring sun. Here and there a hillside, now dwarfed by its loss of a hundred feet of growth, had burned, leaving a black scar against which new growth was struggling to make a showing.

Tom remembered the beauty of those hills when he had last seen them and felt a tightening in his throat. This land was a close neighbor to his own native valley. Seeing it laying bare filled him with sadness. Here no fields were replacing the scars of the cutting. No life was replacing the death of the trees. It was only a trade–off, a prairie of bare and blackened hills for a cluster of big, white houses.

Tom leaned back as his mind carried him back through the pages of history. Denuded Palestine, ravaged South America. Was it man's destiny to take and take with–out putting back?

Nature, in its wisdom, replaces leaf with mould, flesh with leaf and time with time. Only man takes, lives high, and laughs at tomorrow. Perhaps he will someday find that there is no more to take.

He pondered the extent this total destruction might take. Chicago, Detroit, Cleveland, and Buffalo were all easy markets for Michigan white pine and all were grow-ing cities. Could this be the beginning of the end of Michigan's big trees?

His thoughts went back to the hills of his own valley where the trees had always been the pride of the settlers. In his mind he began a methodical roll call of the proper-ty. Most of the really big pines were owned by those early settlers like his father, the Harcourts, the Moreaus, Ole Nelson and Bill and Mary Sugars. They were all holding a section or more of the big trees and would never sell them to be harvested as they were doing it here in Muskegon.

Of this he was sure.

But how about the hills south of the lake? This was still government land. An area of swamp and hill not yet developed in any way. Here timber rights could be bought for a song, and while the trees there were not like the big ones owned by the early settlers, there were a thousand acres there for the taking.

Halvar Brady's bugle sounded its distinctive announcement and the town dogs answered. A flurry of herring gulls screamed down and escorted the stage down the last long slope into town. From up on the driver's seat Halvar's voice came drifting down, "D'ese tam 'Skeegon gulls, dey don' know a stagecoach from a herring schooner. Dey bane sat on sawdus' piles so long de'er all hatched from woaden eggs."

The stage whirled to a stop in front of the hotel with its usual flourish, proper jingling of harness gear, squeaking of leather, and the smell of sweating horse flesh. Tom waited for the dust to settle, then eased his tired back from the leather seat and sought the relief of a short walk around town. The stage, having no other passengers, dropped a mail sack and immediately took off for the livery and a change of horses.

From closer up he could see that the lake and the mouth of the river were filled from shore to shore with floating logs. He watched for a while the rivermen scampering over them like ants, sorting the brands and pushing them on to the boomed off holding pens. From there they were pushed onto conveyors which carried them up into the mills. Even from this distance Tom could hear the steady pumping of the gang saws and the screaming of the big blades. Then from the other end the boards came sliding down a chute to be piled for drying and shipping.

He moved on down the street. At the waterfront two ragged Indians sat cross–legged on the dock. The old man had a whiskey bottle and the squaw a loud and berating tongue. He walked around them. A long–legged hound with sad, brown eyes and a ponderous pair of ears came to stand beside him in friendly silence. His eyes rolled upwards to encourage a friendly pat. In spite of the early season two boys were diving naked from the end of the dock. Behind him two girls peeked from behind an over-turned riverboat and giggled.

Halvar Brady came up. The hound's sad eyes swam to him, the long tail wagging slowly in recognition. Halvar looked down at him and watched as the hound's great eyes swept out across the expanse of treeless hills, then came back again to look sadly at him.

"Sorry ol' boy," Halvar laughed. "Progress, she is sometimes 'ard on all of us." He leaned down and gave the hound another understanding pat.

"Quite a sight, ain't it, Tom? They 'ave a gang saw in there d'at rips up two logs at a time and a circle blade for'dy–two inches 'cross. Hear tell d'ey cut near to four million board feet jest last year."

"And Chicago is using it all?" asked Tom.

"Mos' every bit," laughed Halvar. "Whenever d'ey git too much d'ey jes' burn the tam' place down an' start over."

Tom watched Halvar head back to the livery, then went to meet him at the hotel. As he entered the shadows of the stage, he was surprised to find a new passenger already waiting on the opposite seat.

"Hello!" he finally said, "I am Tom Michaels, bound for the little town of Golden."

"Hello." The young lady's eyes met his with only a hint of shyness. "I am Dana Sharrow. I will be meeting friends in Middlesex. I believe that that is still north of Golden, right?"

"Right," said Tom, then settled back into the leather as Halvar's "Gee up" stirred the fresh team into action and the rattle of the boards on the river bridge drowned all other sounds.

He had planned to take a short nap after they left Muskegon. It had been a wearing two days. But with the rather pretty girl now sitting in the seat across from him, he found his attention divided. One eye insisted on opening and disclosed a small foot close to his. Attached to it was a very trim ankle and above that was the promise of a very pretty calf well concealed in a flowing blue skirt.

The other eye opened and was drawn immediately to the two big brown ones staring quizzically into his. She really was pretty, he thought, in a neat, capable sort of way. And probably friendly, as she gave him an amused smile. But his position, sitting so immediately opposite to her in the cozy confines of the coach required a considerable amount of self–control.

In spite of himself his eyes seemed to insist on indecently wandering from that pair of trim ankles back to the wide–set pair of brown eyes which always seemed to be just turning to meet his and carried a disconcerting placidity which conditions did not seem to warrant. The rather confining space within the now gently swaying coach, after all, pretty much limited their acquaintance to one of direct confrontation from the opposite seats or one of chummy companionship on either the front or the rear one.

Tom contemplated the more desirable of the two, since this arrangement would serve several purposes. It would not only relieve the direct confrontation which seemed more than normally difficult for him to handle, it would also allow for a more thorough examination of the subject at hand without the interruption of those steady dark eyes. He grinned at the thought. Then his eyes rose to find hers again looking questioningly at him. He felt a rush of heat on his neck as he grinned back.

She smiled in a rather knowing way and he believed that he had now determined that, while the brown eyes were the most striking feature, the roll of chestnut hair with the tinge of sorrel showing where the light struck it and the trim cut of waist, breasts, and shoulders were equally attractive. But since she had been so inconsiderate as to take the opposite seat, and he could conceive of no gentlemanly way of correcting the situation, he could only exchange pleasantries and try to interest his own eyes in the view from the side window.

It was Dana who broke the awkward silence. "This is beautiful country, isn't it?"

"It is, especially during this time of the year, before the dryness sets in."

"Do you live near here?"

"Golden," he said, relaxing a little. "It is even nicer there. It is close to the lake where the air comes in sharp and clean." He hesitated, but she seemed interested and he felt more at ease on this familiar soil, so he went on. "My father was one of the first to come here many years ago. He was attracted by the big trees in the valley and by the stories of my uncle Milan. Uncle Milan was no farmer and he thought that if trees would grow two hundred feet tall here, surely corn would grow to at least twenty feet."

"He was wrong?" she smiled.

"Very much so," replied Tom. "White pine trees grow tall on sandy soil when there is moisture deep down that their roots can reach. But during dry years corn, with its shallow roots, withered and died in the August sun. We thought we would have to leave this country or starve."

"But you stayed?"

"Yes, we stayed." He was at ease now. "We stayed and others came. This country gets into your blood. The hills, the lakes and especially the clear, sharp air are things you don't find farther south where the soil is heavier and richer. It is like our neighbor, Bill Sugars, always says, 'Once you live here you become a slave to freedom.' No matter where you go, sooner or later the air begins to lay heavy in your lungs and you begin to hunger for the smell of the pines and the feel of the white sand of the lake shores."

"Is that the reason you are coming back?"

"I hadn't thought of it that way, but it just could be."

"Even if it means being hungry?"

"Oh! I think those days are over. We have learned a bit since then. And with the War between the States pushing prices up, farming is coming into its own."

"You certainly don't look like you were ever hungry." There was a hint of a compliment in her tone, but it also carried a cool note which told him that real hunger was something she also might have known.

He smiled as he recalled some of the lean years of his childhood. He remembered that year when he and his father had cleared their first fields behind old Bess and Bruno, the oxen uncle Milan had driven all the way from Yankee Springs. Slow, hard work it was. And when the fields were finally cleared and crops planted, the long August drought set in and the corn withered and curled in the hot sun while it was still barely knee–high.

That had been the worst year. There was hardly enough corn or wheat to replace the seed they had planted, and the blueberries and blackberries were so small they were hardly worth picking. Before they could put in a store of wild nuts and smoked fish, the winter was upon them. It came that year with a rush of swirling snow and freezing rain, then more snow blowing and drifting over the glazed first fall and piling in drifts as high as the eaves of the new barn. By January their food was gone. If it had not been for Uncle Milan they would not have made it. Milan had gone into the swamps on snow shoes and brought out a deer with the wolves howling at him from the ridges. The tough meat and maple sugar had been their only food for many days.

"Yes, we were hungry many times," he said, looking closely now at this friendly girl. "But we were lucky, too. Father was a fighter. When a fighter gets punched a few times, he learns to duck and swing with the blows. Then he watches for a weakness in the other fellow's style and gets in a few licks of his own. That is exactly what he did. When he learned that corn and wheat did poorly, he planted potatoes where he could irrigate them with water from the creek. They grew large and smooth in the sandy soil. Then he planted apple and pear trees. When he learned that these did well, we dried and canned plenty of fruit. We grazed cattle on the bottomlands along the lake and picked blueberries and blackberries in the hills. Then to make some ready money we started to ship fruit on the schooners to Muskegon and Chicago, we trapped along the streams, and made shingles from the cedar trees. We didn't get rich, but we avoided the knockout punches and even did quite well. And when we finally had time to look about us again there were good neighbors building in the hills, planting fruit trees and learning to live as we had learned. No one talked of leaving again. I guess we finally decided, to hell with getting rich, this is what we left the old countries to find. Peace, peace and land of our own."

The stage swayed out of the tunnel of green south of White Lake and out onto the ridge where the road drops into the valley of the White River. There the river broadens to become the lake, held back from entry to Lake Michigan by a barrier of sandy hills. The sun, dropping low now over the blue wall of Lake Michigan, bathed the slopes of the hills in evening gold and cast long shadows far out into the lake and its watershed. The evening hush had fallen on the valley. The water of the lakes was settling into an evening calm and the ethereal quiet which precedes the night chorus was broken only by the calling of crows seeking their nesting grounds and the distant scream of a loon.

Here again, as Tom looked across the valley, he could see that the hills were being cleared of pines. The smell of burning sawdust, dull and pungent, came to him from the mill at the mouth of the river.

"Damn the cutters," he said, half out loud.

"Why do you say that, Tom?" Her voice came sharp and quizzical from out of the deepening shadows. "Aren't you forgetting that we have soldiers to feed, bridges, to build and schools to pay for?" The subject appeared to be one of interest to Dana, as it was to Tom, and the strength of opposing views, for the moment, led them to forget their discomfort. "It would seem to me that if Michigan is to grow and prosper, it must be done with our trees." She paused, then the fire which had flamed in her eyes briefly smoldered and went out. A smile slowly replaced the fire and she blushed a little and said quietly, in her rich, deep voice, "I'm sorry."

She turned to the opposite window. But only for a minute, then faced him again. The smile was more relaxed now and accompanied by a devilish twinkle. "But I meant every word of it," she added.

Tom grinned, too. The irritation in her voice had amused him. "I guess I need to admit that I am prejudiced," he conceded. "My background is among these hills. Those trees are mostly what brought us here. My family and my neighbor's families worked hard for the privilege of saying, 'These are our hills.' They are not much. They are sandy knobs looking down on unproductive valleys. But on those hills grow trees, the ultimate fruit of years of God's handiwork. To us they are much more than wealth. They are like ourselves, full of life.

"I believe we all knew that someday this time would come and that when it did those trees could bring us fortunes. That is the reason we bought up all the land we could afford to buy. I do not believe, though, that there is one family in our valley who would ever cut timber as you see it being cut here. They will cut only to clear fields or to sell prime trees. All else remains money in the bank and a feast for the spirit."

Even more quietly, he added, "In the eyes of the world my father was not a great man, but the lessons he taught me were the lessons of compassion for my fellow man. 'It is consideration for others,' he said, 'even though they be of another generation, that will produce a prosperous and a healthy nation.' This he believed, and this I believe."

As he spoke, he had leaned forward and thoughtlessly placed a big hand on a blue–skirted knee. Now he pulled it back quickly, grinning a little.

"Where was you father from, Tom?"

"Pittsburgh, when he came here, but originally from Serbia. He had known life under the Turks. It is little wonder he valued these hills and the freedom he found here."

She shifted her gaze to outside the window, and although a hint of resentment seemed to linger in her eyes, she said no more.

Tom remained silent, too. Perhaps he had already said too much. There was no good reason to add sparks to tinder which could burst so quickly into flame. He fingered the roll of stiff paper inside his coat pocket and wished deeply that his father could have lived to know that he had received it.

It was nearly dark when the stage came to a stop in front of Caleb Greene's store in Benona. A lamp was burning in a hanger above the counter, its light barely visible in the afterglow from the western sky.

"You're late, Halvar," called Caleb, as he caught the

mail sack Halvar Brady tossed down to him.

"Yes, dey off white had trowed a shoe back in 'Skegon so we los' an hour. Smiddies up dat way are so busy making new cutters for saw blades, ain't hardly got time to tend a hoof anymore. How's Hannah?"

"Fit," said Caleb. "Here, she sent you a bit of chicken. Don't suppose you got time to eat a bite with us."

"Nope. Got a lady passenger go'n into Middlesex. It be mighty late now tam we make it. Got me another passenger you know, too. Young Tom Michaels, back from college. All growed up and edgicated fer law."

The door of the stage swung open. Caleb Green looked inside and thrust a big hand towards Tom. "Howdy, Tom. Don't suppose you remember me, but I knew your Pa. And a fine man he was. Glad to see you back. Old Judge Littlejohn was through t'other day and calculated he could use a few good lawyers. Welcome home, son." And looking across the stage, he said apologetically, "Howdy, Miss," and closed the door.

The stage jolted forward again, with a complaining of leather, the sound of fluttering chickens, and the stench of fresh horse manure filling the night air.

They rode in silence for some time. They had given each other much to think about and the quiet of the evening and a sense of weariness encouraged silence. Finally Tom relaxed and dozed comfortably in the swaying seat.

It was dark when he was awakened by the touch of a hand on his knee and the girl saying "Tom, Tom."

She had moved back to the seat with him and was calling to him in her low voice. "Tom, you will be leaving in a few minutes and there is something I want to tell you."

Tom came slowly awake. Easy relaxing was one of his pleasures.

"Please listen closely, Tom, and someday you will know why. I, too, have a heritage. Mine is Irish. I came from a good Irish family of some wealth, as Ireland measures wealth. But when the potato crops failed, we grew poor like the rest. My parents are gone now. Hunger and a rough passage were more than they could stand. I suspect now that the food available went to my brother and to me. Now I have only one living relative. He is my brother, Milton, and I love him very much. It was he who paid for the schooling which I just finished. Please remember this, Tom. Please." She tightened the hold on his knee. "Please, Please remember."

Tom looked at her in the shadows. Why was she telling him this?

The stage had stopped now. The horses were blowing and whipping their tails impatiently. In the dusk Tom could see the sandy, twin–rutted trail leading off to the west towards Golden. He was nearly home. He opened the door and slid stiffly from the coach.

"One more thing, Tom. In September, after the harvests, there will be a new school teacher in your valley. Wish me luck. It will be my first school." As she closed the door, she leaned forward in the darkness and kissed him playfully on the cheek.

"Hey up," said Halvar Brady, and the stage whirred into the darkness of the night.

It was four miles from the stage stop to Golden, and two more before he would reach the crest of the hill that overlooked the lake. But to Tom, the miles passed lightly under foot. The days of travel from Ann Arbor had seemed endless. Now, releasing his long legs from the cramped quarters of the stage and his back from the swaying and jolting was pure joy. Besides, he seemed to think more clearly out here on his feet. Here he could kick a stray stone in disgust or fling out a word or two aloud if the thought so struck him. This was freedom as he had known it in the valley. This was home.

Inky shadows had crept out of the woods and blanketed the hills in cool darkness. The western sky carried only a green hint of the faded day, with the evening star blinking brightly in it. The air, moving in slowly off Lake Michigan carried its remembered freshness along with the added eloquence of distant lilacs and the closer pungence of fresh pine. Another mile and he would be entering the familiar valley. Around the next bend was Carl VanBolt's grist mill, with the gurgle of water running under the wooden bridge, and then the cluster of cottages and the short street that was the town.

I wonder, he mused, what the VanBolt girls will look like. Sarah will not have changed much. She will be big and clean and full of song and well on her way towards maturity, unless, of course, some young blade has set off some sparks and put new life in her.

Jeannie, now that one was pretty and tomboyish and full of the devil when I left. She could be quite a beauty by now, and likely as rough on Nancy VanBolt as a spirited stallion. She will throw her trainer and leave some bad bruises before she settles down.

The town would be quiet by now. It was always quiet at this time of the evening. His mind methodically reconstructed the familiar details. Nick Tanner's Blacksmith Shop, Ole Nelson's Store, Martin Brewer's hardware, then a little farther on the Lake road would be the schoolhouse. Then, over one more wooded ridge and he would be home.

What would his mother say when he told her that, at least for the time being, he wanted to work the farm? The smell of the cows and the feel of fresh turned earth under his feet were calling him stronger than all the challenges in the world and he knew that for a while he was going to heed that call. Later on, perhaps?....

The town was not quiet that night. From a new frame building beyond the blacksmith's shop came the glow of lights and the sound of rough laughter. Drawing closer, Tom could hear the muffled clatter of dishes and the restless whinny of horses tied too long at the rail. Tom stopped, tried to read the sign over the door, then, with his curiosity aroused by the alien sounds, he reacted to them with a surge of anger. Like Muskegon and White Lake, the town had changed. There it had disappointed him. Here it filled him with anger and resentment. He crossed the deserted street, opened the door of the new building and stepped inside. In the room was a scattering of tables, several of them occupied by strangers concentrating over noisy games of euchre and tall glasses of Monongahela. There was a well–stocked bar across the rear and from behind this came the greasy smells of a kitchen.

It was a scene strange and repulsive to Tom whose memories of the village had never included a saloon. Stranger, too, was the absence of familiar faces. With one exception, every face in the room was new to him. The one exception was old Martin Brewer, the hardware merchant who occupied a table in the corner, across from a well–dressed stranger.

Tom's first impulse was to turn and leave quietly, the way he had come, but in the back of his mind swelled a curiosity to learn more about these strangers, and the rejection of any indication that he was one who would turn from a new situation. He had left this village a young man, mature in growth but naive in the ways of the world. He was returning a man. He had known the bars and brawls of a college town. He had been hardened by three summers of work with the sailors and miners of the Lake Superior country. He had seen the highs and the lows of human nature and, like his Uncle Milan, he had made his choice. When he walked out it would be because his curiosity was satisfied and the hand of Martin Brewer had been shaken as a neighbor, although he held no great bond of friendship with this old merchant.

Tom's lean height was forced to bend slightly as he shook hands with Martin, who did not bother to rise.

"Milton Sharrow, you meet," he said, nodding to the stranger. "He is a new businessman here."

Tom stiffened at recognition of the name. "How do you do, Mr. Sharrow?" He was not surprised or disturbed when Martin Brewer failed to rise. He was the one person in the town slow to extend overtures of friendliness to anyone. But when the man, Sharrow, also failed to stand in greeting, Tom's big frame stiffened.

"What is your business, Mr. Sharrow?" It was the logical question, although Tom had noted the red sashes of shanty boys in the room and already suspected the answer.

Milt Sharrow shifted his cigar to the other side of his mouth, pulled his coat open as if to expose the richly embroidered vest, and ignoring Tom's question, asked, "Are you the Michaels that lives on the farm east of the lake?"

Omission of civil courtesy Tom could overlook, but when his question was ignored and the stranger's question came back, a slow wave of anger possessed him. He pulled the chair aside and sat down slowly and deliberately at the table, leaned forward and spoke in a voice cool with challenge, "If that is your business, yes!"

Voices in the room lowered. Seconds slipped by. The clatter of dishes from the back of the room quieted, then stopped. Slowly the wave of anger which had enveloped Tom subsided, leaving him more amused than aroused. Seldom had anger risen in him so quickly and possessed him so completely.

It was a full minute before the flush slowly left the stranger's face. When he finally spoke his voice was calm and he smiled weakly.

Immediately the noise at the tables continued. Tom did not choose to press luck further. He picked up his hat and without a second glance at the men at the tables, he closed the door slowly behind him.

Tom walked home in the darkness that precedes the rising moon. Traveling with him were the troubled thoughts that follow a burst of anger. By the time he had reached the bend above the farm, the moon had risen yellow in the sky behind him, then turned to blue–white in the upper heights to unfold a silvery coating on everything in the valley, the neat house with its various outbuildings, a freshly tilled field, the long lane reaching to the forests beyond. To the westward, behind the pines, the lake lay shimmering with blue diamonds and rising from it rose the clean, sharp folds of the sand dunes, rising in combinations of bronze blue and silver. Still farther above and beyond, Lake Michigan stretched away like a blue veil studded with sequins of reflected light. This should have been the end of everything, thought Tom, but it was not, for ever above, like a lovely benediction, shone the mysterious stars.

There was no light at the cottage, so assuming his mother had retired, Tom circled the house, the beauty of the night weaving its spell even more poignantly than in the past. Returning to the scenes, sounds, and smells of his early days was pleasant. He wandered to the barn. The horses whinnied and nuzzled him in the darkness. The old familiar smells of curing hay and rotting manure mixed with the fresh smells from outside urged him to go farther.

He took the path through the feed lot, past the new–plowed field and down the lane bordered by the zigzag rails of a new fence. Beyond the pasture he climbed through the old stump fence he and his father had laid and faced the woodlands standing like a wall of mysterious darkness before him. Tom had liked to walk here at night, especially when he was troubled. Here the sweet smell of pines cleared his head and the great round boles of the trees thrust themselves straight up at the stars. He enjoyed the feel of the ground cushioned by centuries of fallen needles. Here, in the insulated void between the dead needles below and the live ones above, was a darkness and a stillness exceeded only by death itself. It was a silence, heavy and motionless, which by its very sterility seemed to ridicule the strength of any living thing. The great pillars of the trees rising from the softness of the earth were felt, rather than seen, in the darkness of the night, but their strength and size was the strength of the unknown, the odor of the ages, and the majesty of a cathedral.

Tom could remember these same big pines in all of their moods: in the white stillness of winter when they were shaking powdery snow from their high branches; when their tops were hidden in the wet mists of early spring and only the big feet of them came down out of the hidden sky to show their strength; during the summer storms when they swayed and bent like tall grass in the vicious west winds that thundered in off of the lake, their rooted grip against this beating power.

Now, here again in this blue night, Tom found the challenge and, at the same time, the solace that always thrilled and fascinated him. It was symbolic of the test put to Indian boys before they are accepted as members of the clan. He knew now that he had again wanted to feel the thrill of that experience. He wanted to know if the new Tom Michaels was still in command of the emotional inner man as the younger Tom had learned to be.

He was not disappointed. The easy excitement was still there, and perhaps an even greater appreciation of the therapy of silence and darkness. He wanted to think, so, as he had always done, he stretched out on the cool needles and watched the blue of the sky finding little holes in the blackness of the growth. A tree toad twittered quietly and the faint whoo of an owl came out of the distance. Somewhere to his left, something, probably a raccoon, scratched down a tree and melted into the silence of the needles. Farther away a wolf started its mating call, low and tremulous at first, then rising to a sad lonely wail.

His mind wandered back to the girl on the stage. She had been noticeably troubled by his story of the valley and its people. Now the reason was becoming clear to him. Her brother was cutting timber somewhere in these hills.

An almost imperceptible movement of air fanned the tree-tops above him and he watched as a spire of pine one hundred and eighty feet above him swept slowly and majestically in movement, crossed a star, hesitated and returned.

If a kiss was a plea for friendship with Milton Sharrow it held little hope of success. Mr. Sharrow had showed none of the good qualities he thought he had observed in the girl, Dana. But perhaps he could be wrong. He would have to wait and see. The very fact that anyone was cutting trees in the valley, though, troubled him.

The air had become quite cool so he rose and pushed deeper into the blackness of the pines. He felt an uneasiness creep over him. The strange, cool feel of the unfamiliar penetrating the subconscious pattern of the familiar. The call of the wolf had seemed too close. There was an odor in the air that did not belong there. He felt compelled by it to go deeper into these wooded hills.

As the land started to slope downwards towards the lake the temper of the silence changed. The long howl of the wolf came even more clearly, and was answered. Stars appeared ahead of him. Moonlight was appearing where only darkness should have remained. Now he walked out into an opening, scarred by many stumps still reeking with the smell of freshly cut pine. He knew now that this was the odor that had troubled him.

The moonlight seemed bright here after the darkness of the tall timber that he had left. As his eyes slowly adjusted, he could see that the area of cut timber did not stop. Instead, it widened into a prairie of shining stumps and a jungle of cut limbs and brown, wilting tops. It extended from the crest of the hill on down to the shores of the shining lake. A strip of fine timber along the north boundary of their land had been cut as though the giant stroke of a scythe had whipped across it. Nothing was left; no young trees, no birch or maple, nothing but a tangle of discarded trimmings. Included in the prairie of barren stump land, according to Tom's quick estimate, was at least twenty acres of land belonging to his mother. The rest would be the property of Jim and Louise Colby.

For the third time in two days Tom felt his blood surging in anger. He had first felt anger when the girl on the stage had flared up in defense of the lumbermen. Now the course of events during his first night at home had brought the problem close. It was no longer something he could look at from a safe distance but a well embedded thorn in his own flash.

His father had always taught him to live at peace with his neighbors. This he would have to try hard to do, if only out of respect for his father. In the back of his mind he knew that his nature would not allow it. His blood was French and Serbian. Neither flowed cool on the end of a tether.

Chapter Seven

The sun was well up over the eastern hills when Mina Michaels let the back door of the big cabin slam shut behind her. She walked out towards the grain shed, admiring as always the clarity of the morning air. No breeze had yet appeared and, on the western horizon, Lake Michigan was piled azure blue and glassy smooth against the morning sky. The dunes, always their sharpest and yellowest in the morning sun, rose in between and seemed so close that she could almost reach out and touch them. Even Old Smokey, the high peak to the far south, failed to show the faintest wisp of sand drifting over its sharp crest. This tiny flag of sand could be the sign that a bit of breeze was stirring out over the lake. A fair weather flag, Ganus had called it.

"Not a breath of air stirring," she said, half aloud. "Oh! I wish Tom was here. It is so still that the dunes are reflected in the lake."

The granary door squeaked open. She measured two scoops of yellow grain into her apron and proceeded on to the chicken yard. Hired hands are fine, she thought, to till the soil and milk the cow. But the chickens, they are a woman's chore. Make a quick move or change their feed and bingo! There won't be enough eggs to bake a good cake. Hens are too temperamental for hired hands to handle.

Amid the noise of the clucking hens, another noise, a louder clucking, sounded somewhere behind her. She turned to see if a hen had slipped out of the gate. The gate was closed tight so she turned again to her feeding. Again a noise sounded behind her, this time the plaintive bleat of a lamb. A lamb? We've got no sheep, she started to say, then let out a happy cry. "Tom! Oh, Tom! Where are you?"

"Look up, Mother, always look up."

She turned at the sound of his voice, and looking up she saw him, sitting legs a-dangle from the loft door in the peak of the barn.

"Tom Michaels," she laughed. Her laughter was as sweet and clear as ever. "You come right down from there. The idea, sleeping in the loft your first night home from college."

"Now don't start bossing me around," teased Tom. "I might subpoena a witness and hold you liable for intimidation." He reached for the hay rope, though, and slid gently to the ground.

His mother met him there and they held each other close. Mina's arms were hungry for the feel of him and her eyes were misty when she looked up.

Louise was in the kitchen and greeted Tom with the

usual Indian reserve. Tom thought she looked older and a little worn, but the glow in her dark eyes told him that she was glad to see him back home. She accepted his compliments and the arm around her waist with quiet appreciation.

Over a stack of wheat cakes and maple syrup Tom carefully observed his mother. There were streaks of gray appearing in the glossy chestnut of her hair, and she might be a little quieter, but the quick smile was unchanged and the lights that flickered in the dark eyes still danced there. Perhaps they were not so much asparkle as they were a few years ago, but now held more of a deep beautiful glow.

They talked for a long time, of Louise and Jim, of the crops, and the people of the village, and finally of the War between the States. They talked of Lincoln and his call for soldiers and supplies to carry on the war.

"Now tell me, Tom, what are your plans?" Mina finally asked.

"Must I have plans, Mother? I thought you taught me to live one day at a time."

"Yes," she smiled, "but I am sure that you have some."

He looked at her steadily, knowing that the war was on her mind. "Only this, Mother. I will put my law books on a shelf until the war with the South is over. If I am drafted I will go, of course. I will never send someone in my place. If I am not called I will remain here and work the land. Food, too, is important. Does this distress you?"

"Oh no, Tom, no." He could read the relief in her face.

"You do not fear being called a Copperhead?"

"No, Tom, not here among these people who know us. They know what we believe."

"Would you prefer that I use my learning?"

"You will use it, Tom. You cannot avoid using it. It is now a part of you. And what you say tells me much."

"Oh!"

"It tells me that you still do not have the greed which sometimes is acquired with knowledge."

"Oh, but I do!" Tom grinned. "I am greedy for the sight of you, and Milan, and Louise and these hills. I want to see more and more of this good life and these good people."

Mina's eyes showed her pleasure.

"If it were not for this greed I would have volunteered for duty, as most of my fellow students did. Perhaps, if the need continues, my conscience will demand that I join. So far I do not feel ready. I believe that it is father's dislike for fighting that holds me back."

Mina placed a hand on his. She knew full well that the thought of leaving her with neither husband nor son was in his mind. With the deep understanding she always showed, she said, "Tom, whatever you feel must be done, you must do. The world is full of needs, and of men and women to fill these needs. It is for you and you alone to decide where your talents and energies may best be used."

When he looked at her, though, Tom knew that her eyes were saying "stay Tom, please stay."

There had been no mention, so far, of the cutting of the timber in the valley, but Tom could not help believe that perhaps an indirect reference had been made by the need for him to be here at home. This thought brought him closer to a decision, and now he decided it was time to open the subject.

"Tell me now, Mother," he said, pushing his chair back from the table. "Who is doing the cutting?"

"You know, then."

"I know little, but I saw the cuttings last night in the moonlight, and I saw shantymen in town."

Louise stiffened a little at her work, then continued the rattling of the dishes.

"Milton Sharrow is his name," she said.

"I suspected as much. A schemer, that one."

"Mill Sharrow may be the schemer, yes, but his fore-man, Angus McBride, is the real boss. He is a lawless brute, Tom. If you have notions of fighting Mill Sharrow, don't do it. The timber is gone, but the land is still there. Give them that much and let us continue in peace. That is the way your father would want it."

"I am not that sure, Mother. Father disliked fighting because he had seen much of it. But also because much that he saw in old Serbia were hopeless, wasteful wars of pride. Disorganized small communities fighting hopeless little wars against the organized Turks.

"That timber was dear to Father. He had a feeling for it. It was the first solid, worthwhile thing he ever owned. He was proud that he could call it his because he had bought it with money earned with his own hands and he held papers that said clearly, this land is mine, the rocks, the grass, the sky above and the earth below, and most of all, those big pine trees that grow there.

"I don't know, Mother. I think Father would see that this is not like the war with the Turks which had been lost generations before his time. This is a new problem, one that is just being born out there on our back forty, and a hundred other back forties in our state. It is one which we may be able to solve quickly if we make use of the laws and the courts of our new state. But the longer it is put off, the harder it will be to stop it.

"Mill Sharrow is not likely to stop with those twenty acres unless he is made to fear the consequences. We will lose more and more, Louise and Jimmy will lose more, then the Moreaus and the Harcourts could be next. We can't just sit here on our back sides and let men like him bully and steal, Mother. We have to fight back with the tools that our country has given us. If we don't, Mill Sharrow and those like him could become the new Turks and us the bitter exiles.

"I'm sorry, Mom, if we disagree." He placed his big hand on hers. "But I am sure that this is true. Dad's cause was lost, but ours has just begun. Let's not give up all that he gave us unless we have to."

"The logging run is nearly over for this year, Tom. The last of the logs are in the little lake. Some of them have reached the bay and been rafted and hauled away. Soon Jimmy and Milan will be home from their surveying jobs...then...."

Tom saddled the sorrel and rode north down the lane, across the pasture and through the cathedral-like stand of great cork pines, fragrant in the stillness of the morning.

On the barren hillside beyond, he watched three deer herd their spotted offspring to a safer distance. He then set to work to more accurately estimate the size and number of the trees which had been cut. Twenty acres of such timber could well produce 480,000 board feet of lumber. Even at the low price of $7.50 per thousand, this would pay Mill Sharrow a handsome return.

No wonder he is willing to gamble. Twenty acres of that timber south of the lake would not pay a third that well.

Tom continued westward through the tangle of discarded limbs. A black squirrel scampered ahead of him, looking vainly for the safety of a tree. Finding none, he climbed to the top of the largest stump and scolded loudly. Noticing the size of the stump, Tom rode alongside. It was close to four and one–half feet in diameter at the cut and carried such an unusual formation of dark heartwood that Tom dismounted to see it better. The tree had been damaged by lightning or fire while quite young. During the healing process which followed, the bark had folded and turned inward so that the rings of growth were uneven, and down through the center, the dark heartwood had formed into the shape of a mitten, or, thought Tom, the shape of the state of Michigan. He mounted again, then looked back. Yes, it could be, he thought. The blackened heart of Michigan that lay before him.

From the point where the river leaves the lake to where it empties into Lake Michigan is at least two miles. First it travels into a small, shallow lake, scarcely ten acres in size, which formed an ideal marshaling area for Mill Sharrow's logs. Here they could be hauled or floated to be counted and branded, then pushed, in the spring, into the swift current of the river which runs through thick woods for perhaps a mile, then out into semi–open wasteland. Here the towering dunes push relentlessly in from the west, drifting and sliding directly into the flowing stream, crowding and filling it, forcing it to cut and chew into the opposite banks, its swift current fighting to clear its way past the crowding dunes and onward to the blue water of Lake Michigan.

At the point where the river leaves the small lake, Milton Sharrow had built his camp. Tom circled it. Along the stream he rode quietly. Contrary to what his mother had told him there were still plenty of logs in the river. The spring run was still moving and it was the big logs that had been held until last. There were rivermen busy at crucial points, prodding and cursing them back into the swift current. They were much too busy to pay attention to him.

At the point where the dunes rose highest along the north bank, the river was made shallow by the sand which drifted into it. Here Tom stopped, sitting his horse quietly and watching as the largest of the logs hesitated where the lowering spring water allowed it to drag on the sandy shoal. It swung with the current and suddenly its huge bole nudged the bank close to the base of the towering dune. Another log, equally as large, swung around the bend behind it, struck it with a resounding thud and drove it solidly up into the shallow water at the base of the dune. Slowly, as Tom watched, he saw the sand above the log start to slide. Slowly at first, then more swiftly as the dry sand above loosened, and finally, with a smooth surge of power, the entire side of the hill gave way and slid silently over the log. Only the huge butt of it remained to be washed clean by the passing water, and on the butt Tom could see two marks, the circled M S brand of the Milton Sharrow Logging Company, and a patch of heartwood shaped like a dark brown mitten.

Tom backed his horse quickly into the brush, turned it and rode to the top of the nearest rise. From here he could watch unnoticed as the rivermen came shouting to the spot.

The second big log, which had met the first, had swung crosswise to the current and in a matter of minutes, others from upstream came crashing down to drive it against the brushy near bank. Now it was too late. Before the men could turn it again downstream there was a tangle of timber forming behind it. The solid thud of log against log could be heard from Tom's hilltop and, as the force of the rising water drove them on, some of them turned end over end to form the tangled jam-up that rivermen dread.

Tom quietly turned his horse and left the scene. There will be no more logs going to the big lake this season, he thought. Mill Sharrow's greed to cut the big pines he could not buy had been his undoing. The river would carry such timber only during seasons of extremely high water.

Chapter Eight

The logging season was over. The shanty boys had left camp weeks ago and now, with the jam plugging the river and the water dropping lower behind it, Mill Sharrow was forced to quit for the season.

Next year he would build a dam below the jam and by raising the water level he would break the tangle and float them off. The war would likely be over by then and, with prices rising, he could still do well.

He and his foreman were alone at the end of the long cabin which served as storeroom and office. The water of the lake shining through the doorway sent little patches of reflected sunlight dancing on the walls and ceiling. The sound of a horse outside did not disturb them as they prepared the figures for paying off the last of the rivermen.

Suddenly the dancing lights disappeared from the wall, and turning, they saw in the doorway the tall figure of Tom Michaels. He had exchanged his suit coat for a flannel shirt which he wore open at the neck, and heavy leather boots lent a capable look to his long legs.

"I have something for you, Mill Sharrow," said Tom

dryly, and stepping into the room, he handed him a long thick envelope. "It is something," he said, "which I doubt that you have ever received before, a summons to appear in circuit court on November the first of this year."

Mill Sharrow's face reddened and the huge red—bearded foreman, Angus McBride, started forward in anger. Mill Sharrow stopped him with a hand on his arm. The foreman was the physical boss of the outfit. That was clear. And well equipped he was, for while he was shorter than Tom, he was a man of tremendous proportions, thick–shouldered and heavy of neck and thigh. But with all his bulk he moved with the quick, easy motions of a cat, and his eyes, dark above the thick, red beard, shone as vicious as those of a swamp bobcat. The fact that Mill Sharrow did stop him with a word was proof enough that he remained the boss, and to some degree Tom's respect for the crafty lumberman increased.

"What is the charge?" Mill finally spoke, eyeing Tom closely and making no move to read the contents of the envelope which he had tossed loosely on the table.

"The theft of four hundred and eighty thousand board feet of timber from my mother's property and that of Jim and Louise Colby."

"And you can prove that, I suppose."

"Proof of timber theft is a difficult thing," said Tom. "That I grant you. Suppose we leave the matter of proof to the judgment of a court. But the matter of restitution is something for you to think about during the summer. I hope you enjoy it, Mill Sharrow."

"We might pay you long before that," muttered the foreman. But Tom had left the doorway.

The foreman followed him quickly to the door. "Do you hear me?" he fairly shouted. "We may pay you long before that." And as he spoke, he reached to the pegs above the door, pulled down the rifle which was there and brought it to his shoulder.

The survey party had completed its work. Without waiting for a new day, Milan and Jimmy Colby turned their horses to the west. Riding late, they rested briefly during the moonless hours.

They were on their way again at sunrise. Milan was in good spirits. Surveying for the railroad was dull, confining work, not at all to his liking. He was glad that it was finished.

"Next year, Jimmy, mon ami swamp Indian, mebby we run some trap lines. Then we be our own boss. No more of this, 'Farther right, Milan. Now one inch more.' What in hell is the difference if train goes one inch more farther north? A year after it gets there, whoosh! nothing left but stumps anyway."

"Oui, Milan, trap lines more better. Survey man too much, hurry up, hurry up. Maybe nex' year I hunt for Mr. Sharrow. He want me for food Indian."

Milan stopped his horse and turned it crosswise of the trail. "Listen, Jim, you red heathen. You know damn well why I got us this job this year. It was to get you away from that camp of thieves. Three fat venison you get for them the first week, and what do you get? A bottle of cheap whiskey and a big ache in the head. What did your family get? Nothing. Don't be an Indian fool, my fren'. Stay clean of that Mill Sharrow."

Milan heard the quiet, "Oui oui, Milan," but he knew that Jimmy Colby would never be the same. The winter had worn heavy upon him. The confinement of the work and the weight of white man's ways were more than his spirit could bear. He would never again work by time. Milan knew this, and he was not much pleased with it himself. He had done it to free Jimmy from something much worse, and because of the look he had seen in Louise's dark eyes. Perhaps he and Jimmy should quit this country. The freedom was being squeezed out of it too fast for the likes of them. But then, there were Louise and the children.

His mind went back to his winters on the Mauvais. Jim would love that country. He wondered if old Simon Charette still ran a post at Lac Du Flambeau, and if the Indians were still friendly now that the white settlers were showing in their country. Those were good days he had spent there. Especially those spring days like these when the warm sun was driving the ice from the rivers and the snow was melting back among the pines. Those were the days when the ages of rotting pine needles warmed and steamed and gave birth to the green fiddleheads of the ferns and the yellow of adders tongues, and the forest lay blanketed with the pink and white of the trilliums. It was a time when the air was full of the perfume of violets, the songs of a million mating birds, and the sun sent sweet warmth down the middle of his back. At night, the spring waters roared and thundered over the falls of the Montreal, the calumet passed from hand to hand, and the Indian girls flashed dark eyes and quick smiles in the moonlight.

Those were the good times. Good because I was young and tall in the eyes of all who knew me. Life was all fight and song and I was rich with beaver and martin.

Those were good times, but a man changes. Age creeps into his bones and his head and he becomes filled with doubts and questions. It is strange that when a buck is young and has good reasons to be cautious, he laughs and throws his life to the winds for the pure joy of it. Then, when age creeps into him and he has little ahead of him to lose, he becomes shy of every danger and guards himself like a she wolf guards her whelps.

Yes, those were good times, but now there is Mina and the good people of the valley, and new kinds of challenges to be met. With Ganus gone, someone should be in camp, least until Tom gets back from school. It might be that he is home now. But Tom is now the young buck. It is now his time to wander. So if he is home, he is probably about to leave again for somewhere. It might be that stinking Detroit, to practice his law, or find him a woman. But there is a war on too. He might be fixing to join Lincoln's army. If I were not so old, I would join, too. I could still walk the legs off most of these young bucks, and I can shoot the tail feathers off a hummingbird at a hundred yards. Armies have queer notions, though. Only those too young to die are allowed to do it.

A wolf howled its morning greeting in the distance. Male, thought Milan. Female will be in litter by now. A male out hunting for food.

He was back from his dreaming, now. The sound of the wolf made him feel free again. He burst into one of his songs,-

La jeune Sophia
Chantain l' autre jour
Son echo lui repete
Que non pas d'amour...

Jimmy rode up behind him, feeling better now also, free from the drudgery of work. "No trap much beaver nex' year if you make noise like that," he grinned.

By noon of that day Milan and Jimmy had skirted the hills of yellow sand which extend into the forests at the north end of the lake. They crossed the desolate wastes of dune grass and junipers, where the horses labored and sweat through the soft sand of the ridges. They then rode south down the smooth hard sands of the Lake Michigan beach, letting the waves lap at the horses' hooves.

In another hour, they came to the point where the log-filled river entered the lake. Fording it, they rested briefly on the other side as they watched the last raft of logs being chained together in the bay. A little later they pushed their way past the point where the logs had jammed in the river and soon came out into the cedars and birches at the edge of the clearing where Mill Sharrow had built his camp. In the center of the clearing stood a saddled horse which Jimmy and Milan immediately recognized. Walking towards the horse was Tom Michaels.

Tom was still five paces from the sorrel when the burly form of Angus McBride appeared in the doorway. There was the glint of sun on a rifle barrel, and a shot rang out, followed by a hoarse, throaty laugh.

The shot was intended to do no harm. It was aimed low, but close enough to throw a spray of sand against Tom's boots. It was a warning only. A grim warning of the kind of man with whom Tom was dealing. It was the slashing punctuation mark for that throaty, challenging laugh.

But the laugh was never completely finished. Milan's musket came quickly from its place of rest across his knees and swung upward in a smooth arc. The ball slammed solidly into the casing of the cabin door, barely seven inches above Angus' head. His laugh faded into a shocked murmur. Anger burned in his dark eyes, and without waiting to finish his warning, he disappeared into the darkness of the cabin.

The kitchen of the big cabin on the hill was buzzing. Mina and Louise were busy behind a clatter of pans and the smells of baking beans and fresh churned butter. The return of Tom and Milan and the news that young Eber Harcourt was leaving to join the Union forces were reasons enough for a party. Besides, Ole Nelson said, it probably was a plot to get the big wood stove removed from the center of the schoolhouse floor. Others said it was to celebrate the departure of Mill Sharrow and his shanty boys from the valley. Whatever the reason might be, parties in the valley were always fun and the real reasons for having them were often vague.

By mid afternoon Mina and Louise had pulled the big loaves of bread from the oven and sent Milan to the barn to harness the horses. The blackberry preserves were packed, the baked beans placed on hot soapstones in the bottom of the wagon, and soon they were creaking their way towards town.

Tables were already set up under the big elm trees in the schoolyard and the wagons were appearing from all directions. Ole Nelson had closed up the store and Nick Tanner would be along as soon as he replaced a shoe on one of Bill Sugar's big whites.

Most of the faces were familiar to Tom, for this was a meeting of old friends. These were the settlers who had followed his mother and father into these hills and bought up huge sections of land while it was still cheap. Most of them had borne children, and parents had taken land in their names, clearing it and nursing it to productivity. All had known the hardships of the early fight to shelter, feed, and clothe themselves through the strength and skill of their own two hands. All shared the satisfaction which comes to those who have bruised their knuckles in a common fight. These hills, those blue lakes, the towering pines, the yellow hills of sand, and the clear, sweet air were theirs. The joy of life and the grim call of death had been theirs, to suffer and to enjoy, together and alone.

Eber Harcourt was there, signs of young manhood still fuzzing his cheeks, his long legs still coltlike and unresponsive. He found his way respectfully to Tom.

"I want you should meet Judy, Tom. We were planning to get hitched when I got back from servin', but we decided we shouldn't wait. You understand, don't you?" His eyes showed the knowledge of parental disapproval.

Tom took Judy's hand. She was the Nelson's oldest, small but capable, with eyes brown and warm as a yearling deer.

"You know what? We got papers started on a whole half–section of that big timber back of Dad's place. Some of the biggest durn cork pines you ever saw, outside of those on your place, of course. Should be worth a mee-million, time I git back. The war may be a bad thing, but it sure is helping Judy and me."

"You are getting a bonus, Eber?."

"Better'n that, Tom. The foreman of Joe Stronach's mill, up in Manistee, is paying me three hundred dollars to sign draft for his boy. Says he needs him at the mill. Besides that I may get another hundred dollars bounty from the government. I hate to leave little Judy here, but I figger I can stand a stretch to give us a start like that."

Eber sobered a little, showing a mite of the more thoughtful nature of his mother. "Besides, I guess we all owe this country something, and I figger a spell in the army will make me feel that I have squared things."

"Eber says the worst of the fighting should be over time he gets fitted and trained," said Judy. "He hopes he can get into the Cavalry, 'cause he's just like a burr on a horse. Won't he make a handsome soldier?"

Tom looked the skinny form over slowly and allowed that he would. Eber had never been exactly the pride of old Allen's flock. He was tall, bony, and delicate like his Ma, but reckless and scatter–brained like a colt that never figured for harness. Maybe the army would be good for Eber. He had come late, after the hard times were mostly over. Sometimes it takes some lather on a horse to bring out the best in him. Tom hoped Eber was the same. Judy was a nice girl.

The clatter of a wooden spoon on a tin pan called the men and children to the tables. In the absence of a circuit rider, Bill Sugars asked the blessing:

"We thank you, Lord, for this privilege of being together again in this, our valley. We pray that your hand will remain close to those who are returning home, and those who are going away to give their blood, if necessary, to preserve this Union which is so important to us. Cast the shadow of your hand on President Lincoln, that he may plan well the course of action which will gain this goal with the utmost speed. We pray further that this terrible war between brothers and friends may be quickly ended so that all men, both of the North and the South, may return in peace to the mountains and the valleys and the cities they call home, and that future generations may never again find differences so great, greed so binding, or hearts so unyielding that they cannot remould their differences into peaceful valleys of men....Amen."

Bill Sugars was always a good man with words. Surely no hell fireing circuit rider could have done better.

"Amen," said Nick Tanner. "Now for God's sake, pass the beans."

Nancy VanBolt scowled darkly at this lack of respect, but most of the women just smiled, knowing just how good a man old Nick Tanner really was.

Tom ate as he remembered eating in past years, silently and with appreciation. Hunger came naturally in this country. Sometimes it had come from not having. More often, now, from hard work and living in the cool, fresh air.

Soon the sun was disappearing over the distant blue wall of lake Michigan. The wind died to a rustling whisper. The horses and oxen were fed where they were tied. The men lit their pipes and formed their little groups, sitting on the ground cross–legged like Indians. The children romped through the hills and returned. One by one, as they wore themselves out, they were bedded down in the wagons. There they laughed and twittered for a while, like the catbirds in the pine trees, then turned silent.

The men talked of many things: the cutting of the pine trees by Mill Sharrow; of Abe Lincoln and the War between the States; and of the poor showing made so far by the Union forces under McClellan and Pope.

"We will do better," said Bill Sugars, "as soon as we learn respect for Lee and Jackson. We came close to losing Washington, though, in the learning. It's too bad Lee chose to go with the South. He would have made a difference."

The women's thoughts were of different things: the marriage of Eber and Judy;: the shortage of cotton goods on account of the war; and whether the blueberries would be as big as last year up in the hills.

Slowly the evening mellowed. Outlines faded and people became just soft, familiar voices out of the darkness of the night.

Tom listened mostly, listened and watched the last faint green of the fading day frame the evening star, then disappear behind the blue heap of Lake Michigan. The voices, soft and familiar, chuckling and rippling and full of contentment, brought him close again to these good people. He was glad to be home again; glad he was not yet at war; glad he had not chosen to go into the crowded cities to practice his law. Life was good here. It was people like these who were making Michigan a good place to live. They were the good, strong yarn of the mitten.

Now and then a child stirred and giggled from the wagons, or a horse shook a tinkle from a halter ring. The night sounds of the hills drifted close and faded away.

After a while a whippoorwill started its chant down along the sandy trail. As though in answer, Nick Tanner's violin started to whine inside the schoolhouse, then picked up the rhythm of the call and gathered momentum as Milan and his mouth organ joined in for The Chicken Reel.

It was after midnight when Ole Nelson wiped the perspiration from his bald head and went outside for a smoke. Minutes later they heard his deep voice shouting above the din of the fiddle and shouts of the dancers.

"Fire, fire," he was shouting, trying desperately to make himself heard.

Slowly a hush fell over the dancers. The fiddle slowed and squealed to a halt. Out into the blue night streamed the dancers, shivering in the cool night air.

In the western sky a red glow was expanding rapidly. Flames, sometimes visible, were licking upwards into a cloud of smoke which billowed so high it seemed to mingle with the star–lit sky. It grew gradually bright as the little group huddled together in the schoolyard watched helplessly. As it grew brighter it seemed nearer and nearer until Tom knew what he feared was true. It was their farm. Wearily he wiped the cold sweat from his forehead and found his mother, surprised that she was calm in the knowledge of her loss.

"I think it is only the barn, Tom. See how the sparks from the hay float high in the air?"

Holding her close to him, they watched in silence until the shower of sparks told them that the walls had fallen. Nothing could be done now. They might as well remain here and survey the damage in the morning. So standing erect, he shouted, and he could see the pride in his mother's eyes as she watched him: "Well, come on, let's dance," he said. "To-night is a party night. Tomorrow is soon enough to worry about our troubles."

So the violin wheezed wearily under Nick's urging and slowly picked up the rhythm of the dance. "Swing your partner, Bill Sugars. Swing her once again. We've known trouble many times before. We know it once again. Whirl your lady, Milan, you French devil. Alaman left, pretty Nancy VanVolt. Dip for the oyster, Mina Michaels, dip for the pearl. Come on Eber Harcourt. Come on Judy. Get out on the floor. Just one more couple. Good! dance, dance. Morning is still a fur piece! Let her rip! Karl, let her rip!"

But as the dance continued, one by one the men of the crowd tapped Tom on the arm. "We are with you, Tom," they would say. And he began to realize that every one of them knew of his contact with Mill Sharrow and his foreman. They knew, as he did, that somehow Mill and the Irishman had something to do with the fire. It was an alliance of big rough men, each one the owner of his own heritage of the big pines. It was an unsolicited and unsigned pact of war against Mill Sharrow and his like.

Tom knew, as he stood there, that he was being looked upon to lead them. He had hoped to remain at peace with his fellow men, but whether he liked it or not he was now commander–in–chief of his own private little war. Oh, to have the wisdom and the courage of the Union's Abe Lincoln!

"Good day, Eber Harcourt, and good luck."

Chapter Nine

Mina Michaels lingered for a long time where the big doors of the barn once swung. Slowly she bent down and, lifting a twisted piece of metal from the ashes, held it carefully and let the white dust drift out on the morning breeze. It could be that to some people a barn was a lifeless thing. A structure only, of timbers, planks, rough stone, stinking manure and rotting straw. She remembered the many times she had wondered why a barn must be the retreat of every varmint in the hills, porcupines, mice, polecats and woodchucks. Why the hornets must always fly, legs a-dangle, beneath the overhang, and swallows, pigeons and owls frequent its loft.

But now, with the stink buried beneath a pile of sterile ashes, and the swallows circling overhead, she felt a sudden need for that which had once been annoying. Like the hills and the lake and the white cottage, the barn had become a deep down part of her. After they had built their new cottage she had watched Ganus transform the old log house, which had been their first home, into warm winter quarters for the livestock. They had laughed together when old Betsie had turned around and around in the very spot that had been their bedroom, as though there was no more comfort to be found there.

The new part had been added later, board by board and nail by nail, by Ganus and young Tom. And sometimes by me, she recalled. Every stick and peg was their handiwork. Everything had something of them in it. They had roamed the hills with wagon and oxen to gather stones for the footings, and Ganus had smiled because Mina had admired the beauty of the quartz and conglomerate, and had questioned where they might have come from. The beams and the rafters they had cut from straight young pines out of the hills, and Allen Harcourt had come down to help set them straight and true and tighten them in with wooden pegs. Even the shingles of the barn had been split by hand from cedars cut along the river, and fitted and nailed with loving care. When it was done the morning glories were planted beside the door, and they had blossomed there ever since.

Tom was scarcely six years old then, but was already a help, and sometimes a bother, too, with his impatience at being kept on the fringe of things. But a barn is the domain of a boy, and he would rather sleep in the loft than in a clean bed. When the fresh new hay was piled deep in the loft, even Mina liked to climb up and lie in its fragrance and wonder how they could have left so many little holes and let shafts of sunshine come streaming through.

Those were wonderful days, thought Mina, stirring the ashes with the twisted metal. Ganus was big and strong and healthy, not yet bent by the fever and ague that bowed him later. Tom was getting stronger and more mischievous every day, and folks like the Harcourts, the Moreaus, and Bill and Mary Sugars were appearing and taking up land in the hills. Oh, the good times we had! And when the week's work was done we would sometimes go down the hill and bathe in the cool water of the lake and lie, half naked, in the warm sand until the sun dried us and browned us near to the color of the hills.

Of course, all of our living here wasn't fun. Many times we wondered if the barn could remain standing under the weight of the winter snows and the push of those west winds that came screaming up the valley to beat and tear at every crack and shingle until we felt like screaming right along with it. And I guess a few times I did. But Ganus would laugh and say, "Easy, Mina, 't ain't thet bad." And he was always right. Sooner or later, the sun would shine again and the whole valley would lay out below us, a crisp wonderland of sparkling white.

Sometimes deer would come out of the woods and walk right up to the barn, thin and hungry and eager at the smell of the hay.

Yes! That old barn has been a part of me for a long time and I admit I miss the stinking old mess.

Down at the end of the lane, Tom appeared, riding slowly towards her and searching the ground carefully as he came.

I am sure glad the stock was out on pasture, thought Mina. They would be more of a loss than the barn.

Tom rounded the end of the lane and pushed the mare into an easy trot until he reached her side.

"A lot of memories went up in that smoke, eh, Mom?"

"A lot of memories, Tom, but that's about all. That and twenty–four good laying hens. Your dad and I came here young and saw a lot of trouble and happiness. And somehow, things like that old barn get mixed up in the middle of it. But it wasn't really valuable. Maybe it's just as well to be rid of some of the old things. New beginnings can sometimes put new strength in old bones."

Mina toyed with the piece of metal, fighting back the question. But finally it had to come out. "Who did it, Tom?" Her question was blunt, but her voice carried no hint of emotion or fear. She knew the answer, too, but was anxious to know what support Tom had found to tie Mill Sharrow and Angus McBride to the setting of the fire.

"No way to be sure, Mom. Boot tracks down the lane could be anybody's. The camp is empty and locked up, and the last of the logs not locked in by the jam have been rafted and are gone. The sow and pigs are probably well on their way to Muskegon by now.

"Have you seen Jimmy Colby today?"

"No," said Mina. "I haven't seen him since last night at the dance."

"And you haven't seen him since before the fire,

either," said Tom. "His tracks are everywhere. I'll bet he wasn't an hour behind whoever did the setting. If there is anything to know, he knows it by now."

That evening Jimmy and Louise dropped by to chat and smoke, but Jimmy made no mention of the fire or who might have started it. What he knew was locked forever in his Indian reserve and would remain there until proof was available. This was the Indian way.

"Strawberries Are Ripe on Golden County Hills." This was the headline on the front of Bill Sugars' little newspaper the last week of June. Bill Sugars had put it there with solemn intent. Thinkin' small is just as important as thinkin' big, thought Bill. These days when there is a war stirring things up and people are trying to draw the strings together around a new state, it's easy to fret and stew until the little pleasurable things are lost in the stew, so to speak. A newspaper–man has to know where to find the meat, but a little touch of onion now and then makes the meat more flavorful.

Nancy VanBolt rocked quietly in her chair on the front porch of her pretty white cottage that morning and read the item with interest. Wild strawberries make the finest of preserves and she knew where the finest strawberries in Golden County could be found.

Below the item about the strawberries was the meat, the latest news from the war fronts. She read those, too, but without too much interest except where a bit of knowledge struck home.

"Sheridan appointed Colonel of the Second Michigan Cavalry," she read. And who is Sheridan? She had already forgotten that the Second Michigan was Eber Harcourt's outfit.

The article continued: "Four hours after Colonel Sheridan takes command of the Second Michigan Cavalry on May 25, he joins with the Second Iowan and leads them to a decisive victory over Confederate Cavalry units at Boonville, Mississippi. The Mobile and Ohio Railroad was destroyed at this point, trains and supplies burned, and Johnson and Beauregard's retreat from Corinth made difficult."

"And why must they always burn everything in sight?" sighed Nancy.

Farther down the page Bill's comments moved to the darker side of the war: the campaigns in the west. "McClellan's advance on Richmond held up by heavy rains," was the first line, followed by Bill's doubtful comment in small type; "We hope."

Then there was another ominous announcement: "General Jackson's army threatens Washington. McDowell called back to the Potomac."

Nancy dropped the paper to her lap. I suppose the war is the most important news right now but it seems so far away. Those fights in Mississippi or wherever they are. Why, Mississippi is farther away than St. Louis! Why should Sheridan be way down there stirring up trouble when the Capital itself is in danger? Sometimes I wonder if that Lincoln knows what he is doing.

Anyways, I'm glad I have two girls right now, not boys.

Returning to the article on strawberries, Nancy's interest returned. At least Bill Sugars forgot the war long enough to write one small item about the local situation.

"Sarah! Sarah! Where are you now?"

"Here, Mom, cleanin' the parlor like you told me, and singing at the top of my voice. How could you not know where I am?"

"Where's your sister?'

"I don't know, Mom. She ain't singin'. Probably down at the mill pond, fishing. She should have been a boy. Or looking into the water and dreamin' of Nathan Harcourt like she was a girl."

Jeanie was down by the mill pond, fishing and looking into the water. For, at sixteen, a girl can be both tomboy and queen, and Jeanie was more than the usual amount of both, as any quick eye could see.

"Jeanieee-e!" Nancy had left the porch and drifted out onto the side lawn, newspaper still in hand.

"Yes, Ma." Jeanie's voice did not show great respect. Besides, interruptions when the sunfish were biting in the pond were intolerable.

"Jean, go down to the mill and have Dad hitch up Blackie. We're going strawberrying," she shouted.

"Strawberries, whee!" said Jeanie, and scooted off to throw the harness on Blackie herself. No need to bother Dad. I can lift a harness, if Blackie doesn't mind getting one end at a time. Blackie didn't mind, not from Jeanie.

The strawberries on the hill south of the lake were not as luscious as Bill Sugars had pictured them. The weather had turned dry and the grasshoppers were already singing in the hills. Nancy VanBolt was not one to be satisfied with anything but the best. So working her way along the hillside she slipped through the strip of pines bordering Jim and Louise Colby's property and out on a little meadow where the sun shone warm and the cool wind from the lake was cut off by the trees below.

"I'm not going to stay here," said Jeanie. "You know very well, Mother, that these are Louise Colby's berries. She cuts the grass here each fall and covers the plants so that they start late in the spring and bear nice big berries. You and Sarah can stay, if you like, but I won't steal. And I'll pick just as many berries out on the south meadow as you do here," she flung back.

Nancy admired Jeanie's spunk, but she also admired the big, juicy berries. She moved on, nursing her plump figure over the rough ground, disliking the picking but relishing the pleasure she would feel when she displayed her choice preserves next fall.

Finally she could stand the bending no longer, and rolled gently into a sitting position on a smooth glacial boulder, like a gull alighting on a post. As she did, she raised her eyes and found herself looking straight into the stonelike face of Jimmy Colby.

"Berries here belong Louise," said Jim. "Many berries,

south hill, belong nobody."

"Oh! But Jim," said Nancy, in her most intriguing manner, "these are wild berries, the same as those on the south hill, planted by the Great Father so that everybody can have food. Surely you wouldn't want them to go to waste."

"Plants wild, berries tame. Berries made big by Louise. She not waste." Jimmy was not much softened by Nancy's charm. He waved his arm in a wide circle. "White man take land from Indians. Say mine. Jimmy take land, too. Okay?"

"Okay, Jimmy. We pick a few more, then we go. Okay?"

Jimmy did not reply, but sat on a stump, smoking his pipe until Nancy and Sarah gathered up their berries and left. Nancy found it hard to enjoy the picking with Jim's cold, black eyes resting steadily on her backside. The smaller berries would be good enough for jam.

A week later Jimmy Colby was seen walking south through town with a huge crosscut saw over his shoulder. Two husky young boys were trailing behind him, swinging recklessly at each other with an old double–bitted axe, their loose, black hair flying in the wind.

"What is that Indian up to now?" asked Ole Nelson as he watched him pass by the front of his general store.

"Must be a little cutting up goin' on this morning," he shouted to Nick Tanner who was heating up his forge across the street.

Nick left his forge and came to see what Ole was looking at. "Now what do you know!" he muttered. And he has trees by the hundred right in his back yard. "Come on, Ole, let's see what he's up to."

So the store and the forge were left unattended as Ole and Nick drifted along behind Jimmy and the boys.

"No business this morning anyhow," said Ole. "Might as well enjoy a little sunshine."

Down the hill to the south continued Jimmy, looking neither right or left, until he reached the pretty white house occupied by Carl and Nancy VanBolt. It was a fine square cottage of sturdy timbers and white painted siding, built by Carl himself and admired by everyone in the village.

South of the house, perhaps a stone's throw, stood Carl's mill, with the mill pond backing up behind it, forming a beautiful setting. The mill itself stood close to the road and as the water passed over the huge wheel it fell, in a splashing torrent, to pass beneath the wooden bridge which carried the road.

Between the mill and the cottage was a cool expanse of green grass kept neatly clipped by the girls' two riding horses, and shading this choice, grassy area were five huge, hard maple trees.

Without a word or a glance, Jimmy Colby walked past the cottage, out onto the VanBolt's green lawn, and with much unnecessary noise leaned back against the finest of the big maple trees and started stroking the teeth of the saw with a piece of broken grindstone. The sound grated through the morning air and brought Nancy VanBolt clattering out to the big front porch. "Now, what are you doing here?" she shouted at Jimmy Colby.

Jim looked at her briefly, but did not reply. Instead he laid aside the big saw and taking the axe from the boys started serenely whetting the edge of the blades.

Slowly the flame of anger rose, and Nancy, bursting with it, descended the steps like a sputtering firecracker about to explode. "Jimmy Colby!" She now planted herself at Jimmie's feet. "What are you doing here with those vicious implements? And why don't you answer me?"

Jim laid down the stone, ran his thumb carefully over the edge of the axe blade and looked up, completely unperturbed.

"Fur on otter much thick this year," he stated. He waved his arm to the north. "Beaver in north swamp cutting pople trees like hell."

He picked up the big saw and laid the blade against the trunk of the maple.

"Squirrels already looking for nuts. Nex' winter be dam' cold, you bettcha. Indian need much wood."

"And you mean to stand there and tell me you intend to cut that tree for wood?" Nancy was almost speechless with anger.

"Sugar maple make good wood. Burn long, burn hot," said Jimmy, leveling the saw and calling one boy to the other end of it.

Nancy now planted her bountiful form between Jimmy

and the boy and held her ground. "And you intend to cut our tree for your wood?"

Jim took a long minute to survey the tree from top to bottom, then walked back a few paces and appeared to study the proper direction to fell the maple. Finally he returned to the base of the tree, Nancy still sputtering in hot pursuit.

"Oh! no you don't, Jimmy Colby. Not that maple tree."

"Tree planted by Great White Father for everyone to use," stated Jim, innocently. "Indian need much wood. Maple tree best wood anywhere."

Ole Nelson could hold himself in no longer, and not wanting Nancy VanBolt to see them, he punched Nick Tanner in the ribs with his elbow and together they melted back up the hill, shaking with laughter.

Thirty minutes later, Jimmy Colby and the two boys came back up the hill still carrying the big saw. Jim's face was as expressionless as ever, but each of the boys was enjoying a big sugar cookie from each hand.

Ole and Nick watched them from their doorways until they disappeared west down the road towards the lake.

Late that afternoon, after Nick had finished shrinking a new rim on the rear wheel of Jim Moreau's wagon, he let the air wheeze from the leather bellows for the last time and watched his fire. When the coals had faded to a mellow glow, he untied his leather apron and walked across to Ole Nelson's store.

"Hey, Ole, I been thinkin'."

"Hurt any?" Ole grinned.

"You know what I think, Ole?" he asked.

Ole pulled on the weight that lifted the glass cover from the big cheese, cut a generous slice for each of them, and grinned his broad grin.

"Milan?" he said.

"Milan," said Nick. And they had another good laugh.

Tom's first cutting of hay had been made and, for lack of a barn to store it in, he had neatly stacked it in a corner of the field. The corn was cultivated, and if they were fortunate enough to get rain in July, the usual small crop would be enough to fatten the winter meat.

It looked as though he had a few days to spare, so Tom and young Nathan Harcourt hitched up the big team and headed down the lane towards the hills where Mill Sharrow had done his cutting. The horses puffed little explosions of cool morning air and the chains clinked merrily against the whiffle trees.

"How many stumps do you reckon we can pull in a day?" asked Nathan.

"Seven or eight, maybe," said Tom. "These are big fellows, but we have a good rig."

"Will Milan be around to help?"

"Maybe," said Tom, knowing that Nathan hoped he would be.

"Kin I drive the team when we start pullin?" asked Nathan.

"That's exactly what you can do, but you will have to

take it easy. If the stump doesn't come, hold back and wait until I cut the roots free."

Stumping is hard work, and Nathan was not yet the able man that his dad was. But he was ambitious, and even now, at fifteen, was more powerful and more observing than his brother Eber had been. More like his dad, thought Tom, as he rested on his axe and wiped the sweat from his eyes. He will be a big man someday.

Eber, he is more like his Ma, delicate and skittish. Sure hope he comes through the war safe. I'm afraid for Eber. He's not the right set to be a soldier.

The rigging strained as Nathan, anxious to be on, increased the pull on the drag rope. Tom looked aloft to judge the tension on the triangle of the poles which framed the rigging, then stepped beneath the huge stump, cut through the tap root with a few smooth swings of the axe. The stump hesitated, rose again as the last roots were cut, then swung free. It was hard, dangerous work and Tom's muscles, softened by his years in school, tired more quickly than they should.

"Let her down," he shouted, and the stump was allowed to settle on its side to be trimmed. They would pull a few more, then skid them into position to form a fence around the field.

Tom sat on the edge of the hole left by the stump and rested while a locust clattered in the distance. The sun was hot now. He heard Nathan shake the team free of the pull rope and heard the clip, clip of the horses' heels against the empty whiffle trees as they came back to set up the rig and tie onto the next stump.

"I sure wish Dad was here," said Tom. This was a job he always liked. He told me once that to him clearing a new field was like painting a picture. You take a meadow dotted with stumps and framed with green trees. You swing your axe, your shovel, and your oxen like a painter swings his brush. And after a year, or maybe two, of sweat and toil and cussin', the field of barren soil is changed into a picture of greens, browns, and gold, and is again a living, useful thing with pattern and color and depth. What artist could do more than that? Then he might not speak again for days," laughed Tom.

"But he could have painted a better picture if he had picked some better paint." He sliced through the edge of the hole with his shovel, exposing the usual layers of soil: twelve inches of good rich topsoil, formed from the years of falling pine needles, then sand, nothing but sand, clean, white and thirsty.

"Dad knew this, though. Even before he came here he knew it. But he had an idea, and the country held him." He spoke half to himself and half to Nathan, who stood waiting with the horses. "Yes, the country held him, the same as it did Milan, and your dad, and all the others. They all disliked the heat, the swamps, the speculators, and the fever and ague that plagued the country to the south. They all believed that, if they could hold out long enough, someday the timber here would make them rich.

And it did, but not in the way they thought it would. Because when the time came, and men like Charley Mears, and Ward, were ready to buy the timber, not a man in the valley was ready to sell. And I guess I feel the same way.

"Somehow this country makes you feel that you have everything in the world that you want. No money, no travel, no fancy buggies or big houses could add a thing to the pleasures we already have. And just knowing those big trees are there is like having money in the bank, only better. There they are, big as life in front of you, to enjoy and to admire, to listen to, walk under and to smell."

"How about Mill Sharrow, Tom? Do you think we can keep him out?"

Tom knew that question was coming, but was still unprepared for it.

"I can't answer that, Nate. I'm sorry, but I just don't know. I am hoping that he has worked his last round forty, and if my plans work out, and we can make him pay for the timber he took from this one, I believe he will give up.

"But Michigan law is slow, Nate. Judge Littlejohn covers a circuit two hundred and fifty miles long from south to north. Yet I know he will be here to hold court if it is possible. Judge Littlejohn knows that the decision will be important to the whole state. If we should lose, Nate, the lumbermen will cut free and easy across the whole state. But law is law, and the decision will go to the one who can prove his case in the eyes of the written law. No one else.

"The lumbermen are fast becoming powerful, Nate. And while Mill Sharrow is small by comparison, none of the mill or camp owners will want to see him lose. Either by accident or intent, probably every cutter in the state has at some time crossed property lines, and one thing they do not want is a general uprising against them."

Tom was anxious to be shut of the subject. Walking to the stone boat, he lifted the basket that his mother had sent. Inside was a jug of ginger water and some chicken sandwiches. He divided these with Nate, then brought out a small woven basket covered with a moist cloth. This he showed to Nate. Inside, as he drew back the cloth, was a fruit much like the red cherries used for pies. But these were much larger and black. Black as ebony.

Nathan took one, and biting into it carefully, found it to be sweet and firm and deliciously satisfying.

"What are they, Tom?

"They are cherries, Nate. Black, sweet, plum cherries."

"I told you Dad had an idea. Even as far back as Detroit, when he first came to Michigan, Milan's description of this country made him believe that it would be right for fruit. And it was. Our plums, our pears, our red cherries, our apples, and our wild blueberries have been our best crops.

"But Dad was remembering farther back, to the fruit he had known as a boy, back in the hills beside the Adriatic. There the warm winds off the sea held down the winter temperatures so that the trees did not freeze out during the hard winters. And in the spring, those same winds came in cool and fresh off the bays and kept the trees from budding and blossoming until the danger of frost was well past. This, with the belief that these trees would reach their roots far down into the sandy soil and find the moisture, the same as those big pines do, were the reasons he let Milan bring us into these hills.

"But Dad died, never knowing for sure that he was right. Soon after we settled here he sent for some trees, but those first ones died. Later he sent for more. But before they could blossom and bear fruit Dad was taken by the fever.

"But now they are healthy and strong on the hill behind our house and are beginning to bear. Perhaps some day these hills will be covered with them, Nate. I am sure that Dad believed that they would."

"And that is the reason we are clearing this new field?"

"That, and to get rid of the mess that our friend Mill Sharrow left us, yes."

The work seemed to go more smoothly after that. Reasons are important to both men and boys.

Chapter Ten

Bill Sugars looked down between the ears of the big, white horses to where the sandy trail met the horizon and seemed to disappear into the distant, shimmering blue of Lake Michigan. In July, he thought, with the heat sucking moisture from every blade and filling the air with haze, it is difficult to tell lake from sky. The hot sand squeaked beneath the wheels of the wagon, lifted with the steel–clad rims, and slithered back into the ruts. A locust clattered its song from the cedars along the roadside. A white–tailed kingbird took off in the direction of the clatter.

"It takes a bit of self–sacrificin' to close up a newspaper office and go off partakin' in a barn raisin' in this July heat." Bill flicked a fly off of Nellie's rump with a smooth overhand motion of the whip.

Mary Sugars braced herself against Nellie's lurch, watched the smooth sweep of Bill's whip, and spoke with a knowing smile. "Yeah! Especially when the trout are flippin' their fins for a fair ye well in Carl VanBolt's mill pond. Don't tell me your troubles, Bill Sugars. I ain't been sweeping the dirt from under your feet for thirty years without readin' the writing between every line in your book."

Bill grinned in silence. Mary always knew.

"Besides, I don't recall old Ganus Michaels ever hesitatin' when there was a raisin' to be done. Bless his soul."

"And how that man could work," mused Bill, ducking in mock terror as a huge black and yellow butterfly nearly collided with his hat brim, then listening with pleasure for the chuckles of the kids in the back of the wagon.

"Want the shotgun, Dad?" quipped Sandy.

"Not yet, son, but keep it handy."

Queer, thought Bill, relaxing in the seat and stretching one long leg out over the foregate, how kids pass through the age where they are satisfied to chuckle at the other fellow's jokes, then, all of a sudden, like Sandy there, at eleven, they start thinking out ahead and become a part of the act.

Soon Frosty, now nine, would be taking his place in the sun. Then Butch, and someday little Cindy. And the world would certainly be the sweeter for their coming.

"Take Tom Michaels, for instance."

Mary looked at him and smiled, as his thoughts became conversation, just like she was a part of him. And that's the way she liked it.

"It seems like just yesterday when we first pulled into the valley and saw old Ganus setting stumps round the west pasture. There was Tom no bigger'n a pint of cider ridin' on old Ben the oxen's broad back, a-chewin' on a sassafras twig.

"And now he's grown up..."

"And about to get himself cut back to the cider if he keeps on crossing lines with Mill Sharrow and that foreman of his," added Mary.

"Michigan is still young, Mary. Young and strong and sassy. Like the kids back there, she's still laughing at other people's jokes. But she is starting to come of age. She's beginning to get organized. And when she does, cusses like Mill Sharrow won't be having such a free rein."

"And when are all these miracles going to take place, lover boy? 'Cause I got a feeling, that unless it happens mighty soon, the newspaper business, in your clever hands, could be a pretty ripe pumpkin."

"Well!" Bill switched legs on the foregate. "In the newspaper business, that is what is known as an occupational hazard, Mary. And I guess as long as I am in the business I'm obliged to take certain steps in certain directions as my conscience directs me. If someone's feet are not properly removed from that direction, they are just naturally likely to get stepped on."

"Yeah! That's how I thought it would be." Mary wiped the beads of perspiration from her face with her apron. "And some high–minded newspaper–man, with a wife and four kids to feed, starts pickin' type out of the ashes of his office with a peavy hook."

"Aw, Ma!" giggled Cynthia.

The locust started his low chatter, built it to a high

crescendo, which stopped abruptly. The kingbird settled back on his post.

"Seriously, though, Pa." Mary Sugars looked at her husband with real concern in her big, brown eyes. "Don't take sides. A newspaper can report the facts without taking sides."

"I'm sorry, Mary." Bill placed a rough hand on Mary's well–rounded knee. "We all think that we can, and some newspapers might, but I doubt it. With me, my paper is me, Michigan is my state, America is my adopted country. Right is right and wrong is wrong, and the Bible the only true source of our moral judgments. The way words are twisted and placed before people's eyes can make or break a whole country. My paper is only a speck of white on the face of the map, no bigger than a gnat's knee. But as long as I live, it will stay white. Gray is a poor color to leave for those kids.

"Besides, if worst comes to worst, we still have the farm."

"You have no likin' for farm work, Bill. You know that."

"Can't say I have a liking for work, period, Mary," Bill grinned. "But I did it once or twice, and I can do it again.

"Look, Mary. We've been in this country a long time. Only the Michaels, Jimmy Colby, and Allen and Anna Harcourt have been here longer. When we had trouble, we had help. Now it is not just us in trouble. Our whole new state needs help. We are fighting to establish principles of which we are only a small part. Are we going to watch barns burn as we sit idly by, or are we going to tell our story to the world?

"Besides, I don't intend to fight Mill Sharrow alone, and I don't believe Tom has that in mind, else he wouldn't have used that summons to bring him to heel."

Mary smiled a knowing smile. "Or you wouldn't have sent copies of your paper to every representative in Lansing and most of them in Washington."

It was Bill's turn to smile. He should have known Mary would learn of it.

"One thing I am sure of," he grinned. "The more noise I make with that little press of mine, the more likely we are to get help. And I intend to make a clatter that can be heard all the way to Washington."

"And after you make all of thet noise, honey boy, and all of our politickers write a hundred new laws, we end up right back at the beginning, Bill Sugars."

The big whites had topped the hill east of the Michaels' farm and Bill called out a gentle "Whoa!" as the valley lay spread out below them.

The mid morning sun was hot on their backs, but a breeze had stirred a scattering of billowy clouds out over the blue of Lake Michigan and was coming in fresh and sharp in their faces. A wisp of sand was lifting off the crest of the big dune. Blue Lake was blue-gray as the fresh breeze broke up the reflected light from its surface, and the big spears of the pines on the near shore thrust up sharp and tall against the white of the water.

Starting on the south shore of the lake and sloping upward, the hills bore the scars of Mill Sharrow's cutting. An open sore cut across the valley, red with the drying limbs of the giant pines and hazy with the heat waves rising from the sores.

"It's no wonder Tom is fighting to save this valley," whispered Mary. "It's beautiful."

"And no wonder Mill Sharrow is set on cleaning it of timber," said Bill. "There's easy three thousand acres of pine in that valley. All of it an easy haul to the lake. If the price of lumber comes back, and it is sure to after the war, there is a fortune down there. Yet all that he has been able to buy is second–rate timber. I am sure he hoped to do better. His other problem is the river. It's too small and shallow to handle the big logs. If he gets a dry spring, he's going to have trouble.

"Let's see. From where Mill is cutting now, it must be a half mile to Jimmy Colby's place below Tom. Then comes Tom's lake one–sixty, then Allen Harcourt's, then Jim Moreau's. All of them close to the lake, where Mill Sharrow will be itching to cut a few acres. Especially on Tom's where those big cork pines are taller and heavier than anywhere. He already got twenty acres there and he knows well enough what they are."

"Let's go, Bill. See! They are starting to set the timbers."

"Then more of Jimmy Colby's or the Harcourts could be next. Then maybe the quarter section young Eber Harcourt just bought. Unless Tom can scare the hell out of him before that."

"Come on, Bill."

"Yeah! Let's go, Dad. They're starting to set the timbers."

"One thing I'm wondering." Bill loosened the reins on the big whites and they surged forward down the hill. The scent of fresh water was strong in their nostrils. "Who is going to hold rein on that Frenchman, Milan, if Mill Sharrow starts something next year? He may be getting old, but take it from me. There will be shanty boy blood running up hill if anything more happens to Mina or Tom."

It took four days to set the timbers and start boarding in the barn. Most of the help stayed put, the women and children sleeping in the house, the men in the wagons in the yard. A few had stayed at the Harcourts' and some at Jim Moreau's place a mile up the road.

On the fifth morning Tom raised himself from the straw of the wagon bed, stretched muscles unaccustomed to the climbing and lifting required in barn building, then lay back again for another minute of ease. Soon he rose and climbed down over the wagon wheel to the ground.

The sun was showing gentle red over the hills behind him, its rays slanted low overhead. A streak of butter yellow shone across the tops of the highest dunes, pulling them up out of the misty lake to stand out sharp and clear against the horizonless blue beyond. The house, the yard, and the wagons with the men beginning to roll from their blankets were still in the cool shadow of the eastern hills. A flight of herring gulls complained long and loud overhead, the morning sun gleaming off their whiteness. Somewhere out of the mists of the lake a loon wailed its morning call, and was answered.

The air held the sharpness of the lake at this early hour and Tom buttoned his flannel shirt against it, wishing it would speed warmth down into the clearing, yet knowing full well that by ten o'clock heat would be sucking the juices from every pore as they struggled with the last of the roof boards.

Tom could hear the women already busy in the kitchen. Soon, usually by five a.m., breakfast would be served on the new barn doors in the yard. The mornings were quiet and businesslike as men stretched cramped limbs and loosened sore muscles. Not so much of the banter and cutting up as would show later.

Tom heard the squeak of the outhouse door, and saw Allen Harcourt come out and start towards the new building, still buttoning up his drawers. Allen was always on the job at dawn and Tom's approach brought the rumbling, "Good morning, Tom," that sounded so gruff, yet carried a hint of kindly good humor. Then, hanging his long level on his belt, Allen swung his big frame up into the timbers to check the square and pitch of the previous day's work. Tom turned, knowing he would rather be alone, and went to the house to make sure the women had good wood for the big kitchen range and plenty of water in its reservoir.

The tang of woodsmoke mingled with the sharp morning sounds as the men sat for breakfast. Slowly there was a building up of the clatter of good humor that would run through the rest of the day.

After they had eaten, Allen and Tom would set the tasks for each crew for the coming day. Then Allen would take the lead, his shock of white hair identifying him as he stood in the overhead. Each move was a reminder of his years at sea. His voice, never raised above that deep rumble, carried the quiet authority of one who knows what needs to be done and who can do it best. Neighbor was paired with neighbor, agile with agile, plodder with plodder and the work went on. Some complained, some gossiped, some stood helpless from not knowin', some jibed and prodded, but the work went on. The ring of axes, the clatter of hammers, the laughter of the women mingled with the sound of Milan's and Nick Tanner's songs and echoed off of the hills, and the work went on.

Bill Sugars and the big white team were kept busy hauling the last of the boards and shingles from Dan Marsaque's mill north of town. Nathan Harcourt and Carl Nelson would unload it, anxious, at sixteen, to handle a little more each time than was reasonable, to test new strength and to make a good showing.

The young ones would disappear into the pines at the end of the lane and, a little while later, show up down below on the sandy shore of the lake to dig and swim and tease, where the prying eyes of adults took only casual notice.

The women folks cooked, baked, cleaned, and cooked again, happy with their work and the chance to exchange small talk of kids and men and relatives and the war with the South. Of new recipes for cornbread and how President Lincoln would save the Union.

Later they would raid the gardens, gathering peas and new potatoes for the evening meal, and check for late raspberries or early blueberries for pies.

The pump in the yard was kept busy squeaking and clanking out the endless supply of water needed for so large a group, and the women good naturedly complained that the men and boys were never there to stand their turn at the handle.

Nick Vaino Tanner had his own department. Under a maple tree on the edge of the yard he had drawn his wagon and set up a blacksmith shop. His forge billowed black smoke as the small boys pumped air through fresh coal to heat pieces of iron to white heat. The ring of his hammer on the big anvil rang across the valley as he fashioned hinges from horseshoes and latches from the metal salvaged from the ashes of the fire.

Milan and Jimmy Colby helped wherever they could. Milan could be a driving force on a job if he set his mind to it, and Jimmy would follow his every move as if anticipating it in advance. But while both enjoyed the fun of being a part of things, the work weighed on them. Their natures were not tuned to long days of routine work and, like the teenagers, their hearts wandered to the hills.

Eventually Louise or Tom would see this and send them off for corn meal and flour from the VanBolt mill or fresh fish for an evening meal.

Milan would feel better when freed from the sound of the building. The hammering was not to his liking. Out on the lake he would stretch out in the old boat Allen Harcourt had made for them, his ears once again alert to the sounds of gulls and wave and wind. He would open his shirt to the belly if he liked, pull the old hat down over his eyes and listen to the scream of the gulls and turn back the pages of time one by one.

"What you think, Jimmy, my friend?" Milan spoke from beneath his hat, wondering if Jimmy's Indian mind was thinking as he was.

"Heap of doin'," said Jimmy. "Better, I think wait until wind stops blowing fore try to straighten up the trees. Eagle more smart. He kill the snakes off the rocks first, then build nest on cliff. White people funny.

"If we catch perch for supper, friend Milan, better you tend line. I not catch enough to feed whole tam village."

"Haven't made up my mind yet, my friend, if I want to catch perch or not. It will take a heap pile of perch to feed that crowd. Maybe we best try the net for whitefish?"

"Indian like perch sides better."

"Maybe you're not remembering, Jimmy. Somebody has to clean that pile of perch you're catching, and one scale or one black gut in the pan and you are in deep trouble."

"Louise clean. Jimmy no clean fish."

"But what if Mina says we clean?"

"Mina go to hell. Louise clean."

But Jimmy only caught one more line with its three yellow perch, then pulled in his line, coiled it neatly in the bottom of the boat and stepped nimbly to the front of the boat to pull in the heavy stone used for an anchor.

"And now what are you doing?" asked Milan, looking out from under his old felt hat.

"We try for whitefish," said Jimmy, hopping back to his seat with more than necessary rocking of the boat. "They clean easy."

Milan laughed to himself, thoroughly enjoying this game. And, as Jimmy moved the boat to the whitefish water where the river entered the lake, he dozed and drank deep of the smells and sounds of the lake.

On the sixth day the barn was shingled with fresh cedar shakes from the shingle mill, and the women appeared with rakes and forks and baskets to help with the cleanup. The scraps of wood were saved and piled into a neat pile at the rear of the house. Leftover timbers and new cedar posts were used to fence in a new barnyard. And before the last man had climbed down from the roof, the morning glories had been planted on both sides of the new door.

But the doors themselves were saved for last. For a real feed and an evening of talking and dancing was in order before the friends left for home.

That night a yellow moon looked down on hills singing along with Nick Tanner's fiddle and Milan's harmonica as the people of the hills danced around the barn doors piled heavy with cookies, cake, and pie from the busy kitchen. The tradition of work followed by play comes from many countries and blends into a common bond bridging a dozen barriers.

The next morning the wagons rolled from the Michaels' farm as the people returned to their own cultivating and harvest. Tom and his mother watched them leave, feeling more than ever before the strength of the bonds that held close the people of the valley.

Back in his office the next day, Bill Sugars applied his thoughts to the problems at hand. It is one thing to build a barn, he reasoned. It might be another thing to keep it, and the many others like it from the same fate that came to Tom's. One judge, riding a circuit reaching all the way from Allegan to the Sault, can no longer handle our needs, he thought. And the attorney riding with him can be even less prepared to know the details of the events preceding these cases. With this firmly in mind he went into action.

Later, he got into the inevitable news of the war. Bill Sugars had never been one to gloss over the facts. He had established his sources of information as meticulously as a big city editor and was determined to stick to the facts as they were. His only touch was to baste the meat with the layer of optimism that was him, and that he felt was justified by the more deep-seated course of events. After all, the North did have the advantage of their mills and mines, and freedom from the blockade which was strangling the South. The East was rich with the ability to produce the equipment of war and all of the West was a rich source of capable, hard–working men, well equipped to stand the rigors of war and handy with rifles and horses. The thing they seemed to lack were good generals. Certainly these would eventually be found. But as the news of the war came in, Bill began to wonder if his optimism might be poorly founded. Already fine potential generals like Richardson and Roberts had been killed. With good leaders already difficult to find, the North could ill afford to lose men like these.

But his optimism would win over. Periods of need bring out the greatness in men, and surely the likes of Lincoln would find enough talent to cover the need. Perhaps Grant or Buell would be taken from the West to be pitted against Lee and Jackson. Who could say?

It is hard to report a war which seems so far away, thought Bill. Here in the North, things still seem much the same. Roosters still crowed in the warm sun of the mornings. The same wild call of the loon sang out over the lake. Cool breezes came at night, and only the absence of Eber Harcourt, or his once–in–a–while letters to Judy, tied the village people to the country's troubles.

The only other sign was the once–in–a–while singing of negroes, as they straggled through. Usually they were walking the beach or hauling a rickety wagon over the Middlesex Road as they followed the underground railroad into the North.

Once in a while Bill was forced to wonder what would happen if the South should win the war. After all, so far the North had little reason to believe that this could not happen. Only the weak victory at Williamsburg had been theirs in the East. And this had been followed by the long string of bloody defeats outside Richmond. Only in the West had the Federal armies done well. And even there Grant had come close to losing his army at Shiloh. Strange, that under these circumstances, everyone, including himself, clung naively to the assumption that the North would eventually win. Perhaps this was typical human nature. Perhaps this was how old Ganus Michaelovic's grandfather felt when the Turks were sweeping down from the east and his own people were running into the hills. Was this the way Carl VanBolt's father had thought when Napoleon's armies were swarming into the Low Countries? Or was there a point in a man's thinking where he was forced to acknowledge the complete and unquestionable superiority of another force? Bill was inclined to believe that this could not be. But Bill Sugars was Bill Sugars and Carl VanBolt was the Carl VanBolt who left Holland in the stinking hold of an emigrant schooner rather than chance having a boy of his conscripted into the service of another Napoleon. And then his boys all turned out to be girls. Bill Sugars had himself another little chuckle about that. He knew that Carl had never been sorry that he had made the move, except, maybe, when his Nancy had come near to dying on that long hard trip across.

In spite of his optimism Bill had to admit to himself that the Confederacy was strong, unbelievably strong. And with its strength it had Lee and Jackson, Joe Johnston and Morgan, all of whom handled their men with the skill and daring of a Napoleon.

Even now it appeared that Lee and Jackson were on their way north to attack Washington. What if the Army of the Potomac failed to stop them? Would the Confederate armies continue on to plunder and destroy the North, or would a peaceful separation result?

Another thing gnawed at Bill's conscience. Should he, knowing that he had a better than ordinary knowledge of these events, place a hint of warning in his next item? Was it his duty to suggest to his people that a serious defeat was entirely possible?

Neither alternatives set well with Bill Sugars. Perhaps it was his thinking of Nancy Harcourt that prevented it. Anyway, he decided to continue to believe that the Union would survive. It might not be completely realistic but it could keep him from developing ulcers.

And this was the way that he eventually stated it in his paper. It was not exactly in the explosive style of Horace Greeley, he admitted. But perhaps that was the reason Mr. Greeley already had ulcers.

Chapter Eleven

The bench in front of Lyman Corbin's store was empty except for Lyman's old blue tick hound lazing underneath. The sun was warm, in spite of last night's frost, and little go-devils of hot dust were chasing each other down the street.

Bill Sugars was in Hart to meet the stage. He had come early and tied his big whites loosely to the rail in front of the tavern. He wanted to get away from the same four walls for a while and do some thinking out in the open. He had come early so he could set a while and maybe sort something worthy of print out of the gossip of the townsfolk.

Hart was a growing town now that it was the new county seat. The new courthouse was already nearly finished up south of town. Probably Tom's case would be its first, certainly its biggest. Bill found a warm spot on the bench, rubbed the ears of the old hound, and looked upwards towards the new building. It would be big to the whole state if Tom could make his case strong enough to rouse people up. Bill was building it as a case of the people who wanted the cutting of timber to go slow and lawful and at a profit to the state, against the big companies, who were wanting to cut clean and fast while land was still cheap. If Tom could stir people up enough to rouse old Judge Flavius Littlejohn to a strong judgment it would be a blow to the timber barons. He was a good enough Judge and would be fair either way, but Judges are human. When you get down to honest facts, sometimes it takes people a stirrin', people roused up and angry, to spur a judge to make a strong judgment.

Bill Sugars grinned at this thought. He was good at stirring.

An uneven thumping of steps sounded from inside the store and the screen door squeaked open. "Howdy, Bill Sugars, you old pencil–pushing reprobate."

Bill couldn't see the big man who came from the store behind him but he knew John Barr's uneven step, and felt the firm hand on his shoulder.

"First time I've felt the hand of the law on my shoulder for some time, John. How are you?"

"I'm in good shape, Bill, considering the thumping some newspaper–man has been giving to law and order in my district. You and Tom Michaels are sure stirring things up down your way."

Bill slid over to allow room for John on the warm bench. He settled onto it as though it was familiar to him.

"We try, Sheriff, since the forces of law and order don't seem to penetrate down into our neck of the woods."

"Kind of touchy today, aren't you, Bill?" The Sheriff let deep–set eyes slide to him. It wasn't like Bill to speak out strong against old friends. But maybe he had a right. Timber cutting to the people of the valley was like horse stealing to a farmer, theft of both love and livelihood.

"You must know, Bill, there are sixteen townships and three hundred and twenty–eight square miles, more or less, in Golden County. Do you know there are forty–two outfits starting to cut timber in this county alone?"

Bill shook his head. "And every one of them doing it more or less illegally, I imagine."

"No, I don't think it is as bad as that. We still have our good people, and the big outfits like Sands, Stronach, and Mears try to stay clean. They have too much at stake to chance riling people up. It's those little operators like Sharrow that try to cheat. They can't afford to lay out the money for land and leases. They think that cutting the round forty is the only way they can get started. And maybe they are right."

Bill looked directly at him. John was a big man, with deep–set eyes and little hollows in his cheeks that showed he had known his share of troubles. Now he was quiet, and smelled a little of Lyman's strong cheese and hard cider. "What are we going to do about it, John? Stealing from government land is bad enough, but cutting choice trees from a widow's homestead and paid–for land like Mina Michaels? Sure, we have to do something."

"Listen, Old Timer. I guess I can't blame you for your

strong feelings, but remember, Bill, there was snow a-
plenty last January and that lake is back country. That's
how Mill got in there and did his cutting without anyone
noticing. That is why word was slow coming out. The
damage was done and the logs were hauled long before I
even knew about it."

"Did you call on Mill Sharrow?"

"Twice, Bill. Once then and again in the spring."

"What did he say?"

"I got a big horse laugh from that foreman of his and
the usual from Mill Sharrow."

"Like, how do you know that I cut those trees? I suppose," replied Bill. "And the worst thing is they are getting away with it. They and a lot of others."

"Like Canfield, up at Manistee?"

"And then we had the fire."

"Yes! I know, Bill." John's voice was a bit weary. "I reckon they timed that with my leaving."

"But you didn't go back?"

"No. I knew they would be gone. They were most
ready when I saw them the second time."

"And you didn't call on Mina Michaels?"

"No, I would have made a poor show of it, Bill, making
excuses to Mina. There was nothing more I could do. Tom
had delivered the summons."

"Twenty acres of prime timber cut from the hills in
your county, and you know well enough who did it, and
you say there is nothing you can do. The county is wast-

ing its money, John. That's honestly the way I feel. The law is not functioning."

"And I suppose that is the way you will write it into your paper." John's voice was not bitter, just resigned to a sad fact.

"I try to report the truth as I see it, John. And that is sure the way that I see it."

"Our laws operate on two levels, Bill. The first one, of which I am a part, aims to prevent crimes against our citizenry or catch the culprits in the act. Failing this, and I have to admit that our level is mostly deterrent, the second level takes over and tries to rectify the effects of the misdeed through an appeal to our courts. You know as well as I do that this is Tom's best chance, and I am happy as hell that he is out there fighting for us."

"And I suppose you believe that Judge Littlejohn can bring back those trees and set them all up again, straight and pretty on Mina's hillside? Or that he can give Mina what their value might be ten years from now? Or maybe twenty years, when four by fours may be selling for thirty dollars a thousand instead of twelve?"

John sighed in dismay. He had never seen Bill like this. But when he looked back, Bill was grinning again. He had made his point and tested out the lead item in his paper. His hand now went to the big man's knee, as was his way. John knew he was saying, I am disappointed in you, John, but I am still your friend.

He grinned, too, and stretched the lame leg out over the

old hound that had poured itself out like hot butter in the warm sun. Bill was like a baseball pitcher. He argues, not for a change in the present call but for a better deal on the next. Maybe Bill was right. Perhaps he could have done more.

"How about government marshalls, John? Can we get any help from them?"

"They have more than they can handle running down the cutting from government land, Bill. Look how long it took them to get Canfield, up in Manistee. Then he beat them in court."

"But this is different, John. The people here are solid for Mina and Tom. I can bring a hundred people into court for her."

"But are they solid, Bill? How about Martin Brewer? Mill Sharrow has a pretty firm hold on him, I'm thinking. How about a dozen others up there in these hills? Not all of the people of this county have the same feeling for those big pines that we do. Fact is, some of these folks coming in now think that the sooner those trees are cleared off the land the sooner they can settle down to farming and herding."

"Farming, John? You know as well as I do that this country is not farming country. Fruit, maybe, but who wants to live on pears and blueberries? Those trees are our best crop. Without them our future is thin soup and cherry pie."

"I know that, Bill, and you know it. But I reckon it may

be considerable years yet before these new people get the education you and I had. And in the meantime, one of them, or a whiskey–hungry squatter looking for a loose dollar, could raise holy hell with Tom's case. That's the reason I advised Tom against a jury trial."

Caleb's big hound crawled from underneath the bench, stretched, turned around three times and went back for another nap. The stage was due and without knowing he knew it, he knew it.

The Sheriff stretched too, then pulled the big watch from his vest pocket and sprung it open. "Stage should be showing soon." He wondered how the blue tick had known this, too, not having a watch or a vest to wear it in. The hound looked up at him, his faded red eyes full of love and asking. The Sheriff shifted his gun back behind his right hip. The ball he carried from the skirmish at Thames River made sitting uncomfortable. Better to be on his feet. The dog struggled to his feet, too, as if he understood.

"I suppose you are here to pick up your new school maam?" he grinned.

Bill looked a little surprised. "You seem to keep well informed, John."

"I do that, Bill. I suppose you know who she is?"

"Yes. I know. Tom met her on his way up from school."

"Surprises me, under the circumstances, that you folks will have her around."

"Don't guess we should hold it against her that her

brother is a no-good. She was recommended high by the commissioner so I guess the least we can do is give her a chance.

"We were surprised that she would still come, though, knowing that she would be staying in some pretty bitter homes."

"Where is she staying first, Bill?"

"With Mary and me for a while. Reckon if she can put up with those Indians of ours, we can sure put up with her."

The sound of the stage bugle drifted up from the valley to the north carrying Halvar Brady's special touch. The sad howls of the town dogs answered, expressing in their own way that the dullness of the afternoon was about to be broken.

Bill stretched, too, and did a little two–step on the boardwalk. He felt better for his talk with John Barr. Now he knew better what his own job was. Pushing his hat back on his head, he straightened his tie and strutted off in the direction of the tavern. "If'n I don't show for a couple of weeks, John, just tell Mary I had a little something to straighten out down in Middlesex," he called back over his shoulder.

Growing older and having problems didn't change Bill Sugars a whit, thought John, as he shook his head and watched him clowning down the street. Yet under it all there was none better.

The storekeeper's old dog shook himself awake and

trotted along behind.

The stage cleared the north curve, crossed the bridge over the neck of the mill pond and stopped in front of the tavern. "Miss Sharrow?" Bill was on his best behavior now as the young lady hopped lightly off of the stage without waiting for help.

"That's right, but I like Dana better. You are Mr. Sugars?"

"Yeah, but I like Bill better." And an easy grin lit the twinkle in the gray eyes that were starting to wrinkle a bit at the corners.

"Pleased to know you, Dana." He wanted to say more but Halvar Brady was already handing the bags down. He received them and tucked them behind the seat of the wagon. Carl VanBolt had wanted him to use his surrey but Bill figgered the new teacher might just as well get used to their ways and, so far, Carl was the only one in town to sport a buggy. Everyone knew he wouldn't either if it wasn't for Nancy's wanting ways.

Dana was fresh with questions for a while. "How many children will there be in school? Will they have paper? Do they have any learning?"

And how can any child live even a day without learning? thought Bill. But he knew what Dana meant. And he would see that they had paper. Only foolscap, though. And not to be wasted.

"Do they all speak English?

"Strangest English you ever heard, sometimes," said

Bill. But it's English.

"Is Tom Michaels still around?" He could not help but notice the veiled concern which accompanied this question, but he felt it best not to notice. He answered the questions as best he could and finally the talk kind of petered out. Dana had run out of questions and, like Bill, seemed satisfied to ride silent for the time being. Let the big questions come later. After they got to kind of know one another. But Bill knew he was putting it off. There were things that should be said before they reached the valley. He opened his mouth to speak, then hesitated again.

Dana noticed and looked curious, but she also remained silent. Late afternoon was a pretty time of day and Bill Sugars was real nice. No sense to spoil it with a wrong word.

The crows were starting their afternoon flight towards the pines west of town and with the air still and frosty you could hear the soft swish—swish of their wings mingling with the jingle of the whipple tree chains and the soft slur, slur, the hooves of the whites made in the sand of the trail. A lone barn swallow lazed over the mill pond, its easy motions belittling the quick, purposeful speed of its flight.

Nice, thought Dana, that he doesn't feel the need to be entertaining. There is a closeness to be felt in just knowing there is no need to talk. Lord! But this country is beautiful, all trees and sky and hills and water. Sooner or later, though, talk will have to come.

Each knew the other was wondering. Wondering, in his or her own way, how it was going to be possible to bridge the rift that must always lay between them. There could be pleasant agreements on many things, and as Dana looked at the Lincoln–like Bill Sugars, she felt sure that there would be. But no matter how long they journeyed among common interests and pleasant conversations there would always come the time when the road would lead to their differences. Would she be big enough to listen and accept their criticism of her brother? Could she hold from telling reasons? She had told herself that she would. But what if the accusations held traces of narrowness, or hints of challenge, or any of the many other possibilities that human nature could contrive? Would she, or should she, fail to support him, even though she agreed that Milt was wrong? Should she try to tell them that there are circumstances back through everyone's lives which make them what they are? Could these close–knit people who had lived so long away from the troubles of the world outside their own valley possibly understand how these things can happen? She doubted it. Their fathers had freed them from those troubles. They were enjoying a generation of peace and solitude here in an unspoiled land.

And probably if those trees were mine, and I had lived among them as long, I would be just as unwaveringly bitter as they are.

But the subject had to be talked about openly. At least once. Then perhaps it could be pushed aside. But first, she had to know where she stood.

"You started, back there, to make a little speech, Bill. Don't you think we may as well get it over?"

Her brown eyes were big and worry–filled and looking straight ahead down the sandy trail. Perhaps they were a little bit scared, too, thought Bill, as he eased up on the reins and looked steady at her. She was still young and full of fire, but not yet sure of how and where to turn the torch. Bill pulled the impatient whites to a stop and they shook their heads in tinkling disgust.

"Yeah, I had a question. Maybe a lot of questions," said Bill. "But after I met you I began to think maybe I knew the answers. So I've just been thinking, same as you, probably, how nice it would be if everybody could know everybody else better. A lot of the world's problems would just disappear, wouldn't they?" And he smiled that easy smile that Dana liked.

"You are wondering if I still want to go on, aren't you?"

"Yes, I guess that is the big one, Dana. That, and one about trees and is three dollars per week per pupil satisfactory, and why am I the one who has to argue with a schoolmaam who is so dog–gone pretty". He turned and looked straight at her. "Trouble is, Dana, this isn't something that will be over. Not with a trial coming up and people riled. You and I can talk, and I think you and Mary will do even better. But there will be a hundred times in the next year, Dana, when somebody will be asking you: 'Why did he do it?' Do you think you can answer them? Dana, this is the thing that you must know."

Bill was quietly sober, now, not bitter, just concerned, as a father would be, talking to a troubled child.

"Do you think that you can answer them without sharpness, and face them tomorrow, and go back into that schoolroom with no bitterness and teach their kids fairly and honestly the next day?"

Dana lowered her head, touched by the honest concern of this man. It was not the kind of talk she was prepared for.

"All of these problems will be yours, Dana. These and many more. You will be living in their homes, eating their food, and trusted with their most valuable possessions, their kids. They are good people, Dana, and Mina and Tom Michaels are among the best. But we are human, and humans are sometimes weak and self–centered, especially when someone we love is being hurt."

Dana's head turned quickly as he mentioned Tom. Bill noticed but went on—-

"If there is any doubt about you being able to do this, Dana, it might be better for you to turn around now and go back to your friends in Middlesex."

It was a blunt, hard statement. Bill was almost ashamed of his directness with this young woman. But it had to be this way. Better to be open and to make sure all of the cards were on the table.

Dana did not speak right away, but dropped her head a bit. She had thought of these problems, but they sounded different out here in the loneliness of the open trail. They sounded different and more threatening when this strong but kindly man threw them out straight from the shoulder, and harder to answer for his lack of narrowness. Perhaps she had not expected such forceful and yet reasonable people in this far out place. Perhaps she had been vain enough to believe she could defend herself and her brother against them. Now she was suddenly afraid, afraid she was wrong, afraid she could not be as calm and reasonable as they. Whatever she said or did would have to be tempered with reason. It would be a hard winter. They would not all be as easy to talk with as Bill Sugars. It would be hard.

She felt like crying, and knew that this was what Bill would expect. She wanted desperately to put her head on his shoulder and weep softly. She would like to tell him that suddenly, in spite of their differences, or perhaps it was because of them, he already was the nearest thing to an understanding father that she had known. She would like to tell him that, and take his hand. The hand with the long delicate fingers, like those of a musician. She would like to tell him that there were reasons for a man to grow up to be like her Irish brother Milton. Reasons too hard to even talk about. Reasons born of hunger and fear even worse than these people of the valley had known. Times like those make people hard and aggressive and lacking in faith in other people. All people were not as kind and understanding as Bill was. But this was not the time for that. It would have to wait. Perhaps forever.

She lifted her chin and faced straight forward. The sky was turning to the turquoise shades of evening and the air was taking on the sharp coolness of the lake and the coming winter.

After a long time she looked at Bill, who had honored her silence with understanding. Her voice was husky quiet. "I'm not sure, Bill. I'm still not sure. But I think I would like to keep on going, if it's all right with you."

Bill shifted the reins to his left hand and awkwardly held out his right, just as he would seal a bargain with another man. Dana felt that it was also something of a compliment on her choice and a friendly gesture. She took it, surprised again that it was so slender and delicate.

"I figured you would, when I first saw you." Bill was his old self again. "But I wouldn't want you to walk under a bee tree covered with honey. A little preparing won't keep the bees from stinging, but it may teach you to have some soda handy."

"You have done your duty." Her voice was more edgy than she had intended, but Bill accepted it as understandable.

They made their last turn towards the village, the whites dancing in their eagerness to be home. Off in the distance now the sun glittered cold off the water where Lake Michigan was showing between the hills. Bill noticed, and listened to the hushed moodiness of fall in the lake country. He wished he had brought his harmonica. There was something about the deadness of late summer that needed the spirit of good music.

There is an interesting thing about this situation, though, his ever–busy mind was telling him. If this young gal can do the job, these kids in the valley may be learning something that no other school has ever taught, leastwise not the way they may learn it. The bible tells us to 'Love our enemies.' I've got a feeling that some of these kids are going to learn to love this girl in spite of what they hear about her brother.

Judy Harcourt watched, and waved to Bill Sugars as he went by with the new teacher. She had finished drying the evening dishes and was hanging the towel on the line in the Nelsons' big yard. For so late in the fall, the sun had shone warm today. But the days were getting shorter and already the chill of evening was creeping down into the clearing. Judy liked it outside. Her thoughts had troubled her lately. With Eber so far away and his seed swelling daily within her, it seemed as if being out of doors gave her a feeling of peace with the world that was more difficult to find when she was closed in by four walls. She went back into the house, bundled herself up in her warm coat, picked up the new copy of Bill Sugar's paper, and drifted back out to sit in the two–seated swing under the maple trees.

The item about the new teacher interested her. It was

like Bill to welcome her and wish her a pleasant stay in the valley without mentioning the problems that she would surely find here. I wonder what she will be like? I wonder when Mom and Dad will be having her here? I'll bet she will have an eye for Tom Michaels in spite of what he is doing to her brother. And I bet Jeannie VanBolt will have an eye on both of them.

The column about the need for a Judge in each of the new counties did not interest her so she continued on to the news of the war. It had been a long time now since the news of the bloody battle of Manassas Junction had become known. Now, more than a year later, the details of those seven days around Richmond, and the Second Bull Run, were coming back. And the stories were much the same. The North was not doing well. Judy was painfully aware of this.

Were they being badly beaten? This was beyond her understanding. But of one thing she was certain. The war was not going to be over soon. Eber's baby was going to be born without him, and it troubled her. A man should be there when his baby is born, and his woman should know the strength of his presence. But I feel good, real good, except sometimes in the mornings. At least I am glad that he is with Sheridan in the West where things are going a little better for the Union armies.

The air was turning cold as the sun disappeared over the hills to the west. Judy pulled the coat closer around her and retreated to the corner of the living room. Here the heat from the fireplace warmed the spirits and she could still see out of the west window. The heat of the fire after the chill of the outdoors made her drowsy. She closed her eyes, wondering if Eber was warm and well fed down there somewhere in those Kentucky hills.

The baby moved as if relaxing with her and she smiled. It would be fun having it to play with while she waited for Eber.

Outside, a red–headed woodpecker searched a dead stub of the big maple tree, the evening glow shining bright off its busy head. He located his evening snack, tilted his head to estimate the depth of the movement, rapped twice to confirm the location of the cavity in the stub, and started his excavation. Tap tap tap tap tap——The sound rang out clear and sharp across the darkening hills.

Chapter Twelve

Tap tap - tap tap - tap - tap tap. From behind a rough stone fence, Eber Harcourt listened. He listened quiet in the autumn wet and watched a cold, black night slowly take on the steel blue of skyglow. A pale half moon slid out from behind the scuttle of clouds that were the last trace of a rainy afternoon, hesitated, and started its arc across the remains of the night. Sloping down behind him, a stand of pin oak and locust trees settled into a black tangle of brier and rhododendron. A mile beyond, it rose again to a gentle moonlit slope. There, along the Hodgenville Road a glow of fires showed where Sheridan's Second Michigan Cavalry guarded the flank of Carlos Buell's Union Army. They were bivouacked without tents, getting as much rest as possible under pursuit conditions. For days now, they had been searching for General Bragg's Army and today they had unexpectedly found it.

This was Eber's twenty–four hours of guard duty. It was spent in broken intervals of four hours off and two hours on, and he had no liking for it. Rest was hard enough to get in a cavalry unit, and the fight to stay awake after only four hours of rest could be almost as bad as fighting. Seemed as though a man's eyes just closed when the rattle of an incoming sentry would warn him that it was time to be back at his post. Better if they could stay on duty for eight hours and be done with it.

The afternoon drizzle had left the trees wet, and there was the drip, drip of cold water following each slight sigh of the wind through the branches. He pushed the collar of his greatcoat higher with the barrel of his rifle.

Tap tap - tap tap -tap -tap tap. The sound came again from beyond the dark ravine and the moonlit road in front of him. Two, two, one and two. It was a sound Eber had heard down in Mississippi when he was once before face to face with Bragg's army.

Eber twisted off of the stone he had placed to keep his butt from the wetness of the hill, picked up the stick of ironwood he had been whittling on, and struck it lightly against the barrel of his Colt rifle.

Tap tap - tap - tap - tap tap.

He hesitated a few minutes, listening like a robin stalking a worm, then raised his eyes to the level of the loose stone wall, his head reeking with the smell of wet moss and rotting wood. Ahead of him the mottled blue–black of the timbered cut sloped downward to where a quiet run of water muttered nervously in the dark. The ground beyond the run then raised, was scarred by a loose dirt lane and flanked by an expanse of scrubby pasture land.

This in turn drifted downward into foggy distance, cut by ravines and dotted with prickly crab and wild junipers. Somewhere, back in the moonlit distance, was Bardstown and some thirty thousand men who were Braxton Bragg's Confederate Army.

As Eber's eyes cleared the level of the wall a flash of fire burst from the brush across the ravine. He ducked instinctively, his heart pounding a wild tattoo in his chest, and heard the ball thud sickeningly into the tree behind him. There was a split second of silence before the sound of the shot followed on the tail of the ball and echoed from the wet hills. The flash and the sound of the shot were nearly simultaneous, but Eber had learned to measure his distance from a shot by the length of that short interval. Forty, maybe fifty yards, he thought. In the junipers just beyond the lane.

He huddled a moment behind the safety of the wall, angry and puzzled, and tempted to send a few shots back from his repeating Colt. After a short pause, though, a soft laugh came drifting from beyond the darkness of the ravine, carried clearly on the moist night air. "How come you don't answer me sooner, Abe? "Y'all sleeping on guard again? Nex' time ah'll clip the braid raght off'n yore hat."

Eber shuffled a bit lower in his cubicle, knowing the loneliness of post and listening for a change of distance or direction of the voice. He knew it was Poke. Nobody but the Tennesseean could shoot like that in the dark of the night. Slowly the pounding in his chest slowed and he again raised his eyes above the wall. "You nigh got them that time, Poke." Eber tried to hide the sickness the galloping heartbeat left in the pit of his stomach. His mind flashed back to those bodies at Shiloh, laid out in piles, stiff and cold and starey–eyed. Sure he knew Poke wasn't aiming to do him in, but just a few inches of error and it still could happen.

"Did I 'most get them, sure 'nuff?" Poke's voice was as cheerful and confident as a squirrel's. "I reckoned to be about three quarters of a coon's aar hyah than thet. Laghts kinda poorly, tho', and ah ain't been shooting sharp lyghtly, Ain't really been missin'. Just kinda graisin' things."

Eber stretched a cramped leg and listened close for the expected change of direction. A shadow crossed the sandy lane and melted into the wet brush of the draw. "Grazin' don't make good friends, Poke. Specially if I cut loose with this Colts. I might not figger to take another chance on your half a raccoon's ear. Or I might think it's one of your cotton–picking buddies on post. I'm warning you." Eber was serious. He did not relish this kind of war play. "Don't be clipping my braids or I will be shooting: — low and straight.."

"Aw, Eber. Ain't no cause to git all riled up." The voice had softened a bit. "Shucks, Pa and me used to graze each other regular, just funnin'. We know where thet little old ball was a'goin ary time. Reckon y'all jest ain't used to us Tennessee folks." Poke's voice was a bit sad. Eber was just

like those flannel–mouthed cotton farmers in his own outfit. He just couldn't understand that it was a friendly gesture, sort of. Like some people callin' their best friend a
bad name.

Poke settled down into his new pocket beside the murmuring run of water. It had been the same way in the
camp. The men from the cotton country had no feeling for
Tennessee people. Likely, three–quarters of the men in his
outfit were Georgia aristocrats. Cotton gentlemen with
their own fine horses and black servants to care for them.
They were good soldiers when they were sober, but
would rather drink and party than fight. Others were
small farmers who worked in their fields right along with
their slaves, the same as his Pa had done back in South
Carolina. But they were still South, and they thought
South. Tennessee people were different. Poke felt a loneliness deep–down as he wished that he had been left in a
Tennessee outfit. Cotton was not his dish. You'd think to
hear them talk that nothing in the world mattered but cotton and the price of it.

He hungered more for the hills. Dogwoods dripping
with sunny fog in the spring and bittersweet berries hanging like fiery waterfalls in November. Should be busting
out just about now, he thought. I bet Jinny's got a basket
of them on Ma's table. And Ma would be baking cookies
and cornbread in the kitchen, and maybe an apple pie. For
supper there would be ham and sweet potatoes and frog–
eye gravy. Boy! just thinkin' about it made a man home-

sick. And would that range feel good this time of year, with the oak and apple wood crackling inside. Now Ma would be calling out the back door to where Pa was splitting the winter wood. "Cm'ere Pa, and call Poke. I got fresh cookies a coolin'. But don't stuff yourself. Be suppertime soon." But Jinny wouldn't wait for him to show. She would tuck a few of Ma's molasses cookies in her apron and they would sit on the oak log he had been trimming and drink in the sharp mountain air, the cookies, and each other. 'Cuz he and Jinny were that close, real close.

Something there is about Tennessee that brings people close, thought Poke. Probably those rocky ridges cutting every which way so that a man don't rightfully see his next door neighbor. Only the little valleys could be farmed, and all the towns were down below on the river flats. Either the county seat of Winchester or the little town of Jasper, a good three peaks and a right smart way to the east. In those hills you raise your corn and your potatoes and your hogs, and to hell with anyone else. You don't get rich and you ain't rightfully poor. You just have your little meadow in the hills, your family, and if'n it's like mine, your bible to read on the long evenings. Then in the winter you could hunt and make a little likker to sell in town for spending money.

I reckon Pa should know which life is best. He tried them all, thought Poke. Sidling up and carefully peeking the shadows to where Eber was waiting and wondering behind his stones. Let him wait. Don't feel like talking now anyways. I reckon I shouldn't have fired on him like that, but it was so nice to hear the sound of his voice. He settled back down. Virginia; North Carolina; Clayton, Georgia; then Tennessee. Near stayed in Greenville, I reckon. Ma liked it so well. And him almost getting to be a Southern Gentleman. Ma liked it 'cause there was white churches and women to talk to and such. But Pa was irked by the pompous rich. Men should be judged by their value, not their worth, he said. Some of the richest men he knew were of no more value to their country than an empty sardine can. Ma likes Tennessee, too, though, now that she's got settled to it. Jinny does, too. He slowly counted the days since he had seen a calendar. She will be seventeen in a few days, now, and blossoming like a ripe tomato. Sure would like to see that shiny hair again and smell the sweet, clean smell of her. Wish now I had stayed up there and looked after her and Ma. Pa's not as spry as he once was and this war is getting bigger every day.

He looked back to where his own troops were spread across the Kentucky hillsides, then back again to the west where the fires of Don Carlos Buell's Union Army glinted through the trees in the distance. Home and family and the pleasant Tennessee mountains faded away. He was again Private Porter Campbell, sharpshooter, with General Braxton Bragg's Confederate Army, dedicated to breaking apart the Union of States his grandfather and those like him had fought to put together. It didn't make much sense, being here in the Kentucky hills and wishing that he was back home in Tennessee.

I wonder if Eber is feeling the same way? He pulled himself alert, pushed a wet branch slowly down with the musket barrel and took a long look across the draw. "Are you still there, Abe?" He spoke softly.

"For another hour yet," said Eber. "What are you doing?"

"Just thinkin'."

"Thinkin' what?"

"Thinkin' I should never have left Jinny and Ma up there in those hills. Kin I come a mite closer, Abe?"

Eber didn't answer, but watched as a shadow drifted out of the blue of the draw and scuttled up the sides of the wooded cut. He cocked the rifle, feeling for the safety of the cold steel with nervous hands and watched for any other movement on the slopes. None appeared so he backed away and scooted into another pocket, thirty feet up the wall, then turned his attention to the darkness of the run. There was no sound, no shadow, no movement that could be detected, but after a while the voice came from the gloom hardly twenty feet away.

"Whar be ye, Abe?"

"Right here, Poke, and sitting pretty to split yore skull if I have a mind to."

"Reckon you made a smarty move on me, didn't you. Don't fret, Abe, I left my musket back a mite. Just hankerin' fer company, I guess. Y'all know they's times I feel closer to you Yankee timber wolves than I do to those Georgia cotton mouths in my own outfit."

Eber doubted that Poke would be out of touch with his musket, but it made no matter. War was all gamble any way you looked at it. Men lying in cold tents, white with pneumonia and the dysentery. Better to gamble any time on a ball between the eyes than to be laid on a cot in a stinking sick tent. One thing about Poke, grinned Eber, if'n he didn't aim to, he wouldn't miss.

"Are you feared for your folks, Poke?"

Poke settled on a rock behind an oak, and wiggled into instant comfort. "Reckon I kinda am. Didn' rightfully think the South would haid all the way into Kentucky and Ohio. Figgered they would jest hold down there and do their heavy fighting in the East."

"We think Bragg figgered to swing Kentucky people to jine with the South."

"So I heered, but it didn't work out. Kentucky people are more like Tennessee mountain folks. They think independent–like. Some along the roads swung, but most didn't."

"How come you jined, Poke?"

Poke thought a while on that, and scuffed up the leaves with the musket butt he still held handy. "I reckon ah listened too much to the men in town and not enough to my Pa," he admitted. "They made me believe I had only two prideful choices, jine or turn bushwacker. And bushwackin' kind of goes again my grain. Even fightin' kin be honest like if'n you wear your colors and make your intent known. Reckon I still fight like a bushwhacker 'cuz I don' know no other way. Caint see standing out when there's a rock to hide behind or a bush to carry or a ridge to slither. But leastwise I wear my gray" Poke's mind went back again to the hills, listening to the men round the old stove in the post office. "Seems like men don't proper think when they gang up. Blood starts a pressuring up and some big planter with a bay stallion and polished boots talks important–like and the sheep start herding. Hardly a body stops to ask, Where are we a-going? What are we hoping to accomplish, or what happens if we don't? Calhoun and Jeff Davis are doing the thinking, just follow the tail in front of you and keep your nose down. The good Lord might better have made people like Tennessee, all walled in by rocky ridges so they couldn't see the tail in front of them and wouldn't be skeered to be different. Then, maybe, they would all grow up with their own special kind of purty. I reckon I'm a mite smarter now than I was then."

Eber wondered what he would say if Poke asked him why he had joined. Of course the three hundred dollars and the big trees it had bought was the real reason. But that didn't seem like as good a reason now. Saving the Union was a better one.

Poke didn' ask, though, so Eber raised his head to check the hills. A cold, white mist was staining the wash and dropping streamers of fog across the distant pasture land.

They fell into a friendly silence again. Poke's melancholy and the moodiness of the night had unsettled Eber's mind. Poke's talk about Jinny brought his own memories. He wondered about Judy and pictured her here beside him on this far hillside, warm and fresh and sweet–smelling with a peach blossom in her brown hair. I bet Judy and Jinny would make a great pair. But here they were, mountains and rivers and uniforms apart, and no chance for it to be different.

Only a chancy wonder that he and Poke dared scooch here in the cold moonlight, not seeing each other or really knowing what the other looked like. Not always talking, but feeling close to each other all the same. Probably it was because neither one of them were city folks or big planters or storekeepers but just back country farmers, sort of, each in his own way.

Eber was remembering when they had first met, on another black night back in Corinth, Mississippi. Poke had invited conversation across the picket line just as he had tonight. And they had become friends. It is hard to identify the strange chemistry that binds one person to another but between Eber and Poke the cement soon hardened and held. They became friends, friends, unseen and unknown, over the strange war–imposed wall. Only the sound of each other's voices and the little acts of sharing held them together.

But war is fluid, and their roads separated as Bragg left

Mississippi and Tennessee to make his rendezvous with Kirby Smith in Kentucky. But before that day, they set up their tapped–out signs in case they met again. And now they had.

Yet tomorrow, a week from tomorrow or next year sometime, when the snow covered the ground and the cold froze glove to hard steel, and nerves were ragged, when the last hour of sleep seemed days ago and the Parrott Guns were booming from the woods and men were screaming with a mad desire just to get the whole thing over with, then they might, without even knowing it, meet again. It might be on a hillside like this, but under conditions that would not let them hold back. Then it could happen. Even if Poke were his brother, it could happen.

I'm glad Judy isn't here. I'm glad she is safe up there in those Michigan hills, glad she don't rightfully know what it is like down here.

War hadn't sounded so bad from back there. But he had not reckoned on wearing boots that had lost their soles two months ago. He hadn't expected to see the dead, like he had seen them at Shiloh, stacked in piles like cordwood waiting to be laid in a more fitting place. He would not have believed that half of them wouldn't even have the satisfaction of dying out there fighting to save the Union, but would pass slowly on from a dirty bed in a cold, wet tent from the fever or dysentery or the other strange sicknesses that were worse by far than fighting.

He had been lucky. A spell of sickness and dysentery back at Corinth had taken him down. But he had most of his weight back now and was feeling fit. The war was not the same as he had pictured it, though. It was a cold, dreary business. Fighting was only a small part of it. It was the long, lonely weeks of waiting in wet camps, and nights of riding in unknown darkness where you couldn't see a white horse following a black one; the seeing of no friendly lights along the way. It was the eating of sweet potatoes and goober peas instead of good pork sausage and buttermilk pancakes. It was seeing old and dear faces disappear from their places in line and knowing where they had been laid. It was watching new, young, eager ones take their places. It was living a dozen lives in a few short months.

Sure, there had been good times, too, like back at Rienzi. There the Rebs were on the run and talk was light and they had time to play catch with home–made balls, and the spirit for euchre games under the Southern oaks. But it wasn't like home, and he had no idea that Judy would become so important to him.

"Got any coffee tonight, Abe?"

"Just a little, Poke. Here. Catch." And he dug in his coat pocket for the ball of coffee he carried in a pouch of rabbit hide, and tossed it into the shadows. he gripped his Colt at ready while Poke shadowed over to the packet.

"It's been a long time since we were down Corinth way, Abe."

"A long time and a lot of miles," sighed Eber. "You must of nigh wore out your musket tappin' out our sign."

After a while Poke's voice came back again from out of the dark. A dew was forming, laying a cold wetness on the night. Eber pulled his coat more tightly around him. "Wars are hardest on Ma's I reckon. What's your Ma like, Eber?"

Eber tried to describe his Ma, all the time wondering why she sounded so much like Poke's mother.

And then, his Pa. But here the sameness ended and Eber came up wondering that he knew so little about his Pa. And what he did know had been learned in little bits and pieces. A word here and a half–spoken memory there. People in the valley wondered about him, too. Leaving the sea and settling in the Michigan hills like he did. They noticed that he had settled where he could see the sun setting out over Lake Michigan and could smell the clean, fresh air coming off the water. They shook their heads when he put on his big sweater and took those lonesome walks along the lake shore where the seagulls screamed their loudest and the spring winds rolled the breakers high up on the beaches. They could see, as Eber had, that the sea was still calling softly to him.

Once he had met a red–faced man on the docks at Manistee and they had talked with words strange to Eber. They had spoken of Liberia and Dakar, of Dutch traders and of cargoes of black ivory, of riding the trade winds into Rico and Amalia, of chains of Gullahs, and of the coming of the brigs and the brigantines. But his Pa had talked little to him of his sailing days except to say that he got his start sailing out of Liverpool as helper to the ship's carpenter, when he was young. And that he had stayed on for quite a spell. Seems like it was a hard thing for him to talk about to a boy who didn't know the language of the sea. So much remained unknown, hid in the darkness of a strange language and lost times. Events dim and different, hidden in strange ways, like Poke sitting quiet out there in the darkness behind his oak tree.

Probably some day I will try to tell a little boy about how I rode with Colonel Sheridan and those twelve hundred men of the twin Seconds to blow up and burn the railroad bridges at Boonville, and I will probably have the same problem. Already it is fading into the darkness of the past. The fires of war will burn low and smolder into dim rememberings and go out, and a little boy will wonder why it is so hard to remember.

The sky was pinking where the mountains crowded broodingly against the eastern sky. A rustle of wet air drifted up the cut and fought with the gentle gurgle of the run for a part of the silence.

Eber and Poke just sat quiet, now, content in the closeness of a strange friendship. Poke finally stirred. "Gittin' late, Abe. Reckon I better be gittin'." And with Eber scarcely noticing, he drifted down through the gloom of the wash, carefully crossed the moonlit lane, and faded into the shadows of the junipers.

The morning sounds of twittering and rustling worried a new day out of darkness. Then from the brush beyond the road, Poke's voice came back, breaking out in a bit of song, like the moving of muscles had driven his spirits higher,—"Oh Susannah, don't you fret fer me, I've gone to old Kentucky, to ——

The song stopped with a fit of fake coughing. "Reckon I better not be singin' in this wet, Abe." The old humor was back in his voice. "Sort of feels like this night air is tightening up my overlays."

Chapter Thirteen

Dana Sharrow loosened the long coat she had thought she would need in the cool September air. The autumn sun on her back and the brisk walk out to the schoolhouse had warmed her. It was Saturday. She had finished her first week of teaching at the little school and was feeling good. The people of the town had been surprisingly kind to her in a quiet, cautious way. Maybe teaching here was not going to be so bad. The children had all had schooling of a sort, either at home or in the classes which Louise Colby had held during the winters. It surprised Dana to learn that among these people the Indian Louise, who had attended Reverend Slater's school in Grand Rapids, was the best teacher. It surprised her more that many of these children showed more promise and better training than had many of her classmates back in Albion. It was more understandable now that Tom Michaels had successfully completed his law course at the university.

During the first week of school there had been only seven children. The three dollars per week per pupil which she had been promised was hard to find in some of the homes. In others the older boys were still needed for the potato and corn harvests. She felt especially bad that the three children of Louise and Jim Colby had not appeared, but suspected that the nine dollars per week was more than they could bear. I must go to Louise, she thought. Perhaps with a few more students I can lower the charge to two dollars each.

The little school lay quiet and warm in the autumn sun. She went inside. Already the cool silence of the empty building seemed strange. The big eyes looking back at her and the ready laughter of children seemed like a part of the walls. Without them it was lifeless and still.

She hung the new curtains that Mary Sugars had made for the front windows. The wood shed at the back was her next target, so she tied a scarf around her head and started in.

In an hour the old wood was neatly stacked and the odds and ends of brooms and paint were stored into a corner. She was just emerging from the dust of the shed when she heard the clip clop of a horse stopping outside. Wiping a dusty sleeve across her wet forehead she shielded her eyes from the bright sun and looked out. Sitting his horse outside was Milan LaVoy, his handsome face glowing with unabashed amusement. The corners of his mouth were turned down in that smile that turned on the lights in his eyes and pressed a faint dimple into the weathered chin.

"You the new schoolteacher, Ma'am?"

"Yes. I am Dana Sharrow. You must be Milan. I have heard of you." There was no use trying to look ladylike, Dana knew. She was a mess. She tried to brush the dust and chips from her old sweater. Glory, was he handsome!

"Hope you don't have a polecat in the woodshed again," Milan grinned.

"No, I was just shaking the dust off of the wood so I can maybe stay clean the rest of the winter. Do skunks get in here sometimes?"

"Sometimes," said Milan. "But I think probably they have a little help from some of the boys.

"One got in Nick Tanner's basement last year. Nick is an old army man so he sort of hesitated to give it any orders. Said, according to his teaching, anything with three stripes was to be treated with all proper respect. Besides, if he shot it, it might blow a hole in his reputation for keeping a nice, clean, sweet smelling bachelor house."

"What did he do?" Dana smiled.

"Well, finally Ole Nelson says, Neek, you are my friend. And since you are my friend I will tell you the old Swedish trick. It is used many years ago to get the wood-chuck from the root cellars back in old Sveden." Milan swung easily down from the bare back of his horse, tossed the bridle strap loosely over its neck and sat on the step beside her.

"So that night Nick sneak down the basement steps and very careful scatters a little trail of fresh shell corn all the way from the basement out the back door and into the barn yard. Then he leaves the door open just a crack and goes to bed laughing at how he has outsmart the polecat."

"And did he?"

"Well, not exactly," grinned Milan. "He got up the nex' morning and sees the corn is all gone. He feels real good all over so he holler across the street to Ole Nelson. 'Come see, Ole, it works.' So Ole Nelson comes over, sniffing like a blue tick hound on a bear track, and they go down the basement stairs, real slow and careful–like. And you know what they see? Down there, rubbing their bellies and looking happy as can be, are two skunks."

"Oh! Milan, I don't believe that." Dana was laughing now. But whether it was true or not, she would never know. His face was too much a combination of steely strength and sly good humor.

"Now you got the time to pass the peace pipe? Or is there some more dust in there you have a hankering to collect?"

The grin was too warm to make the words offensive, and the eyes too carefree to be concerned with dirt. She placed a hand on his arm. "If you will prime the pump, kind sir, so that I can clean up a bit, then we can talk. The rest of the day, if you like." She could see that he was pleased with this. He liked people who had time to talk.

The pump in the school yard did not need priming, and with an awkward show of French courtesy Milan helped her to wet her scarf. The cold water felt good on her warm face and brought the color into her cheeks. She had some-how hoped that it was Tom Michaels on that horse, but now it didn't matter. This old Frenchman was nice. How much alike were he and Tom. The broad flat shoulders and the easy grin were from the same mould.

The snow apples were ripening on the tree in the school yard. Milan found a pair of good ones. They were still a bit green but sweet and juicy all the same. Dana sat down in the swing that Bill Sugars had hung there for the children. Milan squatted nearby.

After a while he spoke. "I came here to ask a favor."

Dana had felt that there was a reason for his visit. She waited. "How would you like to add three little Ottawa heathens to your classroom?"

"The Colbys."

"Oui."

"I would love it. But I would have to charge. And nine dollars a week? It would take a lot of wolf bounties to pay that."

"Only one pelt a week," said Milan. "But wolves are getting scarce. There is another way."

Dana looked up.

"If you will talk to Louise, I will see that you are paid at the end of each month." Milan grinned. "That way I can get acquainted with the school Ma'am without going to school."

"You would do that?"

"Go to school? No," he grinned. "It is much too late for

that. But I will see that you are paid."

Dana looked at Milan. He had stretched out now, like a dog on a warm porch and spoke from beneath his battered hat. "Oh, sometimes a man does not really know why he does a thing. Perhaps it is just that Jimmy Colby is my friend."

"I like that reason," said Dana.

"Perhaps it is because Louise and the keeds are also my friends."

His statement was again matter of fact, but Dana wondered if she did not detect a bit of hidden warmth in the tone. Something only another woman might notice.

He became more evasive now. "Perhaps I have the feeling that we owe something to these people that we can never repay, and I would like to do what little I can to change this."

This was a thought foreign to all of her neatly arranged ideas about the Indians. Ideas formed from the usual stories of cruelty and ignorance. Louise and her children seemed different, and she wanted to know them and to teach them. Now she realized, though, that she had thought highly of herself for the wanting. It had never occurred to her before that she might owe them anything. Like Tom Michaels and Bill Sugars, this Frenchman had ways of shaking her out of her patterns. It bothered her a little, but also drew her closer to them. "You really like the Colbys and the other Indians, don't you?" she asked.

Milan was comfortable beneath the tree. He pushed his

hat back off one eye and grinned. "If I pick an ear of corn and find a red kernel among the white ones, I don't throw it away just because it is red," he replied. "Who knows? It might be the best seed on the ear."

Dana looked down at him. She had made herself comfortable, rocking gently in the swing. She suddenly felt very feminine. He was all steel and leather on the outside. The hard shell of the voyageur who had known life in its most physical forms. Now the steel was turning gray around the edges. The leather was softening and in its place, still well hidden, was warmth and kindness. She would like to know him better.

"Milan."

"Yes, Teach."

"Tell me about yourself."

"Ho! Ho! Why you say that?"

"They tell me that you were a voyageur. I am a teacher. Voyageurs were a part of our beginnings. A teacher is interested in beginnings. Please, it is still early."

"It is a long story."

"I have time."

But he still hesitated. Should he tell her of his days as a Huguenot boy in Catholic France? Of a father crippled and bent by beatings, and the tired, sad eyes of his mother as she kissed him good-bye? Should he tell her, who was of Irish Catholic background, that the scars he still carried had been received because his family persisted in having a Huguenot bible always open on their table? And of the courage it took to place it there?

But those things were bad history. Here in America life was different. It would be foolish to turn the pages of history back to its bad chapters.

He felt her big brown eyes, full of questions, looking steadily at him. He knew she was waiting for his story so he began.

"The fur trade, Dana, was already old when I reached these shores. Over a hundred years old, I was told. But in Montreal it was still important. There were trappers and voyageurs in town dressed in skins and moccasins and I was told that the market for beaver was still good. Beaver hats were the style among the well-to-do in both France and England and they were buying all the hides that Montreal could ship."

"But where did they come from, Mila?n"

"There were skins to be had from all of the pioneer territories, Dana, but the good fur country was to the north around the west end of Lac Superior and on to the west.

"Our French explorers were the first ones to explore this country, Radisson, Groseilliers, and Father Menard, but it was the English who were the first to see that to come to it by water from the north was best. It was their trading posts at York and Moose on Hudson Bay that made their Company the first to get rich from the fur trade.

"Our French and American Companies sent their men up the Ottawa River then down through Lake Nipissing and Lake Huron and on into Lake Superior. They built their posts there around the west end of the lake, at La Pointe, Fort Williams and on to the west. But to get their furs back to Montreal meant putting the bales into big canoes built for them by the Chippewas and with eight or ten voyageurs at the paddles, bring them some eleven hundred miles back to the LaChine warehouses at Montreal."

Milan stretched his long arms and settled back into his cross–legged position.

"But you still haven't told me about yourself, Milan," Dana persisted.

"I just did," Milan laughed. "I was a voyageur and a coureurs de bois. A paddler of the big canoes."

Milan stretched out on his back and remained silent for a few minutes as if to think, or perhaps to tease the curious teacher.

Dana waited.

Finally he came easily upright again and spoke quietly. "All right, I will tell you more but it is not all the pleasant story. Some of the life of a coureur de bois was also very rough."

"That is the way I have heard about it, Milan, and I wondered if this was true."

"When I saw the big bundles of furs piled on the docks at Montreal and saw the voyageurs in town I say to myself, 'Ho! Milan, you are young and strong and bigger than most of these men. Here is your chance to make money, and maybe find real adventure.'"

"And you did, obviously."

"I did, along with more scars, bruises, and lessons," laughed Milan. "But I have promised my sister that when I get to America I will send her money so that when she is eighteen she, too, can come to this country.

"So I go to the big building at LaChine. They say 'You ever paddle a canoe, Frenchie?'

"I say, 'Sure 'nuff. I work trap for two years up west of Fort Williams.' Of course, I didn't even know where Fort Williams was but a man in town had told me to say this."

Milan chuckled. "I think they know damn well I never have seen a paddle, but they say, 'You look like a strong boy. You have a job.'

I soon found out why. They wanted to send a late canot du maitre loaded with trade goods up the rivers and lakes to their post at La Point before the fall storms and winter ice closed in. It would be dangerous to start out this late and they needed one more stupid Frenchman to make the trip. I guess you know, Teach, who that one was. I had no idea where La Point was. I thought probably we would be there in two weeks, not two months.

"There were six Frenchmen, the white Pawnee Joe Parks, a Chippewa called Wyan Ding and a Scotsman bookkeeper who already looked very scared in our party.

"We were each given a sack of dried corn and a jug of whiskey before daylight the next morning and with much shouting and singing we started up the river.

"Soon the cabins along the Ottawa disappeared and we were in wild country. The river here was wide and the current was strong from the early rains. I learned the paddling easy by watching the Frenchmen but there was more to learn. By the time we make our mid-day stop, blisters are showing on my hands. The Frenchmen laugh. They could tell that I had never paddled before but they did not warn me to wear pads on my hands. They just drink their whiskey, laugh, sing their boatman songs, and paddle on, stopping only once in a while for a short pipe of tobacco.

"By the middle of the afternoon my hands are raw and bleeding and the muscles along my ribs are tired and sore. Now the Frenchmen are wild with the drink and happy to be away from the city. They paddle even harder than ever and shout and sing like wild men.

"When we make our camp that night I am so tired and sore that I cannot eat. I just roll into my blanket and lay there listening to the mosquitoes all around me and brushing the little black no-see-ums from my neck and ears. I am wondering now if I have made the big mistake. France and home were better than this. Or perhaps I should have looked for work in the shops and workhouses of Quebec.

"I wonder if the English country to the south might be better. But it was too late now. I was on my way to someplace far off in the wilderness to the west. I had very little idea where. I just knew I was on my way and I would have no choice but to stay there until the canoes returned to Montreal in the spring.

"The next morning I was hungry. I ate my portion of dried corn and drank plenty of cold water from the river."

He tilted back his old hat and looked up at Dana, wondering if she was believing him.

She only smiled back.

"This corn or sometimes peas is the only food of a voyageur, Dana, except the fish you can catch or the game that is shot along the way.

"I stretch my sore muscles then and find my place again in the canoe. Joe Parks had made me deerskin pads for my sore hands. I put them on. The Frenchmen were quiet and ugly from the first day's whiskey but they don't bother me. Before long, I knew that this day would be worse than the first. My hands were soon bleeding again and my muscles were becoming numb with the hurt. We paddled on, stopping only now and then for the short pipes.

"By late afternoon most of the whiskey was gone, the singing had stopped and the crew was quiet. Only our leader Joe Parks is feeling good. He tells me that we have done well and are now nearly twenty leagues up the river. Soon the country will get higher and rockier and after the whiskey has burned itself out the Frenchmen will be different.

"We camped that night on an island. I ate my pound of corn and went to my blanket. From it I saw the stars appearing through the pine trees and wondered if they were the same ones my parents were seeing back in France. I listened to the pung, pung of the frogs along the river, heard the trout splashing in the riffles and the wolves howling from the hills. I was homesick. It was the first time that I had heard the wolves singing at night and it made me feel alone and lonely.

"After a while I turned to watch the men around the fire. They were talking again now as the whiskey wore off and I could hear Jean Baptiste Dufrene saying, 'It is the boy's fault that we are slow. Like this we will be caught on the big lake when the storms come.'

"Joe Parks, he say quiet like, 'Easy Jean, It is your liquor talking. The boy does well. The whiskey is now gone and the new one grow stronger. We will be at La Point before the storms.'

"But Jean Baptiste was not satisfied. 'No, we go too slow,' he repeated. 'He is only a boy, a Huguenot boy and a weak one. It is his fault that we are still in the swamps,' and he spat at me where I lay in my blanket.

"I know that these men are tough fighters, but fighting I have done before. A Huguenot boy in the hills of south France does not grow up without fighting. We also grow up quick with the temper. I rolled from my blanket quickly and pulled the knife from Jean's belt before he knows what I am doing. I threw it far out into the river and jumped up to face him. I had heard that these voyageurs were fighters with the knife and I did not want that kind of trouble.

"We fought for a long time, I guess. I was too tired and hurt to really know. All I remember is that after a while I see Jean Baptiste standing in front of me. The rest are still sitting quiet around the fire. There is blood on Jean's lips, his shirt is gone and he is swaying back and forth like a tree in a strong wind. He is not raising his arms to hit me any more, though, and when he tries to kick me he falls backward into the fire.

"I was tired and hurt, too. I had never seen men fight like these men fight, with their knees and their elbows and their heads. But I was still standing, and the faces around the fire were still and offering no help to Jean Baptiste, and when he goes for Joe Parks' knife, he holds it from him. I can see that they are surprised and under my hurting I am feeling good, so with all the strength that I have left I pick Jean from the ground, carry him into the river and dump him into the cold water.

"Then I go back to my blanket. I hear the men laughing as Jean crawls back to the fire and I see Joe Parks looking at me. He has his rifle across his knees and I know by his eyes that I now have a friend. That, Teacher, was my first lesson as a voyageur."

Dana leaned back with a tightness in her throat. Milan had not told the story to make himself look big to her. It was a part of the voyageur's life which he felt compelled to relate. He wanted her to know that his life could have ended out there along that river. Perhaps it was also an indirect warning to her brother Milton that he, too, should take care. She did not think that this was his purpose. More likely it was a veiled explanation of his closeness to the Indians, since Joe Parks was the first one to show him respect and friendship.

"Then Joe Parks became your friend?"

"Yes, but Joe was not really an Indian. He was a white boy who had been adopted by the Pawnees and brought up as one of them. He may have been stolen, or his family may have been killed by Indians or disease. Joe himself never knew."

"But he never really became a white man?"

"No. Joe liked better to remain a Pawnee. Changing would have been hard."

The late afternoon sun was cooling now and a riffle of air rattled the leaves of the maples. Milan's sorrel wandered close, nudged the hat that he had drawn down over his eyes to shade out the afternoon sun then sampled one of the windfalls from the apple tree.

"Are you going to tell me more?" Dana finally asked.

Milan was slow to answer. His mind was now filled with memories. Perhaps it was the coming of winter, a time when growth ceases and the world stands still, resting, remembering and waiting for a new life to begin. A time to look back on the activity of the warm months and good years. Or was he feeling age and not wanting the good things of the past to be lost to the future. This young teacher. Who could better carry them than she? He had only intended to make a point, but maybe it was good for her to know the other stories of those years. The good stories.

"We travel up the Ottawa, then across Lake Nipissing and down the French River. After a while my sore hands heal and my muscles get hard and I begin to like the wild country. Joe Parks has given me bear grease to keep off the mosquitoes and the no-see-ums. Wyang Ding make me moccasins to cover my ankles and the Frenchmen taught me their songs. Now I am one of them. Even Jean Baptiste has forgotten and the warm days of Indian summer are here to raise our spirits.

"After we leave the French River we are among the Lake Huron islands. This is the prettiest country, Dana, that I have ever seen. Nowhere else is there water so clear or skies so blue. Here are the islands of stone covered with the green of pine and cedars where we camp, catch the sweet perch and pickerel from the rocky shores and eat well again.

"Farther on we go through the bays and channels of the La Cloche hills, where only Joe Parks can follow the canoe trails. Here there are mountains of rock so white that it hurts the eyes to look at them in the morning light. The water of the lakes and bays is deep and blue, and the Ottaways are everywhere. They trade fish to us for worthless beads and watch us as we paddle along the trails that have been marked through their country. I could not believe that there was so much water and islands and trees and sky in the whole world. Yet Joe Parks tells me that we are not yet half way to the post at la Point.

"It was October before we had traveled through the Sault of the Saint Marie and reached the open water of the Missisawagegon, the lake we now call Superior. There were no islands to protect us here and the rough waters of the big lake drove us to shore many times.

"By middle of October we reached the portage across the narrow peninsula the Indians call Ka-ki-we-o-nan-ning. From here there were islands again and the big humped–up mountains called the porcupines rose up along the shore. In a few days we arrived at the big post of La Point. I was surprised to find here so many people living in good log cabins, a church, and plenty of good food.

"We stayed at the Post at LaPointe for a week, meeting the white people who lived there and listening to the ring-ing of the bell at the Mission. It was hard for me to believe that this place was visited first by Pierre Radisson over a hundred and fifty years before, and the Jesuit Mission was started by Father Allouez in the year 1665, 111 years before America separated from Mother England.

"We left the rest of our party at the fort where they would spend the winter collecting the furs the Indians would bring in. Joe Parks and I paddled on up the Montreal River and into the back country. In three days we were at Simon Charette's Post on the Lac du Flambeau.

"Do you understand the French, Teach?"

"Only a little, Milan, but Lac Du Flambeau means Lake of Flame, does it not?"

"Yes. The French explorers called it that when they saw it on a spring night lighted by the torches of Indians drifting in their canoes and spearing the pickerel that came into its shallows to spawn."

Milan sat up to his comfortable squatting position now. "That is about enough of my story for today, Teach. I stayed in this country for many winters after that. Some on the Flambeau, some on the Court Oreilles farther to the west. I worked for the company for three years and traveled with the brigades of canoes and when they brought the furs back to Mackinac or Montreal. But I do not talk of those years. They were my wild years.

"After those I settled down. For three years I have sent little money to my sister. I have spent most of it for whiskey and good times. I knew that I had to change my ways, and I did. Joe Parks is still my friend. We buy our own traps and guns, beads and knives, and calico and blankets. We go west of the Flambeau to the Court Oreilles country alone. There is still plenty of beaver where we build our cabin. We trap some and trade much with the Chippewas. When we come out in the spring our canoes are well loaded with the best furs, beaver, martin, and fox, and when this time we take them to Detroit to sell we make more money than we have ever seen.

"And this time I do not waste the money. I send it to my

sister first—-then I go into the city.."

Dana laughed quietly.

"Of course, this is a dangerous business. The companies do not like us now and we know that traders who sell furs this way without the license sometimes disappear in the woods or on the lakes. But we have learned much, we have many good friends and we know that it can be done. And we know that we are doing well."

Milan leaned back and ran his long fingers through his tight curled hair. Dana noticed the beautifully turned high moccasins he wore, the unbelievable trimness of his waist and thighs. Only when she looked at the face, crinkled and graying at the temples, and the slight fading of the still bright eyes, was she aware that he was no longer young. She caught him eyeing her closely. He smiled.

"You wonder why I tell you these things, Teach?"

"I really don't care why, or if you have a reason. I just find them very interesting."

"I tell you one reason. For six years I live in Indian country. Except for a few traders there was nothing in all of that territory but the red people, the Chippewa, a few Ottawas, and some Hurons who had already been driven from their country by the settlers and the Iroquois. They could have killed me many times as they killed the soldiers at Raisin River. Even with their arrows on their puggamauguns they could have driven Joe and me from their country. They could have stolen our supplies of corn and trade goods, but they never did. Maybe they were afraid, but I do not believe this. They were our friends and we were theirs. We did not rob them. We did not try to take their land. In return they taught me to live by seeing and feeling and understanding all the wild world around me.

We call them ignorant, but when I would have died of scurvy they made me a medicine of the buds of the hemlock. When they were dying of the white man's small pox I could do nothing. When the traders needed good boats they went to the Chippewas. They made them, sometimes thirty–five feet long and strong enough to carry three tons of furs back to Montreal. The traders could make nothing so light and strong. They taught me to harvest wild rice by beating it into my canoe with sticks as I passed through it, how to trap the big sturgeon from the rivers, how to make snowshoes from the skin of the oriniack, how to keep comfortable and warm in the skins of the wolf, how to make sugar by dropping hot stones into dug out logs filled with the sap from the maple trees, how to travel through the wild country by knowing the stars and understanding the trees and the rocks. We call them pagans but their Manitous bring them peace and comfort the same as our gods. They are ignorant? ho! - ho!

"I spent many a long winter night around their campfires. We had feasts when the hunting was good and the wild rice was full and long. We knew hunger when the snow piled deep and the food was gone. I learned their language and taught them ours. They saved my life many times and, merci Dieu, sometimes I helped them. They were not always wise, honest, or clean, as white men are not always wise, honest, or clean. But they were always generous with a friend.

"I know, Teacher, that all Indians are not like this, but this was the Algonquian way. It was only after the white men came with his whiskey and his split tongue that I watched the Algonquian tribes change. It is a sad thing to see, and now when I look into the eyes of Jimmy and Louise Colby, I am ashamed. We are from a different world. We cannot understand their ways and they can never change to ours. They can only be born to it, like the Colby children. Even then they are like wild deer born among cows. But with our help they will learn."

Milan remained quiet and thoughtful for a long time. Dana did not press him further. She had learned much and she now knew why he had told his story. Finally she walked over to where he still lay underneath the old felt hat. She put a friendly hand on his arm, "I will be very kind to the Colby children, Milan."

They remained there in friendly silence for a few more minutes as the red sun dipped lower against the heap of Lake Michigan in the west.

After a while he stood up, quickly and without effort from a cross–legged position. He was grinning again now as he took Dana's hand courteously. "I guess no one and no people can stand against the streams of change. But changes from generosity to greed are not good changes, are they, Dana?" He was looking carefully at her now.

Was it a reference to the cutting of the trees? This time Dana thought it was. She caught her breath, but did not answer. This man was good and kind, but he could also be blunt and hard and unforgiving. She found herself wondering what would happen if he met her brother, alone, face to face.

She looked up, prepared to be defiant, but his face was again wide with the friendly grin.

"You will talk to Louise about the keeds?"

"I will talk to her."

Chapter Fourteen

Jimmy Colby shuffled quietly to the window of the little cabin. Shafts of warm October sunshine were slanting through the needles of the big pine trees between the cabin and the lake. Looking out between the scaley boles of the pine trees, Jim could see where the brown cover of pine needles ended and the white sand of the lake shore began. Here the morning sun was showing heat and the brown carpet of needles was sending up little wisps of steam. There was a heavy layer of fog spread over the lake, but above it, standing out sharp and clear above the mists, was the clear copper folds of the sand dunes.

There had been rain yesterday, the slow drizzle of autumn that leaves everything dripping, including the spirits of those that feel the wintry promise in it.

But today would be warm and bright. The trees on the hills would lose their wet by noon. By sundown the sand would be warm and dry. "I think I go for a walk," Jim muttered. He said it half to convince himself that he should, and half to tell Louise that he would soon be out of her way.

Louise looked up from the fire she was starting in the little flat–topped stove. "We could use some fresh white-fish, Jim. They are good this time of the year." Louise was not one to make demands, but sometimes a bit of a spark could grow into a fair fire. She struck a store–bought match to the roll of birch bark and closed the damper part way. The flames licked up through the split cedar and birch. She watched Jim out of the corner of her eye as she set the big iron frying pan on to heat. Just being inside at sunrise was unusual for him. No matter what the weather, he had never been one to care for a roof over his head, and the dirt floors and the settling walls of the cabin were witness to his lack of interest. It was a convenient place to eat and sleep, but the freedom of the outdoors was more to his liking.

Lately, though, he was more inside. He seemed to lean more heavily on the words of Louise and show respect for her in clumsy ways. Perhaps the miseries of age were slowing him. Louise knew deep down, though, that Jimmy had other problems. The cutting of the trees was weighing heavy on him. It was another step by the white people. Another step to extinguish the old ways of the Indians. He had lived to see his people driven from their country by the push of the white settlers, and the sale, under pressure, of their wild lands. But here, by his beloved lake, things had remained much the same. He had been able to fish and trap. He could walk in the woods unmolested, paddle his canoe on the lakes. He could still feed his family in the old way, with the fish and wild game and the fruit which he found here.

But without the trees this would change. He could hope that the cutting would stop. But he had watched the white people before. Once they started something they were like the snows of winter. They left nothing unchanged. The trees would go. His sons would not know the good life. They would plow and hoe and cut the trees like white men, and live by destroying the good land.

Mill Sharrow's loggers were appearing again now at the camp on the south lake. They were probably cutting right now up on the south slopes. The talk was that there would not be many this year. The price of lumber was down. The people of Chicago and Buffalo were busy with the war and money was scarce.

Louise watched Jim as he crossed the yard and headed south down the lake shore. She hoped he wasn't going down to the camp.

About noon Jimmy waded the river south of the lake, climbed to the top of a bare sand hill above the still secure log jamb and looked out across the rolling wastes of sand, scrub junipers and wire grass to where Lake Michigan lay out flat and blue in the October sun. If this was Indian summer it was well named for Jim's blood was stirred by the lonely beauty of it. There were the pine trees to the south and the north, with those close to the lake weathered and bent by relentless west winds. Behind him, partially hidden by the crests of the higher dunes, lay the smaller lake, peaceful and protected by its guardian dunes and the pine–wooded hills. Farther back across the lake to the east, the green of the pines slowly mingled with the autumn gold of the birches, the vermillion of the maples and the bronze red of the oaks, as the hills rose fold upon fold in the distance.

Perhaps his appreciation of it was heightened by his knowledge that his years of viewing were growing few. He was not really old yet. He could still walk the hills with the spring of a yearling buck. He could pass through the swamps as silently as a fox and stalk the deer and turkey as cleverly as ever. Perhaps his growing old was a thing of the head. The whimpering of an old woman. A withering of the spirit. He straightened his shoulders. He was still Jim Colby, Amez-cha-kee-keez-chic, Rays of Sunshine Striking the Earth, named so by his mother. His father was the good Ottawa Chief, Cowpemossay, the Walker. Jim Colby is a good Ottawa, with still young children. He will be strong yet for many winters. He will stay here and watch the seasons come and go from these hills. Let the white strangers cut the trees. They would grow back as they had come back after the Ottawas burned them to plant their corn. He is better here with his family than those who let themselves be driven like cattle to the far away Kansas country. There, it is said, there are no trees and few hills, only the prairies where the buffalo and the two–horned deer are already becoming scarce.

But Jim Colby knew in his heart that he was no longer

the strong Ottawa he once was. Perhaps it was not years that were laying heavy upon him. Perhaps he was bending, like those beaten pines along the shore, to forces of wind and weather. Things unseen and unheard, sent by the Great Manitou to test him. Is he still Amez-cha-kee-keez-chic, son of The Walker? Or is he a child of the weak Kibewabose, The Fool?

Jim looked down. At his feet were his good buffalo skin moccasins. He had removed them wisely to cross the river. Now, with the white sands of the warm dunes caressing his bare feet, he was reluctant to put them on. His eyes moved to his left hand and the fine rifle Milan had given him, then to his right hand hanging loosely at his side, and to the already half–emptied bottle of whiskey that it held. It was the pay for a good young deer he had shot south of the camp. The hunting was good there. The cutting of the trees had allowed a second growth of scrub birch and poplar to appear. This was a poor substitute for the big pines, but it was good feed for the deer, and Jimmy knew this. He knew too, that he should have hung the deer in a tree to be picked up later for Louise. He would not always be that lucky. He knew that he should be netting the whitefish at the mouth of the river. A good Ottawa brave cares first for the needs of his family.

But he was not netting whitefish. He had bent with the wind like a slender willow. The call of the white man's Skitty-wa-boo had drawn him to the camp to make deals with the men he hated. He kicked the sand with a bare foot. Jimmy Colby is a fool. Louise had known what he was going to do. He had seen it in her eyes. Yet he could not turn his steps. He was weak. He had bent like those crooked pine trees, turned slowly, but forever, by the west wind.

He looked again at the bottle. "Got–damn whiskey!" He was shouting now, his voice sounding strange in the silence of the sandy wastes. "Skitty-wa-boo!-Devil Water!" He lifted the bottle and threw it as far as he could out over the sand of the big dune. He knew it would not break. He knew that he would go to it and pick it up, and would ever go back for more. He knew it, and the laughing men at the camp knew it. He sat down in the warm sand and cried softly with the knowing.

A mile farther into the wilderness of juniper and dune grass Jim found a warm pocket. The sloping side of a big dune rose up behind him, deflecting the wind. Before him the tops of the weathered pines sloped downward to where the big lake lay stretched out into the hazy distance. He was alone. Alone with his Manitou.

He ran a bare foot down into the sand and wondered why the foot was bare. The sand was warm on the surface but farther down it was cool and moist. It was like being a boy again. It was like those boyhood days, back along the Grand River, when he would leave his people and their camp at the falls, and taking the good orangewood bow, and the arrows his father had made for him, he would travel through the swamps toward the afternoon sun to where he would climb the sand hills there and look down on this same great Lake of the Illinois.

He had heard the old men around the council fire tell of the tribes who lived beyond the water, the Illinois, the Foxes, the Winnebagoes and the Menominees, and farther to the west, the fierce Sioux. He and his friend Windecowiss had talked of going there. There they would be away from the white settlers who were cutting the trees and turning the soil at the rapids. But their fathers had told them that this was not true. Already the white settlers were in the forest of the Illinois and the Foxes, and already the Winnebagoes were being driven to the west. Best to learn new ways to get meat for their fires and to grow the pumpkins and corn as Father Slater teaches us.

So we learned new ways. We learned to hunt the deer at night using torches made of hollow reeds filled with the wax from the bee's tree, then shooting at the deer's eyes from our canoes. We had meat again. But soon the trees were being cut along the river, and there were no more deer. We raised the corn and pumpkins, and even learned to raise the white man's wheat. But the white squatters built their cabins on our garden lands. It was a hopeless fight. The settlers were too many. The Chiefs could see that there was no hope of holding their land so they took the advice of the trader Robinson and Mr. Cass and sold their lands to the Great White Father.

But soon their money was gone and their lands were gone and the soldiers came to drive them, like cattle, to far away Kansas.

Windecowiss was angry. When his clan was told that they could not go to receive gifts from the English at the big island of the Manitou, he said, "Windecowiss is not the servant of the White Father. He will go where he wishes to go." So Windecowiss had shook the hand of his good friend and then gone with Chief Keeshaowash and his people to live forever in Canada in the land of the white rocks. There, in the white rock country, the white man's plow was like a toy. His oxen were worthless and the corn would not ripen before the frosts came. Only the Indians could live well there, for there was plenty of fish and game. There is where Jimmy Colby should also have gone.

He looked again at the bottle. It came to his lips without effort. He felt the last of the hot liquid sear his throat and work into his belly. He was tired. His mind drifted back into the hills of white rocks, green cedars, and blue lakes where the white people would never cut the trees or turn the soil.

The wind came in cool off the big lake, lifted wisps of sand off the ridges, and tossed them carelessly into his little world of loneliness. He closed his eyes to keep out the sand and sat pleasantly cross-legged in the warm pocket.

After a while his eyes opened to narrow slits and settled on the distant blue horizon. Somewhere in that blue distance the good Father of all Indians made his home. "What words do you give to Jim Colby? My Manitou." He spoke out loud, so that the good Father would hear him, but his voice was low. "Should I take my family to the white stone country? My friend Windecowiss believes that it will never change there because no white man's plow can change those hills of white stone. My friend is wise, but this country is good country. The white people who live here are good. My children are happy here and my good wife Louise is happy, and I, Jim Colby, Amez-cha-kee-keez-chic, am no longer young."

The troubled red man's eyes closed again to keep out the sand and the afternoon sun. He rested, sometimes in sleep, sometimes half–awake, waiting for the answer from his Manitou. But in his heart he knew the answer. He was not yet being driven from this country. These sand hills and the people here were good medicine. These miles of sandy wasteland, like the white rock hills of Canada would never see the white man's plow. If Jimmy Colby ran, it would be from his own weakness, and where can one go to escape himself?

For perhaps an hour, he slept. The wind died and little streams of white sand sifted out of the folds of his wool trousers. An eagle circled overhead and screamed as a pair of herring gulls invaded its territory. Jim opened his watery eyes and struggled to bring them into focus. They found the eagle and followed it. It circled twice, as though to make certain that it was seen, then it started a long slow, circling, glide, slid easily off to the west and, stretching wide its legs, landed gently in the top of a tall pine tree. Jim's eyes followed it and noticed that far down among the big pines along the lake shore, this one great father pine stood up straight and tall against the blue of the lake. It was taller, by far, than all of the others and was unbent by wind or storm. Jim looked at it for a long time. He had not seen it before. He did not believe that it had been there before. His Manitou had spoken. Even a tree, made strong by a brave heart and a stubborn spirit could not be bent or twisted by those steady west winds or broken by the snow and ice that comes with the northeast winter gales. He drifted back into a contented sleep.

It was late evening. The eagle had tightened his circle out over the wastes of sand and stunted junipers. Milan pulled his canoe up onto the sand where the faint remains of tracks led upward into the dunes. In the first valley he found the moccasins that Jim had forgotten. They were nearly covered now by drifting sand. Only here and there were the footprints still visible, but the eagle still circled, curious, hopeful, patient.

It was another half–hour before Milan found the little pocket and looked down where Jim Colby still sat, swaying gently and talking forcefully to himself. Milan walked down slowly and sat beside him on the sand. Jim's eyes opened, swam dreamily to his friend, then closed again as though he did not believe them. He continued his heated argument, "Hoah! Jim Colby good Indian, strong and straight like great pine tree. Hoah! Cut pine trees, no!" He shook his head with so much vigor that he tipped himself over. He righted himself. "Trees good. Hoah! Cut pine trees, no!"

His eyes opened again, blinked to a vacant stare and held. "Hoah! Milan. Bon Jour. Hoah! - Hoah! - Hoah!" and his voice trailed off to a whisper, his eyes rolled, and he fell forward on his hands to vomit convulsively into the clean drifting sands.

Milan waited, perhaps an hour, for the fires of the cheap whiskey to die. The sun settled quietly into blue drifts of clouds out over the lake. The eagle gave up its vigil and disappeared into the hills to the north. The air off the water turned cold and Milan started a small fire of juniper twigs to temper the cold. A wolf mourned the rising of the fall moon and Jimmy came alert and repeated its call. The sound, like that of the wolf's, sounded lonely and wild.

After a while Milan squatted beside of his friend and softly began to sing —

La jeune Sophia
Chantait l'autre jour
Son echo lui repete
Que non pas d'amour
N'est pas de bon jour
Je suis jeune et belle
Je veux me engage
Un amant fidele

It was the boatman's song that Jimmy had sung with him many times as they worked at their paddles.

Slowly, unsteadily, but loudly, Jimmy picked up the words. His voice was unsteady and his eyes still closed as, with empty arms, he began the paddling motions of the voyageur. His sickness returned, and passed.

Louise met Milan where the ribbon of moonlight washed the sands in front of their cabin. Their eyes met, but no word was spoken.

There was soup simmering on the wood stove. It tasted good. Milan had had no food since morning. Jimmy drank coffee as the children watched from beneath the railing that protected their loft.

Without a word, Jimmy finished his cup of coffee and went to his bed.

Chapter Fifteen

Dana Sharrow leaned back against the warm wood of the schoolhouse. It was beginning to feel like home to her now. She brushed a wisp of wind–blown hair from her cheek. It was time to ring the bell. Afternoon recesses were short, too short, when she was enjoying some remembering.

From her seat here on the school steps she had watched her flock for eight weeks now. The little group of seven had grown to ten with the addition of the Colby children. Then as the crops were harvested, and good words of her teaching passed over the hills, the older children appeared until there were now fourteen.

A cardinal called from the apple tree. Charlie Colby held the ball for a moment to whistle back, then threw a whistler to Frosty Sugars. Most of the bird and insect noises were gone from the hills now. Only the occasional bugling of a ribbon of southering geese, the rasp of a crow, or the thrill of a bluejay broke the stillness that precedes winter.

From her seat on these steps Dana had watched the

hills turn slowly from green to gold as the first frosts reached up into the birches. Then the maples and oaks had burst into splashes of scarlet and bronze, made all the more striking by the steady green of the pines on the hills beyond.

Now, only the dark parchment of the oak leaves remained. The gold and the red were gone, molding into nourishment for next years crop, or rustling around the corners of the school house. Life was full of cycles, and Dana's thoughts were caught in the flow of it.

The pump in the schoolyard was squeaking. The kids knew recess should be over and were after their last drink. She must ring the bell.

Frosty Sugars was running from the pump, reading the thoughts in her face. "May I?" she asked.

"Yes, but only once, Frosty. This is just recess, not a forest fire."

Frosty rang it three times, then ran quickly inside. After all, there were no brakes on a school bell.

The older boys, Charlie Colby, Jacques Moreau, and Joe Marsaque were still playing catch when the sound of the bell died and the smaller children streamed inside. Dana watched their glances in her direction, sensed the testing of young adult half–sureness and drifted over to put out the fire. Watching Jacque's eyes as they followed the ball, she turned quickly and picked off the throw with a neat left–handed stab. The game was over. The ball was in the hands of authority. Dana waited, with smiling but determined eyes. The boys took a long look, recognized defeat, and ran quickly to the school. At the door Jacques Moreau waited, though. As Dana came up the steps he spoke quietly before he opened it with the French courtesy which made him her favorite.

"Nice catch, ma'am," he said softly. "We should not have done that. I am sorry." It was a fine gesture from her oldest student. Dana patted the sturdy arm and went inside.

The afternoon sun slanted in through the west windows. The children slowly simmered to quiet. Her eyes wandered to the six panels of foolscap which she had tacked to the front wall behind her homemade desk. The first three represented the three foundation stones of learning; reading, writing and arithmetic. The traditional three "R's." there was a big circle around "Reading" which was the foundation stone of all learning. On the other side were three skills which the people of this valley had chosen to add. They called them the three "L's," Living, Loving, and Losing. "There ain't much use of making a living," Mary Sugars had insisted, "if a person don't know what to do with it after it's made." Dana had agreed, so one afternoon a week had been set aside as "L" time.

The children were starting to chatter so she settled her mind to her task and soon a spelldown was in progress. She picked Charley Colby for one captain and little Carrie Nelson for the other. She liked this choice. Carrie could easily be the last one down and this might awaken a bit of spirit in Charlie whose easy–going Indian nature was a drag on his real ability. She knew that it wouldn't, though. Charlie would remain Indian, caring little if he spelled correctly or not. Carrie would end up standing with Sandy Sugars. Only when they tried an art project would Charlie quietly excel.

And so it was. Although they sometimes surprised her, she knew them now, better than they knew themselves. From now on teaching could be a well planned process. The adding of one layer of knowledge onto another, multiplication to addition, fraction to whole numbers, new words to old ones, new ambitions to old satisfactions. She wondered if it might be possible for Jacques Moreau to follow in the footsteps of Tom Michaels. It would be nice if he could.

It was Thursday afternoon of the following week before the routine of reading, writing, and arithmetic was again broken. Thursday had been chosen to be "Three 'L' day" and Dana had special plans in mind. The first small fire was crackling in the stove, dinner pails were stored in a line along the wall, and coats hung on the pegs above them. The air was chill today and there was a threat of snow in the clouds out over the lakes. One peg remained empty, as it had during the morning. Dana glanced at it and wondered. Jacques Moreau was missing. Perhaps his father needed his help in the mill today. Allen Harcourt was cutting a few trees along his west pasture. They would have to start. She walked to the back of the room and shut the draft on the wood stove. The fire felt good today.

Since one's country is an important part of the three "L's" they started their class with a repeat of the Pledge.

"One nation, indivisible, with liberty and justice for all."

Indivisible? Dana wondered if that word could forever remain in the Pledge, and if these children were aware of the near death of it.

She walked back to the front of the room. "Last week I asked all of you about living. What were some of the suggestions that I made?

"Joe Marsaque"

"You suggested that I stay awake during spelling class."

The kids were laughing, and Dana laughed, too. "And now that the cold weather is here, why don't you use the bench across the room from the stove?"

"I really like it here, Ma'am. It's just like home now."

"And when the fire gets good and hot it will be good training for where he's going someday," added Cora Nelson.

Already the fifteen– and sixteen–year–olds were making choices, and teasing was the first sign.

"And what else did I suggest?"

"That we watch and kind of observe how people live."

"And who did Sandy suggest that we watch?"

"Uncle Milan." It was little Frosty Sugars who stated it so proudly.

"No need for that." It was Joe again. "Our Teacher is watching him."

Dana blushed a little. "That is true, Joe. I admire Uncle Milan very much. But it is the kind of admiration I would have for my father."

This set Joe's agile mind off in another direction. He hesitated, then asked a little timidly; "Do you have a father, Miss Dana?"

"No, Joe. I do not. I had one. A very fine one who worked very hard on a little farm back in Ireland. But he died many years ago."

"During the famine, Ma'am?"

She looked surprised. Joe was French, not Irish.

"Yes, Joe. That is right. Potatoes were our life. Without them life was very hard."

"And your mother. Did she die, too?"

"Yes, Joe."

It was impressionable Cora Nelson's voice that said quietly, "Gee!"

"But we must get back to our lesson. Why did Sandy suggest that we observe Uncle Milan?"

They were silent for a few minutes, their minds still busy.

"I think it was something about seeing all of a tree," little Carrie Nelson finally replied. She was obviously a little puzzled.

"That's right, Carrie. Not just a tree like most of us see, but a tree with bark, branches, leaves, and twigs. A tree different from all other trees. A tree with history, growth, and movement, and beauty."

"And with colors in the bark."

"Yes, green and red and yellow lichens."

"And birds among the leaves."

"And songs in the birds."

"And bugs on the bark."

"And itches behind the bug's ears." Joe was having one of his fun days.

But the lesson was getting through. Now everyone was thinking. They were becoming aware that Uncle Milan enjoyed life more than most because he saw more and understood more and heard more than anyone else they knew. Nothing was too small or too uninteresting to escape his eye. It was a good lesson. Dana was pleased. Teaching them to memorize a lesson would last only a day, or a week, and never carry them beyond that lesson. Teach them to be curious, to think, and to analyze, and they will continue learning forever. Of this she was certain.

"So what are we learning?"

"That it is hard for a left–handed bug to scratch his right ear."

They giggled, "Oh! Joe."

"What else? Sandy."

"I think that it is that some people live through life and

some just walk through it. They see only the tree, not the pretty and the promise of it."

Dana smiled. Some of her father was already showing in Sandy.

"Some, like Uncle Milan, see and hear everything. And some, like old man Brewer - -"

"Skip the name, Cora."

"can't even see the end of their noses." Cora was not to be denied.

It was perhaps an hour later and the discussion had become lively and thought–provoking. Dana heard it first. The rhythm of hoof beats down the road. Then the squeaking of wagon wheels and the tinkle of chains as a wagon stopped outside.

It was unusual for a wagon to stop by this early in the day. Dana went to the window to check. Bill Sugars had pulled into the schoolyard and was tying the big team to the hitching rail. There was a droop to his shoulders that warned Dana that something was wrong. Had the war taken a bad turn? Or perhaps Eber Harcourt had been wounded. Or even--.

She had not known Eber, but she had heard much about him and knew that he was the valley's direct link to the realities of the war.

Bill tapped twice on the door, then walked inside. "I would like to talk to the kids for a minute, Miss Dana, Ma'am, if I may." He was dead serious, and the children sensed the troubled tone of his voice. They settled into silence, waiting, as they had done before when bad news had come to them.

The fire had died during their discussion. Dana went to add a piece of birch from the woodshed. The wind was whistling coldly outside now and a few flakes of snow tapped against the windows. Bill waited until the door of the stove clanged shut.

"I understand that Miss Sharrow has been teaching you some things that have not been taught in schools before. Things some of us have not taught you at home. Least not as well as we should. I mean these three "L's," and he turned to look at the sheets of foolscap. This is good. Even if it just means putting names to feelings and making you open your eyes to notice things that are already in your heads. I know, too, that she is planning to add a few classes of loving, kind of mixed in with spelling and arithmetic, and with a war going on right here in our own country it sure is a good time to learn the importance of loving each other. This also means our friends in the South.

"But it is that other word on the wall that we've got to go to for a bit of advanced learning. Losing. Losing is the hardest of all to understand.

Bill stopped, as if wondering if he was on the right track. Then went on.

"Maybe it is because we avoid talking about it. It's like walking around a puddle instead of splashing right through like every kid knows is best. It's acting like we didn't know that everything in this blooming world of ours comes and goes in cycles. The sun comes up in the morning and goes down at night. The seeds sprout out of those hills out there in the springtime and freeze into nothingness in the fall. Nothing is permanent. Nothing is endless. It's just a question of how long. A million years or more like a star, or three hours like a may fly. Everything comes, lives its allotted time, and passes on."

Dana walked to the window and looked out across the cold hills. A lone herring gull sailed noiselessly on the cold wind coming in hard now off the distant lake. The brown slashings of her brother Milton's cutting slanted out southward from the yellow dunes. They were only dimly visible from this distance in the fall haze, but she knew they were there. Had those big pines died before their time or was their cycle completed? She didn't turn around as she heard Bill Sugars go on.

"This morning another cycle ended. A life important to all of us has been taken. - - It is that of our friend, Jacques Moreau."

There was the sound of quick breathing and a muffled cry from Joe Marsaque. Jacques was his friend.

Dana stiffened at the window. This gifted French boy was her friend also. His strong arms and quick mind were meant for the future. Why should he be taken? She turned for a quick glance at the empty peg where Jacques' red mackinaw and familiar blue stocking cap were missing, then turned again to the window.

Bill waited what seemed a long time, then continued. "If Jacques' cycle seems to have ended before it really started, that is one of the great mysteries of life. That, perhaps, will be one of the hard things Miss Dana will help you to understand when she teaches you how to accept this kind of loss. The important thing will be to reach out beyond the loss and remember that here in our hills cycles are rarely completed. One hungry herring gull can interrupt the cycles of a hundred young fish every day. One stroke of lightning or a strong west wind can easily end the life of one of our big trees, and even the sun can disappear in the middle of the day if a dark cloud moves in from over the lake.

But when this happens we do not go bury our heads in the sand hills. Soon another tree grows. The sun always come out again. The fish come back and things go on as before. That is the way it is meant to be, for if the clouds, with their welcome rains, did not appear, our trees and flowers would wither and die, and without the food that the herring provide, the gulls would disappear from our skies. Perhaps if a loss like this one really has meaning and a reason it is that it may strengthen and make better and wiser people of those of us who are left."

Bill could think of nothing more to say. Circuit rider Beard would put different words to it and make much of God's will and the weakness of man. He would likely be reaching for the same result as Bill was, though, to restore peace of mind to the living.

Without looking back, Bill slowly left the room and closed the door quietly behind him. He could not tell them that Jacques had been cruelly crushed beneath a tumbling load of huge logs. Jacques had lived to the end of the cycle intended for him. For the children, he would like it to end there. With the war in the East going badly and a court trial coming up, it would be a hard enough winter for them all.

Dana stayed at the window until the wagon disappeared over the hill to the east. Even though death was not an uncommon thing here, the closeness of these people made the loss seem more personal. Even though she had been here only a short time, Dana could already feel that a part of her own life had been taken. It was as though a page had been torn from a good book.

Little Cindy Sugars was whimpering quietly and back at his bench, Joe Marsaque had lost the mischievous spark in his eyes. They were wet now as he lay his head quietly on the rough table in front of him. Jacques was not just a friend. He was a special friend, a friend to look up to and talk to about personal things. They had walked the hills together. They had fished for trout in the river and swum naked in the lakes. They had secret places and plans that nobody else knew about and secret thoughts they shared only with each other.

After a while, without really knowing why, Joe rose and, walking quickly to the front of the room, slipped the bell rope from its peg and pulled. He pulled hard and long, as though something within him needed to be released. The sound of the bell rang out across the valley, struck the sand dunes across the lake and the hills beyond and returned. When the beads of sweat started to form on his forehead he stopped, hung the rope back on its peg and returned to his bench. He was expecting, perhaps hoping, to be reprimanded by Miss Dana, but she did not say a word. Finally he stood up and looked at his teacher still facing the window. "I'm sorry, ma'am," he said, and his voice cracked a little, as voices do when they are reaching a knowing age. "It just seemed like a proper thing to do."

It was still an hour before the end of the school-day. Dana would have liked to dismiss the children and taken a long walk out on the lonely dunes. But Bill had said that things should go on as before, and that was the lesson she had intended to teach them. She knew that they must go on. They must not walk around the puddle.

At the end of the wearying day it was Tom Michaels who met her at the door. It was the first time she had had a chance to talk to him alone since she had come to the valley, but now she was not in a mood to talk. At the bend of the trail Tom stopped and for a moment held her hands tightly in his own. Her heart was pounding as she waited for him to speak. But no words came. The understandings that flowed so freely between these people seemed to preclude the need for words. For Dana, though, there were questions. Was this an involuntary and overt show of affection? Or did the gesture only indicate sympathy for her in the loss of a favorite and promising student?

She turned and walked slowly up the trail to the humble cottage of the Sugars family.

Part Three
Chapter Sixteen

It was only two days before New Year's when Eber Harcourt's outfit led General Rosecrans' forty–thousand–man army into Murfreesboro and watched them take up positions along the Nashville Turnpike.

Less than seven hundred yards away, astride of Stones River, a thousand campfires of General Braxton Bragg's Army of Tennessee were already sending up curls of smoke out of the scrub cedars and low–cut hills.

All through the next day Eber stood guard and watched Old Rosie's army forming. Trains ground their way into view from the North with raw recruits from St. Louis. The hardened veterans greeted them with guarded contempt. Bounty Jumpers and Johnny Come Latelies, they were labeled. They would have to prove themselves before they could become a part of this man's army. Even so, they were welcome. Shiloh and Perrysville had taken a toll on Rosecrans' troops, and dysentery and disease had taken an even heavier one. Eber's own regiment was at little more than half strength. And many others were even worse off. Any additional troop strength was welcome, but until they were tested under fire their real worth would be suspect.

Horses, mules, and munitions followed the recruits and were unloaded and shuffled immediately to the front lines. Three–team hitches of horses or mules dragged the heavy Parrott guns through the mud of the Wilkinson Pike and up onto the wooded rises. The noise and beat of activity was constant, and the air crackled with the intensity of the action.

The officers were busy all day coming and going from the big log house that Rosie had taken for his quarters. Telegraph lines were being strung along the turnpike and couriers were busy carrying messages to all points along the front.

On the hilltops and houses behind the Confederate lines the curious people of Murfreesboro could be seen gathering in little groups to watch the expected action, and just below them the sutler's wagons were strung out across the hillside.

As night fell and the air grew cold with December chill, 44,000 tired Union soldiers were massed in the area, almost within a stone's throw of Bragg's well positioned 38,000 Confederates, and between and around them the clear water of Stones River moved on its murmuring, timeless way as though no change had come to the quiet valley.

Eber was stationed along the river on the Union's left flank that night. His orders were to stand at horse and report at once any movement in the clearings beyond the river.

It was a bright, moonlit night, cold with mid winter sharpness and pierced with frosty stars. It was quiet for a while except for the continuing distant activity along the railroad and the muffled clatter of the supper hour. The ears of Eber's horse rose and his neck muscles quivered as a Rebel scouting party moved slowly along the opposite river bank, but the good animal made no sound, and they moved on without observing his position. A cottontail fed on the frozen clover along a fence row. A dog barked in the distance.

Then from somewhere across the river the sound of a Confederate band drifted into the still night air. There was the sharp tattoo of drums, quietly at first, then building to a sharp beat as the brass joined in. Eber tightened the reins on his big bay and listened, recognizing the lilting strains of "The Bonnie Blue Flag."

There was guarded cheering as the Rebel music died, then far down on the Union right, beyond the widow Smith's house, standing dark and tall in the moonlight, a Union band answered with a rousing, reckless rendition of "Out of the Wilderness."

The cheering was louder now, and seemed to ripple from north to south and back and forth across the river as each great army joined in, unit by unit, recklessly betraying their positions. Only Eber and those like him, far out at their lonely posts, remained silent and alert.

It was quiet again for a while, as though some 80,000 minds were considering the meaning of the songs and wondering why they had left their pleasant homes to face each other here across these thin strips of cold field and water. Even the rumble of the continuing activity along the moonlit rails seemed to quiet and ponder. Many a soldier knew that he had a father, a cousin, brothers–in–law and brothers facing him across that narrow field. Like Eber, as he wondered whether Poke was somewhere in those hills across the river, many had good friends in the Southern armies.

Eber, now a tough, disciplined soldier, stood his post that night and guarded well that left flank to which he had been assigned. He did it from training and from knowing that a big fight was going to erupt at any moment. He did his job, but he was tense and scared. He had matured much since he had left home six months ago, but at times like this, alone at a distant post, his mind returned to home and he again felt like a small boy, unsure, inadequate, and afraid. What a man can see, even though the odds are overwhelming, he can prepare for and fight. Or, if necessary, he can retreat from it with measured wisdom. This, his training had taught him. But tonight, when the strength and intent of the enemy was still in doubt, when the numbers and positions of the dreaded artillery batteries were still unknown, when the well–trained cavalry units of Wheeler and Morgan could be circling somewhere in the rear, then there was good reason to know fear.

An engagement could start with a cavalry charge across the river, directly at him, or by flanking him on the left and cutting him off from his own troops. It could start with a withering volley of rifle fire from the cedars across the river, or with the thunder of cannon, fired from the trees on the far ridge. Tonight, his mind was busy and his nerves edgy. And well they should be.

But for long periods that evening there was nothing but a tense, busy silence. Then, as the mess hour passed, the sound of drums sounded out again, not far away on the Union left. Eber listened as they beat quiet and slow, as though hesitant to break the silence, then one by one, as though they had finally made up their minds, the brass sections picked up the tempo and the soulful melody of "Home Sweet Home," and the sound echoed out across the hills. "Be it ever so humble," The words ran through Eber's mind with a new significance as a deeper hush fell upon the two great armies. The rattle of chains along the rails stopped. Horses were halted by a quiet whoa, and mess kits and hats were laid quietly aside. This was a familiar sound, loved by everyone. Out here in these uncertain, snow–blotched hills it tugged at every heart.

Then from the Rebel camps, across the moonlit fields, a muffled cheer rippled through the night air. Their bands were slowly picking up the strains and joining in perfect unison. For a few brief moments in the long expanse of human time there was common thought and action on the part of two great military forces. Eber's mind, like those of some eighty thousand others, went quickly back to the hills of home, to mansions and huts, to mountains and seashores, to mothers and sisters, to teachers and lovers. To Eber, the faces of Judy and the other good people of the valley he knew so well came quickly alive. In his mind he saw their lips moving and heard their voices as they joined in the song. Slowly he became aware that the sounds he heard were very real. The voices of eighty thousand rough soldiers from both sides of the river, from the shining rails of the Nashville and Chattanooga Railroad behind him, and from the distant hills to the west where former Vice President Breckenridge's Confederate division guarded the Rebel left. All were joining in the song which was stirring common memories in the minds of the soldiers of both sides.

The sound swelled, grew recklessly louder and finally ended in a loud cheer which tailed off into a rumbling silence. Officers were gaining control of their troops. The revelry was over.

As a cold gray sun reddened the eastern sky the next morning, a barrage of cannon fire burst from the hills behind the Rebel lines. A few minutes later a wave of blue–clad soldiers waded the shallow river and struck the Union right flank behind the Widow Smith's house. All common thoughts were cast aside. The Blue and the Gray were again mortal enemies locked in deadly combat.

For three days the thunder of cannon and the screams

of dying men scarred those placid hills as the two great armies charged and countercharged. Eber had more than his share of the action, riding in and out of the breaking lines and leading charge after charge against the enemy. He saw friends fall. He saw a General's aide beheaded by a cannon ball and saw a Rebel cavalryman charge the Union lines alone after his reins were cut by a rifle ball. He heard the scream of the cannon balls and the crash of exploding canister and grape. He saw the twigs and leaves disappearing from the oak trees as the intense fire filled the air.

He saw the Widow Smith's house reduced to ashes and the smoke from it sweep across the battlefield. He felt the tug of mine balls at his sleeves and coat tails. He saw friends and new recruits falling like scythed wheat and heard them begging for the help he could not give. He had been forced to learn the priorities of war and he observed them as a good soldier must. He felt his second horse falling beneath him and from behind it he fed the last of his ammunition into his good Colt rifle, hot now in his sweaty palms. With only his pistol and sabre left, he had found his way back across the river and rejoined what was left of his company. Through three days of fighting he had emerged totally helpless with fatigue, dirty, frostbitten, and confused, but for the most part unhurt.

After a few hours of sleep on the cold, wet ground, he woke to be fed a bit of soup and be told that General

Bragg and his remaining troops were withdrawing to the south.

Eber Harcourt had indeed been lucky, for after the smoke of battle drifted away, twelve thousand Union soldiers, and perhaps twice that many Confederate dead and wounded were carried from the fields along Stones River. And for what gain? Perhaps a moral victory over Bragg who needed a decisive victory badly. Mostly it would help to open the road to Chattanooga for the Union. Nothing more. The war would still go on and yet bloodier battles would be fought before it would end. But Stones River would live forever in the minds of these men.

During the weeks following Stones River, Eber Harcourt's unit remained active. Now, after six weeks of constant riding, every bone in Eber's body was tired, bone–weary tired. Tennessee was not like Kentucky. Here there were no waving flags and cheering women. Tennessee was Reb country. Here, every move a man made was observed. Each advance was met by some kind of counter measure: skirmishes, pitched battles, harassment. A battery of artillery seemed hidden on every hill. The Rebel Wheeler's tough cavalrymen were everywhere, and somewhere, not far to the south, was General Bragg with his army, treating his wounded and rebuilding his strength.

But even more dreaded than the regular army were the bushwackers. Here they were a real and constant danger. Every ridge, every tree seemed to have its own little band.

Shoot–and–run fighters they were. Shadows of men only. Shooting from so far away that the deadly hiss of the bullet is heard, and sometimes a man killed, before the sound of the shot comes echoing down from the hills. Shoot, shoot and run, with only a wisp of dust in the distance or a mountainside of thicket and rock to mark the source, and sometimes a Rebel yell to taunt the Yankee. Shoot, and perhaps take up the plow or the axe, and wear a cunning smile to confuse and leave a man wondering if a rifle has been covered in the furrow.

Lie down at night, usually without a tent, never knowing if you will be allowed a full night's sleep. Sleep, damn it! Sleep. Even if your bed is only your blanket on the hard ground, or fence rails laid in the mud. Is that "Boots and Saddles" call? It sure is. Open your eyes, Eber Harcourt. Saddle up and move out. Yes! Yes! it's midnight, and it's cold, and only the stars are overhead to light the way. You enlisted for the war, and this is it. The word is out. The enemy has moved up in the night to the next ridge. Mount and move in. Test his strength. Locate his batteries. Drive in his pickets, lose a few. Capture a few. Draw back, or attack with force, as your captain sees fit. Dismount and wait. Wait in the cold blackness of the night for something. You don't know for what or from what direction. Mount again. Draw the Rebel's fire while your infantry and artillery maneuver for position.

All of this is the job of the cavalryman. And then, when you have done the job, you gather up your wounded and draw back so that the infantry and the artillery can carry on, all the time knowing that you will be called upon to fill the gaps, turn the flanks or protect the rear, wherever help is needed

No wonder Eber Harcourt was tired. For weeks now, this pace had been routine. It was a tiredness born long ago along Stones River and tended to like a garden. A little more each day than a man can rightfully stand. Nurtured by a war which was not a war. Thrust and retreat. Push on until it becomes too dangerous to go farther, then draw back and wait. Keep Wheeler and Morgan and Forrest too busy to cut the rails to Murfreesboro. Wait for help sometimes, but mostly wait, tense and alert, until the enemy makes a move. Keep Bragg busy and hungry while something bigger is developing, probably the big drive towards Chattanooga.

Now, six weeks after Stones River, Eber looked down from the hillside where he sat his horse in readiness. Behind him the Tennessee hills sloped upward into wooded nothingness. The kind of nothingness relished by the local bushwackers who knew its trails and lookouts. Spread out below him like a map was the Bradyville Road, bordered by open pastureland and scattered small farms. The shed houses looked small and peaceful in the morning sunshine. Each had its woodpiles, its fields, untidy with the remains of last year's crops, and its thin plume of smoke drifting straight up into the still February air.

The farms were small and somehow looked poorly kept. Hog pens and corrals were strung out at strange angles and the mule sheds were tilted and propped and warmed by corn shocks from the near fields. Not a house in the whole country, thought Eber, that could compare with the neat layout and white paint of Carl VanBolt's place. Or even his dad's or Tom Michaels'. And the hills? They would probably be pretty a little later when the spring green came, but now they were drab and colorless, lacking the warm green of the tall pines back home.

Down the dirt road from the north the long wagon train Eber was guarding inched slowly along. The mules lagged in the harness unless urged into action by the tired teamsters. Faintly, on the cold morning air, Eber could hear the cursing of the drivers and the barking of the farmer's hounds. A pump was squeaking now as a friendly farmer offered water for the mules. The sounds were far away but they drifted up sharp and clear on the mountain air. It would be a long trip, thought Eber. He had not seen a mule or a hog in their two days out, and little corn. The country had already been cleaned, most likely by foragers and Bragg's army. Only the fact that Union foragers paid for what they took made it possible to get some of the hidden stores of the farmers. Besides, with their hogs and mules already gone, they had little need for their hidden corn.

There had been shooting up ahead during the morning. Eber suspected it must have been bushwackers since no real fight had developed.

The long line of wagons moved on and Eber scanned the hills to the south. Time to move on with them. Foraging duty was dangerous. A cavalry outfit likes to be free to move. Move in deep and get out before the Rebs can organize against you. But you can't move with sixty wagons to care for, nor can they be deserted if fighting can save them. He prodded his horse and moved out from behind the apple tree he had used as a shield from the wooded hills. As he did the hiss of a musket ball from somewhere above him hit a branch and sang off across the fields. He spurred his mount into a short sprint, but no more shots came, and he could not even guess the source of that one. Damn this kind of fighting, Eber thought. A man can be killed in his saddle out here in this cold mountain air and never know what happened. Eber had seen more than one horse returning with an empty saddle, and no one the wiser. It was no wonder that few Bushwackers were ever taken prisoner, or that they were hated almost as much by the farmers as they were by the Union Army because of the fire they brought down on the whole countryside.

The day passed, with the wagons scarcely half–filled. They would have to go on. Only the side roads and the little farms up in the hills were still rich with food. Everything else had been stripped by Bragg's men as they retreated out of Kentucky.

They bivouacked that night without cover. They put

out plenty of pickets, though, and cavalry videttes far out on the hills, standing at horse. They were lucky. The night was quiet. If they had trouble it would probably come on the way back to Murfreesboro, after the wagons had been filled.

In the morning they were on the road again, knowing that a Rebel cavalry had crossed in front of them during the night. They were breaking up now, with a wagon or two separating long enough to draw back up the side trails. The country was growing rougher and the little farms high up in the hills were more productive of the supplies they needed. If not for Morgan's constant raids on the railroad from Louisville to Nashville they would have little supply problem. But Morgan's men were doing their job well. It was equally true that if the railroad had not been cut at the Holston River by Eber's own outfit, General Bragg would be getting supplies from the East. Now both armies must forage to feed their men and animals.

By mid afternoon the train was heavy with corn and fodder. Even a few hogs had been found in the hills. These had been tied with leg ties and thrown squealing into the wagons. The main force of the foragers had halted to make preparations to return. The mules were freed of the wagons and were grazing, still in harness, on the grass starting to show green along the roadsides.

Two wagons were making a last pull up into the hills to the east where a muddy trail marked the way. The main body of the cavalry had ridden south, searching the country for any party which might give them problems on their return trip. The Rebel scouting party must certainly be somewhere nearby.

Eber Harcourt shifted in his saddle to ease his tired back. Seems as though there is no level ground in Tennessee and it always slopes in the wrong direction to ease weary bones. The timber crowded close to the trail as it wound up into the hills, so a guard was forced to find his way through the brush and openings of the side hills. Eber found an opening and moved forward and upward the better to observe the progress of the wagons below him.

As he cleared the crest of the next ridge he found himself looking down into the prettiest little valley he had ever seen. On all sides the mountains rose gently to craggy, wooded peaks, with now and then a thrust of bare granite piercing them. Down from the north the valley formed and slowly spread out to an area of possibly eighty acres of gently rolling meadow and rich red soil. Through the center a run of water sparkled clear in the afternoon glow, wandered across in front of a neat but unpainted frame cottage, and dropped down to the south along the trail where the wagons were struggling with the steep ascent.

Behind the house was the usual array of sheds, typical of the country. There was an outhouse, a chicken coop, a smokehouse and a combination barn and pig pen, with the muddy corrals stretched out and up the hill beyond. Somehow it was a mite neater than the usual layout and the plow and harrow were out of the fields and probably under cover.

Something about the place held Eber tight, however. There was a coldness about it that did not fit the neatness of the plan. A mule stood sleepily in the sun of the barnyard. Evidently it had escaped the eye of Bragg's foragers. No hogs or chickens were in sight, though. Bushwhackers would have taken these. There were gingham curtains showing at the windows, but although there was a long woodpile in the backyard, no sign of the usual wisp of smoke was coming from a cooking fire. The corn crib was more than half full, the yellow of it showing clearly between the slats. More than enough to carry them to the next corn time. Eber squirmed uneasily on his mount. He would like to ride down and warn the wagons that things did not look right, then take the other guards to check it out. His orders were to ride the hills, however, to guard against the sharpshooting hit and run bushwackers. Besides, the wagons had their guards and even now they were fording the stream in front of the cottage. If there were Bushwackers set for them they would have fired by now. Eber relaxed. Strange how a man can sense danger sometimes that he cannot see. Sometimes that is not there at all. Maybe that was there yesterday, or last week. The unknown chemistry of the body that says, Watch out! before a snake strikes, or a storm gathers in the western sky.

But the stream was crossed. The wagons were waiting out front. The guards were posted and they were waiting the knock on the door. Eber's muscles were still tight. His Colt rifle was held at ready and his heart beat slowly but more firmly. Somehow this house was different from the rest. More as if it were his own.

There was no answer to the knock and a gun butt was applied to the door. It swung easily open. The near guards drew in as the soldiers inside waved to them, and Eber could see them circling the house, examining the siding, picking at a broken window and moving out to the barn.

After what seemed a long time the guards came from the barn carrying a man, lifeless and limp. Shovels were fetched from the wagons and soon four graves had been dug into the green of the hillside behind the barn. Then from the house came three more quilt–covered forms to be laid gently in the prepared places. Hats were removed and a prayer was said. The shovels finished their work while others moved the wagons to the corn crib and loaded them with the yellow grain. The dead must be properly cared for, but the living must go on. That is war.

Eber, from his place on the ridge, sat quietly and returned his hat to his head. This was not the first such scene the war had exposed him to, but this one stirred him deeply. Perhaps it was the beauty and serenity of this hidden valley, laying yellow and warm in the afternoon sun. He supposed it might have a strange relationship to the hills back home. Perhaps it was the knowledge that part of those lifeless bundles were the women of the house. Something about the way they were carried and the respect of the service told him that they were not Bushwackers, or even soldiers. Strong men far from home have a way of showing respect for womenfolks, especially when they are in their own homes and caught up in the tragedies of a war they never wanted.

Every soldier, even the toughest of them, and every outfit has its share of corruption, but somewhere, at some time all of these men have known the touch of a mother, a sister, or a girl friend whom they hold in a hidden reservoir of memories. A spot that is brought to life and stirred deeply at times like this. It is not the good times that make men, thought Eber. It is the hard!

The day's work was done. Whatever had happened had happened. Now the filled wagons were squeaking their way back across the creek and down the steep grade. A cold green glow was rimming the ridge to the west and already the level of the valley was deep in the cool evening shadows. They would have just time to catch the main body of the forage train before they bivouacked for the night.

Eber spurred his horse lightly and drifted down into the meadow. He was acting against orders and he knew it, but a stronger force was compelling him down into the valley for a closer look. He allowed his horse a drink as he forded the stream where the row of flat rocks had been laid to make a foot crossing. He rode up to the house, noticed the siding splintered by gunfire, dismounted, and went inside.

It was a neat enough home for Tennessee hill country, except for the shattered windows, splintered castings, and signs of fighting everywhere. There were rocking chairs and a quilt–covered sofa, and a buffet well stocked with good English china. Eber entered into the kitchen. It was much like theirs back home, with a big wood range with a well–limed reservoir and a warming oven, scrubbed wood floors, and an oilcloth–covered table. He went through the back shed, with its boots lined up neat and warm coats still on the wooden pegs. Back in the parlor he noticed the overheated andirons sagging into the white ashes of a late fire, the huge black walnut mantel and, to the right, a bookshelf with a small tier of books. There were some McGuffey's Readers, Pilgrim's Progress, Uncle Tom's Cabin, White Jacket and Leaves of Grass. No ordinary hill people these. Only Bill Sugars and maybe Tom Michaels had books like these back home.

Eber turned again to notice the clutter and the dark stains beneath the windows. They had put up a good fight. Then he turned to the last book, hesitated a moment, and opened it. It was a well–worn Bible. On the last page he found what he was looking for. There was a considerable list of names written in a neat script, each with a short description to properly and lovingly identify it. Eber's eyes were quickly drawn to the last two--

Porter Washington Campbell—Born February 24, 1843. Named after his Grandpa Porter, but we call him "Poke" because he was so slow a coming.

Virginia Catherine Campbell—Born October 9, 1845. Catherine for her mother and Virginia because her Pa thought it the prettiest place he had ever lived.

Slowly Eber closed the book, returned it to the shelf and sat on the sofa with his head in his hands. The warning had been there. That strange, cold feeling he had known up there on the hill. He should have left from there. He should have known better than to break orders and come to this broken place. But he knew that he could not have left. Nothing could have kept him from knowing the truth about this remote valley. The whole truth might never be known, but the pieces of the puzzle were all there. The bushwacker in the barn, probably one of several. The presence of their own foraging expedition and its cavalry escort stirring up the people. The Rebel scouting party, probably part of Wheeler's riders, out searching for us. The bushwhackers had thought it was Union Cavalry and opened fire. Most likely they had the help of their evening liquor. The rest, a blind, senseless shootout in the black of the night with an innocent family the victims.

Eber picked up his rifle and walked out into the evening chill. The convoy was out of sight down the wooded trail. His horse stood waiting. But standing

304 • R. Lewis Jessop

patiently with its reins in his hand was an old black man.
Small but sturdy he was, with his hat in his hand and
patches of steel–gray lambswool hair bordering each side
of a shiny bald head. Eber's gun came up in automatic
surprise, but the old man showed no fear. He only looked
down and shuffled uneasily. "Reckon I surprised you a
mite." A bit of humor showed in the twinkle of the dim-
ming eyes.

"A bit."

He shuffled again and looked embarrassed at the asking. "I was kinda hoping, kinda praying, I reckon, that
you might take me with you when you ride. You won't be
stealing, he quickly added. I'm a free nigger. Was freed
down Greenville way and lately been living here with
Mister and Missy Campbell."

"You belonged to them?"

"Not 'zackly."

"You worked for them?"

"Yes, suh, I fixed to work, voluntary–like, as long as
they wanted me." He looked around him, as though leaving the little valley would be a hard thing. His eyes turned
and rested a moment on the four fresh graves on the slope
of the hill, then came back to Eber's. They were glistening
wet in the evening glow, and his voice broke a little. "But
I reckon they won't be a needing me any more."

"Seems as though," sighed Eber.

"I'm old, I reckon, but I'm still strong. I can cook or cut
wood or mend saddles. I got no better place to go, not

now."

The camp could use him, thought Eber. There were others helping. He came down the steps. It would be dark in an hour. They would have to ride to catch up before the wagons reached bivouac. He took the reins and swung up into the saddle, motioning for the old man to mount behind him. But when he looked down, he was standing stiff and alert, as though aware of some danger. Then without warning, he threw his body against Eber's legs, trying vainly to shield Eber's body. It was too late. The sing of the bullet preceded his move and Eber felt the shock of the impact drive dead into his left thigh. His head swam dizzily and sickness crept into his stomach. He was dreamily aware of the old man bracing him up in the saddle. His horse remained nervous, but steady. Good! His right foot was being pulled from it's stirrup and the colored man was swinging up behind him. Strong arms held him swaying in the saddle and they were slowly wading the creek and heading down the trail.

Hang on, Eber Harcourt, hang on. Not much pain, but so dizzy. Come on world, hold still. Hold still and we will make it yet. It has not been a good day for you, Eber Harcourt.

Chapter Seventeen

Deserter Poke Campbell sharpened the stick of apple-wood with his sheath knife and carefully skewered a freshly skinned squirrel onto it. His little fire was now a red glow of embers in the fading light. He nestled the butt end of the skewer under a slice of ledge rock and eased another one under it to hold it over the coals. He leaned back now and let his eyes wander upward into the blue green forever of the evening sky. A crow, separated from the afternoon flock, was winging silently towards its nesting grounds in the hills, pursued relentlessly by two angry kingbirds. "Good luck, old boy," Poke said, half aloud, and wondered if he was talking more to himself than to the bird.

Down below him to the west lay the valley from which he had recently climbed, with the long trail to Shelbyville fading into the shadows of the used–up day.

He turned the other way. Twenty miles to the east the humped up peaks of the Cumberland Plateau thrust themselves up into the red of the afternoon sun. Poke looked longingly at them.

Somewhere off in the shadows of that glow, Pop and Ma and Virginia would be finishing their evening meal. Pop was probably neating up the fire in the big stone hearth and adding the evening log. Mom and Virginia would soon finish the dishes, then they would light the lamps and sit by the fire, Ma with her balls of yarn and polished maple knitting hooks and Jinny with a book. I wonder if they have any new ones, he mused. Virginia must have read those a dozen times by now.

The fire glowed warm in his face. He unrolled his blanket and spread it against the rocks behind the fire to dry and warm. Wish I had a pail of beans, he thought. A bit of a hole with those good coals in it and a pail of beans and sow belly and molasses nestled into them, then covered with more hot coals and a layer of dirt. Boy, oh boy, would they be good come morning! But he had no beans or sowbelly or molasses. Only a measly little gray squirrel sizzling on a spit. Maybe he should feel lucky to have that. Some of the farmers he had seen along the Shelbyville road had had nothing but corn meal for a month, and that from hidden cribs up in the hills.

I wonder how dad is. He had come to worry about his Dad. Poke realized now that he had been looking gaunt for a year before he had joined the army and the fire was fading from the quick gray eyes. Men worry more than people think and he was sure that Dad saw things coming with the coming of a war that most Southern people couldn't see. Dad read a lot and was a smart one for it.

You can't fight a war with cotton, he had told them. It takes steel and steam engines and cannon and gunpowder to win a war. Jeff Davis had best be looking to old England. If England will help the South they might win. If not, those foundries in Richmond and Portsmouth will never carry us through a long war.

Pop won't be reading now, less'n he has a new newspaper. He will be just sittin', looking at the fire with that quiet look in his eyes. He will be thinking about me, most likely, wondering if I'm still down there with General Bragg's big army south of Murfreesboro, and wishing I was home so we could go turkey-hunting up in the hills like we used to.

He bent his lean frame to turn the squirrel, now browning nicely over the fire. Drops of fat were dripping onto the hot coals, sending up the sharp tang of charcoal and fresh meat into the cold night air. With each drop of fat came a yellow burst of flame that flickered off of the rocks behind him and lit up the green pinions of the larch trees out front.

Down through the trees below a lamp glowed in a cabin in the valley, flickered, went out then glowed again. Maybe I could have got me a warm meal and a bed down there, thought Poke. But a man can't be sure these days. The war has set people up. Especially here in Tennessee where no one knows what is in other people's hearts. Some are loyal Unionists, some are Yankee–hating Secesh, and others are not really stubborn either way. They are just drifting, saying yes to anybody and just wishing that the fighting had never started so that they could be on with their business of raising their crops and trying to put food on the table. Here in Tennessee it is hard to know what it is safe to say when a man opens his door to a stranger. War is hell on soldiers, but it can be mighty hard on people at home, too, when they get caught up in the heat and the fear and the hard times of it. Old Eber is lucky. His wife and kinfolks are far away and safe up there in Michigan.

Thinking of Eber stirred old memories. It had been strange, meeting him twice. Once down there in Mississippi, then again up in the hills outside of Bardstown. It was strange, too, that it had been a Yankee from Michigan who, in those two brief meetings, had stirred that strange chemistry that brings people close to one another. Eber had become the one he liked most to talk to maybe because he was a farmboy like Poke. I wish he was here now, thought Poke. I'd like for him to meet Pa and Mom and Jinny. Then he would really understand us Tennessee folks.

The squirrel was ready now. He cut a leg from it and gnawed on it hungrily. He wished that he had some salt, but it tasted good. He had not really ever had a full belly since Murfreesboro.

Murfreesboro, and Stones River. His wandering thoughts left Eber and home and traveled back to those hard days. Those days at Stones River had turned him homeward. He looked down at his tattered gray uniform pants and felt the thin legs they covered. Stones River had been a nightmare that would not leave his mind. The sights and sounds of it stayed with him and the terrible slaughter of those days of battle numbed his senses.

On the third day, when he was already near dead with tiredness, he had watched Breckenridge's division make its desperation charge across that open field on the east flank. Batteries of Union artillery along the river fired straight into the exposed division; the brave men turned and fell like gray leaves before a cold fall wind. Through the smoke and curtain of heavy fire from both sides, Yankee reinforcements had crossed the river, now red with blood and litter. Breckenridge's men were slowly forced back.

It had been a desperate, cruel attempt to salvage a military victory, but from Poke's sharpshooter's vantage point it was a pathetic sacrifice of nearly eighteen hundred good Southern men left scattered across the fields, killed or wounded for a lost cause.

When it was over he had laid aside his rifle and sat for a long time, sick, both in heart and in stomach, from the sight of it.

Since then he had become fearful of lying down at night because both sleep and the lack of it returned him to the battle. The whistle of shot sang in his ears and the cries of the wounded haunted him until exhaustion brought sleep or a rising sun brought a new day.

It was no wonder that his exhaustion and his opinion of the war had turned Poke's thoughts more and more to his pa's words and to the peaceful life he had known on the little farm. Never had his mother or Virginia seemed so dear to him. Their faces haunted him like the faces of those dying men, and the overpowering thoughts of home carried him from the big camp to this mountainside. If he was to die fighting like those others on a bloody, frozen field, or as a deserter at least he would see Mom and Virginia again first.

And damned if it didn't feel good, making his own decisions once more.

The next morning was bitter cold in spite of the oak stub still smoldering on the fire. Frost showed white on the larch trees and long fingers of ice hung from the rocks behind him. Poke Campbell reached from the blankets and slid another stick of oak onto the graying coals. The sun was rising somewhere over the rocks behind him and its glow was sliding down like a curtain into the tops of the larch trees, burning off the frost as it came, leaving them dripping and fragrant in early spring warmth.

He stirred from his blanket, stretched his long legs and sat facing the fire. He was troubled and lonely and homesick.

After a while he swung the remains of the squirrel back over the fire and stood with his back to the welcome heat as he waited for the meat to warm. When it started to sizzle, he removed it and nibbled the remains of the meat from the bones. He would have no more food unless some farmer offered it. His pride would not let him knock on doors while he was still wearing his greys. Besides, he would stick mostly to the hills from here on. He rolled his blanket tightly and tied it over his left shoulder, then checked his gun and started southward through the hills.

By late afternoon he crossed the McMinnville Pike and cut southeastward into the foothills of the Cumberlands. A light wind had come up during the day and here it was sweeping gently up from the valley, rustling the leaves still hanging brown and dry on the oak trees and bringing with it the faint tang of woodsmoke from the farms scattered through the valley. This would disappear soon. If Poke's memory was good, no more cabins or people existed for nigh onto six miles. Then, if his direction was good, he would break down into the back end of their little valley, and down at the far end would be Pa and Ma and the little cabin that was home. His hunger came sweeping back at the thought of it, but he could wait. He was even more hungry to see Ma and Pa and Jinny.

In another hour Poke cleared the last ridge north of home. He had been dead center in his reckoning and now the country was familiar. He and Pa had hunted turkey and deer all through these hills. They had pulled mistletoe for Ma from the oak trees and bittersweet from the briers in the fall. In the spring they had fished the little stream and brought big bouquets of dogwood home when they were late for supper. They had sat by the stream in August, when they knew the trout wouldn't be there, and talked about Pa's adventures. He had told Poke about his Grandpa Campbell who had left the hills of Scotland to become a writer and a poet, and of his own travels to Holland and Norway before he came to the harbor at Jamestown and jumped his ship to work the good land in America. Poke understood now how he had gathered all of the history and common sense that he had tried to teach his son.

It was less than a mile now to the cabin, and the ground along the winding stream was good for walking. Poke did not go that way, though. As he came out of the hills he thought he could see a wagon at the corn crib, and the bustling of blue about the barn. His heart sank. He was hungry and tired from two days of travel with little food. Was there more trouble ahead? Was this why something within him had said - go home - go home? Was this the real reason he had felt he must walk away from the great encampment south of Murfreesboro, even though he knew he could be shot dead for doing it? Was this why those words of his father had refused to leave his mind but had kept repeating to him, "When a man's heart tells him that he must climb a mountain, he should never remain in the valley?" That was the way his father had lived, and although it had led him to be called a drifter, it had also led him to much knowledge and happiness. Especially up here in these Tennessee hills. From old Scotland to England to the high seas to the New World he had always followed the call of his adventurous heart. And he had found his mountain, right here.

Poke's first impulse was to run. Run up that last mile of the valley and face whatever danger was there. But that would have been foolhardy. There was a war being fought and these hills had become a part of it. He must not lose his head. He walked fast, though, his heart pounding, as the thickets of blackberry and sumac tore at his clothing and clung to his skin.

From the side of the ridge east of the house he could see over the tops of the trees sloping downward below him and down onto the roofs of the buildings. A scurry of pigeons was circling above the barn, and higher up the disappearing sun glinted off the wings of a solitary buzzard riding the evening breeze that had now died to a whisper down in the shadows of the valley.

No smoke was coming from the chimney of the cabin. Poke's hands turned cold and a shudder rippled up his back. No cow, no hogs, no mules, and the gate of the corral drooped open and unsupported. Then, through the evening distance, his eyes picked up the fresh–turned piles of dirt on the slope behind the barn. One, two, three and an extra one. Each with its cross of stones laid neat on top. He swore, a long, hoarse string of words which sounded strange to him, and rubbed a torn sleeve across eyes which refused to stay clear. "No! no! no! not Mom and Ginny, too." His whole being surged in disbelief that what he feared could possibly be true. He felt his body sag weakly back against the rock ledge behind him. Felt the wetness of dripping water soak through his clothing, but didn't care. Saw again the knowing circle of the turkey buzzard in the fading light, and sagged to the ground with his head in his hands.

After a moment or two Poke Campbell's head cleared. The truth had struck deep. He had thought this remote valley would be safe, but a war reaches into far and distant places. Why had he ever left it? He should have stayed here with Ma and Jinny. He shouldn't have listened to the talk in town. It was fool's talk, anyway. He should have listened more to his Pa, who really knew. But he hadn't. He thought to help more by joining the armies which were supposed to protect places like this. Thought, like the rest, that the South would quickly win. It just didn't turn out that way.

His eyes were drawn back to the darkening hillside with its story, then to the familiar sheds now looking cold and different, then to the little house.

Now, for the first time, his eyes caught the movement of a horse in the shadows behind the house, a horse and a blue–clad soldier just climbing into the saddle. He had never before felt real hate for a blue uniform, but now his body surged with it. His fifty–eight calibre Bridesburg musket came up quickly, with a mini ball cartridge in place. It could kill a man a half–mile away. The shadows were deep, though. He could barely see his target in the dying light. The nine–pound gun was heavy in his tired hands. He steadied it against a limb. Up now. Up slowly and squeeze. Easy, now, it's near three hundred yards and downhill. Miss and you lose your one chance to avenge this terrible deed. What a strong, useless passion vengeance is. His Pa had taught him this. But it was done.

The shot was off, the crack of it echoing back from the hills across the way. Had he hit his mark? He could not see and he didn't care. Perhaps he hoped that he had not. Maybe it was some young soldier like Eber Harcourt on that distant horse. Someone with a wife so much like Jinny, waiting back there among the hills of Michigan. It didn't matter. It had to be done. They had to learn.

He stepped back down and aimlessly gathered sticks for a fire. He would stay here until morning and take a last look down below. After that, he wasn't sure. He might go back to General Bragg's big camp. But soldiering had lost its call. His war had been lost. His Pa was right, as he always had been. The South was a-going to get licked. Now that Abe Lincoln had called for a freeing of the slaves England would never join with the South, and the blockade would slowly strangle them. England had always hated slavery. That's probably why old Abe had done it although everybody knew he had wanted to all along.

He uncorked the canteen and took a drink of cold spring water. It felt good to his lips but lay heavy in his empty stomach. People had to go on. Walking, lots of walking sounds good. Maybe I'll keep right on walking.

Right past Murfreesboro and Jackson and Memphis and on to the west. Maybe I can fetch me a mountain of my own.

Chapter Eighteen

The morning of the trial dawned cold, the cruel, penetrating cold that settles over Michigan in February. There had been snow during the night and now it was on the move, pushed here and there over the smooth surfaces born of last month's thaw. It tailed out behind the cedars along the mill pond and skittered in ribbons across the patches of blue–gray ice.

Most likely it would stay cold. February, here, usually does. Cold, but sunny and clear. A blue cold that taunts a body to come out into the clear beauty of the sunshine. Come out, but beware, because February deceives. It carries, in its clear blue skies, the promise of spring. But the promise only. The real truth is that the frost is drives sharp and deep. Even Lake Michigan is frozen far out, a jagged sea of broken floes. The ice on the inland lake is now so thick that cutting it for storage is difficult. The man who ventures out now must check frequently for the white skin of frostbite, for in the stillness of February's cold, a finger or a cheek can be found frozen before one is aware of it.

The parties in the sleighs from the valley were well aware of the cold. They had grouped together in the two sleighs so that they could better keep each other warm. They had heated stones by their fires during the night, wrapped them in blankets, and placed them in the straw–covered bottoms of the sleighs. There were plenty of warm coats, scarfs and blankets, and Mina was wrapped in Milan's buffalo robe.

They were in good spirits, though. The fun of the sleigh ride with old friends kept the blood lively. There had been shouting and laughing as they left their homes, but now, as they neared Hart, and the cold began to penetrate, they became quiet. Only the squeak of the packed snow against the runners of the sleigh, the rhythm of the sleigh bells on Bill Sugar's team, and the swish of the horse's hooves competed with the sighing of the cold wind in the pine trees along the road.

Mina Michaels had slept little that night. During February the lake makes its ice, and the stillness of the night had been broken by the thunder of it. It had wakened her first with a high–pitched crack, like the sound of Milan's rifle. Then it had rumbled a little, like the distant sound of heat lightning in the spring. As the pressure of the expanding ice built up, though, it started a thundering roll. First, far off where the cold sides of the gray dunes met the water, then rolling like a battery of army cannon until it reached its thundering climax far down on the south shore.

In the silver moonlight, she had seen the results from her window. A blue, snakelike, ridge of ice had buckled upward from the pressure and now lay glittering and fresh across the whiteness of the lake.

During her first years in this country these sounds had frightened her. The awesome power of it had held her awake, and she would remain awake, waiting for the next crack which might, or might not, come. Usually it did not. With the pressure relieved, the lake would relax and fall back into its insulated silence.

Now the fears had left her. Like the other strange ways of the lakes and hills, this, too, had become a part of her as all the other tumultuous sounds and silences of this country were now familiar to her. Like Milan, her close association with them had become a love affair. Each one, from the calls of the meadowlarks in the spring to the deep, white silence of February, was something to be anticipated, something to be enjoyed anew, a new page to be turned in a good book, something familiar enough to satisfy old longings, but different enough to add a new dimension to the old memories.

Mina had pushed the quilts aside, found a warm robe and slippers and gone to the window. Outside a moon, near to full, was hanging motionless in the southwest. A few wisps of clouds drifted in the sequined beyond. The valley lay, silver blue in the moonlight, framed within its circle of mysterious lake, brooding pine forests, now hanging deep with accumulated snow, and the copper dunes with silver robes. All was unnaturally quiet, except the wild cry of a wolf, somewhere far into the hills to the north.

At the south end of the lake a thin streak of smoke lifted straight up from the camp where Mill Sharrow and his men rested. Another rose from among the trees that hid Louise and Jimmie's cabin on the near shore. All else lay lifeless and still. Except for the white scar across the hills where the trees had been taken, the country was the same as when she and Ganus had come there, twenty–five years before.

Mina knew, though, that that scar was a tumor, born by the lust of men like Mill Sharrow and nursed by the liquor from John Stronach's saloon. It was something that would not go away, neither here in their valley nor anywhere else across their beautiful state. As long as those big pines lasted, the cutting would continue. The trees were wealth, and wealth brought big houses, land, and power to those who lusted for it. Only on land owned by people like her and her kind was there hope that generations of the future might know the majesty and the beauty that was theirs.

Out in the parlor Mina picked up the iron poker, settled the logs into the burned–out fire and added a fresh one on top. It burst quickly into flame. Not wanting to start a fire in the big range yet, she brought the coffee pot to the fireplace and hung it on the iron hook. Sleep had left her. She might as well enjoy the beauty of the night.

The smell of coffee and the crackling of the fire brought

Tom to the parlor, rubbing his eyes at the big west window. "Almost too much beauty out there tonight to waste by sleeping, isn't there?"

"I thought so, Tom. People miss a heap of living by getting into set habits. I only wish your father could have lived to enjoy more of these good years."

"It would be nice, Mom, but wishing won't make it so."

"Maybe wishing won't, but I like to believe that he lived ninety years of experiences, good times, and memories in those fifty years that he walked this earth. After all, time is only one way to measure a life. Years can be an empty bowl unless they are filled with experiences, love, and happiness."

"His bowl was well filled, Mother."

"I believe that is true. But his experiences in the old country were not all good. The scar of a Janizary's sword was proof of that. He knew some of the best of times and some of the worst of times. But perhaps that is what makes for a full life."

"I have been the fortunate one, Mom. No Napoleons, no Janizaries, no religious zealots to mar my years. Until now, we in this country have been a fortunate people. The men who laid the foundations of our country were dedicated builders."

"But, most important, Tom, is that they laid all personal ambitions aside, perhaps for the first time in history, and applied their pens for the lasting good of all people of their country."

"And now, with a civil war being fought, and selfish interests appearing everywhere, we are about to find out if the people of our generation, and generations to come, can continue building, or if they are about to tear apart and bury the stones so carefully laid."

"I am sure we will continue to build, Tom. At least I have confidence in Lincoln."

"I do, too, Mother, but our kind of government is people, all people. Lincoln is only one. Jeff Davis and Calhoun are another kind. Mill Sharrow is another. They are not thinking of the good of all people. I would like to think that, in our small way, this trial will add one more small brick to the building. That is the only thing that is holding me. I have the thought that I should be doing more."

"There is still time."

Tom left the window and stood with his back to the fire, studying his mother. "Then you are not disappointed that I have returned to the valley even though, perhaps, Lincoln needs me?"

"Until Mill Sharrow is fitted to a harness, Tom, the valley needs you."

"And for a while, at least, I need it," admitted Tom. "You raised me an Indian, Mother. An Indian that likes the lonely hills and the feel of the wind off the lakes in his lungs. You raised me an Indian, then taught me law. Your Indian does not adjust well to his profession."

Mina laughed her little laugh. "So now you believe that

you are a misfit. A hawk among the chickadees. But does-
n't every valley need a hawk? Perhaps one can fly as far
from a pine tree as from a tall building."

Tom whistled softly to himself. He had been concerned
that she would not understand. As usual, he had underestimated her. He found cups and poured coffee for both
of them.

"While I was at the university I gave the other lives a
fair trial, Mother. I traveled home with friends to distant
cities. I felt the many walls a prison. I rode in the carriages
of the rich, and saw Milan walking easy across the hills. I
danced with pretty girls in perfumed gowns, and saw
Jeanie VanBolt singing in the VanBolt kitchen. I tasted the
smoke of industry and hankered for the stink of cows
moving out into the morning fog. I ate lobster and cod's
tongue on silver and linen, but longed for buttermilk pancakes and maple syrup, and side pork frying in cold valley air."

Mina laughed merrily. "You know what you have just
told me, Tom? You were homesick. Don't let that alone tie
you to our valley."

"I am tied by nothing, Mother, but a better understanding of people. The ones I saw out there valued wealth.
And as they prospered they became independent. As they
became independent they stopped needing each other
and knowing each other. It seemed to me that they were
tossing aside a lot more than they were catching up with.
We have something good here, Mom. I really want noth-

ing more."

The silver–blue had turned to gray–white as the moon disappeared and a cold, blustery morning set in. Milan appeared, still stretching the galluses on his wool pants. He splashed the cold water of the wash basin over his hands and face and grinned as he wiped dry on the coarse towel.

"Once, up on the Saint Louis River, Joe Parks and I got caught running the rice marshes. It came dark, and we were lost, so we bedded down in our canoe to wait for morning."

Milan helped himself to coffee.

"'Bout midnight the moon came out bright. I hear a noise out in the rice, 'Quack, quonk,' kind of quiet–like. Then on the other side, 'Quonk, quonk.' Then all over the damn marsh they started in, 'Quaack, quonk, quoonk, quoonk, quaack, quaack.' You know those damn ducks don't know the moon from the sun."

"Are you trying to tell us something, Milan?"

"No, Milan sighed wearily. Just thinking of my poor friend Joe. He sure don't get much sleep."

Tom was starting the fire in the big range now. "People who lay awake listening to other people seldom get much sleep."

"Oh! Joe and me, we are not the kind to listen. We pay no attention. Just go right back to sleep.

Mina smiled as she got out the big iron skillet. "What sounds good for a cold morning breakfast, Milan?"

"Mmm, It sure seems like a long time since we've had good buttermilk pancakes, with maple syrup."

"And fresh side pork?" Tom suggested.

Milan rubbed his hands in pure joy, then went to put an arm over Tom's broad shoulders. "And fresh side pork, mmm, mmm."

The sleighs made the last turn around the mill pond and the neighbors wiggled life into cold bodies again as they jingled up the hill and tied up to the hitching rails outside the new courthouse.

Inside, the building was fragrant with the smell of fresh–cut pine. Lyman Corbin had provided both the building and the land as the customary inducement to move the county seat from Whiskey Creek. Since it would be a financial windfall to Lyman's business interests he had spared nothing to make the building a fine one. Many of the sheathing planks, cut at his own mill, were of clear white pine twenty–four inches wide.

This morning the smell of the fresh wood was blending with the tang of smoke from the two big stoves. John Barr had been up at daybreak firing them, knowing the big new rooms would be well chilled by the piercing cold.

A scattering of townspeople were already on the benches when the sleighs poured their loads of passengers out from the windswept morning and into the warmth of the courthouse. There was much stomping and laughter as they removed their outside layers of clothing and huddled around the stoves, now cherry red from John Barr's birch fires.

Tom left the rest and found his way to the plaintiff's table, his broad, flat shoulders looking uncomfortable in his store–bought suit. He spread his notes out in front of him. An orderly array of paper might intimidate the opposition, he thought, smiling. It might also be an embarrassment if the big door at the side of the hall was suddenly opened to the brisk wind. He found pieces of pine from the wood shed, placed one on each end of the notes and glanced up at the new clock, ticking peacefully above the noise of the gathering court. February was a slow month for the farmers and townspeople. They would relish the excitement of a trial. But besides the townspeople and the people from the valley, Tom saw a scattering of strangers. Big lumbermen from Saginaw and Muskegon, he was sure, and reporters from the capital at Lansing and the lumbering centers along with the color- ful Indians from the village to the east.

All had a stake in the coming trial because it was a microcosm of a bigger problem. This trial was perhaps the beginning, or the end, of a trend in behavior of an indus- try throughout the country. Tom felt a new pride at being a part of it, and a quiet determination to win his case.

He looked back again over the assembling crowd. It seemed ridiculous that this trial should be necessary to support their claims of ownership of land and trees, but it was happening, and it could continue to happen unless it was halted at an early stage.

Milan had come in, after helping to settle the horses into the sheds Lyman had thoughtfully provided. As he took a seat beside Mina, his tall figure attracted all eyes. On her other side was the comforting presence of Bill and Mary Sugars. Turning, she could see the other old neighbors lined up on the benches behind her. It would be a tense time for them, but it was nice to see them all solidly together once more. More than anyone else, they were at once involved. If the arrogant moves of Mill Sharrow were not brought to a halt, either he, or any of the other outfits starting to operate in the country would certainly be nipping at those hills where the big pines were so attractive. Almost every one of these old settlers held a section of those big pines. Any one of them could be a future victim of some land–hungry logger.

Tom's mind went back to the night of the party and he remembered the quiet words of assurance as the significance of the fire became clear to them. "We are with you, Tom," they had said. In the anger of the moment, he had been eager to join in the fight to protect the big trees. Now, as he waited for the rest of the court to appear he wondered if he was capable of their trust. He would be carrying a heavy load. He looked again at the clock, still ticking on above the buzzing hum of voices and the crackling of wood stoves. He was anxious to get started. He would be facing older and more experienced men, but let them come.

It was eight fifty–five before Mill Sharrow appeared.

He was neatly dressed in dark wool pants and red wool shirt. Intentionally unpretentious, no doubt. It would not be wise for him to appear too much out of step with the people of the countryside. His lawyers, Warren Clay, of Muskegon, and a stranger, who Tom did not know, were dressed in dark suits. As they made their way to their table, they stopped and introduced themselves to Tom. He stood and shook their hands, but studiously ignored Mill Sharrow who went on to find his place on the opposite side of Warren Clay.

From her seat behind Tom, Mina Michaels smiled quietly. She was aware that, in spite of the smooth appearance of the opposing lawyers, Tom's rangy physical alertness and natural composure left him more than their equal in courtroom appeal.

During the introductions, Judge Littlejohn appeared and took his place on the bench. He was an imposing figure, with broad shoulders and steady blue eyes under bushy brows that swept the room quietly and gave immediate assurance of respect. He waited for a few minutes until the shuffling of feet died and the whispering from the back of the room indicated that his presence had been duly observed. Sheriff Barr now took his place at the side of the Judge's table and raised his hands awkwardly, like a minister calling for a hymn, to indicate that they were to rise and pay proper respect to the Bench.

Judge Littlejohn smiled at the untutored slowness of the response and made a remark to Sheriff Barr which brought a flicker of a smile to his face. Tom could only guess at its context, but suspected that the stoic Ottawas at the back of the room were probably the last to rise.

"Hear ye, hear ye, hear ye," John Barr's deep voice droned in languid monotone. "This Circuit Court of Oceana County is now in session. You can sit now."

From the back of the courtroom, Nick Tanner's high voice came back in reply, "You mean you can sit, sheriff, on the right hand of God, if you like. But we cain't sit back here, les'n it's on the floor."

A ripple of laughter crossed the courtroom. Judge Littlejohn rapped lightly, as though testing the new apple-wood gavel John Barr had made for him. "You may stand at the back of the courtroom for the present. I think, perhaps, the sheriff may be able to find a couple more benches for the next session."

"Let Sharrow furnish 'em," Nick's voice came back. "He's been cutting the wood."

The Judge grinned, but rapped for order as clapping rippled through the courtroom. Tom had won the first round without saying a word. He knew it would not all be that easy. But he was thankful for good friends.

Judge Littlejohn turned to address Harvey Tower, now settled deep behind his book and box of pens. Harvey rose. His new suit was a bit too tight for him. "Case of Mina Michaels and Milan LaVoy versus Sharrow Logging Company is at issue and ready for hearing." Harvey was acting as both clerk and recorder at the trial. The announcement in his high–pitched voice was a comic contrast to Sheriff Barr's rumbling basso. No wonder he was called "Birdie" by his friends.

Judge Littlejohn acknowledged the announcement with solemn lack of emotion, drew his judicial robes up to cover a heavy wool sweater which insisted on showing above the hamlike wrists, and settled down behind his table. Taking his time, he shuffled through the briefs which each lawyer had prepared. He finally decided not to take the time required to read them, but to summarize them verbally for the court.

Taking a sip of water from the glass at his elbow, he faced the courtroom. He had changed little since Tom had last seen him during one of his visits to the university. The shaggy beard, which formed a low border for the craggy face, was still dark and luxuriant. The high forehead tended to take attention away from eyes kept studiously stern but which could twinkle darkly when the occasion warranted it. He was known to be a man of many callings and had served as surveyor, engineer, and geologist back in Allegan before starting his Law practice and finally being elected judge for the ninth circuit. He was a good choice, thought Tom. A less rugged man would fare badly on a circuit which covered twenty frontier counties, ranging all the way from Allegan, well south of the Grand River, to the Sault Saint Marie on the outlet from Lake Superior. It was a circuit he had had to cover many times on horseback or walking the beaches.

"For the benefit of the court," the Judge was speaking now, "the case at issue involves the claim of illegal cutting of timber from private land by the Sharrow Logging Company. The claim is being made by Mina Michaels and Milan LaVoy.

"It must be remembered in a case of this type that Michigan is a pioneer territory. During the development of wild areas, mistakes of identification of lines and areas are frequently made. Among the lands still owned and administered by the states and the national government, have sprung up farms and pastures of immigrant farmers. Many of these settlers have taken little notice of proper survey practices and have, over the years, made use of public lands, and often they, or their issue, have come to assume ownership which is not supported by proper purchase and patent of title.

"Most of you have heard of them, and some of us can recall the early days of the squatters and the land speculators, when every land office was frequented by squatters, or representatives of squatter groups, who were armed with rifles and pitch forks, ready to defend their squatters rights until they could acquire the money to properly purchase the land which they had already cleared, and on which they might have built their homes. It must be held clear that in such cases of assumed ownership the occupant of the land has no more rightful claim of ownership than a new buyer, except as authorized by the proper application of the Preemption Acts of 1830 or

1838, or the more recent Homestead Act of 1862.

"Conversely, many purchasers of property, and lessees of property who are now engaging in the cutting of timber are equally careless, and, perhaps, criminally negligent in allowing their operations to extend beyond the boundaries defined by their leases and patent. The well-termed practice of cutting a 'round forty' is proof enough of this practice, which might more accurately be called cutting 'around a forty'.

"In its initial stages, these cuttings were pretty much confined to public lands, and the government was prompted to add many land agents and U.S. marshalls to control the practice. More recently, as choice timber lands became less available, more contract cutting and more small operators appeared, and the infringements onto private property have appeared. Cases such as this one are the result."

Tom looked out at the snow pelting steadily at the windows of the courthouse and wondered if he could feel relieved by these converse statements of the judge.

"The remaining problem occurring in these situations is to adequately identify the party, or parties, who subjected said timber to its untimely death and to provide proof of its movement and sale. Since the cutting of timber is a practice peculiar, to a large extent, to the winter months, and is carried on in remote areas under snow–veiled conditions, it appears that the cutters, either by circumstances or intent, have often enjoyed a built–in immunity to prosecution. This is especially true since their own employees usually come from long distances and can rarely be successfully subpoenaed as prime witnesses.

"With these facts in mind it is the duty of the court, as well as the judge, to weigh all testimony carefully and the delicate scales which weigh fact against emotion. We must judiciously separate the misleading and artful vehicles with which these clever men of law will attempt to carry us astray, from their true gems of wisdom, and boil the whole thing down to the sugar of truth. Only then can a fair and equitable judgment be made.

"I might add that I am well aware of the nature and value of the property being contested. It was brought to my attention many years ago that the area, east of the lake and behind the protection of the sand hills which stretch out north of it, had escaped the fires which have burned over most of these hills during the ages past. The lake and the sand hills had provided an efficient barrier from the prevailing west winds, and within this area of protection the trees have grown unmolested, except for the axes of the pioneer farmers, for at least two hundred years.

"It was an area venerated by the Indians because of their respect for the big pines. And since the Claybanks area to the south provided them with their garden land, it has always been secure from their fires."

Tom sat back, surprised by the knowledge of this big man. His father was the only one who had ever before told him this interesting theory which could account for the extraordinary size of those big pines.

The judge's voice rumbled on. "It is a tribute to the wisdom of these early settlers that they recognized the value of those trees at a time when trees were often considered a nuisance and were being cut and burned in huge piles in order to clear fields for cultivation. The fact that they did recognize it is attested to by the fact that they took up, at an early date, practically all of the land covered by the best of the pines. I am confident that this was not done without the exercise of considerable hard work and sacrifice."

Tom was pleased by this last remark. It was the first indication that the judge had real understanding of their life here and their feeling for the big pines. This was a factor above the monetary value of the trees and one not easily understood by outsiders. He was sure, though, that this would have little effect on the judge's decision. If proof of ownership could not, in all cases, be adequately upheld, or if the finger of evidence could not be pointed with forceful proof at Mill Sharrow and his foreman, the judge would have no choice but to rule against them. This would seem impossible to those people out there in the room who would judge only on their gut knowledge of the truth and their knowledge of the law's intent. Tom was well aware of the pitfalls of arguing a law's intent. Hard facts and proof the letter of the law had been violated would govern the Judge's verdict. He could expect nothing more.

He had warned his mother of this. He had told her that

there would be sensitive questions asked concerning proof of ownership of property which had not even been surveyed when she and Ganus had squatted there. The laws of disposition of property from husband to wife would be explored and questioned by the defense. There would be repeated attempts, through clever and apparently unrelated questions, to discredit his father's ownership of such a valuable property, and a play made to gain for Mill Sharrow the sympathy of the other holders of poor land.

She knew that the lawyers Mill Sharrow had brought with him would be the best in the state. She knew they would be hired by the big lumbermen from Muskegon and Saginaw who would not want to see the judgment establish a precedent which could forever be used against them.

The judge had finished now. The evaluation of the briefs had been unusual but informative. He twisted to the back of the room to calculate the effect of the judge's warning on the audience. Lyman Corbin was already dozing comfortably back by the rear stove. He had a reputation for finding the most comfortable chair in a house. Or maybe it was that he could look comfortable on almost anything.

The rest of the townspeople were whispering and stretching on their benches, impatient for the real action to begin. They were unaware, as yet, that the case would most likely last a week or more. It was cheap winter entertainment, and something to talk about besides the war.

Just behind Tom, Milan was sitting uncomfortably and

uneasily on the hard bench. Unlike Lyman Corbin, a chair, to Milan, was something to be tolerated but not enjoyed. He was never completely at ease unless he was on a floor or in a canoe.

The judge waited patiently while Lyman came awake and clattered a fresh piece of birch into each one of the big Detroit stoves and the benches were moved back a bit from the gathering heat. With order settling again over the court, the judge looked down at Tom, and then at the table where Mill Sharrow sat sullenly with his attorneys. "Are the councils on both sides ready to proceed?"

Tom swallowed twice. Of a sudden he was wondering if he was truly ready. Perhaps it would have been wiser to have hired an experienced lawyer to represent his mother. It was too late for those thoughts now. He rose to his full height and answered, "The plaintiff is ready, Sir."

Warren Clay rose in his tailored splendor, paused dramatically to display the poise and self–possession of a true aristocrat of the courts. "The defense council is ready, Your Honor. I would like, at this time, however, to present Mr. Cyrus Brigham of Saginaw, who will be assisting me in this case. Mr. Brigham."

The stranger stood and now bowed courteously to the Court.

This is it, thought Tom. The imported expert.

The judge looked back at Tom, obviously unimpressed by the drama and anxious to get things moving. "Call your first witness," he said.

Chapter Nineteen

"The complainant calls Milan LaVoy."

Tom had chosen Milan to be his first witness. He was expecting a play by the defense to discredit ownership of the lands purchased by his parents and more especially by Jim and Louise Colby. It was not unusual in those days for pioneers to take a great deal for granted and to place little importance on the legal aspects of taking up land. This course had often been successful in pioneer courts. It could often bring out questions and weaknesses in the operation of the old land offices and perhaps a crack into which the defense could place a foot. At worst they could divert attention from the real issue.

Tom intended to disrupt this area of defense by firmly establishing the history of the purchases with questions of his own choosing. Milan could do this and perhaps spare his mother the strain of an early appearance.

Milan was as tall and erect as a pine tree as he came forward. He wore the buckskin jacket that Louise Colby had made for him, with wide fringes down the sleeves and across the back. High beaded moccasins showed beneath wool breeches and a red wool shirt. Only the touch of silver in his curly hair betrayed his years. The easy grace of an animal was in his walk as he came to the front of the room.

Harvey Tower intercepted him there, and arching his head back like a chicken swallowing a drink, he held the bible high for Milan's swearing in. "Do you swear to tell the truth, the whole truth, and nothing but the truth, so help you God?" Harvey's thin voice cracked even more when confronted by the old voyageur.

"With or without help, I will tell the truth," grinned Milan, looking down in amusement at Harvey, who blocked his path like a bantam rooster. He was still wondering if Milan's reply was legally adequate. Finally deciding that it was, he padded back to his table and disappeared behind his battery of writing materials.

Milan continued to the witness chair, seeming to lose his animal grace half way down as he settled onto the wooden chair which seemed much too small and stiff for his rangy frame. Ignoringthe discomfort, he relaxed and let his gaze wander over the room until it finally locked on Mill Sharrow. The animal fire glowed briefly but calmly. It was Mill Sharrow who looked away. He then shifted his eyes to the defense councils. Warren Clay immediately became very busy with his notes. Harvey Tower waited nervously. Milan's face showed the slight trace of an amused grin.

Tom rose and smiled at Milan. "When did you first visit what is now Oceana County, Milan?"

Milan leaned back and thought a bit. "I visit the Indians at the Claybanks area about 1822. I brought my furs down to Mackinac Island that year, then watched the Indians get their payoff. After that I decide that, since the weather is good, I would go down the Lake Michigan coast and maybe cross over on the long portage. This way would take me up the Manistee River to the lake at its end. Then, after a carry, I would paddle down the Au Sable and back into Lake Huron. This is the way the Indians have crossed the state for a long time."

"But you did not go that way or you would not have come south far enough to visit the Claybanks."

"That is right. The weather was still good and Lake Michigan so smooth that I can travel safe most every day, So I say, 'I will go visit my friend, Rix Robinson, on the Grand River.'"

"So you visited the Indians at the Claybanks on your way."

"I do, and while I am there they take me to the lake behind the grand saubles and into these hills where we now live."

Tom would like to have asked more questions about the nature of the country at that time. There might never be such a glorious opportunity again, but he knew that he must remain closer to the case at hand. "When did you again visit this area?" he continued.

"I don't remember all of the times, but I visit it several more times." Milan paused, as if searching for the proper words to express his feelings. "The big trees there, and the lakes and hills and the fresh air off of the lakes, they bring me back. Maybe the hills here are more like those I knew when I was a little boy in South France. I don't remember very well, but my sister says that this is true. Anyway, in 1837, when my sister comes to Michigan, I bring her and her husband, Ganus, and their little boy up here to live." Milan stopped here to grin boyishly at his reference to Tom.

"I understand it was a very ugly baby," Tom offered.

"Like an eagle fresh from the nest," laughed Milan.

Judge Littlejohn stirred in his chair. "When the plaintiff has finished his blind search for compliments, perhaps we can be on with the trial." His voice was gruff but there was a bit of a glow in his eyes.

"And they built their home there at that time?"

"A cabin, yes. That cabin later became a part of the barn which was burned last spring."

Tom expected a challenge here from Warren Clay, but he wisely remained silent. He, no doubt, considered it wiser to ignore the indirect accusation than to add fuel to what could be a very hot subject.

"Were there any other people in the area at that time?"

"Only Jim and Louise Colby then. During the next few years, though, Allen Harcourt showed up from a schooner that stopped in the bay at what is now Buttersworth. Then one day Jim Moreau and his family appeared; they came by ox wagon from Ionia."

"Was the property that Ganus Michaels took up purchased at that time?" Tom wanted this question to come from him rather than the defense. It would set better with the people of the area and, perhaps, with the judge.

"No," said Milan," the county has not even been surveyed yet at that time."

"So you were squatters, so to speak."

"Settlers, waiting for our lines to be drawn, I would say." Milan remembered well the words Tom had chosen.

Now Warren Clay was forced to object. "My worthy opponent obviously disagrees with Abe Lincoln and insists that chicken's eggs hatched in an oven will, in truth, produce biscuits. I suggest that our Judge and our intelligent audience would prefer a spade be called a spade, and a squatter a squatter."

But the words were out.

Judge Littlejohn smiled a little behind his studied sternness and accepted the objection.

Tom pressed on. "The land then was unassigned?"

"If you mean it don't belong to anyone else, that is right." Milan laughed, probably remembering the remoteness of the area at that time. "No," he finally said. "It was bought from the Indians at the Treaty of Washington in 1836, but was not surveyed until three or four years later."

"When did Ganus Michaels and Jim Colby actually purchase the land?"

"As soon as it was offered; 1840, I believe."

"Were you with them at the time of the purchase?"

"Oui." Milan's French background became more apparent under the strain of the questioning, but he was calm and personable, as always.

"Was there anyone else with you at the time?"

"Oui, Allen Harcourt, Jim Moreau, and Jimmy Colby. We all go together."

"And where did you go?"

"To the land office at Ionia."

"Was there any problem getting patents to the land? Did anyone else try to assume a prior claim? Had any land speculators made a blind purchase which included any sections of your properties?"

"Their were no problems. Only a few people believed that this country had land of any value at that time. Only the people I have named had seen it, and we agreed on lines before we go. We also agreed not to talk to any strangers about the land until we have finished with our business."

"Were there any problems among yourselves after the purchases were made and the surveys completed?"

"Oui, a few," Milan grinned.

"Can you explain these problems? It may be important to the judge to know that the patents to these properties are in order."

"Well." Milan's love of humor was showing in his eyes. "There was slight problem with Jim Moreau find out that he has planted his spring potatoes in Allen Harcourt's pasture land, and that Allen Harcourt has built twenty rods of good stump fence more than a chain into Ganus

Michael's woodlot. But they are good neighbors and they make out all right."

Milan paused to reminisce. "Allen Harcourt ate Jim Moreau's potatoes and then felt strong enough to pull his stumps back to his own line. Then Allen gave Jim Moreau the wood he cut from Ganus Michael's woodlot to pay for the potatoes, and Jim trades the wood to Ganus for potatoes to replace the ones that Allen Harcourt ate."

"Then everybody was satisfied?" Tom laughed.

"Fair well," said Milan, "until Ganus figured out that it was his own wood that Jim Moreau had traded back to him for potatoes."

By this time the court was around to noisy disorder and Sheriff Barr was rapping loudly with the judge's gavel.

When a semblance of quiet was finally restored, the Judge addressed the court. "A bit of funning now and then is good for the human soul," he admitted. "But let us not forget, this is a court of law. We have a serious case ahead of us, and spring will soon be here. Will the plaintiff please confine his questions to the case at hand, and the witness limit his replies to a simple yes or no whenever this is possible."

"Yes, Your Honor," grinned Tom and turned again to Milan.

"Now back again, for a moment, to my question of problems. Were all of the conveyances properly delivered to the purchasers of the properties?"

"If you mean the patents of title, yes. But it was a long

time before they received them. Nearly three years, I believe. There was much land being transferred in those days."

"Then, to the best of your knowledge, both at that time and through later years, clear titles to these properties have been maintained and nobody has the right to trespass, destroy or remove anything from these properties without the consent of the owners?"

Warren Clay was now on his feet. "Objection, Your Honor, I have been sitting here listening to these insane historical ramblings because they had absolutely no importance in the final analysis of this suit and were doing our defense no harm. But since my historian opponent is now up to the present decade, I must object on the basis that any claim of ownership made by this witness would be based on hearsay and cannot be entered as positive evidence."

There was a murmur in the crowd, but Judge Littlejohn quickly rapped for order. "Objection is sustained. However, if it is the plaintiff's intent to properly support these claims of ownership later in the trial, I will accept this as both time–saving and legal." There was the hint of a smile on the judge's solemn face as he noted the uneasiness of the crowd.

Mina saw it and wondered. Surely Tom had expected the objection. Perhaps he had even invited it. Was it because he knew that the closeness of these people would be underestimated by Warren Clay? The defense would have little warning that a suggestion that knowledge here was not common knowledge could be an irrational assumption to these people. His objection might be a point of importance to the judge, and as such would have to be made. In the minds of the people, however, it could appear belittling to Milan. Tom, feeling that the temper of the people might have an influence upon the judge, and, as important, upon those reporters at the back of the room, was fighting for early rounds. Mina smiled.

Mary Sugars, also understanding, squeezed her hand.

Tom returned to his questioning. Warren Clay returned to his chair. His lawyer's sense told him that he had made a mistake but, for the life of him, he could find no logical support for that feeling.

"You have lived close to these people since their land was purchased. Have you ever known anyone to question the ownership during those years?"

"Nevair," replied Milan. Warren Clay did not object.

"And that property owned by Jim Colby. Has that ownership been in question?"

"Not yet," Milan grinned, looking directly at Warren Clay and his companion.

Tom was more at ease now, and ready to switch to another subject. "Do you recall where you were on the afternoon of April 25 of last year?"

Milan was surprised by Tom's quick change of direction in his questioning. He looked out over the little room filled with friends to where the snow still blustered against the frosted windows. The stoves were cherry red at the base of the fire pots. The warmth of the room oppressed him. The memory of that spring day when he and Jimmy Colby had watched the rafts of logs being formed at the mouth of the river swept back to him and he knew what Tom was about to expose. "Oui, I remember," he replied.

"Will you tell the court what you saw on that day?"

Milan crossed his ankles and hooked one moccasined foot behind a chair leg. This seemed to help, and he leaned back. The chair complained noisily and a ripple of expectancy came from the front rows of people and mingled with the crackling of the fires. "I remember, continued Milan, because on April 24th, Jim Colby and I had finished our work with the men surveying for the new railroad. We were anxious to be home so we traveled west until dark, then we hobbled our horses and sleep for a few hours in the sand above Lake Michigan. After the moon comes up we ride the lakeshore to where the river from Blue Lake empties into the bay. Then we sleep again until morning. This would be the 25th.

"That morning we watched, for a while, the men chaining together the logs coming out of the river. They were making the rafts, or what they call peegs. After they get two, maybe three, peegs ready they chain them to the tug, or sow, and away they go off towards Muskegon. They are good men and we watch, maybe two or three hours. After a while we rode east along the river, watching the men driving the logs down towards the bay, and wondering where Mr. Sharrow find logs so big on that land south of the river."

"I object, Your Honor." Warren Clay was on his feet again. "The matter of log size is an opinion, unsupported by proof, which is obviously being used to influence the Court."

"The objection is accepted, but I am sure the influence is of no major importance, Mr. Clay. Continue, Mr. Michaels."

A gust of wind sent a swirl of dry snow past the south windows. Milan unwrapped one foot from the leg of the chair, amid more creaking of wood, and carefully adjusted the other one in its place. Mary Sugars' whispered voice came from the crowd, "Good Lord, he doesn't sit in a chair, he puts it on." The judge rapped quietly as laughter rippled through the room.

"By maybe ten o'clock," Milan went on, "we reached the clearing at the end of the lake where Mr. Sharrow has built his camp. There was a horse standing in the clearing and Tom Michaels was walking towards it." Milan hesitated, as if wondering if the rest of his story should be told. It was something which he and Tom and Jimmy had kept to themselves, up to now. They had thought it better that the people of the valley, especially Mina, be spared the details of an act which could easily be overplayed. But it was probably the proper time now to make the big foreman's actions a part of the record. Time had mellowed the anger of the people while not the extent of their determination.

It was nearing time for noon recess and Judge Littlejohn was becoming impatient of small delays. "If the witness has not lost himself in his forest of recollections, will he please continue."

Milan's quick temper surged for a moment at the impatience of the judge. He hesitated a long minute before he went on, looking steadily at His Honor. Finally he cooled, smiled a little, and continued.

Tom relaxed, and let out a long breath of relief.

Judge Littlejohn smiled to himself. He had known Milan for many years. He would be careful not to strike flint to such perfect steel again.

Milan's steady eyes now locked on Mill Sharrow. Mill fiddled with his watch chain. The courtroom became tensely quiet.

"As Tom walked out of the cabin, this man's foreman, Angus McBride, I have heard him called, follows him to the doorway. There must have been gun pegs above the door, for all at once a gun shows and he lays down a shot in Tom's direction."

A murmur ran through the hall.

"He don't try to hit Tom, but his shot is close all the same and I can see the sand fly up against his legs."

"And what was it he said at that time?" asked Tom.

"I do not hear what Tom had said, but I hear the foreman say, 'We may pay you long before that.'" Milan paused. "And he did. It was just two weeks later, in the middle of the night, Mina's barn was burned to the ground."

This time Warren Clay was pounding the table in mock fury. "I object, Your Honor, I object, I object, I object. This statement is slander. It is pure slander. The witness has no sound basis for believing my client was in any way responsible for the fire. I insist that the statement be withdrawn from your mind and stricken from the records of the court."

Judge Littlejohn fondled his new gavel and waited until John Barr had quieted the hall. With a new seriousness in his voice he then upheld the complaint. "The objection is supported and the clerk will strike the witness's final statement from the records. As for my mind, it has a slow withdrawal rate. But I will not be unduly influenced by the witness's statement."

Harvey Tower looked helplessly from his papers. He was already so far behind that there was nothing to strike from the records and he was sure the Judge was aware of that.

"I must also remind the witness and the council that any accusations which cannot be supported by subsequent proof have no place in a court of law. They can truly be considered slanderous, and will carry no weight when my final judgment of guilt or acquittal is made. I remind you further that the case at hand deals with the theft of timber only, and all arguments should be directed strictly towards the resolution of that claim, and that claim only."

Milan was not impressed by the intricacies of legal processes. Supported or not supported, the judge must know, as well as anyone, that the fire was not an accident. "You don't have to see a polecat to know he's been under your house," he added, loud enough to be clearly heard.

During the excitement that followed, the back door opened a crack and John Barr's wife, Hannah, slipped quickly inside. She now found her way to the judge's table, brushing the snow from her cape as she came, and handed him a slip of paper. The Judge looked relieved. The court was getting out of hand. A break in the procedures was needed. He stood up. The studied sternness was gone from his face. He now became Flavius Littlejohn, the man. With a hint of a smile on his broad face, he announced, "I have just been asked to tell you that there is a warm meal waiting for all of you in the basement of the church. I can think of no better reason for adjourning this court. We will meet here again at one p.m. Until then, this court is adjourned."

At one p.m. Tom was again at his table and the court was ready. The stoves, a bit overzealously fired in the morning, had been allowed to mellow and now a cold draft could be felt along the floor. There could be no real comfort in the building as long as the wind outside was pouring sub–zero gusts against it. The trial would have to proceed.

Milan was recalled to the chair and Tom resumed his

questioning. "After you left the camp where the shot was fired, and you and Jim Colby and I rode on towards our homes, please tell the court, Milan, what you saw as we rounded the hills north of Jim Colby's cabin."

Milan thought for only a minute. "We leave the camp and ride north on the sand along the lake shore. We come to Jim Colby's cabin, but Tom says to Jimmy, 'Don't stop now, Jim, come a little farther with us.' So we all rode on until we rounded the shoulder of hill north of the cabin. Here there is a small stream coming down from the back end of the Michael's property and running through a low ravine along the north line of Jim and Louise Colby's property."

"And this ravine is not visible from the Colby cabin?"

"No, it is a long way and the big pines on the ridges between are far too tall and dense to allow this area to be seen."

"Then the only view of this area would be from the dunes across the lake?"

"Right, or maybe from the old Indian camp area on the north shore."

"Good! Now tell the court what you saw when this ravine became visible to you."

"As we rode the beach, Jimmy Colby stop twice and listen. We wait. He says nothing but we can see that he is troubled by something. Maybe the sounds of the lake are different or the wind is speaking to him. When we come around the hills, though, we see what it is that troubles him. All along the ravine and up the sides of the hills for maybe half a mile the trees have been cut clean. We figure maybe thirty acres of the biggest pines are gone and only the big stumps and brush are left. Now I am thinking I know where those big logs came from that we saw in the river."

Tom chose to ignore Milan's last remark. "Are you familiar, Milan, with the property lines in this area?"

"I know that there is a base line marker near the lake, where the north line of section twenty–nine meets the lake. That line is, maybe, a quarter mile north of the stream."

"And that marks the north line of both the Colby and the Michael's properties?"

"That is right."

"And beyond that is the one–sixty which Eber Harcourt recently purchased?"

"That is right."

"Would you say that any trees have been cut from the Harcourt property?"

"Maybe a few, not many. But he could be next."

There was an objection, but it was drowned out by the angry mutterings of the crowd as they became aware that Eber and Judy Harcourt could, in fact, lose their trees while Eber served his country.

"Then there is no government land available in this area, and no land on which cutting of timber has been authorized?"

"There has been no slash cutting of timber authorized. This we all know."

"Yet, how many stumps did we count in this cut over area during the next hour?"

"We count eight hundred and eighty stumps."

Milan was uncomfortable in his chair. Tom was finished with him as his first witness. He looked at Warren Clay, sitting quiet now, at his table. "Your witness," he said.

The courtroom was hushed now. The frivolity of the morning had passed. The drafts of cold air were uncomfortable and the tension was mounting.

Warren Clay was whispering guardedly with Cyrus Brigham. There was disagreement in their attitudes and Brigham was holding firmly to Warren's arm. Finally he stood and addressed the Judge. "No questions at this time, Your Honor, but the defense reserves the right to call the witness at a later time."

Tom was disappointed. The defense was holding back. He was now like a prizefighter forced to keep fighting for points, forced to show his style, his knowledge, his art, while the defense held back, hoping to find defects, weaknesses and openings through which to land a telling blow. His mother was the complainant, the challenger, so to speak. He had no choice but to go on.

Outside, the wind had eased. The beat of it against the windows, now frosted by the warm breath of the crowd inside, had gentled and a glint of afternoon sun made

golden frescoes of the frosty panes. Harvey Tower fidgeted with his pens. He had long since given up a verbatim
account of the proceedings and could think of nothing
more to add to his notes. Judge Littlejohn was studying
the clock. He would like a cup of coffee but it was much
too early to recess the court. He pulled the robes again
down over the big wrists and looked at Tom. The early
sparring of a trial seemed wasteful. Too bad that they
could not be a simple matter of record so that the real
meat might be more quickly skewered over the fire.

Tom checked the time. There was an hour left. He
would call one more witness. Perhaps his plan to show
prior intent to steal would agitate the defense into some
show of action. A charge of premeditation could not be
effective as a weapon but it could be an irritant. Another
fly to buzz around the head of Milt Sharrow and Warren
Clay. Perhaps enough flies would break Warren loose
from that restraining hand of Cyrus Brigham. He would
give it a try.

"The complainant calls Allen Harcourt."

Allen came forward, unperturbed and inscrutable. He
was a quiet man by nature, unconcerned with pretense or
appearance. His wool shirt was open at the throat and the
rolled neck of a seaman's warm woolens showed comfortably over the big expanse of chest and shoulders. He
was a larger edition of Mill Sharrow's foreman, Angus
McBride, except that his slow and easy manner lacked the
cat-like qualities of the lumberman. He is a lot like Father

too, thought Tom. His thoughts do not come quickly, but once they are formed they are like the rocks of a hillside, permanent and indestructible. For all of their years together, there was still not the sense of closeness with the Harcourts that Tom felt with Bill and Mary Sugars, but, no matter, they were good and faithful friends. Perhaps it is good that a few walls are maintained.

Harvey Tower completed the swearing in and returned to his seat.

"Your name, Sir?" Tom smiled at Allen.

Allen looked surprised, as if wondering if Tom could be serious. There wasn't a man in the county who did not know him. But finally he answered, his voice rumbling like a distant storm rising out over the lakes. "Allen Harcourt, it is."

"Mr. Harcourt, where is your property located in relation to the area of cut timber of which we were just speaking?"

"My property extends east of the cuttings and north of the Michaels property."

"And the property which Eber bought would border along the north edge of the cut over area. Is that correct?"

"It is. That would be the south line of section twenty–nine, and west of our property."

"This property has a growth of very fine cork pine. Is that true?"

"Some of the best in the state, I have been told."

"As trustee for your son Eber, has anyone ever offered

to purchase the rights to cut timber from this land?"

"Yes."

"Do you remember who this person was?"

"Yes, it was our friend, Mill Sharrow."

"The defendant, who is sitting at the next table?"

"That is right." The thunder had taken on a slightly more defiant rumble, but Allen remained quiet and thoughtful, not quite sure yet the reasons for Tom's questions.

"When was the time of this contact with you?"

Allen took his usual time to properly consider the answer. "I would say about the second week of November, a year ago last fall. About a week after the shanty boys started to appear at the camp."

"Did you accept the offer for Eber?"

Allen chuckled a little and shifted his bulk more comfortably on the chair. "No, I talked to Judy and we agreed that the answer should be no."

"What did Mr. Sharrow say to that?"

"He appeared quite upset and reminded me that a bad storm or a fire could easily destroy the trees, and that we were foolish to gamble on the future. But I told him a farmer gambles every day on the future. That is a part of our business."

"Would you say that his manner was threatening?"

Cyrus Brigham was anticipating this question and objected immediately. The Judge allowed the objection.

Tom would have rephrased the question, but Allen

Harcourt was not to be denied. His low, but resonant, voice continued clearly above the objections of Warren Clay and the rapping of the Judge. "I did not think of it as a threat at the time," he said. "But after the cutting of the trees and the burning of Mina's barn in the spring, I have had to change some of my opinions. I now believe that it was."

Tom was surprised and pleased at Allen's quiet insistence on being heard out, and with his mellow bass voice he had succeeded, in spite of the uproar.

When there was quiet again, and the final sticks of wood had gone into the stoves, Tom again turned to Allen. "So, inspite of the warning," Tom stopped and grinned a little at the furious attorneys for the defense, "you refused the offer?"

"Yes." Allen was smiling quietly, too. "In this world we all gamble, especially us farmers of sandy hills. Sometimes we win. It seems that more often we lose. Over the years, though, most of us have found that it is sometimes hard to tell whether we have lost or won. When we win it has meant a few dollars for a new dress for the Mrs. and shoes for the kids. When we lose it's more beans and berries and less meat and potatoes. Maybe there is a lesson there. Maybe it was good that we got good and hungry a few times, Tom. Now we know how to appreciate what we have."

Allen had finished now and saw no reason to remain. He rose without invitation and lumbered back to his place beside Anna.

Tom turned to face the Judge. Allen had been a good witness. He felt a new closeness to the old neighbor. "That is all, Your Honor."

The Judge looked at the defense. They had the right to cross-examine, but Cyrus Brigham's hand was still on Clay's arm and he smiled his consent to Allen's abrupt departure.

The sun had disappeared again and a sudden gust of wind whipped against the building, sending a fresh scurry of snow against the frosted windows. A poorly fitted casement whined a long, sad crescendo that quieted again as the wind passed on.

Now it was Judge Littlejohn who checked the clock. The valley people still faced a long cold trip home, although Martin Tyson had been thoughtful enough to bring in the warming stones, which were now piled close against the stoves. Judge Littlejohn accepted the warning of the wind. "Court is dismissed until nine a.m., tomorrow," he said, and the courtroom slowly emptied.

It was not until after the noon recess of the second day that the defense evidently felt that they had learned enough to choose a line of defense and the restraining hand was finally removed from Warren Clay's arm.

Tom had called Louise Colby to the stand to show that she, like Allen Harcourt, had been visited with an offer to lease cutting rights on the Colby property.

"Do you recall the date on which Mr. Sharrow called on

you?" Tom asked.

"November the ninth," Louise answered without hesitation. "He came late in the evening and the foreman McBride was with him."

"We don't need a life history," growled Cyrus Brigham, doing what he could now to disturb the witness.

"Was your husband, Jimmy, at home?" asked Tom.

"No. This was the winter that Jim and Milan worked with the surveyors up east of Buttersworth. They had been gone only a week."

"What did Mr. Sharrow ask you?"

"The first thing was, 'Would you like a bottle of whiskey?'"

"And the whiskey, did you take it?" Tom was grinning now, knowing the feelings Louise had towards strong drink.

"Yes, I did," was her surprising reply. "I had four loaves of hot bread cooling on the kitchen table and I could see these men drooling from the smell of it."

Tom expected an interruption by the Judge, but he glanced in that direction and saw nothing but patience and anticipation. A female obviously had certain rights and privileges in Judge Littlejohn's court.

"So you traded bread for whiskey?" Tom teased.

"Not exactly," smiled Louise.

Tom scratched his head. "You are confusing both me and the court of law, Louise."

Behind his pens, Harvey's eyes showed his agreement.

How much of these court wanderings was he expected to preserve for posterity? And why did nobody object?

"When I went for a loaf of bread," Louise continued, I cut a groove across the top of the loaf with my knife. Then I slowly poured the bottle of whiskey down into it. Their bottle I now handed back to them with the bread. I now owed them nothing.

"The rest of our business was completed quickly. I refused to sell the timber, then bid them good night. By then my boy, Charlie, was sitting on the edge of his loft with Jimmy's bird gun across his knees. They left."

Mary Sugars giggled loudly, otherwise there was an unnatural quiet in the courtroom. If the story was humorous, it was also serious. And the obvious lack of respect which Louise carried for the men told much. The fact that she had still found a way to follow the age–old custom of the Ottawas to share what she had with a stranger was equally interesting.

"I have just one more question." Tom was anxious to get this one on the record. "Were there any words of threat made by these two men?"

"No."

"Then you do not feel that their intent was to pressure you to sell them timber?"

"Yes."

"Your answers appear to conflict, Louise. Will you explain them?

She was silent for a moment.

"There are many ways a person can be made to feel fear, other than by the use of words. The wolf, by his presence outside a chicken house, poses a threat, even though he does not sing his warning or scratch on the door. The very stillness that comes to the wood before a storm is its own silent warning." She hesitated, as though reluctant to go on, then continued. "When Mr. Sharrow and his man entered my home with a bottle in their hand they were like the wolf at the hen house, or the silence that speaks. They were reminding me of a weakness. A weakness of any thoroughly beaten people, and the willingness of others to profit by that weakness. That act, without words, was their threat, I am sure of it."

Harvey's eyes were wide and pleading. How could he possibly record the wanderings of such a trial. Words with strange meanings, and threats with no words at all. He could only look helplessly at the Judge.

Judge Littlejohn smiled his understanding.

Now, however, Warren Clay was stirring. Here was the witness they were waiting for. Tom could see him fidgeting with his notes. The defense was going to overlook the cutting on the Michaels' property, for the time being, and try to free themselves of the remaining charge. He went quickly on a mental search of more questions to ask Louise. He would like to hold Warren at bay for a few more minutes, but there seemed to be no more questions left. He looked straight at Cyrus Brigham, hoping to irritate Warren Clay into some small rashness, and said quietly, "Your witness, sir."

Warren was more than ready. He was a man on a ladder, savoring the opportunity to be heard by the big town reporters and resenting the holding action imposed on him by his colleague. His first question told Tom much about the future trend of the defense; "Mrs. Colby, you are an Indian. Is that right?"

"I am an Ottawa by birth. My father was Keeshaowash, of the Grand River tribe. My mother was of the Crockery Creek clan." Louise was neither apologetic nor arrogant, but the name, Keeshaowash, fell from her lips like water rippling down a rocky hill. If no other word had been spoken her ancestry would have been established by the sound of it.

"Your husband's name is - ?"

"Jimmy."

"Only Jimmy?"

"Jimmy Colby. His father was Cawpemossay, of the Flat River Clan."

"I understand that the main part of the Ottawa nation lives in the area of the Ottawa River, in Canada. Did your tribe once claim property there?"

"Perhaps. The stories of the old ones told of wars with the Iroquois, who drove our people from the land east of the big lakes long ago. Some went north to the Ottawa River highlands of which you speak. My clan came on to the Grand River valley where we have lived for many years."

"Then the Iroquois are enemies of the Ottawa?"

"The Iroquois are a different nation. They do not speak the Algonquian tongue as do the Ottawas and most of the other tribes who live around the great lakes. They are different in other ways, too. They pass their property and their Chief's rights down through the woman's family, not the male's, as the Algonquian tribes do. It is also said that they are much more cruel and warlike."

"So your clan settled in the Grand River valley and eventually claimed ownership of the land there. Is that more correct?

Louise hesitated, and Milan became more alert in his seat beside Mina. It was a loaded question. One difficult for an Indian to explain. Louise finally made her reply.

"In the way that white people own property, no. Indians have never looked upon property as being owned. It is occupied, used as a source of food and comfort, shared with friends and protected from enemies, but no papers are signed, no stakes are driven and no records are kept."

"So when your people were driven from your country east of the lakes they merely look for land which was unoccupied, or perhaps occupied by a tribe which you were able to overpower?"

Louise smiled quietly. "That is right. The same way that white people do."

Warren Clay smiled his respect, and continued. "But when your people sold the Grand River property you were paid for it and also given use of property along the Pentwater River and offered land west of the Mississippi. Was this not a fair deal?"

"After one watches the sun rise in the morning and set at night for many years over a land called home, and when you have seen it buried beneath the winter snows and born again under the warm skies of summer for generations, a land becomes a part of people. The home of the living, the resting place of the dead and the hope of the future. That is how we felt about the Grand River valley. It is the way we all feel about our valley west of here where the big pine trees grow. To lose a part of one's self, without choice, and we Ottawa's knew that we had no choice, can hardly be considered a good bargain."

"So you and Jimmy chose to buy land in what you call, The Valley?"

"Yes. My father was one of the chiefs who went to the land west of the Mississippi to estimate its worth. He advised us, and all of our people, to refuse to go there. Besides, we liked the people who were settling here and believed that we could better ourselves by leaving what was left of our tribe."

"When your husband bought the property," Warren asked this question slowly, "did he acknowledge that he was Ottawa?"

"Both Jimmy and Milan have told me that the men at the land office in Ionia were very busy and did not even ask. If they had asked, Milan was prepared to make the purchase."

"And the ownership of your property was never contested?"

"Until Mr. Sharrow appeared, no. The people of this area have been good to us. We are like one family. Until outsiders came in, there was no problem." Louise hesitated, her mind going back over the hard years, "Except for the finding of food and clothing for our children," she added.

"From where did you find the money to purchase some one hundred and sixty acres of land? Is this not an unusual amount to be accumulated by an Ottawa?"

Tom was on his feet to object, but Louise held him back with a motion of her hand.

"According to the Treaty of Washington, which took our lands, a cash payment of five hundred dollars was due to each chief. Lesser chiefs, like my father, were to receive two hundred dollars. When this money was paid, at the big council at Grand Rapids in 1836, my father at first refused his payment. He regretted that he had been a party to the signing of the treaty and did not want the disgrace which accompanied the payment. On second thought, he took it, and knowing that it would disappear quickly from his hands, he gave it at once to me. We bought our land with that money."

"And you have claimed ownership since that time?"

Louise looked at Tom. It was a question they had hoped would not come up at this time. Now Warren Clay had tossed it out, routinely, without thinking that it could be of great import.

Tom could only nod his head in the affirmative. Perhaps it was just as well this way. He had intended that the question would come from his own lips and at a time of his own choosing. No matter, though. Now it would leave Mill Sharrow with one less road to follow. One less hope to nurture.

Louise was still waiting, so Tom nodded again. But Judge Littlejohn interceded. "Since there appears to have been a private intermission occurring, I suggest that the defense restate the question."

Warren Clay now awoke from the depths of speculation over the sudden importance of his routine question and fished helplessly for the exact words he had used. "Have you and Jimmy retained constant ownership of this property since you first purchased it?"

"No," Louise answered, simply. It was a reply neither expected by the defense nor by many others in the courtroom.

"Are you the present owners of the property?" Warren countered. He was now noticeably concerned.

"No," Louise replied, and now there was a twinkle of amusement showing in her dark eyes.

"Were you the owners of the property at the time the timber was cut?"

"No." The twinkle was showing.

Mill Sharrow had become alert at his table and now

leaned forward on his elbows, his fingers roving deep into the graying hair of his bowed head. He felt his case falling apart. Somewhere he had erred. The defense was dwindling to a fight to clear a charge of simple theft. He had hoped to build it into something much more complex. Why had Warren Clay not discovered this transfer of title. That is what he was being paid for.

Warren Clay was also disturbed. He had examined all of the old records at Ionia. The records there clearly showed Jimmy Colby to be the owner of the property. It was Mill Sharrow who had claimed to have checked the more recent ones at Whiskey Creek. Where had he gone wrong?

His patience thin now, he looked again at Louise. Tom knew that her inscrutable calmness was galling him.

"When, then, did you dispose of this property?" he nearly shouted. Louise spoke slowly. She was not beyond intentionally irritating this arrogant man with controlled candor. "During October of the year before last. Just before Jim and Milan left on their surveying trip."

Warren Clay left the floor now to talk briefly with Mill Sharrow and Cyrus Brigham. Judge Littlejohn waited, toying with his gavel. Tom saw no reason to object. Obviously the slowness of the county clerk to record the transfer of title had worked in their favor. Mill Sharrow had taken precautions, but the gods of fate had worked against him. Tom's luck had been all good, so far.

Warren Clay returned to his questioning, but his back

was broken as far as his present course was concerned. He could satisfy his curiosity, perhaps, but it would avail him little unless the sale was to another Ottawa. "And to whom did you sell the property at that time?"

Louise showed just the hint of a smile. "We sold it to our good friend, Milan LaVoy."

"And what mysterious intuition prompted you to sell at this particular time?" Warren was back in control now and trying hard to make a show of good humor before the court.

Judge Littlejohn had been busy taking notes, but now raised his head with new interest.

Louise was slow to answer this one, so Tom rose to object. "Your Honor, I see no reason for the question except to satisfy the curiosity of the defense. Only the proof of ownership can be of importance, not the reason behind the transfer, and I can assure you that the ownership can be adequately supported."

"Objection is sustained. Are you through, Mr. Clay?"

But Louise had again raised her hand. She evidently felt that no information should be withheld. "I will tell what I know of the reasons. Any more will have to come from my husband, Jimmy. It was he who felt that we should dispose of the property. Only some of the reasons do I know. Some of them are strange to me, for he prizes this property very much. This I do know. He did not want to sell the land, or lease the timber rights, to Mr. Sharrow. Yet he knew that, in a moment of weakness, he might do just that. Perhaps for the same reasons that our fathers sold their tribal lands, back in 1821 and 1836. Perhaps he feared that, one way or another, the land would be taken from him."

Tom glanced back to where Milan sat beside his mother. They all understood the fear that was in Jimmy's heart. It was a tribute to the old Ottawa that he had both the foresight and the fortitude to put the property in the hands of his friend.

"Are you to remain there and live as though you still own the property?" Warren Clay made much show of this apparent fact.

"That is the agreement," said Louise.

Warren's head was shaking in disbelief. Some piece must be missing from the puzzle. But if Tom could support the transfer of patent, the missing piece could change nothing.

Judge Littlejohn was becoming impatient. There was nothing to be gained by pursuing why. "Are you finished with the witness, Mr. Clay?"

"I am finished."

Tom smiled at these words, knowing how true they might be.

But Warren caught a signal from Cyrus Brigham and turned again to the Judge. "However, if the court will permit, I would like to recall Milan LaVoy to the stand."

"Do you have any objections, Mr. Michaels?"

"None at all, Your Honor," Tom replied.

The witness sworn, Warren Clay wasted no time in getting the meat over the fire. "When you were previously on the stand, you swore to tell the truth, the whole truth, and nothing but the truth. Is that not correct? Mr. LaVoy."

"Oui," Milan grinned. "I also swore to try to do so by saying yes or no."

"But when you were questioned before, you spoke of traveling over Jimmy Colby's land and observing the trees cut from Mr. Colby's property. At no time did you venture to inform the court that this land was, in truth, your land, and that you were, in truth, the complainant, along with the Michaels. Not Jimmy and Louise Colby."

Tom was now on his feet waiting to be heard.

"What is it now, Mr. Michaels?"

"I would like to make it clear, Your Honor, that the complainants are, and always have been, recorded as Mina Michaels and Milan LaVoy. At no time was Milan asked who was the owner of the property. At no time did he, or myself, directly state that the property, other than the cabin on the lake, was owned by Jim and Louise Colby. If the defendants have allowed their streams of thought to run freely into the river of their established line of preparation, it has not been through deception on the part of the complainant, although I have to admit that it brings me some satisfaction to observe the disorganized nature of the defense."

The Judge was shuffling through his notes and Harvey Tower was searching frantically for any clues to the nature of the former statements made by Milan. Finally the Judge seemed satisfied. "I find no reason to dispute the claim of the complainant," he confirmed. "Please continue, Mr. Clay."

Warren again faced Milan. "The fact remains that you did fail to tell the whole truth. Is that not true, Mr. LaVoy?"

"It is true," said Milan. "It is also true that I failed to tell the whole truth that the temperature was, on that day, eighty–five degrees and that the wind was blowing steadily from the west."

As if the mention of it had suddenly turned the key, the west door of the courtroom suddenly burst open and another old Indian came in. Blinking at the darkness, he brushed the crusted snow from his eyebrows, leaned a beautifully fashioned pair of snowshoes against a far wall and found a place to squat on the floor where the other Ottawas beamed their silent recognition.

Warren Clay waited for the door to close, then turned again to Milan. "But the fact that you acquired ownership of this property was a fact of direct importance. A fact which you had no right to withhold under oath. I see possible foundation for you to be charged with contempt."

Tom considered objecting, knowing that he had the right, and that Warren's threat could only be an attempt to put pressure on Milan. Perhaps to bathe him in a bad light before the court. Only Tom's confidence in Milan allowed him to wait.

"The only matter of importance that I see," Milan was speaking now without invitation, "is that trees were stolen. Who they were stolen from should matter little. If they were stolen from Jimmy Colby it was a theft. If they were stolen from me it was also a theft. If the whole truth is important, as you say that it is, why don't you now admit to the court that your client stole the trees. We all know that this is true, and it would save us a lot of time."

Judge Littlejohn was rapping steadily now and the room was buzzing with excitement. A frontier court has strange ways of stretching the normal rules of procedure, but Judge Littlejohn was equal to it.

Warren Clay was quick to counter this attack and spoke loudly now above the noise of the court. "But it is important and proper that proof of ownership be shown. Do you have such proof, Mr. LaVoy?"

Tom was prepared for this and now came forward with the patent papers to the property, thankful that the period of waiting for such papers was no longer three years, as it had been when his father had first purchased his land here. The Judge marked the papers for identification, then allowed Clay to take them to the table where he and Cyrus Brigham examined them carefully and made notes of the dates of the transaction. Mill Sharrow also asked to see them, and shook his head when he was finished. The recorded date was scarcely a week after he had visited Whiskey Creek. Now they were given to the Judge for his examination.

Tom felt sure now that the question of Indian owner-ship was passed. He had known that there was plenty of precedent to be found to show that Indian ownership of property had often failed to stand the test of time and court actions. The plea of the southern Cherokees was a prime example. He had been concerned about this, but now it was past. From now on it would be a new ball game.

And so it was, for suddenly Cyrus Brigham was on his feet. "With your permission, may I continue the examina-tion of this witness, Your Honor?"

"You have already been certified by the court, Mr. Brigham. Any objections, Mr. Michaels?"

"No objections," Tom replied. He knew, however, that the remaining innings of the ball game had been turned over to a new pitcher. He would have to face a whole new pattern of curves and fast balls. He knew too, that they would prove to be a superior caliber to those of Warren Clay.

"You are the Milan LaVoy whose name appears on those papers?" He motioned to the papers now in the Judge's possession.

"Oui," Milan grinned.

Cyrus Brigham looked at him for a long moment. "You do not speak the English language, Mr. LaVoy?"

Milan's smile hardened and the color rose slightly in his cheeks. He looked directly at the lawyer until Cyrus Brigham turned and sought refuge in his glass of water.

He recovered quickly and returned. "You do not speak the English language?" he repeated.

Milan replied slowly now and with precision. "I speak what I believe to be an understandable mixture of the languages of which this country was made. If you wish to hear only English, you should have remained in the courts and clubs of England. If you dislike French, you perhaps belong in the Southeast, where it is rarely spoken. If you lack the ability to learn or the patience to compromise with the variations of frontiers, it might be safer to retreat to the libraries of Boston. What I speak is American, perhaps frontier American, but American."

Judge Littlejohn was rapping lightly. Lightly enough so that he could hear out Milan's outburst, thought Tom. But his mask of sternness was firm. "Will the court return to, and continue on, its proper course of searching for the truth. I find Mr. LaVoy's grammar sufficiently understandable."

Milan grinned. He was relaxed again now that he had relieved the pressure.

Cyrus Brigham had returned to his seat and was dramatically waiting for order to be restored in the court. Now he returned. "I will go back to my former question--"

"If you do, you can go to hell," Milan grinned.

Cyrus waited for quiet. "Since you have owned the property, Mr. LaVoy, have you cut, or allowed to be cut, timber for your use or for sale?"

Tom's breath came in sharply. This man would be trouble. Switching defenses came quickly and naturally to him.

"Yes," said Milan. And with that challenging grin, he looked at Cyrus Brigham. "Is that more understandable?" he added.

"It is, Mr. LaVoy. Thank you," and he made a polite bow.

"Now!... If you have allowed timber to be cut from the property, will you please explain under what circumstances this has been allowed?"

Tom stirred uneasily in his chair, knowing that once again his case could be slipping from his hands.

Milan was reflective. Aware of the implications of the question, but aware also that the truth must be stated. "Since these hills have been settled, trees have always been cut. First they were cut to clear fields for use. This practice has slowed down since the original farms became established. I recall no such mass cutting and burning to clear land during the last ten years. Since then the cutting has been confined to the cutting of hardwoods for fuel and the selective cutting of mature pines as they are needed to supply the farmers with lumber to build and maintain their farms."

"Is there a mill in the immediate area?"

"Dan Marsaque owns a small mill north of town. That is the nearest."

"You have made general statements, Mr. LaVoy, but what arrangement do you have with Jimmy Colby in relation to the property on which he lives, and which you own?"

"We have never talked of this matter," said Milan. "I am sure it is understood that Jimmy will cut as he sees fit. The land is essentially his. He is free to use it as he likes."

"If he chose to start at the lake shore and cut every tree from the property, would this meet with your approval?"

"He won't."

"But you have no agreement to prevent this?"

"No." Milan grinned, unconcerned by Cyrus Brigham's dramatic disclosure of his poor business methods.

Cyrus shook his head, then was off sniffing on a new scent. "And what amount was involved in your purchase of this property?"

"Objection, Your Honor."

But before Tom could complete his statement Judge Littlejohn held up his hand. "I appreciate your concern about bringing land and timber values into the action at this time, Mr. Michaels, but we have committed ourselves to whole truth and this must be considered a part of the whole truth. Continue, Mr. Brigham."

Cyrus straightened his shoulders in satisfaction and repeated the question with added directness now that he felt the joy of judicial support. "What amount, exactly, did you pay for the property, Mr. LaVoy?"

Milan looked at Tom, but Tom could only shrug.

"It was agreed that I pay one dollar only," said Milan.

Now it was Warren Clay's moment to smile as he

watched his colleague put the best acting of Edwin Booth to shame as he writhed in mock consternation at Milan's quoted figure. Warren would see to it that the papers back in Lansing and Saginaw made much hay from this despicable treatment of a poor Chippewa.

"Obviously, Mr. LaVoy, you either did your friend a serious injustice, which borders on outright robbery, or you both have a very low opinion of the property which you now appear to protect so zealously. Or is it what it appears, a transfer of convenience to place the property in a more secure position?"

Milan did not hesitate. "When wolves are about, lock well the henhouse door," he said. Then he smiled a little, his mouth corners turning down in amusement.

His brief sojourn into the area of values now completed, the defense now shifted abruptly, as seemed to be Cyrus Brigham's style, back to what would obviously be the heart of his defense.

"You stated, Milan, that Mr. Colby was to be allowed to cut timber from the property at will, right?"

"That is right."

"And is it true that he has cut a considerable amount during the last two years?"

"He has cut some."

Brigham was drawing a tighter string around his new defense now.

Tom felt the pressure mounting and his fighting muscles tighten across the small of his back. There was little

Milan could do to ward off this attack. It would simply have to be counted as a round for the defense. He would have to counterpunch later.

"Would you say, Mr. LaVoy, that he has cut fifty trees, one hundred trees, or more than one hundred?"

"My estimate would be near to seventy," said Milan. "But Jimmy has one hundred and sixty acres of land of which at least one hundred and twenty is in trees. It would be difficult to tell if a hundred trees had been cut from one hundred and twenty acres unless they were clear cut, as Sharrow and most of the camp operators are doing."

The defense pressed on. "Are you aware, Mr. LaVoy, that during the fall months for the last two years, Mr. Colby has had the help of a certain Indian friend from the village east of here who, along with his oldest boys, have helped him cut a considerable number of trees and pile them on the shores of the lake?"

"Is considerable, one hundred, two hundred, or three hundred?" grinned Milan.

"We will disregard the amount for the moment. Are you aware that he has cut trees?"

"Yes. I know this."

"But you do know how many trees were cut?"

"No, but I do know that they were only mature and crowded trees, and were cut selectively from the hillsides near to the lake where they could be easily skidded to the water. Even with help they could not have handled them from the area from which trees have been stolen."

"But during the winter in question you admit that you were working many miles to the north."

"Yes, but so was Jimmy Colby."

"But were his sons, or the helper who he so often used and who is said to have come in the winter with oxen to move some of these logs while the snow was on the ground to make it easier? Were they there, Mr. LaVoy?"

"They were not," sighed Milan. This man could skin a bobcat and sell it for beaver.

Cyrus Brigham now went to his table and returned with a long, black–covered book. Opening it, he selected a page and presented it to Milan. On the page were the records of Mill Sharrow's log scaler showing the number of logs bought, number of board feet per log, and date of purchase. Across the top of the page was neatly printed, "from Indian Jim Colby". Milan's eyes followed the figures to the bottom of the page and rested momentarily where the columns had been totaled. Here the final figures held his attention. They read—-

> *Logs- 1,490*   *Board feet- 278,630*

Milan now returned it without comment.

Cyrus Brigham now handed it to the Judge, who marked it for identification and thumbed through it, making notes as he examined each page.

The clock said four p.m. and the buffeting at the windows seemed to predict another blustery February night. Lyman used the lull in the action to fire up, once again, the big Detroits. He had become so engrossed in the questioning that he let the fires burn low and the room was decidedly chilly.

Tom took his turn at the ledger, examining it carefully, especially the pages where the entry which could be so important to him had been made.

Judge Littlejohn waited until he had finished, then rapped gently. "It has been a long day, ladies and gentlemen, and many of you still have a long way to go. This court stands adjourned until nine a.m. tomorrow."

Tom and Mina would stay in Hart with John and Hannah Barr for the duration of the trial and some of the others were staying with friends. Only the families with children were still making the long trip in Bill Sugar's sleigh with Milan riding as escort.

That night at John Barr's table, Tom wrote down the figures as he had seen them entered in Mill Sharrow's ledger. The long lists of entries which were the record of logs which the scaler had recorded as they passed the river head Tom had ignored, except where there was one of unusual size. Now Tom called John's attention to some of these.

"Great balls of fire!" said John, looking at some of these large figures. "Ten hundred and twenty–four board feet. And here is one of sixteen hundred. That means forty–four–inch logs. Those are mighty big trees to come from that property he owns, Tom."

"They didn't," said Tom. "I rode over his cut–over hills

last summer. There were some nice pines there, but nothing as big as that. The largest stumps on his property won't run over thirty–four inches. Those logs had to come from either our property or Jimmy Colby's. Neither were they cut by Jim. He has too much respect for those trees to cut the big ones, and too little ambition to try to move them. He has cut only the smaller trees that he and his friends can handle."

"Do you think the judge knows that, Tom?"

"Probably, but what he knows in that old head of his will carry little weight if an appeal should take the case to a higher court. These company lawyers could make him look like a fool. It is my job to make the case tight enough to defy the examination of any future court. The Judge knows this, and I know it. And what solid proof do we have? Two–year old–tracks on the ice, logs on a riverbank and two thousand acres of silence to tell us where they came from. Oh, if those hills could only talk!"

"Or if some shanty boy from two hundred miles away would come forward with the truth. You have tried to locate these men, haven't you, Tom?"

"For two months last summer," said Tom. "Sharrow was smart, they came by boat from Illinois. That is all I could learn. And he hires a different crew each year."

Tom leaned back in the creaking chair. "This makes it a difficult and interesting case. This and the danger that losing could leave the whole state fair game to these kinds of lumbermen. I sure hate to think of losing, John," Tom leaned forward on his elbows and rubbed his forehead against his folded hands, "yet I can see only a small chance of winning."

John Barr's eyes went to Tom. The fire from the fireplace sent flickering shadows across his lean face, making him seem suddenly older. He then looked at Mina and Hannah sitting in front of the fire. He was surprised to find Mina smiling knowingly. She had heard Tom's remark, but showed no distress. For the first time he realized that losing the case was a definite possibility, and Mina and Tom knew it.

Tom stretched his legs, then pulled the kerosene lamp closer. "Look here, John." He pushed the piece of paper that he had been figuring on in front of the old sheriff. "Milan estimated that Jimmy cut seventy trees and sold them to Sharrow. Seventy trees would produce approximately 420 logs, and 78,400 board feet of lumber.

"Now look here! Sharrow's record shows that Jimmy is credited with 278,630 board feet of lumber. Do you follow me?"

John looked again at the figures and scratched his head. "I guess I don't see it, Tom."

So Tom put the two sets of figures together so that a better comparison could be made——

My estimate: 420 logs = 78,400 board feet from 70 trees

Sharrow's figure: 1490 logs = 278,630 board feet

"See what could happen if a person, sharp in the computation of log production in terms of board feet, added a

2 to the front of Jimmie's actual footage, and a 1 to his number of logs? Up comes a perfectly logical figure to cover about nine acres of good pine. Just about the amount stolen from Jimmy and Louise's property."

"By God! you're right!" said John. "And that's not counting Nancy VanBolt's maple trees." John pulled the paper to him and did some quick figuring. "That could be about three hundred big trees. About the number that Mill Sharrow stole."

"But more than Jimmy could cut and haul in six years," added Tom. "Still, it gives Cyrus Brigham solid figures to show the court, and figures and signatures are hard things to dispute."

"You know, Tom, every day I spend in court scares the hell out of me. You lawyers can make a man doubt daylight."

Chapter Twenty

The temper of the courtroom had changed when the benches filled again on Thursday. Copies of newspapers from the south had come back on the Wednesday stage and had passed from hand to hand. The Saginaw Press had stated flatly, 'Lumbermen Favored in Oceana Suit.' The Grand Rapids Republican had been less blunt, and the Detroit Christian Herald had spoken what was coming to be a common belief: 'Sharrow Probably Guilty in Oceana County Suit, But Can Attorney Michaels Find Sufficient Proof to Support This in the Face of Steady Opposition from the Lumbermen?' It was apparent that doubt was beginning to appear that Judge Littlejohn would dare rule against them, and the concern in the faces of the people reflected this and brought a hush to the courtroom.

The weather had cleared. It was still cold, but sunny and bright. The country was now spangled with glistening ice and snow crystals, and outside the new courthouse, the warmth of the two big stoves had given birth to huge icicles which draped the eaves and in some places extended the entire twelve feet to the drifts below.

War action had slowed since Murfreesboro. Winter had swept over the central states and the whole country lay quiet. Big armies were licking their wounds and building their reserves as they waited for the increase in the action that would come with spring. The feeling in the North was that the Union armies, after so many crushing defeats, were finally finding the leadership they needed to carry the war to the enemy. Lee, Bragg, and VanDorn had now been turned back at Antietam, Perryville and Corinth. The Union's Grant and Rosecrans were showing real fight. Perhaps 'sixty–two had been the turning point.

But how about Eber Harcourt? They all knew that he had been with Rosecrans at Nashville in December. Since then there had been no word. Now news was coming back that Rosecrans had lost twelve thousand men in a cold December battle at Murfreesboro. Everyone was filled with silent concern, but nobody spoke of it. Time would have to answer their questions. Judy must feel the strength of their faith.

The steady tapping of Judge Littlejohn's gavel slowly brought the gathering to order and separated Tom from his wandering thoughts. Like the country, he was ready and waiting. He had covered most of his points now, including the questionable figures in Mill Sharrow's record book. He had done his best. He knew that the defense had yet to put on their biggest show. Probably today would be the day. Good! Let it come. He also had one final card to show. Then it would be over.

Judge Littlejohn was standing now. He looked taller and more stern as he addressed the room. He was aware of the responsibility which this case placed upon him. He was a servant with two masters. He must justly uphold the public trust by seeing that justice was done. He must also answer to the letter of the law as it might be interpreted in a high court.

Not so much different than the responsibilities we all face, thought Tom, except that the consequences could be vastly greater.

The judge cleared his throat and looked out on the full courtroom. "This trial has now extended itself through a full week. We have listened to many details which are necessary to lay a foundation upon which the case rests. This is important, but I am sure we all know that sooner or later we must start to build on that foundation. What I am saying is that to spend more time sparring and waiting for one side to make a mistake, or for the other side to make a bad move is, in my opinion, poor application of the practice of law. At this point most of us are aware of the courses left open to both complainant and defense. I would hope that we can now hold to these courses and bring this trial to an early close."

If was brief and to the point, and pleased Tom, who was ready to make such a move.

The Judge rapped again, three times. "The defense has requested several witnesses for re-examination. Are you ready, Mr. Brigham?"

"I am, Your Honor. I call the complainant, Mina Michaels."

Mina showed neither fear nor defiance as she took the stand. She was dressed comfortably in the warm wool suit which she and Louise had made. Only the high, fur–lined moccasin boots which she preferred in cold weather set her apart from any fashionable Easterner. Tom felt a new warmth for her as she glanced quickly his way, showed a brief reassuring smile, then turned calmly to Cyrus Brigham.

Cyrus was all gentleman in her presence. "Mrs. Michaels, your home overlooks Blue Lake in its entirety. Is that right?"

"Except where it is hidden by the big trees in between, yes."

Tom smiled.

"Did you, at any time during the last winter, observe logs being hauled across the lake towards Mr. Sharrow's camp?"

"No," said Mina, "I did not."

"If logs had been hauled east from the area where the trees were cut last year and transported on sleighs to either the Marsaque mill or to Middlesex, could you have seen them?"

"No," admitted Mina, "I could not."

Cyrus Brigham bowed politely. "Your witness, Mr. Michaels."

Tom stood up quickly and faced his mother. "I have just one question. "Would it have been possible for teams with sleighs to haul logs west across Blue Lake last winter without you seeing them?"

Mina spoke without hesitation. "Yes. We have many days, many weeks and even months when snow falling or blowing hides the lake completely. They could have also been hauled at night or along the near shore. Here they would have been hidden by the over–hanging trees. During December and January it is quite dark by five o'clock in the evening. Even the tracks would be drifted over by morning."

"Thank you," said Tom. "That is all."

Cyrus Brigham arose quickly, pressing eagerly on this important track. "I would like Louise Colby to return to the stand."

He is using our best witnesses to tear the case to shreds, thought Tom.

"You live in the cabin on the east shore of Blue Lake. Is that correct?"

"That is my home," replied Louise, "but during the winter you are interested in I moved my children and myself into the Michaels' home."

"While you were living at the Michaels' house, did you at any time see logs being hauled across the lake?"

He was pressing, now. Giving the witness no time to wander beyond the question.

"No. I did not," admitted Louise.

"If logs had been cut and hauled east or north from the area of the cutting, perhaps to the banks of the Pentwater River or to the lake at its mouth, could you have seen them from the Michaels residence?"

Louise thought for a minute, picturing the open fields behind the Michaels house and the tall forest beyond. "No," she said finally said, "only to the southwest and west across the lake, is the view open."

"Thank you, Mrs. Colby." And again Cyrus Brigham bowed politely.

"Back to you, Tom," the Judge gently prodded, using Tom's first name with no apologies.

"Louise, would it have been possible, during the stay at our home, for the lumbermen from the camp and the south shore of the lake to have traveled to the area of the cutting, cut the trees from the sides of the ravine, and hauled them back across the lake without you seeing them?"

"Very easily," said Louise. "Like Mina said, there would have been weeks at a time when blowing or falling snow could have completely blocked the view of the lake. There is also much frost on the west windows at this time of the year, yes? This is a wild area in the winter, close to the big lake like it is. It could easily be done. Perhaps without even trying to conceal it."

"Were there any unusual reasons for you moving into the Michaels' house during this period?" This question came late to Tom's mind, but it seemed a timely one.

Louise did not hesitate. "Yes, two reasons. Both Mina and I knew it would be a long, lonely winter with Milan and Jim away working, and with you at school in Ann Arbor. Living together would make the winter more fun for both of us and make it easier for the children to get to school."

Louise was quiet for a moment. Tom waited, feeling that she had more to add. Finally she continued.

"I had another reason, too. After the two men, Mr. Sharrow and his foreman, visited me in the fall to ask for cutting rights, I became uneasy. I guess I felt that both Mina and my family would feel safer living together while our men were away."

"Thank you, Louise," said Tom. "That is all." After noting the nod from Cyrus Brigham he fondly escorted her back to her bench.

Cyrus Brigham was again on his feet, eager to move on. "The defense calls Thomas Michaels to the stand."

There was a buzzing in the courtroom at this announcement. Tom, too was surprised. This was a show of arrogance on the part of the defense which he had not expected. It could also be a bitter blow. With the wily Cyrus Brigham filling the air with questions which could have only one answer, Tom knew well that the truth, when drawn forth by an array of well selected questions, could be made to appear embarrassing.

Judge Littlejohn was rapping again. It was only ten o'clock. The Judge still had visions of winding up the questioning today.

Sorry, Judge, Tom was thinking, but I do not intend to be a docile witness.

"Any objection, Mr. Michaels?"

"Would it make any difference if I had?"

"Probably not," the Judge replied. "Since you are personally involved in the action, I would have to overrule any objection. I will, however, suggest that you allow one of the lawyers I have with me to assist you while you are under oath. Would you like to have a few words with your support before the questioning starts?"

"I would like that, Your Honor."

"We will recess for fifteen minutes. You people may stand and move about, but please be in your seats again;" he glanced at the clock; "by ten twenty–five. Mr. Howland, will you kindly act, temporarily, as council for the complainants?"

Cyrus Brigham was ready and waiting as Harvey Tower squeaked through the swearing–in.

Back on the front bench, Milan was doing a little pantomime to show that he was enjoying seeing Tom made a victim of his own profession. Even a trial must have its light moments, in Milan's eyes.

Back farther, Nick Tanner was showing the same elation. He and Milan were two of a kind.

"Your name, please?"

Now, even Allen Harcourt snorted a little.

"Thomas Michaelovic, by birth, sir. But this was legally

shortened to Thomas Michaels when I started college in 'fifty–seven."

Mr. Brigham showed some surprise, but did not question the change.

"You studied law at the state university. Is that correct?"

"It is."

"You know, then, through your study of the history of law, that there was once a time when a man was considered guilty of an offense, as charged, unless he could prove himself innocent. Do you agree with that concept of law?"

"No! Definitely not."

"Will you tell the court, briefly, why you do not believe in that concept?"

"No! I will not," Tom flashed back.

Judge Littlejohn was quick to grasp the unusual situation. "Mr. Michaels, as a witness, you have no legal right to refuse to answer a question unless that right is given to you by the court. If there is an objection to the question it must be made by your council. Not by you."

Tom was grinning in his boyish way, now, and Webster Howland stood waiting patiently to be heard.

"If it is my turn now, Your Honor, counsel objects. The answer to the question would, of necessity, be only an opinion."

"Objection sustained," the judge quickly ruled.

"You also believe, as the Atheneans did, that every man

should plead his own case." Cyrus Brigham was obviously proud of his knowledge of legal history. Without waiting for an answer, he continued. "You do believe, then, that the present, or perhaps it should be called the English concept, that a man should be considered innocent until and unless he is proved guilty, is a logical and moral concept?"

"I do." Tom failed to believe that the defense could hope to sway old Judge Littlejohn with this approach. Perhaps, however, it was a wise move on the part of the defense to help the Judge to justify an unpopular decision. This must be Cyrus Brigham's aim.

He continued more swiftly now, deftly changing the subject, as he liked to do, to the real bellringer. "Do you agree, Mr. Michaels, that it would be possible for someone, perhaps any one of the sixteen or more professional cutters now operating in the county, to cut trees from the tract in question and transport them to the shore of Lake Michigan?"

With the word, possible, firmly implanted into the question, Tom now found himself in a legal corner. He parried. "It is possible for a man to drown in a river which is only six inches deep, but it is very unlikely that this will happen."

"And a peck will not a bushel hold," Cyrus countered, "but if a peck is carried four times, a bushel is moved. You did not answer my question, Mr. Michaels."

"I think that I did. An act which can be considered possible can range to a very remote distance from the logical exercise of effort."

"But you do admit that it would be possible. Right?"

Tom hesitated, torn between the truth ethic he had been brought up to honor and the knowledge of the importance of his answer. It would be over two difficult miles around the dunes north of the lake to the shores of Lake Michigan. It would be difficult, but it was not impossible. He decided that he had no honorable choice. He must answer. "Yes, it could be possible," he said.

"Thank you, Mr. Michaels." Cyrus Brigham was all smiles. He had won a very big point.

And probably a share of the winner's branch, thought Tom.

The courtroom was buzzing now, and the doors of the big stoves were clanging as though relieved of the pressure of the big moment.

It was still only eleven a.m. Cyrus Brigham had struck hard and fast. It had taken him just an hour to play havoc with Tom's case.

The Judge was speaking again, softly, as he ran his big fingers through the scrubby fringe of beard. He had long ago ceased to be concerned about the appearance of his heavy sweater. "We have two hours before recess. Do you think you can complete your argument in that time, Mr. Michaels? It is not my wish to limit you or the defense as long as there are points of importance to present. I see no gain, however, in continuing to beat the bushes after all the hares have been driven."

"With your permission, Your Honor, I have one more important witness to present. This will take some time, but I believe that I can finish easily by one o'clock. Then I will rest my case."

The Judge settled back in his chair and it squeaked loudly in protest, the noise competing with the crackling of the wood stoves and bringing a ripple of laughter from the people of the front benches. "Proceed, Mr. Michaels."

Tom now nodded to Milan and Sheriff Barr and they retreated to the back room.

"My next witness will not need to be sworn in," said Tom, "Yet I believe that it may be my most eloquent witness. One which will offer indisputable proof that the Milton Sharrow Logging Company did, in fact, steal timber from my mother's property."

There was the sound of scraping now and Milan and the sheriff entered carrying between them the severed cross section of a large tree. It had been cut into a section, perhaps six inches thick, to make it light enough to be handled, and the surface had been oiled and rubbed to a beautiful golden sheen. It had obviously been cut from a huge cork pine, fully five feet in diameter. So large that it completely hid the witness chair against which it was placed.

"I present my next witness, Your Honor, and request that it be stamped as an evidence exhibit."

"It may be so received and marked," the Judge said.

Harvey Tower trotted forward, looking puzzled as to how to mark the huge slab. He finally succeeded in working his identification onto the back side.

Tom now stood beside the exhibit. "Actual identification of this exhibit is only a formality," he said. "I am sure the Judge knows, and I am sure my honorable opponent knows, that, like the fingerprint of a man, there is not, and there never will be, another tree exactly like this one. It was born on a hillside east of Blue Lake exactly two hundred and seventy years ago. That would have been the year 1593, fourteen years before Captain John Smith established the first permanent English settlement on a remote island in Chesapeake Bay and called it Jamestown, and only five years after mother England, and Sir Francis Drake, defeated the Spanish Armada."

"The tree was just twenty–seven years old, and this big," Tom now ran his finger around a six inch core of the big slab, "when the Mayflower Pilgrims landed in Massachusetts Bay and founded Plymouth Colony.

"While the Pilgrims were in a life–or–death struggle to survive that first hard year in this country, this little tree was having a struggle of its own. A fire suddenly appeared along the lakeshore and swept up the hills to the east. Perhaps it was started by Indians camping on the lake shore, to clear land for planting. This does not seem likely, though, since the good planting grounds at the Claybanks area are centuries old and offer better soil for gardening. More likely a flash of lightning, or sparks from a campfire fell on dry leaves. Whatever may have caused it, it was the last fire to burn across those hills, for the trees show no more scars like the one which twisted and blackened the heart of this one back in the year 1620.

"Growth was slow during the next few years after that, as the tree struggled to survive, and the growth rings are barely large enough to separate. Then in 1630, about the same time that New Amsterdam, the city we now call New York, had grown to be a thriving frontier village of three hundred people, the growth rings started to widen and the pine which had been struggling for thirty years found its feet covered with protective needles and its branches reaching to the sun, The same as the thirteen new colonies which were taking form along the Atlantic coast.

"The rest you can see. The tree and the country grew up together. They have both had good years and bad years. There are wide healthy rings, formed during years with good rainfall, and there are narrow, pinched rings, like those made in eighteen thirty–seven and –eight, when my mother and father were struggling to stay alive out there on those same sandy hills where rain would not come when it was so badly needed."

Cyrus Brigham was restless. He knew that Tom's long description could merit legal interruption. He knew also, that the people, and more importantly the judge, were enjoying the colorful descriptions. He held his tongue. Tom relaxed and continued.

"Do you wonder why I am taking the time to tell you these things? It could be to help you to know as these people know, who bought the land covered by these big trees, that, besides wealth, they have those elusive values that are history and beauty. The trees belong not just to them and to the moment, but to the ages and to all who look upon them. The wealth they represent has been drawing interest from deep down in the soil of those hills for ages and deposited to an account which our children and our grandchildren should honor. Land ownership was the dream and the privilege for which our fathers made the hard journey to this country to enjoy. May our laws never fail to protect that right from the Turks and the Napoleons who may rise up among us, and may the true value of the fruits of that land be equally recognized and protected.

"Another, and more pertinent reason I bring this exhibit to you is to prove beyond any possible doubt that the thumbprint of this tree, which is the cross section you are looking at, is uniquely its own. A million trees could be cut, and sections laid alongside this one, but there would be a thousand differences in each one. The outer contour, the date of birth, the scars of fires, wind, and lightning, and the shape and width of the rings would all be vastly different. And especially unique in our state.

"So when I say that this section exactly matches a stump which remains on the hillside of a cut-over ravine on my mother's farm, believe me, I have ample and positive proof. What's more, I will prove it to Your Honor, or to any among you who care to make the trip."

Now Tom looked outside to where a sudden timely gust of wind had carried a swirl of snow from the courthouse roof and sent it rustling against the window. Then he turned and grinned. "Do you, Mr. Sharrow, or Mr. Brigham, or Mr. Clay?"

"We will accept your word that this is true, Mr. Michaels, but we fail to see that this adds greatly to your claim of theft."

"That brings me to my second point of interest," said Tom. He motioned again to Milan and Sheriff Barr. They came forward again and slowly turned the heavy slab so that its back side now faced the court. Immediately a rumble of surprise and anger swept through the room, for there on the rough surface of the unfinished log, the log mark of the Milton Sharrow Logging Company stood

out clearly above the twisted heartwood shaped liked a provocative brown mitten. Tom had finally reached the heart of his case.

"Any questions, Mr. Brigham?"

"None, Your Honor."

For once Cyrus Brigham was facing a witness he did not know how to challenge.

Chapter Twenty–One

The weather remained clear on Thursday but on Friday the blustery winds returned. The stage from the south managed to get through, despite the drifts which were now piled deep and solid in the cuts of the Muskegon Trail. It pulled up in front of the tavern unannounced at five p.m., four hours overdue, and the horses were exhausted.

Halvar Brady declared at once that he would go no farther. The horses were liveried and two more reporters from Coldwater and Grand Rapids found a bed at Wellington Hart's Tavern.

According to Nick Tanner's later account he had asked Halvar Brady why he had not blown his horn in his usual greeting upon entering town.

"You t'ink I'm dom' fool?" he had replied. "I try d'at wonce in 'fifty–nine when the weather was sixteen below nothing an' I couldn't no let go of dat dom' horn until John Barr t'awed us both out."

"Yeah," Nick had added, "I remember that time. And after John finally got you separated from your horn we hung it on a peg behind John's stove and as it thawed out the damn thing played bugle calls for two hours.

"We kept track and figgered that they had starting freezing in 'way back at Yankee Springs."

The weather continued bad on Saturday but, in spite of this, the courtroom was crowded when Tom arrived.

The Ottawas, who had filled the back of the room since the trial began, had left their snowshoes outside today, and many of them were standing along the wall or sitting comfortably on the floor.

From his position up front, Tom turned to inspect the gathering. From his mother and Milan and the close friends up front to the less familiar townspeople farther back he could feel a new glow of respect after his good showing on Thursday. It was a pleasant feeling.

There were new faces today, too. Jeannie VanBolt, home from prep school and looking more and more mature and pretty in a new fur–trimmed jacket, had appeared this morning, riding her horse in over the road from the west. As her eyes met Tom's, they glowed warmly, not with the carefree fire of the schoolgirl Jeannie, but with a deeper message of concern and desire. For what? Tom was not sure. Possibly it was for the success of the trial and the humbling of Mill Sharrow. Jeannie had too much spirit to be a good loser. She was changing, though. God! How she was changing! She looked more like her mother, now, but vastly more interesting. She waved a slender arm, and he smiled back at her, then looked on to the back of the room.

Nick Tanner was still back there, probably so that he could steal a chew now and then and get rid of the spit in the big stove. Anyway, he had accomplished one thing. The room was now supplied with as many benches as it could possibly hold.

Harvey Tower, Cy Brigham, and Warren Clay appeared now, and Mill Sharrow was finding his place at the defense table. I wonder who will make the defense summary? mused Tom. Chances are it will be Cyrus Brigham.

John Barr was rapping now. Everyone stood, as the room quieted and the judge took his place. After a few moments of reflection he raised his head and spoke quietly.

"If some of you city reporters find our procedures here somewhat informal as compared to your city courts, do not be disturbed. Our aim is honest justice, the same as theirs. The difference is mainly that very few of us here are seeking elective office. This frees us from some of the displays of eloquence and elegance which often clutter the courts there." The judge did not smile. Only the twinkle in his deep-set eyes softened the ice of his judicial composure.

"We have now come to the point in this trial where we customarily review the evidence which has been presented." He looked at Tom. "Is the counsel for the complainant ready?"

Tom stood, his Indian-straight back stretching his English tweed coat snugly against broad, flat shoulders as he turned to the judge.

"We are ready, Your Honor."

"Then let's get started."

Tom took time to smile back at his Mother. "Our plea, Your Honor, has been based from the start on proof of two things. One, that my mother, Mina Michaels, and her brother, Milan LaVoy, were in complete and lawful ownership of property from which eight hundred and eighty large cork pine trees were stolen. Second, we set our hands to proving that the person, or persons, who caused these trees to be cut and transported from the property, was the logging company controlled and operated by Mr. Milton Sharrow.

"In order to enforce our claim of ownership we offered adequate and indisputable evidence that all patent papers were properly filed and recorded and all payments were made. While we admit that squatter's rights were exercised during the period prior to government survey, we have proven that there were no contesting claims made by either the defendant or the government. These properties have remained in undisputed possession of the owners since 1837 except for the recent transfer of title of the Colby property to Mr. LaVoy in the fall of 1861. A transaction which has been proved legal and binding.

"So having proved the ownership of the property from which the trees were stolen, we moved on to the proof of our accusations that the theft was a deliberate act on the part of the Milton Sharrow Logging Company."

As Tom paused, the back door of the courtroom swung

open and a rush of cold air and flying snow swept through the hall. Lyman Corbin, who had been tilted comfortably back in his own private chair, came quickly awake with a thump and hastened to close the door. As he did so, he came face to face with a young woman struggling to get through the doorway carrying a huge pair of trapper's snowshoes in her snow–covered arms. She was nearly smothered in a long overcoat which Tom recognized as belonging to Bill Sugars, and hidden by a colorful wool scarf wrapped snugly around her face and tied beneath the turned up collar of Bill's old coat. On her head she wore a bright–colored stocking cap which Tom immediately knew was Dana Sharrow's.

He was tempted to laugh, for the moment, at the comic picture she made wrapped in Bill's old coat. Then the truth struck home. This girl had walked alone, the four miles from the valley in very nasty weather. It was doubtful if she had ever before attempted the art of handling the clumsy snow shoes which she carried. Well, she had made it! He was glad for that. As her eyes swept the room they met his and a smile lighted her face. She had experienced a sample of the hardships known so well to these people of the hills, and was showing the joy of knowing that she was equal to it.

The judge was rapping gently now, trying to get things moving again. Tom waited. Dana had smilingly refused the offer of a seat beside the Sugars. She chose, instead, one made available to her by an old Ottawa in the back of the room. That she wished to remain neutral in the court was clear. Perhaps, even in her own mind, she was not prepared to take sides. Tom could only sympathize quietly with her position. Mill Sharrow was giving her an unfair burden to bear.

His mind wandered back to the time, many months ago, on a warm June night, when she had kissed him in the darkness of the stagecoach and her voice had come out of the night, saying: 'I have only one living relative, as far as I know. He is my brother, Milton Sharrow, and I love him very much."

The judge was rapping louder now. "Are you ready to continue, Mr. Michaels?"

Tom glanced at his well–worn notes. He had lost his train of thought. He would never be a good lawyer. He was too easily led astray by concern for people.

"Yes, Your Honor. After we presented to the court sufficient proof of ownership we set our hands to offering equally conclusive proof of the theft of eight hundred and eighty large and valuable trees from these properties. We well knew when we brought suit of timber theft into court that the burden of proof would be a heavy one. We are aware that many similar suits have failed to adequately prove theft by seemingly well identified parties. We are familiar with the Canfield Case in Manistee County, where the people themselves aided and abetted timber thieves to evade the law and to continue to cut timber from government land. It is a sad commentary to observe that some people have not yet equated stealing from their government with stealing from themselves and their children. We believe, however, that these conditions do not hold in this area. The exception, of course, being the employees of the Sharrow Logging Company. Only a few of these could even be located, and those who were lived far away and steadfastly resisted our efforts to subpoena them as witnesses.

"We are also familiar with the case of Stephenson versus Little, which is similar to this case. Here the confusion of goods, or the mixture of legal and illegally cut logs became an issue. Here a good judge ruled in favor of the complainant and fair retribution was ordered and paid.

"I mention these cases both to show the complexity of some of the prior suits, and to show, with clarity, that our complaint is no less or more muddied by such complexities. The people of the area are both cooperative and singularly honest. The location of the theft is, in spite of the claims of the defense, too isolated to permit practical transportation of logs in any direction other than towards the lake, and the Sharrow Logging Company was the only party in the area capable of cutting and transporting the total of eight hundred and eighty trees, cut into approximately six thousand and sixty logs, from those hills. For the defense to claim otherwise is to belittle the intelligence of our good judge and the people of the court.

"But let us allow, for a moment, that, as the defense claims, these six thousand and sixty logs could have been cut and trimmed and transported the some two and a half miles which would be the most direct route possible to the Lake Michigan shore. If we are naive enough to believe that this could happen, how! and I repeat, how! could the log which I have displayed to the court as exhibit two? How could it have found its way from a hillside on Mina Michael's farm where its roots still rest, into the river which runs from the Sharrow Logging Company camp on Blue Lake, have buried itself beneath a sliding hill of sand along the river, and how! does it just happen to bear the clearly defined log-mark of the Milton Sharrow Logging Company? A mark which is accepted throughout the business as saying clearly and with authority, 'Hands off, I am the property, and in this case the stolen property, of the Sharrow Logging Company.'"

Tom wanted to make one more plea. He wanted to make the judge, and those reporters out there who contributed so heavily to the thinking of a nation, understand that this might be the last chance for a great new state to correct a growing wrong. It could be the last best chance to save some of those hillsides covered with big cork pines to be saved for the eyes of generations not so fortunate as this one. It might be an opportunity to curb the greed of a new generation who had tasted the heady fruit of prosperity but had not yet learned the futility of gorging themselves. His mind went from the iron–fenced mansions he had seen being built in Muskegon back to the musty halls at Ann Arbor and the words of Plato came to his mind, "Could a man from all the world all wealth procure. More would remain, the lack of which would make him poor." And those of another eastern philosopher who said, "Poverty comes not from a decrease of one's wealth, but from an increase in one's greed." He would like to place these words before the court, but this was a court of law, not a lectern. He was sure that Judge Littlejohn, the scholar, was already familiar with these gems of wisdom. But Judge Littlejohn was a Judge first, and second a scholar. His duty was first to his law books. He was not only enlightened by them, he was also shackled by them. Perhaps it was sad that these good men could not be free, like Moses, to act as their wisdom and conscience directed them. He returned his glass to the table and turned again to the judge.

"My plea rests," he said.

Tom's closing argument had been fairly short and to the point. The judge was checking the clock and the blustery weather outside.

"I believe, since the weather is not conducive to short walks, that we will call a ten–minute recess to allow you good people to stand and stretch your legs, then we will hear the defense summary. Court is recessed until ten forty–five."

Cyrus Brigham was at his dramatic best for the defense résumè. He wasted no time with the question of ownership, pressing only the point that the Michaels land was purchased under the name Michaelovic. "Michaelovic," he correctly stated, "was the Slavic surname meaning Son of Michael. The enforced use of such names was an attempt on the part of the Ottoman Turks to disinherit their Christian subjects by forcing a constant change of the family name. With this in mind, I can understand the high value this family places on the ownership of property."

Tom was forced to admire the depth of knowledge of this man. Under other circumstances he might find his company most interesting.

"It is fortunate for the Michaels family that our country has a much more liberal attitude concerning the disposition of property than most. Even under the laws of the United States, however, certain rules of notification and publication govern the changing of names, and little proof has been offered by the complainants to support this point. The defense, however, has not and does not at this time wish to pursue this.

"We do not feel that it is necessary to chase other foxes, since the fox of real truth has been treed and is waiting, to feel the sharp axe of justice. I am now referring to the proof, uncontested by our honorable complainant, that there are at least sixteen other logging companies, and other private parties, cutting timber within this county alone. We have offered proof that the logs in question could have been hauled or floated to any one of the big mills operating along the Lake Michigan coast. We have easily supported the fact that several of these companies, or combinations thereof, have equipment and the labor to cut and move the logs in this manner. Yet the complainant has offered no proof that they did not, or could not, do it, holding only to the thin supposition that, since the Sharrow company was the logical suspect in terms of proximity, and the weak evidence that one log among the hundreds cut was found among those belong to the Sharrow Company, that they were all cut, hauled and sold by the defendant, Milton Sharrow.

"In the eyes of the complainants, Mr. Sharrow has already been tried and convicted. I thank God that the laws of our country do not allow this attitude to prevail. Thankfully our systems of checks and balances, and organized searches for justice, do not accept hearsay and unproven accusations as tools by which honest men can be separated from the freedom for which they fought. Proof, sound unquestionable proof, untarnished by the possibility that it could have been any other way, is the only evidence that our laws accept. This is the way, I am sure, that our country and you good people want it."

Milan's muffled comment was followed by quiet laughter from those around him.

Over hot coffee and big plates of neighborhood stew, served piping hot in the church basement, Tom and his mother considered the summaries.

"Mr. Brigham can be very convincing, Tom. He almost has me believing Mill Sharrow could be innocent."

"Oh, he is guilty enough, and you know it! He worked hard, though, to prove to the judge and the reporter that it could be otherwise. That is what he hopes to do."

"You don't think that the judge really believes this, do you?"

"No, certainly not. Judge Littlejohn knows the country and the people here too well. Someone would certainly have seen men coming and going to the area and would have talked. The judge knows that. But what the judge knows is not our problem."

"More coffee, Tom?" Mrs. Barr was keeping the cups filled.

"The problem is that the judge knows very well that what Cyrus Brigham claims, could be true. And he also knows that, with the backing of the big loggers, any decision he makes against the Sharrow Company will be appealed to a higher court. When this happens, all of his knowledge about the area, the distances, the conditions of the trails and the character of the people will be lost. Some judge, or perhaps a jury, back in Lansing, who has never seen this country and cares little if all the trees in the north are cut, will listen to Cy Brigham and be convinced that the evidence we have is not conclusive. This is the problem the judge faces, and no judge likes to have a decision overruled."

Milan had appeared from the kitchen where the laughter of the town women indicated his presence. "Mighty good stew," he proclaimed, patting his flat belly. "Even Joe Parks don't make it so good. I think his would have been better if he had skun the polecats."

The courtroom was overflowing after noon recess. The whole town knew, by now, that a decision was due. When all who could find standing room had found a place, the doors were barred. Lyman Corbin clinked a last split of wood into each of the stoves and cut back the drafts as the hall was rapped to quiet.

Judge Littlejohn remained seated at his table and referred frequently to his prepared notes as he spoke. His thick fringe of beard bobbed gently and his deep voice, reminiscent of that of old Ganus Michaels, filled the room. Only the rustling of the wind against the windows and the murmur of the fires competed with him for the silence.

"As most of you are aware, the case of Michaels and LaVoy versus the Sharrow Logging Company carries implications and responsibilities far beyond the boundaries of this county. We, here in our frontier court, are being watched, as our nation has been watched, to see if and how we are going to make our form of government work. During this trial I have felt this responsibility as never before. A responsibility in some small way similar to that which our Abe Lincoln must be feeling up there in his big, lonely office in Washington. Yet, by comparison, my job is simple, to listen to the facts from both parties, sort out the heartwood from the sawdust, and search for a just decision. Abe listens to Generals, I listen to lawyers. Abe hears excuses, half truths, and promises. I listen to accusations, white lies, and then, just when the real truth is about to emerge, a protest. Such are the ways of governments and courts.

"This case has been ably pled, however, and many truths have been made evident. The first truth to be made clear to the satisfaction of the court was that the land in question was properly patented and recorded in the names of the complainants. As to the two questions raised by the defense, I can only answer that squatter's rights were properly followed by acquisition of legal patents to the land and since no persons appeared to protest the operation of those rights of preemption, the land can be considered legally purchased.

"Concerning the question of continued legal ownership after the change of the complainants name from Michaelovic to Michaels, I can only say this. In this young country, family name changes have been common. The zeal to cast off all bonds with the past and to take up the ways of the new is typical of many emigrants. This has, admittedly, made the administration of the laws relative to disposition of the property and payments of debts an occupation filled with complexities. Only the fact that our laws have evolved around a very liberal stance in this respect and that most of our American immigrants have been notably honest has made it possible to avoid many unfair decisions. My decision, in this case, is based on the proof that the new name has been consistent and permanent, the relationship of the old to the new is close and reasonable, and the defense, in effect, acknowledged this by failing to attempt to purchase or lease under the old name."

Tom relaxed a little. At least he had weathered the first obstacle.

The judge took a sip of water, glanced at the frost–encrusted window, and went on. "We can now pass on through the maze of supporting evidence which our men of law so ably presented and address ourselves to the charge that eight hundred and eighty trees were stolen sometime during the months of January and February of last year from the properties now established as belonging to Mrs. Mina Michaels and Mr. Milan LaVoy. How this solid figure of eight hundred and eighty trees can be supported is something I have to question since it has been admitted that the former owner and present resident of the LaVoy property, Jimmy Colby, had been cutting trees in the manner of a small contractor and selling the logs to the Sharrow Company.

"So we are now faced with a new question which, in the eyes of the court, has not been, and perhaps cannot be, positively supported. This is, how can the court accurately differentiate between trees cut from the property legally by Jimmy Colby and trees which may have been cut by the Mill Sharrow Logging Company, or possibly some other thief."

There was a clatter in the back of the room as Nick Tanner jumped to his feet. "Amen! He's guilty. Court's adjourned," He fairly shouted.

The ripple of laughter started slowly, then traveled across the room as the implication of His Honor's last remark struck home.

The judge looked up questioningly, then realizing that his words had betrayed his real feelings, he showed the restrained hint of a smile, rapped the court to order, and continued.

"This also brings up the point that, since the court can find no reason to question the fact that trees cut from the Michaels property were indeed stolen, would it not have been more logical to have filed separate claims, rather than initiating a joint suit?"

Tom closed his eyes and rested briefly with his elbows on the table and his head in his hands. He had strongly considered this route, but had preferred to gamble for all or nothing. He had not wanted either Milan or the Colbys to think that he was any less concerned about their loss than he was his own. This was the way of the valley. He could do it no other way. He had allowed personal feelings to override good judgment. This was not the way of a successful lawyer. Now the judge was about to throw out any claim from Milan's property for lack of conclusive evidence and inseparable admixture of legal and stolen goods. Now, would his mother's claim suffer the same fate?

"As we move on to the property owned by Mina Michaels we have some new circumstances appearing. For one, the position of the property places it farther from the lake which is the natural avenue through which the logs would be expected to move. It is more adequately concealed from view from all direction except the west and northwest. That would mean that cutting could have gone on there at a leisurely pace during the winter months with little danger of detection. Only hunters might wander into this area, and that would not be likely since the hunting would be much better to the north."

Tom looked back at his mother and Milan. The knowledge being shown by this old judge from down state was a thing to be marveled at. It was a good bet that sometime prior to the trial he had ridden those hills with an eye for detail that rivaled the quickness of Milan himself.

Mina smiled. She looked tired, Tom thought, as though she was wishing it was over. Back beyond were the Sugars, the Harcourts, the Nelsons, the VanBolts and all the others. They were offering the steady support they always would, but were looking puzzled now that they were beginning to understand that this thing was not as simple as it should be. Even old Judge Littlejohn, who they all respected, was hedging. He was telling them, in roundabout ways, that Mill Sharrow might not be held strictly accountable for what they knew was outright theft. There was disappointment and disbelief showing in their eyes. Here and there, where the fire burned hotter, as it did in Milan, there was anger. Back farther yet, Tom's eyes met those of Jeannie VanBolt, and here, as in Milan, the fires were smoldering deep and hot and questioning, and more beautiful than ever before. Perhaps he had not done as well as he should have, thought Tom. Perhaps he had let them down. Perhaps an older and wiser lawyer could have won for them the support of the judge and stopped forever the plunder which was sweeping across the state. He knew that this was not true, though. He knew the judge's problem. He knew that he, Tom Michaels, had done what could be done.

The judge had finished his drink and was probing on. "The position of the land raises another possibility. This is the one so strongly pressed by the defense, the contention that logs could have been hauled across the lake to the north and on to Lake Michigan. I am not truly ready to accept this possibility as fact, since the movement south-west across the lake appears more likely. I cannot, on the other hand, exclude it as impossible." The judge paused, knowing full well the importance of his last statement.

Tom knew it, too.

"So since neither party in the suit can completely prove guilt or no guilt, the court is left with the innocent unless, principle, or perhaps the need for a Solomon-like decision, which it prays that it may have the wisdom to provide."

"But something remains. The one solid piece of evidence which this case has produced. I refer to the single log which carries the undeniable relationship to the stump on the Michaels' property. The section which was so well presented to the court and which I must consider adequate proof of its theft from Mina Michaels' hillside.

"In my experience with these types of suits it has been rare that a solid piece of evidence has been produced. The fact that the attorney for the complainant has produced such evidence, a witness which cannot lie or be offset by counter evidence, is unique. It could well be a factor in reducing promiscuous log theft in the future. This evidence I accept as satisfactory proof of theft by the Sharrow Logging Company and this man, Milton Sharrow, who now sits accused before us, from the complainant, Mina Michaels."

Tom acknowledged his mother's smile. He also shook his head in warning. The judge was not finished yet.

"Does it follow, however, that proof of the theft of one log is sufficient proof of theft of the other three hundred and ninety trees which were stolen from the Michaels' property? Or does there remain the possibility that other parties could have also been involved? This is the final question which confronts the court. It is a question which conflicts with the need of the times, to more adequately enforce our laws. It is a question which hinges heavily on the, 'innocent unless,' principle. It is a basic conflict between the human rights of individuals and the rights of the community to enforce order."

The judge pulled the sleeves of the heavy sweater down more comfortably over the big wrists and ran his fingers through the fringe of beard. He was leaving his prepared text now, yielding to the temptation to philosophize to a captive audience. "Like many others I was once convinced that individual freedom was the greatest need of mankind. But as I grow older I have come to see that order, either attained by disciplines developed in youth, or by fair and equitable laws enforced in adults, is a greater need. For I know now that without order there can be no freedom.

"The law, however, sets definite limits on the freedom with which it may be interpreted. If those limits are breached, it falls to the authority of a higher court to mend the fences, so to speak, and restore judgment to the letter of the law."

This is the real meat, thought Tom, knowing that he was losing. He is telling me that he cannot convict Mill Sharrow of the total charge. He could not deprive him of his freedom or his income when there was lack of conclusive proof of his guilt. And he, Tom Michaels, could not produce that undeniable proof.

Perhaps he should have asked for a jury trial. A jury is not bound by judicial knowledge and technicalities of law. A jury can more freely, if not more accurately, judge people. It can act on the strength of those subtle truths that personalities make self–evident.

Suddenly Tom felt very lonely. The wind, gusting a hard snow against the window across the room, suddenly had a cold yet welcoming sound. He would like to put on his big coat and go out into it and walk and walk and walk. His mind slowly drifted back to the courtroom.

"With these questions remaining unanswered by the processes of the court," the judge was speaking again, his voice sounding low and far away, "I can only fairly make these judgments. First, the Milton Sharrow Logging Company is hereby freed, for lack of sufficient evidence, of the charge of stealing logs from the property of Milan LaVoy. Second, it is also freed from the same charge against the property of Mina Michaels, with one exception. That exception constitutes a separate judgment, and one which should not be underestimated in its importance." The judge's voice had now taken on a steely edge.

Tom came slowly alert to the change.

"I refer to the single log which carries the undeniable mark of the Sharrow Logging Company and the equally clear relationship to the stump on the Michaels' property." He hesitated now, his head bowed in thought, as if seeking the proper words. "Stealing, whether it be one log or many, identifies the defendant as a thief. The dictionary explains the word very simply as 'one who steals.' Not one who steals much, or one who steals often, just, 'one who steals'. It follows then in the eyes of the world, that the Milton Sharrow Logging Company, and Milton Sharrow in particular, as the owner and the manager of that company, must now be considered dishonest. And I, for one, so consider him. And the fact that he is free from a portion of the charge brought against him in no way alters that judgment."

"It also follows, that some consideration should be

accorded the complainant, Mina Michaels, in payment for the loss, however small it may be in relation to the total loss. It is also evident that the cost to the complainant of pressing charges to recover that loss is equally as great as though the defendant was proved guilty of the theft of the entire eight hundred and eighty trees."

Tom began to smile gently at these words.

"I therefore charge the defendant Mill Sharrow Logging Company and its owner, Milton Sharrow, to pay to Mrs. Mina Michaels the sum of two thousand and five hundred dollars. This amount is the court's estimate of the cost of pressing charges against the Sharrow Company plus the value of one fifty–four inch cork pine. A one–year sentence in the Oceana County Jail is suspended pending the payment of those costs."

The old judge's fingers went slowly through the hair of his bowed head. Then the big frame straightened. He was rapping now, gently, then louder, his stern old face showing no trace of the satisfaction he must have felt in the judgment made.

"This court is now adjourned." Tap, Tap, Tap.

Out in the courtroom the silence which had followed the judge's last statements was now swelling slowly to whispers of understanding.

Tom was pressing his mother's hand, knowing better than most the wisdom of Judge Littlejohn's course. The wily old judge had left Milt Sharrow little chance to profit by an appeal. But at the same time he had found a way to award the Michaels family a fair consideration for their loss, an amount which would leave Mill Sharrow's adventure decidedly barren of profit. Especially since a fair amount of those logs were still piled high on the sides of the river behind the jam.

The Indians still sat, silent and without understanding of the strange ways of white people.

The wind rattled the dampers of the big stoves and tapped steadily now at the windows.

Tom was writing now on a piece of notepaper. When he finished, he walked slowly to the defendant's table and placed it before Milton Sharrow.

Mill unfolded it and read these simple words of Philo, "Prefer loss before unjust gain, for that brings grief but once."

Chapter Twenty-Two

Where the deep green crest of the big lake melted against the hazy blue of the spring sky a wisp of cloud rose, rolled itself into a ball of white cotton and moved slowly north. The rest of the sky was clear. So clear the blue of it stretched up and on into the dizzy nothingness of space.

High up. So high that Tom Michaels' eye sometimes lost them in misty distance, two eagles rode the warm thermals rising from the sandy waters of the lake plains. Theirs was not the studied circle of hungry birds searching the ground for food. It was the lazy drifting of satisfied bellies floating endlessly in the freedom of space.

A shadow appeared over the top of the near dune, moved across the sand and flickered on as a herring gull sidled swiftly by, his black–tipped wings bowed to catch the faint breeze drifting in off the lake. From the south, where the hills had been bared by Mill Sharrow's loggers, the faint high-low calls of the meadowlarks could be heard starting their spring chorus. All else this morning was breathlessly still.

The sun, low on its April arc, had picked this rare day to beat warm on the sands. The breeze, usually cool off the lake, was whispering softly from the south, and smelled of fresh–cut pine and bursting buds.

Tom stretched back into the warm sand, searched space again for the eagles and found them, still on the same wide circle, probably equally interested in this invasion of their lonely hills.

At his side, Dana Sharrow spoke, without taking her eyes from the wings overhead. "Whatever led your father to this wild place as early as 1837, Tom?"

"Directly, it was Milan. He had been here before and believed this country to be the prettiest and the healthiest he had seen. As I look back, though, I think many other things led them here. Things farther back; way back in the old countries. Things which turned them away from people and led them to welcome the peaceful quiet of it."

"The religious and political troubles in France?"

"Yes, but more than that, the Turks. Father had seen bad times in old Serbia and Bosnia. When he was small, the good Turk, Hadji Mustapha, was a well loved Pasha. The Turkish janizaries disliked him because of his good treatment of his Christian subjects, and, when he was killed, they turned on the Christians, as the Catholics did the Protestant French. Father watched the tax collectors measure the fields, before his father was allowed to gather the grain, and saw him pay a tax equal to one third of his crop. His family could wear only dark clothing, to indicate their servile condition. They were never allowed to wear green, the color of the Prophet. There was constant fear of arrest, and it was not perjury for a Moslem to falsely testify against a Christian. Finally, my grandfather was found one morning, hanging from the very bridge my father had to cross on his way to school."

"Now I understand why your mother likes to wear bright colors", said Dana.

"They were the favorites of my father, but she also wears them well."

"She is beautiful."

"To be fair, though, Dana, the Turks hated the Christians for a reason. Father knew that. The Moslem Turks, whose religion stressed abstinence, blamed the Christians for introducing the drinking of alcoholic beverages to their Moslem young people."

Tom rested quietly for a moment, watching the single puff of cloud drift slowly to the north. "Isn't it easy to believe that my father might be attracted to a country free of all people?"

"Do you think that here they found what they were looking for, Tom?"

"Probably not." Tom thought for a moment. "But they came close. They were looking for a new beginning. I am sure, maybe consciously, maybe without knowing it, and here they found it. The nice thing was that the people who followed them here were so much like them, even though they were from many different countries. Or perhaps it was that only compatible people stayed. Some, I remember, came and looked and moved on, to Manistee where there were always saloons, or to Buttersworth where there were jobs in the mills. Not everyone had the spirit to stand the hardships here. But the people that remained learned to help one another, and that life suited Mother and Dad. And while they did not really prosper, they managed to live well. Land was cheap and available. By living frugally and working hard they managed to accumulate more and more, thinking always of leaving it to me. To them, land was wealth. Land and peace of mind. Here they found both."

"Then a man called Mill Sharrow came and took away the pleasure of land ownership." Dana's voice was neither bitter nor sad. She had changed much since that day when she and Tom had ridden the stage together out of Muskegon. She had been sure then that the cutting of the trees was going to make this country wealthy, and that that wealth would bring schools and churches and prosperous farms. Now she was not so sure.

The hills of old Serbia had produced their wealth of wood and rich farmland many years ago. But now, in 1863, many generations after this wealth had ceased to flow, only four out of every hundred people in Tom's father's land could read and write. Yet here in this valley, with its wealth of trees still standing, and it's soil thin and dry, were men like Tom, Louise, the musical VanBolt girls, and, had he lived to reach his promise, her favorite student, Jacques Moreau. It certainly had not been wealth that had produced these people. There was no real wealth in these lonely hills.—Or was there? This was the question that kept coming back to trouble her. Was that wealth inside of these people? Tom called it peace of mind; Louise called it inner peace. Were they rich in the natural resources of active minds, untroubled souls, and contented spirits? It was an interesting thought, and if their wealth was indeed there, inside of them, then the little bare schoolroom she did her work in was enough. The rest had already been provided by the country and the good people of the valley, the Sugars, the Michaels, and Louise Colby. The bread had been moulded and leavened. She had only to light the fire, add the texture of broader knowledge, the crust of confidence and a dusting of technical skills to make it top quality. Sale of such a product was of no concern. Perhaps an education should be less concerned with the earning of bread, and more with the adding of flavor to every bite.

"Tom."

"Yes."

"Do you feel competitive?"

"Do you want to wrestle?"

"Yes, I mean no, no!" and she laughed. "I mean, did the valley give you a good education?"

"Must be it didn't, Dana. I lost my first case."

"But the valley did not teach you law, it only prepared you to learn law."

The eagles slid slowly northward, disappeared in blue distance, then reappeared at a lower level. They had still not moved a wing since Tom had been watching them.

"I don't know how to answer that, Dana. The valley taught me to be considerate of my fellow man. Being considerate of Louise and Milan probably cost me my case. As a lawyer, I failed. As a person, I won, because I feel that I fought for them as though their property was my own. My mother feels the same way. The valley, then, taught me to be a good man, maybe not a good lawyer."

"And my brother's background taught him to be a good businessman but a poor neighbor. Interesting, isn't it?"

Tom wanted to answer, but thought better of it.

"And now I am becoming the product of two conflicting cultures. My early lessons told me that opportunity knocks but once, and there may be other people at the door. A smart person steps up quickly, turns the knob and makes a wild dash for the feeding trough of success. But now, after living with the Sugars family, and with you and your mother, I see that there is another way: Turn the knob, hold the door open for the other people to enter, then sit down to share peacefully together as much as is available. I never thought this would work, but here it does."

Tom laughed. "Now you know how I felt when I visited Buffalo with my college friends. It was another world."

"But you were not taken by their ways. I think I am

becoming fond of yours. It reminds me of my history lessons back in Albion. We were reminded often that the Chinese culture and their dynastic governments survived for centuries. Since 221 BC, I believe. While the Ottoman, the Greek, the Roman, and the Napoleonic empires came and went, the Chinese lived calmly on. Sure, they were invaded and conquered many times, but each time the invading armies were slowly absorbed by the stronger culture of the Chinese until the invaders became indistinguishable from them, and the Chinese life went on as before. I feel that is what is happening to me. I am being absorbed."

"Welcome to the first dynasty of William Sugars," laughed Tom.

Between the high dunes flanking Blue Lake and the shores of Lake Michigan lay the wastes of rolling sand hills, dune grass and low junipers the settlers called Colby country. Dana was seeing this lonely area for the first time. They were making the trip for a purpose. She had wanted to see the stump and the buried log which tied her brother to the stealing of the Michaels' timber. They had looked at the big stump with its dark center as they walked around the lake. Now, with the unusual spring day flooding the hills with early warmth, Dana had wanted to go on.

The distance from the high dunes to the big lake is deceiving, and the sand, softened and dried by the warm sun, gave and slid with every step, wearing the body and tiring the spirit.

It was near to noon when they came over the last crest of sand and looked out upon the cool expanse of Lake Michigan. They were tired and hungry, but had brought no food. Tom took out his knife and made a neat cup from the bark of a birch tree. They drank the clear water from the lake. They rested again on the sands of the beach, then took off their shoes and waded in the water, still cold from the winter ice. The shore was lined with wave–washed pebbles, and like children they searched for agates and gray Petoskey stones, polished smooth by the waves.

They rested again where the river slid out from between the dunes and lost itself in the bluer water of the lake. It was warmer here in the protection of the cedar trees and Dana relaxed. It was mid-afternoon when she awoke. Tom's jacket was over her and she was comfortable, although the wind still carried the chill of early spring. Above, the sky was blue and deep and cloudless. An occasional gull slid by, coasting sidewise to follow the line of the beach in search of food. A song sparrow gentled the sweetest of all music from a birch tree. She fell back asleep, tired, contented.

After a while she woke again. The wind had shifted to the west and the sound of waves washing rhythmically on the pebbly beach held her pleasantly alert. A long ribbon of geese drifted north, flying high, their bugling barely audible above the wash of the waves.

Finally she pushed off the deerskin jacket and sat up,

relishing the smell of woodsmoke and frying whitefish. On the near bank of the river, in the protection of a clump of young cedars, Tom was frying the two sides of a fine whitefish on a slab of flat stone over a rich bed of coals. On the opposite side of the river Jimmy Colby crouched, still as a statue, waiting with a long slender homemade spear to add to his catch. As she watched, he made a quick thrust with the notched pole. Carefully, he pulled up another good fish and fell upon it as it slid across the grassy slope.

Tom laughed at the sight of Jimmy chasing it on his hands and knees, but Jimmy was the winner and soon he was adding it to a willow branch which already held two other nice fish. After the stringing was carefully done, Jimmy looked across the river at Tom. "You laugh, ha! ha! ha! at old Jimmy, friend Tom, but without him you starve in the woods like Milan." He picked up his long spear and the string of fish and melted into the woods, his amused laugh still coming back "haa! haa! haa!"

Tom was aware of her watching him. "Come on, Dana. I couldn't even find a fiddlehead fern for a salad, but whitefish we have."

Dana laughed at the crude tools Tom had made, but she loved whitefish, and this was as good as she had ever tasted.

"There have been a lot of those eaten here, Dana. Back behind those trees to the south there are signs of old Indian camps. The bark–covered lodges are gone now, but they were still there when I was a boy. You can still find pieces of their pottery and old tin dishes they bought with their skins."

"And a ton of fish bones, I bet. Where are they now, Tom?"

"Scattered, I suppose, Kansas or Canada, dead of the smallpox or cholera, or living in the villages up in the northeast corner of the county.

"The good fishing is gone. Gathered up by the big nets of the white fishermen. The best of the hunting grounds, the maple woods where they made their sugar and the berry swamps, are on white man's land. There is little left of their way of life. Still it is better here than farther south where most of them came from.

"Sometimes I feel we have done the same thing to them that the Turks did to my father, and they have no place to go. The last frontier is out there somewhere to the west, and that is rapidly being settled."

"It is a westward world we live in, Tom. Our families and our civilizations have moved steadily west. Even the sun rises in the east and moves to the west. Where have the Indians been pushed? To the west. And the American people follow them, always west. Only the wind goes east."

"And politicians and taxes," added Tom.

Refreshed by the whitefish, they left the lakeshore and headed east along the river. The trail was narrow and here and there patches of snow still melted in the hollows. The willow branches were blood–red along the river banks and the birches yellow–tipped and ready.

Tom was puzzled by the lack of activity on the water. This was April. The ice was gone. It was past time for Mill Sharrow to be breaking the jam and moving the logs into the bay. There were no rafts being formed in the bay. No men or tugs to be seen, and no logs showing in the river.

Tom stopped, and stood suddenly silent, amazed at his own lack of understanding. As Dana looked at him with puzzled eyes, he searched back. There had been snow a-plenty in February, but March had been mild. With the ground covered with a deep blanket of insulating snow since last fall, there had been little frost in the ground. The sun had moved higher. The snows had melted, but the water from the spring melt had settled slowly into the soft ground. There had been no frost to hold it back and the usual runoff had not occurred. That was it! The river, even now, was scarcely higher than it was last August. This was going to be the spring Bill Sugars had predicted. The one when the river was refusing to carry Mill Sharrow's logs. Unless something happened to change this, Mill was in trouble. A million or more board feet of cut timber were behind that big jam, yet Sharrow could not get it out.

He hurried ahead. At the bend of the river where the highest dune crowded in from the north, the big log with the dark mitten in its center still lay partially buried in the sand. Behind it, the jumble of the jam lay piled against the flow of the river with only a lazy trickle gushing through.

Dana saw the big log from the high bank on the opposite side of the river. Even from that distance she knew
well enough that Tom was right. The section of log which
he had shown to the court had most certainly been cut
from this log. She had always known that this was true,
but she had to see. Her spirits fell. Until now she could
still hope to see some reason not to believe this one piece
of evidence which linked her brother to the theft of the
Michaels' trees. Now, with that distinctive swirl of dark
wood showing so clearly, she could not doubt it. He had
cut the timber, and most likely all of it. Possibly the foreman, Angus McBride, had urged him on, but that did not
matter. He had lowered himself to steal from a widow.
Regardless of their differences in respect for the big trees,
it was an inexcusable act. She suddenly knew that she was
no longer in his corner. The people here were now her
people.

She thought of the words of Confucius which Bill
Sugars had recently repeated in his paper, "Where there
is righteousness in the heart, there will be beauty in
character. Where there is beauty in the character, there
will be harmony in the home. If there is harmony in the
home, there will be order in the nation. If there is order
in the nation, there will be peace in the world." Her
brother had fallen far short of having righteousness in
his heart. He had broken the chain before the first link
had been welded.

Bill Sugars had gone deeper, to say that if the people of

this nation had seen fit to live by those words, there would have been no slavery. There would have been order in the nation and the Civil War might well have been prevented.

Above the bend of the river the water ran deeper and here lay the heart of the great jam of logs which had piled up behind the sliding sand. The little lake was also filled with logs, and there were more in big piles waiting to be rolled into the water. Dana was amazed at the extent of the piled–up timber.

At the camp, voices could be heard from the big building. Mill had kept men to run the logs to the bay if the opportunity came and the jam could be broken. If there were no heavy rains? Tom shrugged his shoulders in the comfort of the leather jacket. It might be a real bad year for Mill Sharrow.

Dana showed no interest in calling at the camp office, so she and Tom circled the clearing. They walked in silence out past the barns and their rotting manure piles, past the dump where the cook had tossed his trash and on along the sandy shore of the lake.

Up to the south the hills unfolded, lower here and cut by ravines and patches of swamp. The trees had been swept clean from these hills. Down out of them circled the bare ruts of the logging roads, cut deep by the pounding hooves of the four big teams which Mill kept for this use. The sides of the hills were covered by a desolate mixture of brown pine stumps and row upon row of withering pine branches, each one showing by its pattern where one of the big trees had fallen, been stripped of its branches and hauled away.

Tom looked on this with concern. Those limbs, dried in the summer sun, would burn like paper if a fire ever started among them, and there was little to stop a fire this side of the village. The protection of which Judge Littlejohn had spoken was being bridged by a desert of drying branches. The danger would be there until time turned them again to soil.

Along the lake, they walked quietly. Dana had lost the enthusiasm with which she had started the day. The evidence she had seen was convincing. Tom respected her silence. It had been a long day. They had circled Blue Lake and gone on to the big one. The blue green waters of it could be seen again now, heaped up against the sky to the southwest. To the west and northwest the view was blocked by the dunes. From here, at lake level, they looked higher and more majestic, lying quietly in the afternoon sun. They were cool and blue now on their shady side, warm and butter–yellow where the sun still bathed their peaks.

The trail up to the Michaels' lane led through the big trees where Tom had wandered during his first night home from college. Now the carpet of needles was still damp and fragrant, and patches of February's snow still lay deep in the shady ravines. A faint warm breeze rustled the tops of the big pines and they stopped to watch as an afternoon cloud drifted overhead, making the trees appear to be marching smoothly westward.

Where the trees thinned and melted into the Michaels' pastureland, Dana found Tom's hand and turning him towards her she locked her hands behind his back and pulled him close to her. "It has been a good day, Tom. I have not been the best of company, but you have been understanding. Perhaps we can do it again sometime when I am one of you."

"Perhaps you are one of us," said Tom "We have no rules."

"No. No rules, no restrictions, and no penalties. You are just good people. Even Martin Brewer you treat with kindness, even though you despise his saloon and his ways."

"Don't guess any of us are without faults," said Tom, lifting her chin and grinning down at her. He had been made serious by her mood. In the half light of the pines the brown eyes seemed darker. A little tired, too, and maybe brooding a little. She was feeling disappointment in her brother yet was torn by a sense of disloyalty.

She looked up at him with questions in her eyes but could not put them to words, so turned her head to his chest and clung there tightly.

The whisper of air off the lake was turning cold. Up ahead, the trees were silhouetted against the brightness of the afternoon sun slanting down across the open pasture-land. Beyond, the white cottage and the new barn lay peaceful against the softness of budding maples.

In the yard, two horses were tied to the hitching rail. One was John Barr's roan. The other was a stranger to Tom.

Mina heard them on the porch and opened the door. In the darkness inside, Tom saw John Barr and Mill Sharrow sitting at the dining room table. His mother brought them coffee and sugar cookies, and Tom laughed as Dana took two and pulled up a chair beside her brother. It had been a long, hungry day.

"We have some business to cover, Tom. We've been a-waitin'," said the sheriff. "Your mother thought it best that you were here."

Mill Sharrow waited, saying nothing, but looking long at Dana. They had seen little of each other during the past year and their eyes showed hunger for each other. Yet, there was a wall between them that would not yield.

"Mr. Sharrow has some problems, Tom. One of them, of course, is the two thousand five hundred dollar settlement which he owes to your mother. The judge appointed me to see that this is paid, and that I intend to do."

"A damn heavy penalty for a case I won," said Mill.

"And a light one for one you, in truth, lost," replied Tom.

Sheriff Barr was holding both hands over his head for silence, and grinning knowingly. The steel in Tom's voice was new to him. "The trial is over and past. The penalty, fair or otherwise, is set. There ain't nothin' to gain here by questionin' the right or wrong of it. What we need to work out is ways and means."

"And the meanness of the weather is hampering the ways," grinned Tom. His bursts of anger cooled as quickly as they heated. This was more like Milan, thought Mina. Ganus would be more slow to flare up, but equally slow to cool.

"That's exactly it," said the sheriff. "Unless something happens to raise the water in the river there will be no logs reaching the mills this year. And the weather is failing."

"And even if I get them out, I still could not sell them," added Mill. "The market is gone. The war has taken care of that."

"Do you want to explain that to them, like you did to me, Mill?"

"Without going into figures, I will try," said Mill. He spoke quietly now, without looking up. He was a man with many troubles, thought Tom. But troubles of his own making. Let him sweat it out.

"I started thinking of timber back in 'sixty," he said. "I could see that logging was going to be a big thing in Michigan. It had the rivers, it had the big lakes for transporting the lumber, and it had the trees, big and plenty. I wasn't wrong, but I didn't figure on the war."

Tom listened, and began to know Mill Sharrow.

"I saw Crapo doing well in Saginaw. Mills were getting started in Muskegon, and Chicago was buying lumber. If

I could get a start, I might be able to set up a mill of my own in a few years, and the Middlesex area looked like a good spot.

"I had nothing, but money was not hard to get. Michigan banks were regulated close, but in Illinois, where they were mostly wildcat banks, I could get money. So I borrowed. I bought the cheap land south of the lake and in the fall of 'sixty I hired men, built the camp, and bought horses and grub.

"The money went fast, like borrowed money does, and by the time we were ready to start cutting, I was pretty well out of funds.

"For a new outfit, we did all right that first year. No matter what you think of him, my foreman, McBride, is a good man. He gets things done."

"The wrong things, yes!" Tom spoke quietly.

"Damn it! Do you want to hear, or no?"

"Go ahead. It's your story," said Tom. "And watch your tongue. You are in our house."

Sharrow's eyes raised to the window now, troubled and blinking. He looked out, unseeing, at the hills, gray and blurred in the fading light. The arrogance was gone from him. He knew, indeed, that he had a problem.

"It looked like 'sixty–one could be another good year, so in the spring I borrowed again, heavy, figuring to buy more land. I hoped to get some of the really good timber, but the Harcourt boy beat me to the land on the northern shore and the rest would not lease.

"I was back in Michigan again in April when word reached me that the money I had borrowed was worthless. Like I said, Illinois banks were wildcatters. By themselves, they didn't have a nickel of backing. Those banks were funded by state bonds, and most of those bonds were owned by the Southern states. Cotton and slave money. When Fort Sumter went down on April fourteenth of last year, my money went down with it. The Southern states disowned all debts owed to the North. My bank notes were worthless. In Illinois they burned them, or threw them away by the bushel. I was dead broke."

Tom's nature was to feel compassion. He held back, though. Something told him that only a misfortune, such as this, would bend this man to think of another. Only the knowing of what it is like to be in boots that pinch would weld a link of brotherhood between himself and another man. It was a hard way to think, but he felt the truth of it.

"1861 did not look so good now. The war had changed everything. No money meant no building. The price of lumber dropped from sixty–five dollars to nine dollars per thousand. Almost overnight most of the mills closed down and the mill workers and shantymen threw down their tools and marched off to war. We had two choices: sell our horses and equipment and get out, or gamble that the war would be a short one, and go ahead and cut. Most predictions were that the South would not hold out long. So we gambled.

"We had a good cutting season and plenty of snow to

move them. We got about half of the logs out-"

"But one of them, you didn't," added Tom.

"All right, one big five–and–a–half footer. And about two thousand others behind it. That one log caused a jam we could not break. The water was going down, and without plenty of water, and dynamite, we could not break it up. We had about a million board feet out, but that was not enough."

"So you could not pay the men?" It was Dana's worried question.

"Not right away. But I had good men. They understood the bank situation and stayed with me until the lumber was milled and sold. Six dollars and fifty cents a thousand was a giveaway price, but I had to take it. It paid the men."

"We did not try to work the woods last season. The war was still on, there was no credit and no market, and I had a trial on my hands.

"This spring, though, I had to gamble again. There were still over a million feet of timber in those logs, and, with all of the snow we had in February, I figured there would be plenty of water. I rounded up rivermen and we built a dam below the jamb to help raise the water. But I had not noticed the early snow that had kept the ground from freezing. Without frost in the ground the snow melted from the bottom and went straight into that damn sand.

"You know the rest. The best river hogs can't move logs

without water, and it's not coming. If I could have held on, got the timber out, and stored it until the war was over, I still might have done well."

He turned his head to the window again. His voice was bitter at the thought of the lost years. He had felt the need to make his story known, but he disliked the presence of Mina and Dana. This was man's talk. A man should be able to have his say in private, without womenfolks around to spread it far and wide.

It was not a new story to Tom. He had heard it often in the cities. Some men were born to gamble, and many in this new country had done it successfully. Many others had not.

The Sheriff clicked open the cover of his big watch and checked the time. The light in the room had grown dim as the long slant of the sun faded into blue–green and gold out over the lake. Mina did not light a lamp, though. The evening was too beautiful to spoil with lamplight. The privacy of shadows seemed fitting.

The Sheriff cleared his throat. "What Mr. Sharrow is a–sayin', Tom, is that there is no money to give. He's borried his fill and he's about reached the end of his tether."

"Unless he's lying to us," said Tom, looking straight at Mill. "His reputation for telling the truth don't stack up too well in this country."

Mill did not look up. "If I had cash I would pay off the rest of the men, now, and get to hell out of this country."

"You don't figure to get the timber out, then?"

"That river had more water in it last August than it has now. With no frost in the ground, only a week of heavy rain could bring it up. That ain't likely."

"How much timber do you have cut and waiting to be moved?" he asked.

"It figures out at one million one hundred and fifty thousand board feet. Maybe a little more."

"You own six hundred and forty acres south of the lake. Is that right?"

"You seem to know," said Mill.

"About half of that is cleared of timber?"

"Less than half. More like a third."

Tom was busy now with pen and paper. Mina watched him, glad that he was here to help, not down there in Tennessee or Virginia with Lincoln's armies. She needed him, too. Surely Lincoln could understand that. Mill Sharrow would be a hard one to handle if it were not for Tom.

He had finished now and laid his pen aside. He left the table and wandered to the window. He was thinking of what he knew about the war. Although he could not bring himself to leave his mother and participate in it, he and Bill Sugars followed it closely. They marked the movements of the armies on the big map in Bill's office. They studied the reports which he received with each mail, and they always marked the movements of Eber Harcourt's Second Cavalry with a blue pin.

He knew now that General Grant was about to move

on Vicksburg. If he was successful, the entire Mississippi Valley would belong to the Union, and the Confederacy would be split in two. Eber's Second Michigan Cavalry, with General Rosecrans, was certainly preparing to march against Bragg, and hopefully on to Chattanooga. What would happen in the East was less predictable. For the first time, though, it appeared that the Union armies were gaining the upper hand.

The land Mill owned was not choice but it would raise good fruit and be worth the eight hundred dollars that he paid for it. The timber now, was worth nothing. When the war ended, however, it would become valuable again. Perhaps it would bring twelve or fourteen dollars per thousand board feet.

But could he get it out? This spring it did not look possible. Any time, breaking a jam and making a river drive is a job for tough, skilled men. Would he be able to find them? He believed that he could. Besides, he was not in debt like Mill Sharrow. If those logs did remain there in the river and in those piles for another year, they would still be good timber, and the price would most certainly be higher.

He turned from the window and stood behind his mother. She looked up at him, knowing his thoughts, and in the dim light her eyes said, yes, to his unasked question. She just wanted Mill Sharrow out of her hills.

Chapter Twenty–Three

Milt Sharrow spent an hour the next morning walking the river banks between his camp and the bay of Lake Michigan. What he saw was not reassuring.

Now he stood on the cut bank where the river made its bend below the camp. Below him, in the gravel of the river bottom, was the stake he had driven two days earlier. It stood, dry and clean, a full foot above the flowing water. "Down another two inches," he swore softly. With the price of four by fours at only nine dollars he had troubles enough. Even if he could get his logs to the mills he could barely pay off the men and clear himself with Tom Michaels. The times, bad luck, and a dry spring were closing a trap upon him. He was an animal being squeezed between the need for cash and the relentless tide of fair weather which prevented him from acquiring it.

He thought back to other years when the end of March had seen the breaking of the ice and the rivers had run full and high. April was now half gone and the frost and ice had melted away with hardly a half–foot of rise in the river. On the Muskegon or the Manistee Rivers it wouldn't matter. Those streams always carried enough water. But here, with the lake filled with those big, heavy logs, he needed all the water he could get. To get it now would require a miracle, and Mill Sharrow was not one to believe in miracles.

He spent another half hour at the river; then, with mind made up, he tossed a stray stone into the clear water and turned back to the camp. Like Sheriff Barr had said, Mill Sharrow had reached the end of his tether. He had asked Tom Michaels for another week to get the logs out, but hell! There was no use in waiting. He was finished and he knew it. Keeping rivermen in camp at two dollars a day while the water only dropped lower was useless.

Within the hour he instructed Angus McBride and the clerk to pay off the men. He was closing the camp. If Tom Michaels wanted the money for his trees he would make him earn it. Take it from the rough rivermen, or get his own logs out. The thought somehow comforted him.

It was past sundown before the camp was cleared and the last of the River Hogs were on their way. A few had started early and would walk the beach to Middlesex. They were the family men, the ones who were buying land or supporting families. The rest had other ideas. If Martin Brewer's saloon was not open, they sure enough would open it. The cook had already dug out the two bottles he had hidden in the flour barrel, and with this for the road and money in their pockets, they started the long walk into town.

Over on the dark east shore of the lake, Jimmy Colby stepped outside the little cabin. He liked to take a walk along the lake shore before he turned to his blankets. The night was mild, even with the wind coming in off of the lake, and the thin beginning of a moon blazed a faint, shimmering path across the water. As his eyes adjusted to the night, the dunes loomed up dark and mysterious above the silvered water. A tree toad creaked merrily in the darkness of the pines, and somewhere up the shore, two raccoons were quarreling over their evening meal. Jim was full bellied and content, but uneasy. The spring run of whitefish had kept his table well stocked. Charlie was big enough now to be good help, and without the lumbermen in the forests during the winter, his troubles with their whiskey, and with Louise, had been few. He stood proud now, like the pine tree. Since last summer's harvest moon he had stood strong. It had been a good winter for him.

But now the rivermen had returned to the camp at the end of the lake. The sound of their voices and the dull ring of axes came sharp across the water in the cool, wet of the mornings, as they built the new dam. Slowly he had grown more silent and irritable.

Now he stood in the darkness, looking up at the shadowy dunes, then south across the lake to where the tops of the big pine trees pointed upward at the stars. He let out a defiant grunt. The night sounds of the lake answered, chirping and rippling in the darkness. A door slammed shut in the distant camp and Jimmy turned, curious. By standing on a point of sand he could see lamplight as the door opened and closed. After a while it closed and remained closed. A little later the light in the window also went out and the camp was dark. Only the thin moon and a sprinkle of stars worried at the blackness of the night.

He was about to return to the cabin when he heard the sound of men on the trail to the southeast. Several men, their voices clear now in the night air and noisy, as he remembered them during the winter cutting. Noisy, and then quiet again as they topped the ridge towards town.

The old hunger swept over him. He wiped a trembling hand across his face and said, no! But his feet turned south along the lake shore and he followed, eagerly and helplessly, into the dark silence of the pines and on to the needled trail which led upwards to the village.

Out of the shadows of the cabin, young Charlie Colby watched, heard, and understood and felt a loneliness in his heart.

The saloon was closed and Martin and Martha Brewer were in bed when the sound of loud singing and a pounding on their door brought them awake. Lamp in hand, Martin opened the door to face big riverman Jans Troy. "Ve ave da beeg dry, ole man. Better you open op de bar or dese boys shorr bust heem down."

Martin looked up for a minute at Jan's big apologetic grin, then on at the circle of faces showing dim out of the fringe of lamp light. Out in front a step or two, he could see the florid face of Jug Bateese. Jug was a small man, but was a heavy drinker, and with whiskey in his belly he could be a troublemaker. Martin hesitated and Jug took another step forward. Refusing was out of the question.

"I come," he stated simply, and padded back into the house to dress.

A fire was soon blazing in the kitchen stove at the saloon and Martin's cheap whiskey was flowing freely, whiskey bought and delivered by Mill Sharrow.

A half–hour later, Angus McBride and the camp clerk came in out of the night and joined the rest. The party was now complete.

The sliver of moon was high in the blackness of the south sky as Tom went to stand thoughtfully at the window. The light wind that had come up while he and Dana were on the beach the day before, had continued. Now it worried at the window and rustled the bare lilac bushes in the darkness. Dana was curled up in front of the low fire, reading silently by lamplight. Mina had said her goodnights and turned in, tired and disturbed by yesterday's meeting with Mill Sharrow. Nobody knew where Milan was. Nights were the same as days to him and he had ridden off into the darkness.

Out of the blackness of the night, Tom became aware of a light flickering among the trees below him. It disappeared, and then, a few minutes later, appeared again from the trees along the path which led downward to the

Colby cabin on the lakeshore. It took form, and he could finally see that it was Louise and her oldest boy, Charlie, carrying an old coal oil lantern.

Tom looked at the clock above the fireplace. It was nearly eleven o'clock. This was an unusual hour for a visit by Louise. He slipped into the woodshed, drew on his buckskin coat and stepped outside. Dana was deep in her book and was only half aware of his departure.

It was near to midnight when the door of Martin Brewer's saloon again creaked open and Tom Michaels stepped inside for the second time. Except for one game back in the corner, there were no cards to-night. There was money to spend, nothing but travel tomorrow, and more interesting entertainment. In the center of the room, two tables had been pushed together, and here most of the men had gathered.

Tom waited in the darkness of the entry until his eyes had adjusted to the lamplight. The room was hot from Martin's cooking fire, hazy with tobacco and woodsmoke, and rank with the stink of hot grease and cheap whiskey.

As his eyes adjusted to the light he saw, between the men standing around the table, the face and broad body of Angus McBride sitting at the end of the table. Beyond him, with a drunken, silly smile on his dark face, sat Jimmy Colby, polishing awkwardly one of Martin Brewer's battered brass cuspidors. On the table in front of him were lined up two more dirty spittoons, and between each one, a half–filled glass of whiskey. A bottle, still one quarter full, was in line behind the last brass container.

"I have two dollars that says he never gets to the bottle," laughed the foreman, laying two more greenbacks on the table.

"Good money, or more of that Illinois paper?" shouted one of the card players.

"Good money. Keep shinin', Nigger. It's not clean enough yet."

Jimmy looked at the next glass, resting only an arm's length away, his eyes rolling pleadingly from the glass to the face of Angus McBride. The men laughed loudly, enjoying the show.

There were only two men in the room who had seen Tom close the door. One was Angus McBride, who sat facing the door as though anticipating the visitor. The other was Martin Brewer. He was standing at his stove, but glancing often into the room where Jimmy was being humbled. His watery eyes were ashamed and pleading as he looked at Tom. Although he and Martha had never fitted into the ways of the village, Martin held a silent respect for its people. Now he suddenly realized that he considered Jimmy a friend. He was without the courage or the strength to stop this game, though. He knew that the victim could easily as not have been himself. His venture into the logging business had gotten out of hand, the same as it had with Mill Sharrow, and it had gained him little, for Sharrow was the real owner of the business. Now he could neither get out or profit greatly from it. Mill

Sharrow had seen to that.

"Now the inside, Chief, and the drink is yours." McBride was not only enjoying the humbling of the Indian, he was making a dollar doing it. A fair wager is a fair game. And the real fun was still standing there at the door. He raised his big hand, "Come on in, Michaels. Come in and join the fun."

Tom was aware of his position as he saw the Irishman's eyes come to him. He could not back up. In just coming to this place, he had made his choice. His voice was sharp and clear as he called through the noise of the room, "Sorry, McBride, the game is over." Then more quietly, "Get your coat, Jimmy. We're going home."

Jim's eyes swam to Tom, as the room took on a stiff quiet, but he found neither the power or the will to move. Tom found his coat on a hook near the door and stepped into the room. The circle around the table parted. Only Angus McBride remained, his hands wide on the table, his feet pulled back in readiness. It was the little river-man, Jug Bateese, who spoke. "Get heem boss!" he hissed, and his voice sounded loud in the stillness of the room.

With catlike quickness, Angus McBride was on his feet. In one motion, he sent the tables spinning across the room towards Tom and lunged after them. This was the moment he had hoped for.

The rush came too quickly for Tom to avoid. He threw Jim's coat full into the charging face and ducked. A flailing arm caught the side of his head and he went down.

They were both up quickly, but, in the tangle of tables, Tom could not maneuver and he went down again as McBride went spinning across the room.

This was backwoods war. Butting, kicking, and gouging was the style. This was new to Tom, but not unexpected. He was on his feet now and ready. The rush came, and a hobnailed boot caught him as he stepped aside. It tore the leg of his pants to shreds but it missed his groin, and the force of it again sent Angus to his knees. Tom made no effort to follow the advantage.

More cautious now, the stocky foreman hesitated, then charged again, ducked to the right, then came in with his left boot swinging high. The little river rat, Bateese, had slid in next to Tom now, and between them they forced him against the wall. The rest of the men scattered, to give them room, and Jug Bateese shouted, "You got heem now, Boss, fineesh heem."

Tom heard, and felt the wind leave his body as McBride's head came in hard against his middle. He fought the sickness in his stomach as he brought his own knee up into the big head and sent McBride spinning again across the room. He waited against the wall, fighting for consciousness, unaware that Angus McBride was doing the same. The lamps made a slow, wide circle and the thick smoke scorched his lungs as air came back into them. As though from a great distance, he saw the door open, saw the face of Nick Tanner and young Charley Colby briefly where the lamplight slanted into the night, saw a shock of curly gray hair above the crowd and heard Milan's voice fill the room.

"Get back along those walls, you ring–tailed bob–cat." Milan's voice cracked like the lash of summer lightning, and the look in his eyes was something to see. Age had dulled but little the power that once was his.

Tom gulped the fresh air that came in the door, braced his legs and met McBride's desperate charge with the only weapon he had been taught to defend with, a straight arm in the face of the moving target. The effect was startling. Caught unprepared for it, the big man took the full force of his own rush directly in his face. He staggered back as blood flowed from his brow and ran down into his eyes. In the middle of the floor, he stood swaying gently. For the first time, he seemed aware that he might be in trouble.

Tom's head was clear now and the lights stopped their circling. He heard Milan again as he warned the red–eyed Jug Bateese: "Stay where you are, Rat!" He side–stepped another rush and again whipped the left hand into the solid jaw. He heard Milan's "Good boy!" as the Irishman came in again, trying hard to get inside of that long left hand, drive his head against Tom 's chest, and those steel–clad boots into his groin.

He saw Jug Bateese sliding over again, trying to keep him from dancing away from the charges. From the corner of his eye, he saw Milan palm his big knife, handle forward, and bring his hand quickly upward. Jug stopped, a surprised look on his face, as his arm was suddenly impaled against the wall. He did not move again, but stood looking at the blood dripping slowly from his finger–tips. The room was still except for the panting of the two men and the thud of heavy blows. Tom was in command now. He met each rush with that long left arm and the power of the wide, flat shoulders. He was using his right fist now as the foreman backed away. Angus McBride had met his match and he knew it, but the big, quick body fought on.

Finally Tom met a blind rush with a left which brought the big man's head up, then, stepping aside, he drove his right fist hard where the ribs parted above the stomach. He heard the air whistle from McBride's lungs, smelled the sour smell of whisky, then watched as the arms went limp and the big foreman reeled backwards, gasping for air, swayed for a minute like a big cork pine and slid awkwardly down against the far wall.

Someone in the crowd shouted "Timberrrr!" and it was over.

Tom found a chair and sat down. His arms were unbelievably heavy, his knees were weak and tired, and the blood was pounding in his temples.

He saw Milan walk across the room to where Jug Bateese still stood upright against the wall, standing tall to ease the hurt in his arm. Working the sheaf knife from the wood and flesh, Milan wiped it dry on Bateese's own shirt. Then turning him roughly toward the door, he said

"Geet." And Bateese got, out into the night, holding tight to his bleeding arm.

"I bring you water," said Martin Brewer, and gave Tom's shoulder a respectful pat. Tom washed the sweat from his face and the blood from his legs where the nailed boot had torn the flesh. Milan was beside him now. "Where in hell you learn to use that left hand like that?" he smiled.

"Captain Summers," grinned Tom. "You forgot that I spent my vacations working on the survey boat on Lake Superior. The gloves were always there, hanging on the wall of old Cap Summer's cabin. We learned."

He looked down to where Angus McBride still sat. He was aware, but sick and unmoving on the floor. He knew he would never again lead a crew of shanty boys into the woods. A logger never hires, as foreman, a man who has been beaten in a fair fight. In this country, he, like Mill Sharrow, was finished.

The rest of the men had set up the tables and were already dealing out the cards. It still was a long time until morning.

With head clear now, Tom remembered the reason for his being here. "Where is Jimmy?" he asked.

Milan laughed, and big Jans Troy answered, "He back here, all fine."

There Tom found him, sleeping soundly on a table in a corner. He had missed the best fight these hills had ever had.

Chapter Twenty–Four

It was a dull and breathless morning. The sun had come up red and sullen over the hills to the east and now burned hot on their backs as Tom and Milan worked steadily setting young cherry trees in the new field. The horses fidgeted nearby, bobbing their heads, stomping their feet into the dry earth, and whipping their tails at the flies that pestered their flanks. No wind had shown and Tom watched as Milan stopped his work, wiped the sweat from his eyes and fixed a steady, sweeping gaze into the west as if wondering at the lack of it.

The dunes lay out purple and gold in sunlight that couldn't quite burn off the haze, but bored through it instead, sending heat waves shimmering up between lake and sand, making the dunes appear suspended in space. Milan went to the water jug, drank his fill then wet his kerchief, laid it over his curly hair and pulled his hat down over it. "Damn hot for May," he muttered.

They talked little. Milan was moody or troubled. No gain to waste conversation when he was like this. He did his share of the work but made no show of liking it. Tom just waited. After the day's work was done, or before, maybe, his mood would change and he would break into a song.

For now, however, Tom was satisfied with the silence. He, too, felt the weight of the heavy air, so unusual in these hills, and found little joy in his labor.

At noon they turned the restless horses homeward. They would have a bit of lunch, dig a fresh bundle of the little trees and fill the barrels the horses skidded along behind them on a stoneboat, with water from the pump, taking turns sweating at the wooden handle. Usually they could fill them from the water tank at the barn, but, without wind, the wooden mill stood silent. They would have to pump for both trees and animals.

Milan's voice broke the silence as they filled the barrels, "I'm betting we will have more water than we need by tomorrow."

"Maybe so," Tom replied. "But unless those trees have it today, what they get tomorrow won't much matter."

When their barrels were finally filled they unhitched the horses and, leaving them in harness, they put them in cool stalls, threw down hay from the loft, then went to the house for lunch.

It was mid afternoon when Ole Nelson finished putting up a basket of groceries for Mary Sugars and walked out to the front of the store for a breath of fresh air. The day was hot, humid, and still. Across the street, the singing of Nick Tanner's hammer rang out clear and bell-like in the still, moist air. A rooster watched over its harem as they scratched the dust of Main Street, lifting its head often in instinctive worry over signs it was too dull to understand.

Out over the roof of Nick's little shop the country slid down towards the west, one wooded hill against another. The low bell tower of the schoolhouse, a mile out of town, could be seen this time of year, standing up through the budding oaks and maples. On beyond, but hidden by the hills, lay the farms of Mina Michaels and Allen Harcourt, and in the distance, over the rounded humps of the dunes lay Lake Michigan, hazy, gray and mysterious in today's dead calm.

Ole stepped down into the dust of the street and looked to the north, where Martin Brewer's saloon and the little hardware store beyond were without life. With the rivermen gone, perhaps for good, the town had settled down to its old quiet. Up the hill, a half mile to the north, a team of horses pulling a wagon plodded listlessly towards them. Most likely it was Jim Moreau headed for Carl VanBolt's mill with a load of grist. To the south, the road sloped gently away to pass over the little bridge at the mill and disappear into the wooded hills.

Ole sat down on the bench out front and lazed in the dapple of shade made by the wooden awning at the store front and the budding branches of the big maples to the south. The stillness of the air and the countryside made the day unreal and troubling. The usual clear calls of the meadowlarks were stilled. No gulls sailed overhead; no robin warbled a spring greeting from the maples. Only muffled twittering of chickadees from the lilacs along the side of the store and the soft talk of crows back in the hills mellowed the unusual silence.

Slowly the rhythm of Nick Tanner's hammer slowed and Ole could hear the sizzle of hot iron dipped in water as Nick finished the shaping of another shoe. He waited for him to appear out front. "Come 'ere, Nick."

Nick could not hear above the dying roar of the air through hot coals but he knew that he had been called. Dropping his hammer, he made a dramatic sweep of his brow with a forefinger and flicked the sweat into the dust of his shop, then cupped his hand to his ear.

Ole chuckled at the pantomime and motioned again, "Come 'ere, Nick."

The bellows wheezed quiet and the last sounds, saving the squeak of wheels to the north and the twittering of the birds, died as Nick settled heavily on the bench.

"Notice anything, Nick?"

He sighed, tired from his hammer, then grinned. "Notice ye ain't a-workin' overly hard this morning."

"Could be. Anything else?"

Nick settled back. "Tarnashun quiet, ain't it?"

"That's what I mean. Reckon we're in for a storm."

"Been due for weeks. It's drier than the fur in a camel's throat. Lucky we ain't had fires, with all that dry brush a-layin on the cuttin's. Lightin' could fire it too, less'n there's plenty of rain with it. I'm bettin' there will be.

We're overdue some wet."

Ole went into the dark of the store and came out with crackers and cheese on a piece of meat paper. He laid them out on the bench.

Jim Moreau's wagon eased up the street from the north, the wheels squeaking wearily and raising little ribbons of sand that streamed back into the ruts with scarce a stir of dust. Jim took a generous wedge of cheese and sat quiet, looking steady out into the west. "Tink it's a-going to rain, Neek?" he finally asked.

"I think if it don't, were in fer one damn long dry spell," chuckled Nick.

Jim shook his head. "Damdest country, these. Nothing it does by halves. When the rain comes, she come all at once and plenty. Then in August, when we need it, nothing but a long dry. Not enough wet in all these hills to stick a postage stamp. Even the owls cain't pucker enough to whoo. And winter? Sacre Dieu! how eet ees cold. For you Feens and Sweeds it's maybe like home, but we Frenchmen, we have the warm hearts." Jim helped himself to another piece of Ole's cheese and looked again to the west. "Last week I plowed my east ten. Eet was so dry then that the dirt blow right off my plow and clean into Elbridge County. Now look," and he nodded his head to the west," a man don't know best to plant or eat his seed."

"That's the life of a farmer, Jim. I wasn't smart enough to outguess the weather. That's why I ended up in this here cracker emporium. Now, if I don't stop to figger out my profits at the end of the year, I live happy. Near as I can figure out last year, I ended up with fourteen bushels of potatoes, seventy quarts of canned pears, two sheep that I don't know what to do with, one hundred and twenty–two horseshoes, and forty–two cents in cash money. If Halvar Brady ever stops bringing cheeses up from those Dutchmen in Grand Rapids and trading them for Nick's horseshoes, I'm out of business."

Jim Moreau took another look to the west. The dim line between lake and sky had disappeared now. Only the dunes still lay sharp against the near trees and the darkening sky.

"I get lots of entertainment, though. Yesterday Nancy came in. I had a good fresh tongue - a heifer's, I mean, not mine,- but Nancy says no! I couldn't eat anything that came from a cow's mouth. Give me a dozen eggs."

While Jim and Nick chuckled, Ole Nelson went back into the darkness of the store to close the windows. Jim Moreau was squeaking on towards the VanBolt mill when he returned. Nick straightened on his bench. "Looks like a real Oskosh a-coming, Ole. Here, have some more of this horseshoe cheese. It just might be our last meal."

Tom stood at the window and spoke over his shoulder without turning. "I'm thinking our dry spell is over, Mom, but I don't like it. A little at a time would be better. This one could be a buster."

The afternoon work had been called off. Tom had ridden up to the schoolhouse to have Dana send the children home ahead of the coming storm. Now they awaited its coming, Mina, Dana and Tom, with Milan standing behind them.

Lake Michigan had disappeared now and in its place, out over the tops of the dunes, a roll of dull blue cloud was spreading across the western sky. Blue-black below and white above, like a big wave, it came, rolling and turning from bottom to top. Above, the sky was still blue, but dull and fast disappearing in wisps of haze. All of the country lay still. No bird, no leaf, no twig stirred. Everything waited, tense and expectant for the unleashing of the storm.

Off to the north a solitary wolf let out a lonely howl, let the sound trail off to a sad, soul–searching wail, then tried again.

"Damn wolf don't know if to sing or to pray," laughed Milan, then hurried off to set something right that he had forgotten at the barn. Mina followed, trusting no one with her chickens. She threw them some extra corn while she was there. She didn't know why, maybe an act of kindness to ease the trouble that was coming.

When she left the chicken house she felt a cool, sharp wind starting to whip down over the hills to the east, and by the time she reached the back porch it pushed her along and sent her apron streaming out ahead of her. The Lord has strange ways, she thought. Out in front of her was the storm, fast approaching from the west, yet that cool wind was streaming down out of the east, sharp and notional, first from one side and then from another, striking like the flat of a hand against her skin, chilling the perspiration that was still there, and sending cool little shivers up her spine. She swept the persistent flies from the screen door, felt it slam shut behind her and went to stand with Tom.

The big roll of cloud was close now, so close that they could see the dark of it rolling up from down under to turn gray-white where the fading daylight hit it. It rolled over the tops of the tall pines along the lake, bending them like marsh grass beneath it, and over the tops of the dunes, where the quick plumes of wind–blown sand were quieted at once by the lash of rain. They could hear it now, a deep, steady roar of wind and thunder, and could see the flashes of lightning from cloud to dune top.

The lake below had lost its gray calm now and became a writhing, tormented monster of black and white as the winds buffeted it into foam. The little cabin of Jim and Louise Colby would be feeling it and the trees along the lake bent and swayed drunkenly then disappeared as a curtain of rain moved over them.

The back door slammed again and Milan was beside them, grinning now and ready to sing. The tension was relieved now for him. Battle was joined and he relished the fury of it. "Gonna be a real whistler," he grinned, pulling a willing Mina into the refuge of his arms as darkness like night enveloped them. "I remember one like this up on Lake Superior. Nothing but rocky cliffs along the shore and Joe and I—

"But he did not finish. Down on the first ridge a streak of blue white crackled from cloud to ground and the big sentinel pine, which always stood up sharp against the lake beyond, exploded into a ball of blue light, and disappeared. The crash of thunder came immediately and, from the safety of Milan's breast, Mina shuddered and heard the dishes rattling on their shelves. At the same time the rain reached them, beating first at one window and then another, driving hard until it shut out all view beyond the glass. There was another earth–shaking explosion, a flash of light, and another roll of thunder, then it settled down to a steady tumult of water, wind, and slowly receding thunder, as the crest of the storm moved slowly on towards town.

On the front porch of the VanBolt cottage Jeannie pulled her cape more closely around her as the cool wind whipped down from the east. Out at the mill she could see Jim Moreau driving his wagon of grist into the protection of the VanBolt barn as her father struggled to remove the second plank from the dam which held back the water of the mill pond. The dam had been made of stone and mortar, but near the top he had wisely left a notch sixteen inches deep and four feet wide, flanked by three inch slots into which two stout oak planks could be dropped. By removing one of these planks the high level of the mill pond could be lowered eight inches, or if both were removed, the level would drop by sixteen inches at the point where the water fell into the wooden sluice which led to the turning wheel.

The water in the pond was low now for this time of year, but with a bad storm approaching, her father would wisely remove the second plank so that if the water in the pond should rise too fast there would be less danger of it flooding the green lawn and perhaps washing out the dirt fill around the sides of the sturdy dam. Later he would replace them and allow the pond to rise to its full capacity.

Jeannie was about to go out to help him with the heavy plank when Jim Moreau appeared and they soon had the job done. The big mill doors were then shut and barred.

She had watched earlier as the school children had appeared, shouting and singing through town, and was glad that Dana had seen fit to release them. Even then, the Colby children had two miles to go to reach their cabin, and directly into the path of the storm. Wet or dry, they would make it, though. They were sturdy kids. Once they had found their way home in a blinding blizzard, tied together in a line with a cord of moosehide.

The big rolling cloud could be seen clearly now as it rolled up over the dunes and advanced slowly towards them. Buffeting gusts of wind swept down Main Street, rattling the shutters on Ole Nelson's store and sending little pinwheels of dust swirling off into the trees to the south.

Jean smiled to herself. A storm was kind of fun. It made

her blood run hot and filled her with the excitement of anticipating the fierce power of it. It was a challenge to the strong and a humbling influence to all. It made people like her mother look for safety in a familiar place. Probably her bedroom. It brought a self–comforting, low song to easy–going Sarah, cool, organized action to her father, and sent Jim Moreau's finger automatically to his breast to cross himself many times.

Thinking back, as the raw wind streamed at her, she pictured the other people she knew so well. Mary and Bill Sugars would be tending to the necessary preparations with their children helping them. They would be closing windows and barn doors, making a witty remark now and then to hide their concern, and tightening things up in the little building where they printed the paper. They would probably be joking about the time the wind blew the office door open and scattered paper for a mile into the countryside. "Best distribution my paper ever had," Bill said afterwards. Allen Harcourt would be out in his big oilskins and southwestern hat lookin' off west and reading the sky like the pages of a book, knowing the portent of each curl of cloud and brush of air against his weathered skin. In his quiet way he would have known long ago that it was coming and would have everything ship–shape and ready.

Her mind carried her on over the rest of the people of the town and back to past storms and the stories that built up around them. The thinking made her more aware that

she, Jeannie VanBolt, was one of these people, and somehow more than just one of them. She, like Tom Michaels,
the Harcourt boys, the Nelsons and the others, had grown
up here. From a skinny–legged little girl with pigtails and
freckles to Jean VanBolt, a woman. Only nineteen years
old, maybe, but a woman all the same. She let her eyes
drop down to where the wind pressed the cotton dress
and the light cape against her and was pleased with what
she saw. She had changed much during the last year and
she knew it. The pigtails were no more and the dark curls
that were left were soft and womanly. The body below
was full and capable, and her thoughts were different,
too. She thought more and more about Tom Michaels. Not
as the big brother-like boy she had known in school, but
as the man who had held her close at the dance the night
the barn had burned.

Up the street to the right, Jean saw Ole Nelson and
Nick Tanner walk out into the dust of the street to search
the sky for signs of a dangerous funnel cloud. They
returned to Ole's store.

She laughed a little to herself. Under the influence of
the coming storm her mind kept straying off like that of a
person who knows that death is near. The awesome
power of the elements makes one consider more deeply
the paths they walk and wonder with more concern if
they are moving in wise directions. She was aware now
that the realities of life and death and change are driven
home more forcefully when the skies darken and the

forces of nature tug at the human soul. To Jean they were not so much frightening as stimulating. They reminded her that nothing remains untouched by change. Just as the storm would batter, break, and cleanse the countryside in minutes, so would time also bring change. She had listened as the men of the town talked of the war that was spreading through the South. It was a big, important war that was taxing the minds and the strengths of the whole country. Good men were dying out there by the thousands, and they scarcely knew the reason they were fighting. They only knew that the Union was broken, and that they were fighting to bring it back together. Perhaps that was enough. Eber Harcourt was one of them, facing dangers he had never dreamed of, and risking the chance that he might never see his own son, because it was important that the Union be preserved. Could this be foolish resistance to change? or was it wise resistance like the closing of doors and the removing of mill pond planks against the coming of a storm?

Jeannie found herself puzzled as to the right or the wrong of it. The only thing which her mind seemed sure of was that changes seemed to be bad changes when the human weakness of greed became a factor. Then she smiled, admitting to herself that she also was greedy. Otherwise she would have returned to the new prep school at Benzonia. But was it greed or proper and understandable precautions against bad weather that would not let her leave these hills while Dana Sharrow remained. She smiled again, well knowing her reason, and well knowing that she would stay.

She looked up again, as a blackness like night swept over the town. She saw a stream of sparks carried from Nick Tanner's forge and saw Nick's silhouette as he hurried to cover them with sand. A flash of light was followed by a quick roll of thunder as the tree was struck west of the Michaels' house. She heard the muffled scream that came from her mother's room and noticed that Sarah's song had stopped.

"I hope it wasn't the schoolhouse," said her father's voice from the darkness. He had come out onto the porch and put a strong arm around her thin waist.

"Or the Michaels' new barn," laughed Jean. "One fire a year out there is enough.

"Still west of there, I think, but it's coming fast. Better come inside, Jeannie. That rain will be here in a minute or two."

"I'd like to stay for a while, Dad. I'm just getting acquainted."

"Acquainted!"

"Yes, with myself, and maybe with God. A storm does that to me." And she kissed her father playfully on the nose. "You go inside. If I get wet, I will dry off later. I don't know why, but I just like it out here. Milan always says that weather is only bad weather when you sit inside and cuss it, and I think he is right." Then she turned again, a bit more serious, "How is Mother?"

"She will be OK," and he squeezed the thin waist. "Don't judge her too harshly, Jean. When the going is bad, she stiffens. I still remember those fifty two days we spent on the little three–masted schooner coming over here. 'Twas a bad trip, Jeannie. Fifty–two days crossing, and two of those weeks a hell in the hold of that broken–down old schooner with nothing but cold food and sick people. The storms and the high seas were terrible. Most of the women spent their time sick in the filthy cargo hold. Seventy–five of us there was on that little boat, but only sixty–nine when we arrived. If your mother has a fear of storms, it is with reason.

"Yet, when it came time to pass the tests at quarantine, your mother and the others, too, got out of their beds, dressed in their best clothes and their bravest smiles, and stood to pass the tests that would let them enter this country. And every last one of them did. It's a god thing to remember, Jeannie. Castle Gardens never saw a better show."

Jean recognized the mild rebuke. Dad, Like Bill Sugars, had ways of teaching that humbled argument, even before it became words. Past is past, though, and now is now, and she and her mother danced to different music.

After the heart of the storm had passed on and the rain came thundering down, Jeannie pulled off her wet cape and went into the house. Sarah was lighting a fire in the kitchen range and building music from the rhythm of the rain. Jeannie added to the rhythm by whacking her on the rump as she went by, then scurried into her room to dry.

All signs of daylight had disappeared from the Michaels' house as the full fury of the storm settled over them and the black cloud joined with the hills to the east. Mina lighted a lamp with a brand from the fireplace, then returned to the window to watch. The rain was coming now in great sweeping surges, the big drops lashing at the windows and running in shiny waterfalls from the eaves. In the blue–white of the lightning flashes, the outlines of the big maples could be seen, wind–lashed and glistening against the blackness of the storm. Afterwards came more thunder, not as loud or as close as before and after a while the tumult of it tired, and quieted. The wind and the flashing lighting slowly passed on to the east and the thunder rumbled and echoed against the wet hills.

The rain, though, continued as though the heavens had determined to release, all at once, all that had been stored during those long, dry weeks.

The air was cooler now and Tom rolled a log onto the coals. The bright leap of flames was a reassuring hand against the dullness of the storm.

The evening came without new light and the morning followed. Still the rain came down, not so hard or so steady, but still it came.

Not until the evening of the second day did the sun slant out from beneath sullen clouds far out over Lake Michigan to light a countryside clean and glistening wet, completely soaked with moisture and already turning richly green from the wealth of it.

Chapter Twenty–Five

Tom looked north from the big log that topped off the south wing of the new dam. Across the river the hills of yellow sand rose up sharp from where the water flowed against them. They were wet now and solid as concrete, but they would dry fast. There was a light wind flowing off the lake to the west. It carried the fresh cool of May and the pleasant smells of wet woodlands and budding willows.

Tom looked up again at the sharp crests of yellow sand. "Suppose they will hold if we raise her one more log?"

"I think so," rumbled Allen Harcourt, his deep voice booming above the roar of the spillway. "As long as we keep the current from eating at them."

Tom looked upstream to where only the top of the big log showed from beneath the sand. The river was up, up over the dark heartwood so familiar to him and nearly to the top of the fifty–four inch butt. It was pushing the water out, protecting the base of the sand hill from the strong flow of water. A trout rose from the eddy behind the log, dimpled the surface, and slid back into the shadows.

Behind the jutting log the jumble of timber making up the jam it had caused, rose like a carelessly laid wall across the river. Here and there a huge log had been driven end over end to remain pointed like an accusing finger at the tops of the yellow dunes. Water now flowed through and around the barrier but it still held firm against the rising flood.

"I hope that jam don't break too fast," Tom shouted. "It could take this dam with it if it does."

"Good rivermen will take it apart a log at a time," rumbled Allen. "A charge of powder at the south end and good men to move them out. That will do it. It's a good dam. Let's raise her one more.

Between them they added one more ten–incher to the spillway, pinned it down, and watched the water rise against it.

Below the dam the river narrowed but ran deep and hard against wooded banks. With a bit of luck and the help of the dam to get the logs past these shallows they might make a late spring drive. "We'll raise hell with Jimmy's whitefish catch, though," laughed Allen.

It was ten p.m. that night when Tom and Milan left the hard sand of the beach. Their horses labored up the soft sand of the hill separating Buttersworth from the open waters of Lake Michigan. At the top they stopped to look down. Below them the lone street known as Sawdust Avenue was outlined by the scatter of yellow lights slanting from the crude houses. Behind them the dark spread of the Pere Marquette River gathered the water from the hills into a fair–sized lake before breaking through the sand ridge to their left and sliding out into Lake Michigan.

The river which lay in the valley below them bore the marks of this turbulent past. The Indians called it Not-a-pek-a-gon, or place of the skulls. East of this point in 1725 a battle between the Ottawas and three thousand retreating Mascoutins had resulted in an ambush by the Ottawas and the death of the entire group of Mascoutins. Tom had heard this story many times and had seen the remains of some of the skulls that had been placed on posts along the river banks to warn any new invaders.

Now the Ottawas, too, had had their day. Their skulls were not on posts along the river, but their spirits were. Their bodies were in the reserves set aside for them here and in faraway Kansas. Change had come, and unlike the waters of the big lakes, they were not able to change the direction of their flow.

As the Indians disappeared, this spot had become a crude pioneer gathering of fishermen and trappers. It remained quiet and isolated for another twenty years, but now it, too, was changing. Chicago, Detroit, Buffalo were growing markets for good pine lumber and here the ages had produced it. Big, aggressive men like Charles Mears, Jim Ludington, and Pat Donaher were walking Sawdust Avenue. The saloons were bright and noisy and the town was full of strangers. The quiet solitude of those wooded hills stretching to the east and the ancient pulse of the lake to the west were being broken. Lumber was here, enough good pine to build a dozen cities and fortunes for those who could get it out. The war had slowed the pace and held back the explosion of need that was sure to come. But these men were hungry for wealth that could be theirs and were already here preparing for it. In twenty years they could destroy what it had taken seven thousand years to produce.

Tom nudged his horse. They dipped down out of the hills and stopped at Burr Caswell's.

"Just tie them to the rail, Tom. I'll freshen them up and you can pick them up when y'er ready. Heered you had a little altercation down your way." He pulled Tom into the light of the doorway. "Ye look fit. How aire ye, Milan?"

Tom grinned. "I heal real fast."

"He looks better than the Irishman, that's for sure," laughed Milan.

"Best ye watch your step here. We got a passel of those river boys drivin' the last of Charley Mears' logs down the Little Sauble. They're good boys, but when they have money they get playful."

"Thanks, Burr. Is Jans Troy with them?"

"Saw him yestiddy, big as life. Probably at Wheeler's place, end of the Avenue.

"And Pat Donaher?"

"Try Jim Ludington's. He's got a room there."

The sawdust, wet and fragrant from the storm, stuck to

their feet and only hid the rutted mudholes of Buttersworth's main street. Across the lake the Bean and Baird Mill stood out black above the glitter of water. They could see a scattering of logs darkening the river behind the big boom links that stretched across it. Ahead of them the windows of Jay Wheeler's saloon glowed yellow and the sounds of men and the tinkle of glass reminded Tom of Martin Brewer's. Farther up, beyond a wide puddle of standing water, another building, new to Tom, glowed with the same friendly lights and sent the sweet pungency of burning pine drifting on the cool night air. A walkway of rough planks led up to the doorway of Wheeler's place. Tom led the way.

Jans Troy was not there, but they were greeted with friendly faces. They talked a while with Jay Wheeler as they freshened up with some of his good fried potatoes and ham.

At the logger's inn they were met at the door, "You want talk to Jans Troy, he's back dere," grinned old Dick Hatfield. Tom wondered how Dick knew that they had Jans on their mind. Jans was there, sober and full of stories. Tom and Milan waited.

"Dere 'e was," Jans was saying, "The clumsies' tam Svede dat ever roll a log, standing on dat big one as stiff as a scared possum, an de white water of the sluiceway a dunderin' up at him. We haul heem out of da deep water below de dam an I ask heem, 'Why don you yump, Ollie?'

'Yump, Yans? Oow een 'ell could I yump ven aye ain't

got nodding to stand from?'"

The rivermen laughed loudly at the often–told tale and a circle of well whiskied Indians in the back of the room joined in.

"Vell! Vell! our friends from the Sharrow camp," grinned Hans. "How you be?"

The next morning three wagons filled with men left the village and clinked their way westward towards Mill Sharrow's old camp. The words passed so quietly at the party the night of the fire had been sincere. They had said, "We are with you, Tom," and mostly they had meant it.

It was afternoon of the next day when Tom and Milan joined the men at the camp. A short time later Hans Troy appeared from downstream. With him were twelve good rivermen, including Jug Bateese, sober and smiling.

"How's the arm, Bateese?" Milan laughed.

"Sore lak hell, but I do my job," Bateese replied. He was a good riverman. He would be a welcome hand.

"No pay till the job is done or we run out of water to float the logs, Jug."

"Good!" he laughed. "No money, no more sore arms."

Tom now took charge. "We will work as three separate crews," he said. "Jans Troy, you will take the rivermen and the river work. Use your men as you see fit. Break the jam, run the timber down, and raft it in the bay. If you need more help along the riverbanks, some of our young men like Nate Harcourt and Charlie Colby are available. Pay to you rivermen will be two dollars per day when the job is finished. Their will be a tug waiting to haul the rafts to the Bean and Baird Mill. Jans, you know the size of the pig that a tug can work into the river. Their are plenty of chains and tools in the barn. Think you can break that jam by tomorrow, Jans?"

"Ve break her. Mebby today."

There was a twinkle in Allen Harcourt's eyes as he watched Tom. He looked on to where the river worried against the twisted pile of logs that filled the channel from sand hill to wooded bank. With the rising of the water there seemed to be a nervous movement now among the big timbers, a gentle rising and falling with the steady surge of the water built by the storm. Still it held solid. It would be a show to see these men blow it loose. He looked beyond to where the hazy sun was darkening the pines that hid the big lake. Somewhere out there his own flesh and blood was doing a job, too. Eber had not really known what a war was when he left home. He only saw that it was a way to get land and trees of his own. By now he knew well enough what it was like. Too well, perhaps. In his quiet way, Allen was concerned. Eber might take chances. Maybe, like Tom, though, the hard times he was knowing was making a man of him.

Tom felt awkward as he turned to face his old friends from the village and the farms. Speaking up to tough rivermen was one thing. Talking to these people who had left their own work to do a job that seemed much his own was another. Direction was needed, though, and they were looking to him to give it.

"We ain't here just to watch, Tom." Bill Sugars could read his thinking. "Rolling logs may be a bit new to some of us but we've tried most everything else. Just set us up with a job and stand back and see what happens."

"Might be a good idear to stand wa-a-y back, " chirped Nick Tanner.

"All right," Tom was ready now. "We need two groups. Allen, you take the bigger one and the teamsters and start those logs moving into the river. There are close to thirty–five hundred of them waiting to get wet. It will take all of the horses and plenty of hard work to get them down to the bay before this water drops. Most of all, be careful. We all know what happened to Jacques Moreau. We want no more of that. The rest of you will go with Bill Sugars. He's got some new ideas about what this camp should look like."

At five o'clock Bill Sugars' wagon, with Mary at the reins of the white team, appeared over the hill east of the camp. It was filled with an ample supply of food and women to serve it. Nothing could have looked better to the camp full of hungry men.

Already a steady flow of logs was splashing into the river below the jam as Allen Harcourt and his men did their job.

Out of the tangle of logs making up the heart of the jam big Jans Troy stood high as Jug Bateese and his helpers pried away at the key timbers, freeing some and pushing them out into the current. Other river hogs were standing waist deep in the cold water, using their long pike poles to pull and push these logs and the ones Allen's men were hauling out into the fast water where the spillway thrust them into the air and dumped them into the river below. The drive was under way.

By dusk the key logs which held the jam locked so firmly against the river had been identified and two kegs of black powder, waxed and fused, were in place. The force of the explosion would be downward against the bottom logs and Bateese knew this well.

"By Gar, we still gat a hour afore dark. Let's let her reep," said Bateese, as he finished stringing a fuse down to the lower face of the jamb.

From his high post on the top of the logs Jans Troy looked at the sun sinking low in the west and down at the dam another quarter mile downstream. The rest of the men had left the jam now. Only he and Jug remained. He hesitated only a moment, then his big voice boomed out across the water. "Fire in the hole!" he bellowed. "Move your horses back. We're going to set her off."

By the time Jans had reached the downriver side, Bateese had two big logs ready to ride out and the end of the fuse frayed and ready.

"Touch her off," said Jans and stepping onto one of the logs he rode it out into the current.

Bateese held the other log ready with one spiked boot and struck fire to the fuse. It glowed, then sputtered to life.

From a safe distance on shore Tom and Allen Harcourt watched as the two rivermen rode the logs out from the base of the jam. "Moving damn slow, seems to me," Allen rumbled.

"The current won't pick them up until they get farther out," Tom spoke as much to himself as to Allen. Then he turned as Bill Sugars came up to stand beside them.

"Horses all set?" He asked.

"All back in the woods." answered Bill. "Everyone is ready but the women back in camp. They were a-gabbing so fast I couldn't get a word in so I figgered to let them be surprised."

Tom looked at him. "Didn't try too hard, did you Bill?"

"Not too hard," he grinned.

"I figger there was about six minutes of fuse there," said Allen. "If that's right they will never make it to the dam. That current jest ain't that fast."

Jans and Bateese were facing back at the jam now, riding their logs erect and easy as though they were on solid ground. They knew it was about time, and they were none too far away. They would have to ride the surge of water that would follow the blow.

"There she goes!" It was Bateese's wild voice carrying out across the water, and he had timed it perfectly.

Before the sound reached them, Tom saw the logs at the base of the jamb lift and turn end over end into the air. There was a gentle buffeting in their faces and then the heavy dull boom of the exploding powder.

It was a moment or two before the flying bark and black powder smoke cleared. Tom glanced in the direction of the two rivermen and saw Jans pulling Bateese to the safety of his own log. Bateese's log had been caught swinging sidewise to the force of the blow and it had thrown him like a bucking horse throws a rider. He saw the other rivermen, already with pike poles in hand, moving out to intercept the moving logs, then his eyes came back to the site of the explosion.

At first he feared that the charge had not done its job. After the first moment of power which had sent the huge timbers wrenching upward and out from the tangle of the jamb, they had settled again, splashing back into the water and sending cascades of spray high against the setting sun. The echoes of the blast joined with the shrill sound of women's screams from the camp kitchen, bounded from the wet hills like answering drum calls and finally settled to a deep quiet, broken only by the long, lonely call of a wolf. The logs heaved gently up and down with the returning waves and slowly swung into the flow of the current and moved silently and majestically downstream.

"Beautiful," murmured Allen Harcour.

The word, sounding strange coming from the big man, was a heartfelt tribute to a job well done, the appreciation one skilled craftsman has for another.

The log Jans Troy was riding had reached the dam now and he jumped to the safety of it as easily and gracefully as a big cat. From here he directed the movements of the rivermen, and before the pale moon lifted into the eastern sky the river behind the dam had filled from green bank to yellow dunes with a manageable covering of the big logs. The drive to the lake would begin in earnest at day-break on the morrow.

From where they stood in the deepening dusk, Tom watched the last green tint leave the western sky and turned to see the yellow glow of the lanterns that marked the trek of the womenfolks back over the long east slope. He put a big friendly arm around Bill Sugars' narrow shoulders as they found their way back to the camp.

"Ever slept in a muzzle loader, Bill?"

"Never."

"Seems like a good time to start."

Part Four
Chapter Twenty–Six

Like two wrestlers locked in a final show of strength the North and South fought on through 1863 and into 1864. There were the big battles at Gettysburg and the simultaneous fall of Vicksburg to Grant. But these were only great convulsions of giant muscles which strained the bodies of each but did not break either. The South lost over 62,000 men in killed, wounded, and missing in those two battles, and the Union nearly 30,000. But the Southern army drew back and the body remained unbroken.

In the fall, Chicamauga, Missionary Ridge, and Lookout Mountain added 26,000 and 21,000 more casualties to the sad totals and Bill Sugars moved his pins to the southeast of Chattanooga. Now Rosecrans was replaced by General Thomas as commander of the Army of the Cumberland, and Grant, Sherman, and Hooker joined him. The Northern armies had done their job in the West and Bill was certain now that they were preparing to make the drive through Atlanta that would cut the south in half. The Southern arm was bending. 1864 might see it break.

During the fall and winter months there had been no

word from Eber Harcourt. There had been a letter over a year ago, saying that he had come through Stones River without a scratch, then nothing. If he was still attached to the Army of the Cumberland, he was now in northern Georgia. Perhaps his letters were not getting through.

Little Todd Harcourt was walking now and keeping Judy busy. Maybe it was a good thing.

Spring came to Michigan early that year and now the countryside, refreshed by two good spring rains, was fragrant with spring flowers and bursting with the caroling of meadowlarks and the tinkle of bob-o-links. The robins were already plastering their nests with mud, and the clear sky was streaked with returning geese and clouded with the big flocks of passenger pigeons.

Mina Michaels' new buggy was squeaking gently in the schoolyard as the horses, unused to the new rig, turned from the rail to study it reproachfully.

The rest of the conveyances which carried the villagers to church were lined up neatly. Most were horse drawn now. The days when oxen were used because their tough feet were better suited for breaking pioneer soil were gone. Only Dan Marsaque still held to oxen. His dull animals were lazily munching their cud in the woods behind the school.

Inside the school, circuit rider Beard was warming to his task, wondering at the same time why it was difficult for some people to follow in the path of the Lord. His high– pitched voice rose and fell like waves on a beach, slowly lulling the unwary to sleep, and arousing the dedicated believers to hope and action.

From his place beside Mina, Tom listened with understanding interest and felt that perhaps both divisions of the congregation were certain to receive some benefit from the words of the good man. Even a spot of rest could be a heavenly blessing.

The text today was from Proverbs, and the passion in the voice of the good parson was a reminder to all that these words of the wise King Solomon were his favorites. His voice rose to the crest of a new swell.

Allen Harcourt struggled, one eye half open. The preacher was looking the other way. He closed it again.

"These are days of war and peace, the same as they were in the time of Solomon."

The same as they have been since history began, thought Tom.

"A time of war for those who answered the calls of Lincoln and Jefferson Davis and now face their brothers in our own great Civil War. A time of peace for those who, even in the midst of war, are able to grasp the word of the Lord and hold tightly to it. 'My son, forget not my law, but let thine heart keep my commandments, for length of days, and long life and peace shall they add to thee.'

"Here in chapter three, verse two, the word peace appears again. And here, as it so often is throughout the scriptures, it is the key word. For without peace, and I refer to that quality of peace of mind which our Indian friends call inner peace, we probably will have difficulty keeping the commandment; we will most likely shorten rather than lengthen our lives and our days will be less filled with the joys of living."

Mina was alert as always and thinking Beard's a good point. A little more peace down in Virginia and Georgia would help, too.

"But how do we acquire this inner peace? Do we get it by accumulating worldly goods?"

"No! Certainly Peter and John and the tax collector did not acquire peace of mind by this method. On the contrary, they sought it by disposing of their wealth. The scribes of Israel and the monks of the Middle Ages who translated and copied the good words of the Scriptures were notably poor, but rich in spirit and long in years of life."

The parson's voice rose on another wave, and Mary Sugars poked a sharp elbow playfully into Nick Tanner's lean ribs. He came awake with a muffled snort that brought subdued smiles to those around him and a whispered admonition to Mary: "Gentlemen yearn for peace, but there is no peace."

High over the spring hills the eagle, now a resident of the valley, stretched white–tipped wings, looked down on the little schoolhouse, and searched through the thickening cover of the fields and forests. Two herring gulls drifted by beneath him. If hunger had been strong within him, he could have tipped sidewise, as he so often did, dropping like a stone upon one of them, and come from the scattering of feathers with a satisfying meal in his strong claws. He was not hungry, and if he had been, the sturgeon were spawning in the shallows of the bay. Fresh fish were a banquet compared to a feathery gull. Peace of mind was his.

The capricious thrust of a thermal of warm air rose off the sandy dunes to the west, pushed against strong wings, and carried him on its rising flow, up, up, up another thousand feet, until to anyone below he became a mere particle of living dust drifting in a directionless void of misty spring sky.

His eyes focused again on the expanded horizons below him. Only God himself could enjoy an overview such as this, and only the eyes of an eagle could still see deep into the beauty of the peaceful countryside spread out below him. North of the small lake, blue as polished turquoise from a half mile high, the yellow dunes changed to wooded hills, then crested to a small grassy clearing. To the west they sloped downward and fell into the open sandy wastes of the Lake Michigan shoreline. A mile off shore a sleek lumber schooner glided south loaded with iced fish and piles of milled lumber bound for Chicago. Father north the speck of white of Burr Caswell's fishing sloop was setting nets off the south rocks. Back at the crest of the hill two figures mounted the wooded path and settled comfortably onto the grass high in the solitude of the hills and rich with the expanse of pine, sand, and water spread out below them.

Church services had never suited Milan. "Religion?" he

replied once to Mina's query. "Certain I have releegion. Anyone who place the good of all people above his own, has releegion." Mina had to agree that the basics of religion were there, and that he practiced them. But church? No. It was his practice, rather, to wander into the hills on Sunday to find his peace where he understood it best, in the song of a bird and the freshness of the wind. As for the hereafter, he had said, "Hell! Mina, I know people who worry about the hereafter thet don't know what to do with yesstide's rainy afternoon. I'm tinking that if I do a proper job with the here, mos' likely I can't do much more about the hereafter."

Meanwhile, the preacher continued. Mina looked at Tom, happy that Tom had chosen to accompany her to services.

Up in the hills Milan lay back and watched the speck of black circling slowly above him. This, to him, was the ultimate peace. Joe Marsaque had discovered this habit of Milan's and had thereafter found excuses to join him on Sunday mornings. "What are you lookin' at, Milan?"

Milan hesitated. Joe would never get his eye on that drifting speck and would give him no rest until he did.

"I see the maple branch. It hang from my left, heavy with new life no preacher, no doctor and no one else, now or ever, can explain."

"You mean the seeds with the wings?"

"Oui. Wings to carry them away from their mother to new, good soil." He hesitated. "The same as your feet carry you."

There was a long silence, then Joe raised up again. "I think I will climb up and get some." He was gone and Milan rested.

After a while he was back. "Can I borrow your knife? Milan."

There was a long interval while Joe cut apart seed after seed, searching carefully for the life he knew was there. Finally the knife snapped shut and Joe lay again on the warm grass, silent and thoughtful. The eagle had dropped lower now and Joe's eyes finally caught sight of it. He only said, "Gee."

"How did you climb that tree, Joe, head first or feet first?"

"Head first of course."

"Best way to climb trees is feet up," said Milan. "Then if you fall you always know jest exactly how far it ees before you are going to hit the ground."

"You're funnin', ain't you, Milan?" The eagle swept off towards the east. Something had attracted i's attention.

"You know, that seed is just like an eagle's egg, just needs warm and proper time. Find the answer to one and I'll bet you would have the answer to t'other."

"Oui, maybe, but you still wouldn't know how a trout finds its way back to it's home stream to spawn." Milan pointed his long stem of grass at a ribbon of geese throbbing steadily north. "You still won't know how those geese get two tousan' miles south and back again through fog and rain and snowstorms without getting lost, or how the frog lives all winter in the mud without food."

Milan sat up and looked out across the tops of the big pines onto the white sands of the lonely wasteland and on over the blue gray of the big lake. "Damn me, Joe, if I don' think there are more sermons out there in that pretty, and down there in those seeds, than any parson or pope will ever dream of. And in their own way they are telling us that there are certain t'ings we were never meant to know. Maybe in the knowing we might lose more than we would gain. Like a rainbow, the knowin' couldn't make it no prettier and not knowin' feeds the mind."

Milan made a mark in the sand with a stick. "Out there nothing really dies." Joe looked up at him. "It just changes, from dust to wood and flesh and life back to dust again to start all over. Guess probably that is all life is, and man is not so beeg and mighty that he can ever change it. Egg to flesh, seed to substance, and round and around we go. Have your fun, do your good whenever you can, and don' worry about things you can't change or understand. Talkin' don't make rainbows and a bundle of gold won' make your dust no richer."

Milan leaned back again into the fragrant grass. The fresh smell of budding pines was drifting up on the lake air. "I'm thinking that that hereafter the preachers talk about is already here. Right here in our hands if we will only look. And thinkin' this might make us value today the more and be the better for it."

The eagle had drifted out of sight to the east now. Something along the trail had caught its sharp eye. It was two men, one on a shining bay mare and the other plodding slowly alongside. They both looked dusty and tired, but slowly they plodded on, working their way over the hills and down the sandy trail that would, after a while, bring them across the bridge at the VanBolt mill and up into the village, now lying quiet and deserted in the Sunday sunshine.

The bird tilted its wings lazily westward again, noted three deer feeding on the spring brouse in a clearing. They were out of the swamps now, where a diet of bark and buds had kept them alive during the winter, and busy mating and fattening on the lush new graze. He checked again the two figures on the hilltop, noted a she–wolf and four whelps warming in the sun outside their hillside cave, then picked up the thermal from the sand plains again, rode it playfully into the heights and out over the big lake. His nesting mate would be in need of fish or fresh meat by now. As it is with all living things, peace is made more dear by the obligations that interrupt it.

Down in the schoolhouse Parson Beard was still quoting Solomon. "The fear of the Lord is the beginning of knowledge, but fools despise wisdom and instruction.' So in the absence of wisdom," he went on, "man substitutes war and children abstain from their schooling. My son, if sinners entice thee, consent thou not, for the turning away of the simple shall slay them, and the prosperity of fools shall destroy them."

Allen Harcourt stirred for a moment and grinned a half–awake grin. He was thinking of his own philosophy, "The first step to acquiring knowledge is silence." Then he relaxed back into half–awake rest, not much caring that the parson's eyes were turning again his way.

"Be not wise in thine own eyes. Fear the Lord and depart from evil."—

As the good man continued his preaching, the horse-man and his companion entered the school yard and stopped outside. The tall one dismounted from his horse stiffly, as thought he had known a long journey and brushed the dust from his clothing. The other one flipped the bridle reins around the hitching rail and turned to walk beside him to the door of the schoolhouse. It squeaked gently. They entered, they stood quietly inside, hats in hand, waiting for their eyes to accustom to the lesser light of the interior. Slowly their vision cleared and with a halting, thumping gait, that allowed one hand to push the thumping wooden leg forward, the tall one took a few steps down the aisle, his eyes searching the crowd as a man dying of thirst searches for water. Alongside, the little gray–haired colored man waited, as though ready in case the tall one stumbled.

The parson now had raised his eyes, and looking out saw the tall man in the blue uniform searching the backs of the villagers. His voice dwindled to a whisper then stopped, as he recognized the man in the dusty blue coat with its stiff collar laying open and the gold buttons glittering in the slanting light. It was a bigger, taller, different Eber Harcourt, home from the war.

The rest of the hill people turned now and one by one gasped as recognition came.

Up front a gentle, muffled cry cut through the room as Judy's eyes told her the truth. Yet strangely enough, she hesitated. Was it really him? He looked so different. Could it be true? Then she was in his arms, but only tears, tears of pent–up sadness and joy would flow from her.

There would be no more of Proverbs today. The return of the prodigal son was, to these people, deeper reason for thanks. The rest of the sermon would wait.

Mary Sugars took control of the situation. "I believe," she said, as the gathering quieted, "that this is a day to be celebrated. But first I think it is more fitting than ever to close our service in the usual way.—- "Her mellow voice called, and the beautiful tones of Sara VanBolt's soprano led on—--"Praise God from whom all blessings flow." The gathering joined reverently in, the words suddenly having meanings never before recognized. "Praise him all creatures here below. Praise him above, ye heavenly hosts. Praise Father, Son, and Holy Ghost."

"Now," said Mary, "there has to be a celebration. How about tomorrow evening at the old Sharrow camp?" There was a murmur of approval.

Like the others, Tom was standing now, his straight, broad back showing above the rest. His eyes clung to the soldier for a long time, noticing the quiet maturity in Eber, and saw with sadness the stub of wood that was now his leg and the deep set of his eyes that was a record of the suffering he had known. He looked to the ageless, little colored man, neat for all his travel and time worn clothing.

Eber was introducing him now. "Meet John Legg, folks, the best companion a man could have, outside of little Judy here, of course," and his arms again brought her close.

"Howdy do, howdy do," the little man was saying, turning his hat nervously round and around in small, rather light, hands, while his eyes fairly shone with enjoyment of life. "We all, we all decided, since another leg seemed kind of in order, and since I was plumb out of employment, that we were the perfect partners." He shifted nervously from one foot to the other as was his way, but the good humor in his face was like a light shining in a dark room. Only when his eyes fell on old Allen Harcourt did they change. Tom held his breath for a moment as a fleeting look of fear and wonder flickered across the dark face. It was as though something from out of the far–away past, or a fear of the future, had struck the inner recesses of the sharp brain and held it for a brief moment. Then it was gone and the light returned to the happy face. Tom could not help but smile. This man could be a savior to the crippled Eber Harcourt.

Tom's eyes now circled the room, fascinated with the faces of the people. Allen and Anna Harcourt were all proud smiles. Nick Tanner was fidgeting to get into the

center of things but his lack of height was making it difficult. The big, blue eyes of Jeannie VanBolt were, like his,
enjoying the scene, but stopped, as they so often did, to
rest on Tom. Tom smiled. Jeannie had certainly grown to
be a pretty girl.

The Nelsons, the Marsaques and the others were calmly waiting their turn to greet Eber. Louise Colby, with her
brood growing tall and straight beside her, was silent and
unreadable as the hills. Dana Sharrow, who had not
known Eber, stood quietly to one side.

The sunshine was making the room warm, and the air
from the open window smelled of lilacs. Tom found his
mother and together they went with Mary Sugars to plan
the party.

The sun was scarcely past its highest arc the next day
when the wagons began to appear over the hill east of the
old Sharrow camp and jingle their way down the sandy trail
towards the little lake and the river that flowed from it. This
was to be the best party since Eber had left for the war and
there was still work to be done before things were ready.

Soon there were rough tables being set up in the yard
where bullets had once spread sand against Tom and
Milan had made quick reply. The bunks had been torn
down from the west end of the building and on the smooth
flooring that Bill Sugars' men had laid during the log
drive, bright homemade rugs were spread. The fireplace
was newly cleaned and the smells of dirty underwear and
tobacco juice were gone. Judy Harcourt and Dana Sharrow

had sewn curtains of bright calico from Muskegon. The windows were glassed and swung open to let in the clean air from the distant lake. Mill Sharrow's office was now a kitchen, not really finished yet, but it was a start.

Behind the house a few young apple, pear, and cherry trees already blossomed, and back up the hill a cow with calf grazed. Part of the stumps left by Mill Sharrow were already pulled and lined up for fencing. The work of their friends and the turn of the wheel that had driven Milton Sharrow from the valley had provided Eber and Judy with the beginnings of a home; perhaps the pleasantest in the valley. With plenty of land already cleared, they would have a good start.

When Bill Sugar's paper appeared the next week there was news a-plenty, The stories Eber Harcourt had told to Bill would make good reading for months.

To Tom Michaels, it was Eber's assurance that the outcome of the war was now certain, that settled his mind. It had always worn on him that he was not doing his share, that he was not properly answering the calls of the country that had given him and his people so much. He had always been on the verge of going to Muskegon or Grand Rapids to sign up for his blues.

Now his mind was made up. Unless he was drafted, or a greater need appeared, he would stay. There were other ways of serving. The days of Judge Littlejohn's three–hundred–mile long circuit were about over. Soon new judges would be needed in each new county. These hills would grow and prosper once the war was over.

He folded the paper and laid it aside. Bill Sugars had already told him the rest. The second page would tell him that a good friend, Jean VanBolt, was leaving soon to study at the new prep school of Benzonia. He was sure that Jeannie had known for a long time that this was the way it must be.

Then there was the rest of the war news. Grant's promotion to Commander of all Federal Armies, the positioning of his 118,000 men between Lee's 60,000 Confederates and Richmond, the terrible fighting in the Wilderness east of Fredericksburg, William Tecumseh Sherman's costly, but steady, advance towards Atlanta.

It bothered Tom that so many good men were dying, or being maimed like Eber Harcourt, fighting for a cause that was long ago lost. He raised the big, flat shoulders that had known the board and the willow basket those long years ago and went to stand between his mother and Dana Sharrow at the big window. A big, strong arm went warmly and naturally around each.

Far out over the tops of the big pine trees the lake was sparkling like diamonds on blue velvet. Beyond it the dunes rose sharp in the morning air, their yellow slopes turning to violet in the shaded folds. On the crest of the highest, where the fresh spring air off Lake Michigan was sending little banners of good–weather sand curling over its sharp crest, two figures stood looking out across the big lake, far beyond it, probably, beyond the Lac Du

Flambeau and the Court Oreilles and on to those storied, craggy mountains of the west, where there were still beaver by the thousands and the rivers sang on to God knows where.

Tom smiled to himself. Then a pang of sadness crept slowly over him. He knew, like Milan, that these hills would continue to change. The post-war boom would bring more Mill Sharrows, men who would see here only fortunes to be made, not the quiet beauty of it all. Would the day ever come, when his feet, too, would turn west-ward, away from the buzzing of saws, the clanging of hammers, the smell of sawdust?

But what about Mina, and all of their good friends and neighbors - Jimmy and Louise, the Sugars and Harcourts, the VanBolts, Dana, and Eber - back from the war? They were like family, woven together by the yarn of common experience, and a deep and abiding faith in each other. Besides, Judge Littlejohn's ruling had given them fresh hope. At least, the valley would likely be spared from the cutters... for a while, anyway. And the fruit trees were just beginning to bear.

Tom had to smile, now, at himself and his wandering thoughts. After all, his father and mother had traveled halfway around the world to find this place. What a fool he would be to leave it.

A Moving Tale About Michigan's Earliest Years, Written by one of its Native Sons!

The Yarn gives Michigan's early history a profoundly human face. It begins in 1837 when Ganus and Mina Michealovic step off the lake steamer Chippewa at the port of Detroit. It builds to a trial which pits loggers against homesteaders in the state's northern section and an equally poignant struggle between a young Michigander wearing Union blue and his friend from the hills of Tennessee wearing Confederate grey.

Questions or comments about *The Yarn*?
Send them in or e-mail us at davis_rs@juno.com.

_____

_____

_____

_____

Like to order additional copies?
Check with your local bookstore or order directly.

Yes, I want additional copies of *The Yarn of the Mitten*. Send me _____ copies at $24.95 each, plus $3.00 shipping and handling.* We offer a 10% discount for orders of 3 or more.

Make check or money order payable and return to: L.A. Davis
52 Valley View Trail
Sparta, NJ 07871

New Jersey customers please add New Jersey sales tax.